SECOND CHANCE

DAN MONTAGUE

SECOND CHANCE

A DUTTON BOOK

DUTTON
Published by the Penguin Group
Penguin Putnam Inc., 375 Hudson Street,
New York, New York 10014, U.S.A.
Penguin Books Ltd, 27 Wrights Lane,
London W8 5TZ, England
Penguin Books Australia Ltd, Ringwood,
Victoria, Australia
Penguin Books Canada Ltd, 10 Alcorn Avenue,
Toronto, Ontario, Canada M4V 3B2
Penguin Books (N.Z.) Ltd, 182–190 Wairau Road,
Auckland 10, New Zealand

Penguin Books Ltd, Registered Offices:
Harmondsworth, Middlesex, England

First published by Dutton, an imprint of Dutton NAL,
a member of Penguin Putnam Inc.

First Printing, July, 1998
10 9 8 7 6 5 4 3 2 1

 REGISTERED TRADEMARK—MARCA REGISTRADA

LIBRARY OF CONGRESS CATALOGING-IN-PUBLICATION DATA

Montague, Dan.
    Second chance / Dan Montague.
        p.   cm.
    ISBN 0-525-94420-6 (acid-free paper)
    I. Title.
    PS3563.05372S4   1998
    813'.54—dc21   98-12908
                                    CIP

Printed in the United States of America
Set in Caslon 540
Designed by Stanley S. Drate/Folio Graphics Co. Inc.

This book is printed on acid-free paper.
∞

For our children
Daniel, Melanie, and Martha,
and for two remarkable dogs,
Bear and Clara

ACKNOWLEDGMENTS

My thanks to Carolyn Jenks, good friend and agent, for her sound advice, and to Al Silverman, my editor, for his availability, patience and guidance.

Richard Hollander, with the International Poster Gallery on Newbury Street in Boston, was most helpful in introducing me to the fascinating field of poster art and its influence on political history.

Andrea Turner, Commercial Assistant at the British Consulate General in Boston assisted me with phrases and expressions from her native country, Wales.

Tom Wong, Museum Designer, lent his imagination, wit and experience to my creation of a fictional art museum.

Two books were invaluable in helping me to understand the lingering effects of childhood abuse and how its scars can be healed: *The Invisible Wound* by Wayne Kritsberg, and *Secret Survivors* by E. Sue Blume.

And, as always, I am indebted to Zoë, my wife, and Melanie, our daughter, who read every page and every rewritten page with careful eyes, sharp pencils and good suggestions, until the three of us thought we had it right. Also, for permission to use Zoë's dog, Bear, and Melanie's dog, Clara, as key characters in this novel.

ONE

Chuck Carver arrived a day late for his father's funeral. That was the way he wanted it. He wouldn't have come at all if the lawyer hadn't suggested he be there for the reading of the will. Maybe, after all these years, his father had remembered he existed.

He wound his Mitsubishi 3000GT Spyder along highway 1-A through Salem, Massachusetts, looking for the address of the lawyer's office. The car's top was up against a steady April rain that made it difficult to see out the side windows. He rolled his window down a few inches so he could see the street numbers. The houses looked more residential than business, big Federal-period homes. Then he noticed discreet plaques by the doors indicating offices of architects, doctors and lawyers. He spotted the number and parked his car. Chuck uncoiled his six-foot four-inch frame from the ergonomically designed seat that embraced his body like the enfolding arms of a woman, and popped a spring-loaded umbrella over his head.

Under his leather jacket, the collar of his turtleneck sweater disappeared beneath his gray beard. His tightly curled hair matched the color of his beard and made him look older than his forty-two years. Walking with a smooth, lumbering gait toward the lawyer's office, he had a vague childhood memory of visiting a witch museum here in Salem. Must have been more than thirty-two years ago, he thought, because he was ten when he and his mom escaped from his father and fled to Rochester, New York. Marblehead, where they'd lived with his father, was next door to Salem. Chuck pulled the collar of the leather jacket together as a gust of wind sent a wet mist against his face and rattled the bare tree limbs over his head.

The brass plaque by the door read, LAW OFFICES, PATRICK CONSTANZA, ATTORNEY. The building, a large white wooden house, needed paint. He went in, wiped his feet on the mat and closed his wet umbrella. Down the hallway a door on the left opened into a waiting room where a young man sat behind a desk.

"Have a seat," the man said without looking up from his computer. He wore thick glasses and had a mop of black hair. "Mr. Constanza will be with you in a minute."

The man's eyes shifted back and forth from the screen to a document lying on the desk. Behind him several storage cartons were stacked in the opening of a swept-clean fireplace, while neat piles of papers lined the mantel. One entire wall was lined with legal-looking books, and another had two windows looking out on the scraggly remains of a garden. A row of straight chairs had been placed across from the desk, and Chuck took the first seat by the door.

Two people were seated at the other end of the row. Chuck gave them a cursory glance, a young man maybe in his mid-twenties and a woman a little older. Did this mean they were ahead of him, that he had to wait for Constanza to deal with them before he could get to him? If so, why did the lawyer tell him to be here at four o'clock? He sneaked another glance at the pair, who were reading magazines. They looked like brother and sister. Same nose and mouth.

The intercom buzzed and the secretary listened into the receiver.

"Mr. Constanza will see you now." His eyebrows gestured toward the door to the inner office. "Right through there."

The couple got up, crossed in front of Chuck and went into the office.

"You, too," the man said with a toss of his head toward the door. "Right in there."

Relieved but puzzled, Chuck got up and entered the office of Patrick Constanza.

The attorney, standing as they entered, was dressed in a dark blue suit, white shirt and blue tie with red stripes. He wore glasses and had wavy white hair. Loose skin on his pallid face was marked with brown age spots and made him look at least seventy. He rounded the desk, greeting the two with extended hands.

"My deepest condolences on the passing of your father." His voice was soft and genuine. "He was a dear friend of mine for more than thirty-five years."

What's this "your father" stuff? Chuck wondered. But he did allow his right hand to be grasped by Mr. Constanza's two hands.

"Please, won't you have a seat?" he said, indicating the three chairs in front of his desk. His office was bigger than the waiting room and had two large windows that faced the street. The walls were covered with diplomas, awards and pictures of Constanza shaking hands with smiling politicians.

Who are these two people? Chuck asked himself. Why are they here?

The woman spoke. "Mr. Constanza, I assume this is Charles Carver Junior, but Josh and I have never met him." She turned to Chuck and studied his face carefully.

Chuck stared back at her. She was well dressed in brown slacks, beige blouse and suede jacket, an attractive and confident woman, but there was sadness in her expression. The man she'd called Josh, who sat next to Chuck, had brown hair pulled tightly around his head, tied in a ponytail extending about five inches down his back. He was dressed informally in a pale blue sweater and dark blue slacks with pleats and cuffs. His face was strikingly handsome but, like the woman's, traced with sadness.

The lawyer looked confused. "I didn't realize," he said. "I assumed you knew each other. Uh, Vivian Hammersmith and Josh Carver, this is, uh, Charles Carver Junior. Charles, this is Vivian and Josh, your half-sister and half-brother."

Chuck was shocked. "My . . . what?" he said with a scowl.

"You didn't know?" Constanza said. Now it was his turn to be shocked. "You didn't know your father remarried and had a family?"

"No" he said, angry at the surprise they'd sprung on him. "I know nothing about him."

His caustic tone fell like stones on Vivian and Josh, vulnerable in their grief. Hurt tears formed at the edge of Vivian's eyes. Constanza, perplexed, fumbled for words.

"Ahh, Mr. Carver . . . Charles, please don't take offense. Your father never told me you didn't know. Or perhaps he didn't know you didn't know."

Josh turned toward Chuck. "Dad never would have kept you in the dark. He wasn't that kind of person. We always assumed you knew about us because he told us about you. In fact, he talked a lot about you."

Chuck's head was fixed at an angle that walled off Josh's appeal.

Vivian took a tissue from her purse and touched the corners of her eyes. "When we were growing up we always expected to see you one day, that you'd come by the house. Then, when you never came, we thought maybe you'd died."

"Sometimes," Josh added, "we even thought Dad imagined you. That you never really existed."

Chuck Carver, who never could hold his anger for long, let his jaw relax. He folded his hands in his lap and drew a long breath. "Well, I exist and I think we ought to get on with this."

"Good idea," Mr. Constanza said, glad to just do his job. He shifted papers on the desk, then looked at each of the children of Charles Carver Senior to be sure he had their attention. "We're here for the reading of your father's will." He cleared his throat and began. " 'Being of sound mind and . . .' "

Chuck's thoughts wandered as he listened to the legal phrases and clauses, the words about family trusts and codicils. Why was he here at all? Why had Constanza been so insistent about his coming? Surely a father who had driven his wife and son from their home and never made any attempt at reconciliation wouldn't have anything for him in his will. Chuck tried to picture what little he knew about his father. All he could remember were the things his mother had said about him after they moved to Rochester, how unfair he was and how he'd hurt her. The picture was too painful, and Chuck shook the memory from his head.

" '. . . all stock, bonds, mutual funds and cash shall be divided equally between my daughter Vivian Hammersmith and my son Josh Carver.' The latest estimate of the value of his investments and cash," the attorney said, "means that each of you will receive approximately eight hundred eighty thousand dollars." He paused to let that sink in.

Vivian put her hand to her throat and gasped. Josh smiled and shook his head in disbelief.

"Of course, there will be taxes as you draw on the funds that were tax-deferred by your father, but because of the trusts, the inheritance taxes will be only the minimum."

Then he turned to Chuck. " 'And to Charles Carver Junior, I leave my property at number 9 Cove Road, including the house, furnishings, personal effects and all other contents except the painting of Jacqueline Carver, which goes to her daughter, Vivian, and boxes stored in the basement marked as the property of Josh Carver.' " He looked up at Chuck, who stared back at him, amazed at the words he had just heard. "The appraised value of the property, as of three years ago when he contemplated putting it up for sale, was approximately $1.2 million, not including the furnishings." Chuck's face froze in amazement. "Oh, and you're also to have the sailboat, an O'Day 22, and the 1996 Ford pickup truck."

The three sat in stunned silence. Finally Vivian spoke. "I wasn't aware Dad had accumulated that much money. The house I knew to be worth quite a bit because of its location on the water." She hesitated. "I'm overwhelmed."

Josh laughed. "I share a Back Bay apartment in Boston. I drive a five-year-old Honda Civic. I sell real estate. If I make thirty-five thousand a year I'm lucky. I can't imagine eight hundred thousand."

Chuck, stone-faced, said nothing.

"Of course, it will take some time to make these transfers," Mr. Constanza said, "but as executor I will begin immediately. You should know, Charles, that the current value of the house may be less, its true value determined only by what a buyer is willing to pay. I have the keys here and I see no reason why you shouldn't take them right now. And Vivian, you can take the portrait of your mother. Josh, you can pick up the things you've stored there any time that's convenient."

"If we're through," Chuck said abruptly, "I'd like to get going."

"That's it for now," Mr. Constanza said. "But give me a call, Charles, and let me know where I can reach you." He walked them to the door.

Vivian turned to Chuck. "If you wouldn't mind, I'd like to pick up that portrait now. We live in Weston and it's a bit of a drive to Marblehead."

Chuck, uneasy around people he'd just met, said, "Sure. That'll be okay."

"And I'd like to get an idea how much stuff I've got stored there," Josh said. "We could lead you there in case you don't remember where the house is."

"Remember?" Chuck laughed bitterly. "I haven't the slightest idea."

"Then let's go," Josh said. "Vivian, you go first, and Charles, keep your eyes on my Honda."

"Call me Chuck."

"Okay, Chuck," Josh said with a smile.

Twenty minutes later the three-car caravan circled Quiet Cove in Marblehead and turned the beams of their headlights onto Cove Road. Chuck looked through the rain-splattered windshield for landmarks, but saw nothing he remembered. He followed Josh's car as it turned onto a long, curved driveway that came up to a double garage beneath the left side of a house that Chuck now apparently owned. Josh got out, pulled his raincoat over his head and came back to Chuck's car. Chuck lowered the window.

"Did he give you the garage door opener when he gave you the keys?" Josh said, hunched over and talking through the window.

Chuck fished in his pocket and pulled out a ring of keys on which there was a small rectangular casing. "This?"

"Yeah, I think so. Push it there." Chuck did. The right garage door opened and the lights went on.

"Come on," Josh said to Chuck, "let's make a run for it."

The three of them dashed into the garage past the Ford pickup. Chuck looked at the truck he'd just acquired. It was black and had an extended cab.

"Let's go upstairs," Josh said, removing his coat and shaking off drops of water. The other two did the same and followed him up and into the kitchen. Josh, excited with the prospects of showing his newly found half-brother the house, turned on lights and adjusted the thermostat to a warmer setting. Vivian walked into the living room, where the portrait of her mother hung as it always had over the fireplace.

Chuck was last into the kitchen. He dropped his jacket over a chair and slowly lifted his eyes, cautiously letting them wander around the room. His muscles tensed, his jaw tightened. Guardedly, he squinted at the cabinets, stove, sink and refrigerator as if a familiar sight would suddenly lash out at him with some horrible memory of his father. Nothing happened. It was like any other modern kitchen. There was nothing here he remembered. It must have been remodeled and updated. There were, however, dirty dishes in the sink, as if someone had stacked them there before putting them into the dishwasher.

He heard the furnace come on and the beginnings of hot water moving through the system. Carefully, he went through a still-dark dining room and into the living room. Josh and Vivian were standing beneath the portrait. Squinting like a frightened child, he looked around the room, guard up, ready to defend himself from the past.

Vivian came to his side. "This is awkward, isn't it? Too much all of a sudden."

Chuck sighed, appreciating her understanding of his feelings. "Yeah."

"I don't know about you," Josh said, "but I'd like a drink. Dad's usually got some beer and wine around. Probably something harder, too. How about it, Viv?"

"I'll have a glass of wine. It's been a hard day," Vivian said, resting her hand on her brother's arm and sighing from fatigue. Josh gently patted her hand. Chuck watched the tenderness. He liked the way Josh had called his sister Viv. What would it be like to have a brother and sister, he wondered? Quickly, he put aside the thought. He wasn't going to get involved with these kids.

"Chuck?" Josh asked.

"Scotch, if it's there. With ice."

In five minutes Josh was back with the drinks and a beer for himself. He'd found a pressed log, which he put in the fireplace and lit. They sat down and watched the log catch fire, adding a warm focus to the room.

"I can't believe he's gone," Vivian said softly. "He called me last week saying he was going into the hospital for some tests, nothing serious, nothing to worry about. Then, two days later, the doctor called saying he'd died of a massive heart attack."

"It doesn't seem possible, does it?" Josh said. "I've sat here so many times by this fireplace with Dad. He'd ask about school or my work. We'd talk." He paused for several seconds, then added, "I feel like he's still here, like I should hear his footsteps on the stairs and see him come into the room."

The thought made Chuck shudder.

"He was the best," Vivian said. "Oh, there were times when I could have killed him for things he said in front of my friends. And he was a pain when I started living with Carl before we got married. But Dad was from a different generation, kind of old-fashioned."

"I had trouble, too," Josh said. "When we talked it was what he wanted to talk about. Not the things I wanted. I don't think he ever really understood me. But I knew I could count on him. He'd never let me down."

Chuck stared at the fire and sipped his scotch. They can't be talking about my father, he thought. There's got to be some mistake here. He wanted to shout that their father, his father, had been a selfish, inconsiderate man. But he said nothing. Why hurt them with the truth?

"Where do you live, Chuck?" Vivian was asking him.

"Uh, in Alexandria, Virginia. I've got a condo there."

"Married? Family?"

"No, just me."

She let her eyes rest on him. Her smile was accepting.

"What kind of work do you do?" Josh asked.

"Consultant." Chuck kept his eyes glued to the burning log. "I design computer programs for banks and financial institutions."

"And now you're the owner of a big house on Quiet Cove in Marblehead," Josh said with a slight laugh.

"Yeah. It'll be a while before I believe it." Then he added, "Does it bother you that he left the house to me?"

Vivian thought for a moment. "It's not so much that I feel bothered. I'm still getting used to the fact that you really exist. As for the house, well, it never occurred to me that Dad would die and . . . not be here anymore." The words caught in her throat. "I've got wonderful memories of this place, growing up here. When Mom died ten years ago—both Josh and I were away at college by then—it was like a black cloud settled over the house. Over Dad, too. He loved her so much." She paused, sighed, then continued. "Anyway, Carl and I have a nice home in Weston, out beyond 128."

"And you, Josh?" Chuck turned to look at him.

"Oh, I thought a lot about the house," he said. "I always wanted to come back here one day."

"And how do you feel now?" Chuck asked calmly.

"Okay, I guess. Certainly, I'm not mad at you. You had nothing to do with it." He took a pull at his beer. "Actually, I'm not surprised he left you the house. I always thought you were his favorite." Chuck shot him a look of disbelief. "Sometimes I even felt jealous of you when we were growing up."

"Me too," Vivian confessed quietly.

Chuck frowned and shook his head.

"It had to do with your room." Chuck looked at him. "Your old room. When you left, he closed it, locked it. Kept it just the way it was when you lived here. Of course, it was cleaned when the cleaning lady came and sometimes he'd let us go in there and look around, but only when he was with us."

Vivian turned to Chuck. "It became almost an obsession with him. It was strange. That's why we thought maybe you were dead. That he was keeping your room as a kind of shrine."

Listening to his half-siblings, Chuck shook his head slowly from side to side. "I'm afraid I can't help you with any of this. I knew nothing about it, and frankly, it doesn't fit the slightest with how I picture him. All I can remember, and most of that is what Mom told me, is how much he hurt the two of us."

They listened, shocked.

"Frankly," he continued, "it sounds like we're talking about two different people."

The room fell silent except for the rain against the windows and the whistle of wind over the chimney.

"I'm sorry about the house, Josh," Chuck said. "I doubt if I'll keep it. Probably put it on the market." He thought for a few seconds. "You can have first crack at it if you want."

"Thanks, but the truth is I haven't enough income to keep it up."

Again, silence extending to the point of awkwardness filled the room. Vivian got up. "Well, I'd better be going. I've got a family to feed."

"Children?" Chuck asked. Vivian smiled as if pleased to see him coming out of his shell.

"Yes. Three. A boy six and two girls, four and two. Their baby-sitter must be going nuts with them by now."

"Here," Chuck said. "Let me help you with the portrait." With ease he reached up above the fireplace and lifted the frame off the wall.

"Give me your car keys, Viv," Josh said. "I'll move yours into the other side of the garage so you can put the painting in it without getting it wet."

Chuck carried the portrait to the basement and Vivian and the painting got settled in her car.

"What will you do now, Chuck?" she asked her half-brother through the open door.

"First off, I'm going to try to find an inn here in town. Then come back here tomorrow and have a look at the house in the daylight."

"If it's okay with you," Josh said, "I'd like to come back tomorrow with a U-Haul van and pick up my stuff."

"Fine by me."

Josh went to his car and Vivian started her engine.

"Be careful. It's slippery out there." He waved good-bye, and the cars drove off into the rainy night.

Turning back into the garage, he went up to the first floor. The house was deadly silent. Only the wind and the rain. He crossed from the kitchen through the dining room, then from the living room into the front hall, where he looked up into the darkness of the second floor. Somewhere up there was the room with the locked door. His room. He shivered slightly and returned to the living room.

Quickly, he checked the fireplace, lowered the thermostat and turned off the lights. Back in his car he pushed the button to close the garage door and, for the second time in thirty-two years, fled from the house of his father.

TWO

D awn Ireland leaned across the empty seat next to the window of the British Airways 747 and lifted the shade an inch. Light streamed into the darkened business-class section, diffusing the movie on the screen. When her eyes became accustomed to the glare, she peeked out at the barren coastline of what was probably Newfoundland, then closed the shade again. The movie was some idiotic thing about cars chasing cars and blowing up in great bursts of exploding gasoline, not one she cared to watch.

Only a couple more hours, she sighed. She was on her way home after spending two weeks in Europe, mainly in Berlin. She looked at her watch, still set on London time, where she had changed planes. Six-ten, she said to herself, and already I'm exhausted.

Sinking back into her reclining seat, she noticed the passenger who had been sitting in the seat across the aisle from her. He was returning from the galley and carrying a drink. Since boarding, every time she happened to glance in his direction, he met her eyes with a hopeful smile. He was well dressed and about forty-five. She knew it was only a matter of time before he'd try to strike up a conversation. Sooner or later, most unattached men did. A few attached men, too. When you're thirty-three and attractive, men notice you. Dawn was used to it, especially in business class, which most male travelers considered to be their private club.

"Not much of a movie, is it," he said, sliding into his seat. "I took my kids to see it about a month ago. They liked it."

Dawn said idly, "How old are they?"

"Twelve and ten." He sat askew on his seat so he could face her. "Can I get you something from the galley?"

"No thanks."

"On your way home?" His smile seemed genuine.

"Yes."

"Same here. I've been away for four weeks. I can hardly wait to see the family." He sipped his drink. "It's amazing how much the boys grow in just one month."

"I know. My son's fifteen. Every time I see him he's grown another inch."

"Fifteen?" He looked surprised. "You don't look old enough to have a fifteen-year-old."

"Thanks."

"Where's home?"

"Just north of Boston." He seemed safe enough, so she added, "In Marblehead."

"I've heard of it. Never been there, though. We live in Montpelier. That's Vermont. Have you been on a vacation?"

"No. Business."

"What company?"

"My own."

"Really!"

She loved it when men looked surprised. "I'm an art dealer."

"Well, that's something! Your own company and a fifteen-year-old son!" He paused, waiting for her to say something. When she didn't, he asked, "So, do you buy or sell art?"

"Both." Okay, buddy, she thought, it's time to end this. Maybe if I tell him what I do, he'll go away. "I specialize in old posters. Buy them in Europe and sell them in the States. And right now I'm publishing a book and mounting a show at the Boston Museum of Art."

"That's impressive." He sat up in his seat and leaned toward her. "I'd really like to know more. When we get to Boston, I've got to wait three hours for my flight to Montpelier." Oh-oh, she thought. Here it comes. "If you don't have to rush home, what say we have a drink together and you can tell me more about the posters?"

"No thanks. I'm going home."

"I could even stay over for another night in Boston." His voice was eager, insistent.

The bastard. So much for missing his wife and kids. She closed her eyes and settled into her seat.

"What do you say?" Now he was pleading. She didn't answer. After a few minutes, she heard him get up. Through narrowed eyelids, she watched him head up the aisle toward the galley. I hope that's the end of him, she said to herself. Then she let her eyes drift closed.

Swallowing to clear her ears, she listened to the relaxing drone of the engines. She was tired, too tired to be excited about returning home. Brian was away at boarding school, so he wouldn't be there to greet her. At least there was Clara, her dog, and her next-door neighbor, Charlie. He was like a father to her, understanding, a good listener. As soon as he saw her lights go on, he'd be knocking at her door and inviting her over for a drink.

She hadn't intended to come home so soon. Her plans called for her to go to Paris after Berlin. In a moment of weakness, however, when talking by phone with the curator at the Boston Museum of Art, she mentioned that she hadn't yet located the Russian owner of the poster that was to be the centerpiece of the exhibit. Immediately he exploded in a fit of nerves, saying she was upsetting the entire plan for the exhibit and they might as well cancel the show. When she couldn't calm him down, she decided to come home and meet with him in person. This meant the loss of one week in her schedule and the expense of an extra round trip.

That was the downside. The upside was she'd get a chance to see her son. If he couldn't come to Marblehead, she'd go up to Brighton Academy and see him.

She tipped her seat back as far as it would go and curled up as best she could. It wasn't just the long flight that was tiring. It was carrying the whole load alone. Hopping from city to city across Europe had been fun when Gareth Davies was with her. They were a great team, researching the book and gathering posters for the exhibit. Five years before, when she had attended that seminar on European history given by a visiting Welsh professor, she could not have imagined that they would one day be collaborating on a book. At the end of the seminar, Professor Davies invited her for coffee and, after that, for a walk along the Charles River. He talked about life at the University of Wales in Cardiff, and she about the European political posters she bought and sold. She loved his ruddy Welsh complexion, his accent and the way he held her arm as they stepped from a curb. In his mid-forties—almost twice her age—he had wavy gray hair and wore narrow-rimmed glasses. When she laughingly suggested they co-author a book on European poster politics, he said that might be a good idea. A month after he returned to Wales, he wrote her. Was she still interested in writing a book together? Could she locate posters that highlighted various political movements during the first half of the century?

That was the beginning of their work together. At first it was a business partnership. Dawn was married and had a ten-year-old son. It was two years before they became lovers.

Now, with Gareth no longer with her, everything had fallen into her lap. The book, *European Poster Politics: 1910–1940*, was to be published in September, concurrent with the opening of the exhibit.

Dawn squeezed her eyes tightly shut and moved her right hand onto the armrest of the empty window seat. Gareth had always taken the window and she the aisle. He liked to look out. She liked not being confined. When they took off or landed, she would grip his arm and he would look at her reassuringly, guaranteeing her safety. In the air, they would raise their armrests and Dawn would cuddle to his side, placing her head on his shoulder to take a nap.

In the darkness of the cabin, she could barely see him sitting beside her. But she could feel the soft skin of his hand, smell the pipe tucked in the breast pocket of his coat and hear him breathing long, deep breaths. She moved closer to his seat and leaned her head against his shoulder. His head came down so his cheek was pressed against her forehead.

"You okay, luv?" he said.

"I'm okay. I'm with you."

"That's my girl." She knew he was smiling.

She awakened with a start as the engines changed pitch, and realized she'd been asleep. Quickly, she closed her eyes again, hoping to capture a fragment of the dream, but it was gone.

THREE

It was eight o'clock when Chuck awoke in his room on the top floor of the Harbor Light Inn, his eyes gradually focusing on the exposed roof beams of this pre-Revolutionary home. Last night, as he drove through the rain-darkened streets of Marblehead's Old Town, he'd come upon the inn, its sign blowing back and forth in the wind. Fortunately, they had a vacancy. He checked in, stowed his bag and went looking for a restaurant. Down the street and around the corner he found The King's Rook, located in another pre-Revolutionary building. He got a grilled chicken sandwich and was back at the inn by ten o'clock, crawling into his big fourposter bed.

But he hadn't slept well. The tension of the long drive from Alexandria to Salem, the discovery of his half-brother and sister and the sudden responsibility of a $1,200,000 house kept him awake most of the night. It had happened too quickly, shattering what he liked to think was his carefully structured and controlled life. He worried that maybe Josh and Vivian, after they'd had a chance to think about it, might raise legal objections to his disproportionate share of the legacy. That could delay the sale of the house and waste a lot of time. His consulting business in Alexandria required his full attention, and he needed to get back to it.

But there was more. By leaving him the house, his father was stirring up memories that Chuck had long since buried, not just of events that were still a blur in his mind, but of feelings of fear and

15

anger. His father had driven him and his mother from the house, forcing them to make a life of their own in Rochester, and Chuck hated him for it.

He dragged his tired body out of bed, showered, shaved and dressed, then went downstairs. As he neared the dining room, his sour spirits were lifted by the aroma of hot coffee and freshly baked bread and rolls. Maybe there was some hope for the day.

Soon he was back in his car, driving to his newly acquired house. The rain had departed for Nova Scotia, and the sky was blue, with fluffy white clouds. Using a map the innkeeper had given him, he followed the narrow road past Colonial-period homes, around sharp corners where lots were filled with the hulls of sailboats and fishing boats resting on their winter cradles, arriving finally at Quiet Cove. The road circled the head of the cove and was separated from the beach by a rail fence. He stopped his car and got out. There it was, the house—his house now—on the other side of the cove.

It was large, with blue-gray shingle siding and white trim. The landscape sloped from the right side of the house to the left, so that the basement garage could be entered from the driveway on the left side. The first floor had large windows for a view of the cove. Above this floor was a long sloping roof with two double window dormers for the second floor and one for an attic room on the third floor. A wide porch stretched across the front and wrapped around the left side above the garage.

Between the front yard and the cove was Cove Road, heading out to the end of the point. Other houses set on large lots were partially visible behind trees. The embankment below the road was composed of huge granite rocks and showed a high-tide mark a full nine feet above the current low water level.

The tide was out, exposing a mud flat beyond the stony beach. A tree-covered island a couple hundred yards beyond the mouth of the cove sheltered it from the wind and waves, making it truly a quiet cove.

This was where he had lived for the first ten years of his life. He looked for things he might remember. The wide, sloping lawn in front of the house, possibly. The apple trees in the side yard, maybe. The island just offshore, perhaps. Chuck Carver usually remembered everything, but his memory of the house and his childhood seemed completely blocked.

A horn tooted behind him. He turned to see Josh waving from the driver's seat of a U-Haul van.

"Good morning," Chuck said, walking to the van. "You're up early."

"We've got to get back to town," Josh said. "I've got afternoon appointments. Oh, this is my roommate, Cliff Banister."

Cliff leaned forward in the passenger seat and hollered a hello. He seemed to be about Josh's age and was African-American. Chuck was annoyed with himself for feeling surprised, but said nothing.

Josh filled the embarrassed silence by asking, "Is the garage open?"

"No. I just got here. I was looking around to see if I remember anything."

"Do you?"

"Not much." Then, turning to his car, "Follow me."

They pulled into the driveway and Josh turned the van around, backing it up to the garage door. On the left side of the garage were several boxes and a few pieces of furniture marked JOSH and stacked against the back wall.

"What is all this stuff?" Chuck asked.

"Books, mainly," Josh said. "Some pictures, clothes, I don't know what all."

"I wouldn't have minded if you kept it here."

"Thanks, but it's time I made the break from the house. We've got storage in our basement. The lamp and drop-leaf table we'll use in our apartment." Chuck couldn't detect any disappointment in Josh's voice about not getting the house. Maybe he was worrying unnecessarily.

Chuck helped Josh and Cliff carry the boxes to the van. Cliff looked to be six-two, about four inches taller than Josh. He wore Levi's and a plaid shirt with wide white suspenders. He had close-cut hair, wide-set eyes and a strong jaw. His slim build, broad shoulders and strong neck made Chuck wonder if he lifted weights. Josh had dressed for the task in a khaki shirt and dockers.

"Put that box over there," Josh was telling Cliff. "Then bring that lamp and we'll fit it into this space here."

As Cliff carried the lamp past Chuck, he rolled his eyes.

Chuck laughed. "Is he always this bossy?"

"You should see him at home," Cliff said so Josh could hear him. "Everything has to be just so. One cup out of place and he has a fit."

"All right, you two." Josh smiled as he returned to the stack of boxes. "Stop giving me a hard time. If we pack it right, it won't shift around."

Chuck watched them work. He liked the compatibility of the two, found himself even envying their close friendship. What if they're gay? he wondered. At first he felt uneasy with the thought, but he quickly relaxed and acknowledged how strong old prejudices can be. So what if my half-brother's gay? he said to himself.

The van was loaded in less than thirty minutes. As they made ready to leave, Josh thanked him for his help and said, "Come by and see us the next time you're in Boston."

The invitation caught Chuck off guard. Immediately the prejudices kicked in, then just as quickly evaporated. In its place was a longing to share in Josh and Cliff's comfortable camaraderie.

"I'd like that, but I doubt if I'll be getting into the city."

"Please try. We'll have dinner." His smile was genuine.

"Nice meeting you, Chuck," Cliff called through the window.

"Same here. See you later." He waved good-bye.

Chuck watched the car until it was out of sight. He thought, Well, Josh has got his stuff. Vivian's got her portrait. That's the last I'll see of them. Suddenly feeling alone, he turned into the garage and began climbing the stairs. What would it be like to have a brother and sister? he asked himself.

In the kitchen, while he prepared coffee, he wondered about the dirty dishes still in the sink. There was a frying pan, a small plate with toast crumbs, jam and bits of bacon on it, a juice glass half-filled with water and a cup and spoon with the hardened remains of a soft-boiled egg stuck to them. My father's last meal, he thought, before he left for the hospital. I'm doing my father's dishes. Chuck felt a wave of nausea hit him. But he rinsed the dishes and added them to those already in the dishwasher from some previous meal. His eyes wandered to the refrigerator. A note was stuck to the door with a magnet.

Mrs. Crippen,
Thank you for coming. Don't bother with my bedroom. It's a mess. I'll do it myself when I get home. The money's in the usual place.

Charlie

The cleaning lady, Chuck thought. And my father's handwriting. A little wobbly. How old would he be now? Certainly in his mid-seventies. But he's gone and I'm living in his house. Well, not for long.

He filled a mug and set off with his coffee to raise the thermostat. How different the rooms looked in the morning sunlight. They seemed friendlier, almost inviting. He looked at the vacant space above the fireplace where the portrait had hung and could see its silhouette where the wallpaper was cleaner and not so faded. He touched the back of the sofa where he'd sat the night before in front of the fireplace. It was leather, the same as the two large chairs flanking its sides. Bookcases were on either side of the fireplace, and to the left were the front windows. For an instant he saw a small boy curled up in the chair on the right side of the sofa, reading a book he'd pulled from the bookcase, then the memory was gone.

He walked into the entrance hall and looked upstairs. He'd check on his bedroom later. Now he needed to find a bathroom. He discovered it between the kitchen and the dining room.

He was settled on the commode when a phone began ringing. There was no way he'd be able to get it before they hung up, so he let it ring. On the fourth ring he heard a voice.

"Hi. Charlie here. Leave me a message and I'll catch you later."
Suddenly, words flashed into his mind.
"*. . . you can't catch me! I'm the Gingerbread Man.*"
Chuck gripped the edge of the sink. He felt dizzy, faint. Then, as quickly as it came, it ended and his head cleared.

"My god, where did that come from?" he said aloud. "Gingerbread Man? What's that all about?"

Then he heard a voice coming into the answering machine.

"Mr. Carver, this is Kendall Kennels calling, please give us a call." This was followed by an electronic voice saying, "Wednesday, 11:18 A.M."

Chuck hiked up his pants, washed his hands and went to the kitchen looking for the phone and answering machine. It was in the opposite corner of the room from the sink and he hadn't noticed it. The message light was blinking; there were four messages. He pushed the message button and the machine's tape whirred.

"Mr. Carver, this is Mrs. Crippen. My husband pulled his back yesterday and I'm taking him to the chiropractor today. I'm sorry I won't be able to make it, but I'll be there for sure next Friday. Uhh, good-bye." The machine followed with, "Thursday, 9:08 A.M." That's last week, Chuck thought.

"Hi, Dad! It's Vivian. How did the tests go? Call me." Then the machine, "Friday, 10:16 A.M." Poor Vivian, Chuck thought. He was probably dead by then.

"Well, where were you this morning?" It was a man's voice. "How can we have a foursome when only three of us show up? Give me a call. It's Harry." Pause. "You okay, Charlie?" And the machine, "Friday, 11:23 A.M."

Chuck stood over the machine adding up this new information about his father. He played golf with friends, he had something to do with a Kendall Kennels and his cleaning lady couldn't make it last week. I wonder if I should call the kennel? No, he decided. They'll call me if they need to.

He refilled his coffee mug and went to the stairs. The father who had been only a vague but unpleasant memory was beginning to take the human form of an old man who apparently had an active life. He'd left here for the hospital one day last week for tests and had every intention of returning the same day, but he never made it. As Chuck had done so many times in the last twenty-four hours, he tried to resolve the conflict between his feelings toward his father and the way other people pictured him.

Halfway up the steps he heard the phone ring. Not knowing where other extensions might be, he ran back to the kitchen, picking up the receiver just before the answering machine came on.

"Hello."

"Is this Mr. Carver?" a clipped voice asked.

"Yes." Then he realized they meant his father, but before he could explain, the voice went on.

"Well, this is Kendall Kennels. Have you forgotten about your dog? It'll be a full week today that he's been here."

"I . . . I didn't realize."

"It's okay with us if you want to keep him here longer, but we thought it was going to be just a day or two."

"Well," Chuck hesitated, "I'm not sure what I should do."

"It's up to you, but so far you owe us four hundred dollars."

"Four hundred dollars?" he gasped.

"That's right. Our weekly charge, that is if you pick him up this afternoon."

"Okay. I'll be by after lunch. Where're you located?"

"Don't you remember?" the voice asked.

FOUR

Dawn stood next to the baggage carousel in the customs section of Logan International Airport. Behind the wall she could hear the rumble of carts and the plop of heavy bags dropping onto the conveyor belt. Today, no one would be outside the customs door to greet her. Charlie, her friend from next door, often drove down from Marblehead to pick her up, but her stopover in London was so short she hadn't called him. He'll have a fit that I didn't telephone, Dawn thought.

"You should have called, Dawn," he'll say. "So it was six in the morning my time, I wouldn't have minded."

She usually did call, even though she felt she was imposing on his kindness. And when she did, he was always there, waiting with the crowd of greeters. Tall, gray-haired and wearing his old leather flying jacket, he'd wave to her.

"Hi, Dawn. Over here." And she'd go to him to receive a welcoming hug and a kiss on the cheek.

"You're good to pick me up."

"It's no trouble, Dawn," he always said, the lines around his eyes crinkling as he smiled. "When you get to be my age, it's nice to have something you really want to do."

Charlie, she thought. I love him!

At seventy-three, Charlie was a handsome man. When she and her mother had moved next door to him on Cove Road, he was fifty-four, a senior pilot with TWA flying from Boston to Europe several times each month. His daughter, Vivian, was twelve, only two years younger than Dawn. Ordinarily Dawn, a teenager, wouldn't have bothered herself with a youngster two years her junior, but she was lonely. Vivian, on the other hand, was in awe of her tall, blond neighbor who was already developing the body of a young woman. She invited Dawn swimming in the cove and always included her when her dad took her sailing. The friendship that developed that first summer between the two girls never waned.

And Charlie—she never called him Mr. Carver—was the father she didn't have.

"Charlie, if I carry the sails down to the boat, will you teach me how to rig them?" she asked one day.

"Sure," he said. "I've got to get the truck washed and then we'll go. Find Viv and see if she wants to come, too." Off she ran into the house, as if it were her own, to find her friend. In a minute she was back, Vivian in tow.

"Can we help you wash the truck?"

If it wasn't washing the truck in the summer, it was carrying wood for the fireplace in the fall, shoveling the walk in the winter or helping him plant his garden in the spring.

The second summer, when Dawn was fifteen, Vivian said, "Mom's jealous of you. I heard her telling Dad that he was spending more time with you than he was with her."

"Jealous of me?" They were sitting in Dawn's bedroom looking at a scrapbook.

"Yeah." She paused, then added, "I feel that way too, sometimes. I think he likes you more than me."

"That's crazy. He's your dad, not mine." Dawn let her eyes drop to the scrapbook they had open on the bed. She turned a page. "This is my dad."

Vivian looked at the book. There was a picture of Dawn as a little girl with her mother and a tall, lanky man, all in bathing suits. Another picture showed Dawn blowing out candles on a cake with her dad grinning in the background. Vivian turned some more pages. Here were photos of Dawn's father in his flying suit and holding a helmet as he stood at the nose of an F-14 Tomcat. There was one formal portrait of him in uniform beneath which was printed "Lt. Commander Robert Olson." The last page of the book had a newspaper clipping describing the crash of an F-14 on a routine training mission over the Gulf of Mexico and a long obituary about Olson. "Lt. Commander Olson is survived by his wife, Ellen, and daughter, Dawn."

Vivian read the entire obituary, then turned to Dawn and began to cry. "I couldn't stand it if Daddy died. It must be awful for you."

"I wish he'd never been a pilot," Dawn said angrily. "I wish he'd been a businessman and stayed on the ground. Then I'd still have him."

"I never thought of my daddy crashing. He's flying all the time."

"It's different if you're flying passenger planes. They're safe." As Dawn took the book a sheet of paper fluttered to the floor.

"What's this?" Vivian asked.

"An old poem I wrote." Dawn picked up the paper and was putting it back in the book. "It's nothing."

"Let me read it."

Dawn hesitated, then gave it to her. "Okay, but don't tell your parents or my mom about it. Promise?"

"I promise," Vivian said. She took the poem and read it aloud.

Icarus's Daughter

Icarus had a daughter who sent him on his way.
She made his life unbearable by what she wouldn't say.
She wouldn't say she's sorry, she wouldn't say good bye.
So off he flew to find the sun, to find a way to die.

Dawn Olson
9th Grade
Warrington High School

Vivian looked at a penned note scrawled across the bottom, then asked, "Why did your teacher tell you to see her after class?"

"She thought I was screwed up." Vivian looked puzzled. Dawn sighed and went on. "Do you know who Icarus was?"

"Is he the guy who made wings from bird feathers and tried to fly to the sun?"

"Yeah."

"And he had a daughter?"

"I made up that part."

"It's a good poem. Why don't you want your mother to see it?"

"It's none of her business." Dawn took the note, shoved it into the scrapbook and slammed the cover shut.

At the carousel, a man elbowing his way past Dawn to grab his bag brought her back to the present. Her bag followed his on the track. She picked it up, extended the handle and pulled it toward the customs inspector, who waved her through.

As she opened the door to the Terminal C concourse, she couldn't help but search the crowd for Charlie's face.

Forget it, she told herself. He's not here.

FIVE

Chuck pulled into the parking lot of Kendall Kennels and saw why it cost $400 a week to keep a dog there. There were several well-maintained buildings, including a veterinary office, a pet supply and gift store and a comfortable waiting room with young, smiling attendants all in identical blue smocks. He waited for an elderly couple to pay the bill for their golden retriever and to hug and kiss the dog. The dog licked their faces excitedly and peed on the linoleum floor. Chuck grimaced.

"My name's Carver. You called about a dog that's here?"

A man got up from a desk at the rear of the office and came forward. He looked at Chuck questioningly. "Mr. Charles Carver?"

"That's my father. He died last week. I'm his son. Same name."

"Oh, Mr. Carver. I'm sorry." Chuck recognized the same clipped voice. "We didn't know. When he didn't come by for the dog we were worried and called several times."

"Yes." Chuck chose to ignore his exaggeration. "Well, I'd like to get him now."

"Of course. Jane . . . no, Mike, please get Mr. Carver's dog." Mike, who looked like an NFL tackle, left through a back door to the kennel area, while Chuck reluctantly wrote out a four-hundred-dollar check.

A minute later thunderous barks were heard behind the door, which flew open as a monstrous dog plunged into the waiting room

26

with Mike in tow. Chuck drew back. The dog had heavy, jet-black hair with a white patch on his chest. His wild eyes were brown and set deep in his large and powerful head. A full tail wagged vigorously, sweeping magazines from the waiting room table as the dog continued his stentorian barking.

"He's glad to see you," Mike said, gasping for breath.

"Really? Lord, but he's big," Chuck declared.

"Yeah," the attendant said. "It's all muscle too. No fat."

"How much does he weigh?"

"It was about a hundred and forty, wasn't it, Jane?" Mike called over his shoulder.

"One forty-two," she answered.

"What's his name?"

"Bear. He's half Newfy and half Lab."

"Well," Chuck said, resigned, "let's go home, Bear."

"Can I help you?" Mike offered.

"No, I'll manage," Chuck said, taking the leash from Mike.

Instantly Bear charged for the outside door, spun Chuck around and pulled him out into the parking lot. Skidding on the gravel like an ice hockey player coming to a stop, Chuck thought he'd gained control. But no. Bear had stopped to express his outrage with Kendall Kennels by relieving himself on the back tire of one of their trucks. He stood on three legs for a full minute, a sublime expression on his face. When he finished, he allowed his new master to lead him to the Mitsubishi.

Chuck got a blanket from the trunk and spread it over the narrow backseat, then pulled the seat forward for Bear to get in back. The dog looked at him indignantly, flipped the seat back with his nose and climbed into the front. Chuck started to protest, then gave up and got in. He looked at Bear, who was sitting beside him on the seat, hunched over with his head pressed against the ceiling.

"Tough luck, fella. You're either going to ride that way or lie down in the back."

Bear ignored him.

Chuck started the car and headed out onto the road for the twenty-mile drive back to Marblehead. They hadn't gone a hundred yards before the car hit a bump and Bear's head came up against the retractable roof with such force that Chuck was afraid he'd break the hinges. He stopped and pressed a button that folded the top back into the trunk.

They started again, this time with Bear holding his head high and looking over the top of the windshield. As they picked up speed, the wind caught his jowls, flaring them open so it looked as if he were smiling.

When they pulled into the driveway, Chuck pressed the remote to open the garage door. Bear leaped over the side of the car and raced into the house, barking. Chuck followed.

On the stairs to the kitchen he could hear the dog charging from room to room, then galloping up the stairs to the bedrooms. Finally he stopped running and came to the top of stairs, where he looked down at Chuck. He barked one loud, questioning bark, then lay down and cried softly.

Chuck, who kept his emotions on a leash stronger than Bear's, was touched.

"He's not here, big boy. I'm sorry."

Bear raised his head and looked at him. Then he came down the stairs to the living room chair on the left side of the sofa, where there was a reading lamp and a magazine rack. With his head on the seat of the chair, he let his body thud to the floor, then emitted a long, rumbling, sad sigh.

Chuck sat on the arm of the chair. He began rubbing the dog's head and digging his fingers into the thick fur of his neck. Bear rumbled another sigh, but this time it sounded like a purr.

"You loved him a lot, didn't you?" Bear opened his eyes and looked at Chuck.

"You and everybody else. Everybody but me." He continued rubbing and Bear continued looking at him. "Why did I miss out?" Bear didn't answer.

Chuck sat with Bear for a few more minutes, then got up and went to the kitchen to see what provisions were in the refrigerator and pantry. Not much. He'd have to make a trip to the grocery store. And what about the dog? Did he have food? He searched the cabinets under the counters and found a large bag of dry dog food and several cans. Bear's pretty well set, he thought.

Meanwhile, Bear had gone to the front door and barked one

demanding bark. Chuck stood up from examining the dog food. "Now what?" Bear barked again.

"All right, I'm coming. But let's get this straight." Chuck was talking as he walked through the living room and into the front hall. "I'm sorry you're sad, but you're going to have to adjust your life to mine, at least for a while."

Chuck opened the front door and Bear lumbered off across the porch and into the yard. He circled the entire house with Chuck trying to keep pace, ending up in the garage, where he sniffed every corner.

"Still not convinced, huh? Think I'm trying to fool you?"

Bear went up to the pickup truck and stood on his hind legs to look into the driver's-side window. On two legs, Bear was more than six feet tall.

"What are you trying to do, make me cry?" Chuck said as he got the leash from the front seat of the Mitsubishi. "Come on. We're going for a walk." He hooked up the dog and together they went down the driveway, Bear obediently walking by his side. "That's a good dog," Chuck said. He suspected Bear was thinking, "That's a good human."

The tide was coming in and Quiet Cove was filled with water halfway to the top of the embankment. When they got to the narrow beach that was still exposed, not seeing any other dogs or people, Chuck unhooked the leash. Bear ran into the cold water, stopping to look approvingly at Chuck as if this human did have some sense. He swam out into the cove with only his head and tail above water. Guess he knows what he's doing, Chuck thought. Probably waited all week for this. After a few minutes Bear swam back, and walked up onto the beach.

"Hi," a voice said behind him. As Chuck was turning around, another dog rocketed past him, bounding onto the beach and racing toward Bear. The dog, half Bear's size, grabbed the fur on Bear's neck and, growling fiercely, wrenched it back and forth. Chuck started toward them, alarmed.

"It's okay," the woman said buoyantly. "They're friends. That's how they say hello." Glancing first at Chuck and then at Bear, she frowned. "Where's Charlie?"

Chuck stared at her, lost for words.

When he didn't answer, she asked, "Is something wrong?"

"I'm Chuck Carver." He was stalling, searching for a way to tell her. "You're a friend of my father."

"I live next door." She waved a finger toward the house to the right of Charlie's. "Then, you're his son." Her voice broke. Some message was coming through to her. As if clinging to the hope that she might be wrong, she added, "He's told me about you. I'm Dawn Ireland." She stopped. Her face hardened. "Tell me. What's happened?"

"My father died last week. While he was in the hospital for tests. It was a massive heart attack."

Her eyes filled with horror. "No!" Her mouth began to quiver. "Not Charlie. Not another one." Then she sank to the ground. Chuck picked her up gently and carried her to a concrete culvert near the road, where he carefully set her down. Her eyes opened. Braced by his arm and leaning against his chest, she began to cry until her whole body was convulsed with sobbing.

The two dogs relinquished their play and sat in front of them, each whining softly.

Gradually her crying subsided, and she relaxed against Chuck's arm. After several moments of silence, he thought she might have fainted again. Then she spoke.

"This isn't fair to you. He was your father and here I am doing all the crying."

"No. It's okay." But he was embarrassed. He could breathe in the scent of her hair as her head lay against his chest. "You were very close, I guess."

"He was more than a friend. He was like my father. Someone I counted on." Her voice broke again. "My best friend."

Chuck felt awkward. He didn't know what to say. A glance at the road and his eyes met the disapproving eyes of a woman pushing a baby carriage. More embarrassment. He returned his gaze to the blond head on his shoulder, wondering what the relationship had been between this woman and his dad. He tried a few avuncular pats on her shoulder. This seemed to help. She sat up and dried her eyes with the back of her hand.

"I think I'd better go." She stood, unsteadily.

"I'll walk you up to your house," Chuck offered. They started up a path to the road.

"I've been away . . . on a trip. I got back about an hour ago and came over to Charlie's to say hello. When I couldn't find him, I went back home and took a nap. Then I looked out my window and saw you down here with Bear. Your leather jacket—at first I thought you were Charlie. He's got one, too. Then I could see you're much bigger. But I wondered, why would someone else be walking Bear?" She shook her head. "I'm sorry. I'm rambling."

She stopped when they came to the beginning of her driveway, giving Chuck a chance to look at her. Her tear-stained eyes were blue and her face slender. She was maybe ten years younger than he. Her hair fell across the collar of her black nylon jacket and reached halfway down her back. She wore a pair of faded jeans that were torn just above the left knee and Nike running shoes. Her long, trim figure, what he could see of it, was that of a runner.

She looked up at him. "Your jacket—the leather smells like Charlie's, but his has a sheepskin collar." Abruptly she turned to look back at the cove, as if the physical movement would help her gain control and redirect her thoughts. "I'm sorry for going on like this. You're the one who's lost a father. It's just that it's so sudden. I can't believe it. Charlie was my anchor and now I've got no one." She started to walk toward the houses. "Come on, Clara!" she said, and the dog bounded to her side.

Halfway up the drive, she stopped, then waved. "Good-bye," she called.

Chuck asked, concerned, "Will you be all right?"

"I don't know." The lines in her face contorted, and turning quickly, she went into her house.

SIX

Dawn stood at her kitchen window gazing at Charlie's house while she opened a can of dog food for Clara's dinner.

I can't believe he's gone, she said to herself. If I went over there, I'm sure I'd find him. "Charlie, are you home?" "Be right down," he'd say. She had crossed to his house so often she'd worn a path. When she was discouraged or filled with self-doubt, Charlie, in his quiet, unassuming way, was the one who restored her. When she was happy, Charlie was there to share her joy.

Standing there with a half-opened can of dog food in her hand, she saw Chuck open the front door and come onto the porch with Bear. He was examining the decking, scraping up pieces of chipped paint with the edge of his shoe. He and Bear walked the full length of the porch, stopping occasionally to scrape more chipped paint. Eventually they went back inside.

So that's the mysterious Chuck Carver, she thought. Charlie had told her about his first marriage and his son Chucky. What must he have thought of me down there on the beach, fainting and bawling like a crazy woman? Now that I think of it, he seemed to take it pretty well. Even asked if I'd be all right. And Bear seems to like him. I'll have to apologize the next time I see him.

She turned from the sink to see Clara sitting expectantly behind her, head erect, ears alert and tail sweeping back and forth across the tile floor.

"I'm glad you're here, sweetie," Dawn said as she reached down to pet Clara. The dog folded back her ears and raised her forehead to cherish the full stroke of her mistress's hand. "I'll bet you're hungry."

Dawn had adopted Clara a year after she and Paul divorced. With Brian away at boarding school, the house was cold and empty when she returned from her trips. Paul, who had moved out of the house to an apartment a few blocks away, was furious with her for getting the dog. It was one more thing he'd have to take care of when she was away. The house, Brian and now a dog. She didn't know why he put up with it, but he did. He could have gone his own way and she wouldn't have blamed him, but he continued to help her out in the same begrudging way he had when they were married. In winter when the car wouldn't start, he'd come by and get it going. When the toilet continued running, he'd fix it. And for each thing he'd correct or get to work, he'd shake his head disgustedly, reaffirming his belief that she was totally incompetent. When they were married, this look made her burn, but now it amused her.

On her way home from Logan Airport she'd asked the taxi driver to go by Paul's apartment so she could pick up Clara. Paul was out, thank goodness. The dog was so excited to see her, she left a wet circle on Paul's carpet. Dawn thought for a moment about leaving it, but decided to clean it up, knowing she'd have to ask him to take care of Clara again in a few days.

Dawn fed Clara and, fighting the urge to give in to jet lag and take a nap, went to her bedroom to finish unpacking. Clara followed her.

"Can't sleep now, Clara, or I'll wake up in the middle of the night." She hung up her dark blue business suit and three dresses and tossed her dirty clothes in the hamper, then sat on the bed. The dog put her head on her lap and Dawn scratched her ears.

"I never got a chance to say good-bye," she said to Clara. "He was out when I left for England." Dawn stared at nothing for several moments, tears forming in her eyes then took a deep breath, wiped her eyes and carried her laundry hamper to the washer-dryer down the hall. Returning to her room, she stopped at Brian's bedroom, which had a view of the Carver house. In the waning light of late afternoon, the house looked like a gray mausoleum.

I'd better call Brian, she thought. Paul must have known about Charlie, but I'll bet he didn't tell Brian. She telephoned Brighton Academy and left word for her son to call her as soon as possible, then went to the kitchen to fix dinner for herself. In the freezer she found a frozen veal parmesan dinner, which she put in the microwave. As she finished setting the cooking time and pushing the START button, the phone rang.

"Hi, Mom, what's up?" His cheerful voice immediately lifted her spirits. Brian, like his mother, had inherited his great-grandparents' Norwegian blond hair and blue eyes. His slim body was still growing into his tall frame, but already his shoulders were broadening and his jaw was assuming a masculine firmness.

"Well, for starters, I'm home."

"Oh, yeah. How was the trip?"

"Okay, but I had to come home early. How are things at school?"

"We had our last hockey game on Sunday. We won by two goals, and I got one of 'em."

"Good for you. What'll you do now that hockey season's over?"

"I don't know. Might study for a change," he laughed.

"Did your dad call you about the news from here?"

"Haven't talked to him. What's happening?"

"Well," she paused, "I have some very bad news. Charlie died at the end of last week."

There was no response on the other end of the line.

"I'm so sorry, darling. I didn't learn about it myself until just a little while ago."

"So that's why."

"What do you mean?"

"He called last week and said he'd be here for our last game." His voice began to break. "I kept looking at the stands. I couldn't find him. He . . . was . . . already . . ."

"Brian, do you want to come home?"

After a moment he spoke. "No." Pause. "Got a test first period tomorrow. I'll be all right."

"Do you want me to come up there?"

"No, but I'd like to come home this weekend." Those were the last words Dawn wanted to hear.

"Darling," then she paused. She didn't know what to say. "I've got to go back on Friday. I won't be here." The silence on the line bore into her heart like a dagger. "I don't want to, but I've got to go."

"Where this time?"

"Paris."

"How long?"

"It might be two weeks, but then I'll be home for a while."

Again silence.

She asked, "Are you free tomorrow afternoon? I can come up and we'll do something together, then have dinner."

"Could we go to Freeport? I want to get some pants at L.L. Bean."

"Sure. What time?"

"My last class ends at two-twenty."

"I'll be there. And Brian, I'm sorry."

"I know. It won't be the same this summer."

"I mean about being away so much."

"Yeah, I know. Me too."

She set the phone down but didn't move from the chair in the kitchen. No, she thought, it won't be the same this summer. From the time Brian could go out of doors alone, he'd cross the yards to Charlie's to look for his friend. When Brian was seven, Charlie retired and he and Brian became a full-time team. It was the same year Charlie's wife, Jacqueline, died, so Brian's companionship meant as much to Charlie as Charlie's did to Brian. One day they'd be building something in the shed, the next they'd be sailing on Charlie's boat. He never missed a trip to the hardware store with his friend, and he always came home with some treasure Charlie'd buy him, like a neat pulley or a tiny screwdriver or a length of rope, important things a boy needed. About the only time they weren't together was when Charlie played golf once a week.

Brian was twelve when his parents divorced and his father moved out. Unlike other children who suffer through a divorce, Brian was relieved. It brought an end to the arguing and bickering over the amount of time his mother was spending traveling with her new business. When she was away, he stayed at his dad's apartment but spent his days with Charlie. When she was home, life was perfect.

Last year when he started high school, Dawn decided a private boarding school was the best thing because she knew she couldn't count on Paul to take care of him while she was away. That first year was hell for everybody. Dawn felt guilty for not being available to Brian, the boy was lonely and missed his friend Charlie, and Paul fumed every time he had to write a check to Brighton Academy. By the second year Brian had made friends and become a star on the junior varsity hockey team.

Knowing she'd see him tomorrow eased some of Dawn's guilt. Why is it, she wondered, that every time I do something for myself I feel like I'm stealing it from someone else? Or doing what I want means I'm depriving another person? That's how it was with Paul when she was still married, and he'd never let her forget it. But she could live with that. Brian was another matter. The balance she'd struck between being his mother and a dealer in European poster art needed to lean only a fraction of an inch toward her business and she felt guilty.

Tomorrow morning, after walking the dog, she'd phone Joel Rabinowitz, her editor. He might be able to tell her what to do about the poster for which she didn't have copyright permission. Next she'd go to Boston and calm the fears of the BMA. Then off to Brighton.

She remembered her dinner in the microwave. She'd been sitting there in the kitchen so long it had gotten cool, so she zapped it for another minute and a half. She poured herself a glass of chardonnay and sat down to eat her dinner.

If only I could talk with Charlie, she mused. How hard it was to have him gone.

She finished eating and went upstairs with her briefcase and a glass of brandy. At the top of the stairs she turned into Brian's room again for another look at Charlie's house. As she peered through the few trees that stood between the houses, she could see lights go on and off in one set of windows on the second floor, then in another set. Chuck must be going from room to room exploring the house. I wonder if Charlie left it to him?

SEVEN

Chuck fed Bear, then locked him in the house and drove to Crosby's Market in Marblehead's Old Town. Accustomed to living alone, doing his own cooking and shopping for food, he had no trouble buying bacon, eggs and bagels for breakfast, lunch meats and bread for sandwiches and steak for one evening meal and salmon for another. He topped it off with vegetables and the makings for salad. He was now set for three days, which was as long as he planned to be in town. To make that night's dinner easier, he bought a barbecued chicken.

As he was getting in the car, he remembered he hadn't checked out of the Harbor Light Inn. Now that there was Bear to take care of, he'd decided to move into his father's house. He parked behind the inn and went to the desk. Yes, they were still holding the room for him, but having heard about his father's death and that Chuck had inherited the house—it was a small town—they expected him to be moving to Quiet Cove.

"There'll be no charge for late checkout, Mr. Carver," the owner said. "You've had enough to think about, I'm sure."

"Thank you," Chuck said, thinking how nice people were in Marblehead. He got his overnight bag and briefcase from the room and went to the car.

Bear met him at the front door as if he'd been gone for a week and followed him into the kitchen. Chuck set the barbecued chicken on the counter and went to the refrigerator. Bear sat by the chicken, unwrapping the stay-warm package with his eyes. "Oh, that's it," Chuck laughed. "Just when I thought you were beginning to like me."

He poured himself a double scotch from his father's liquor cabinet, moved the chicken to the back of the counter for safekeeping and went to the stairs. Bear followed.

"So, big guy, we're going to be roommates for a few days." Bear bumped along beside him. "I'd better go upstairs and find a place to sleep."

As he started up, he realized this was the second day he'd been in the house and he hadn't ventured upstairs. During the day, with sunlight filling the rooms, the house hadn't been so foreboding. But now it was getting dark outside and shadows filled the corners. The sense of anxiety he had first felt returned.

A balcony circled above the entrance hallway and had several open doors and another hall leading from it. Chuck took a sip of scotch and tried to remember which room had belonged to his parents. Bear looked at him and started off around the balcony to an open door toward the front of the house. He walked in, collapsing on the floor with a thud and his customary deep resonant moan. Chuck entered and turned on the wall switch by the door. A bedside table lamp came on. The room was large, with a king-size bed against the back wall, windows on the outside wall facing the cove, a long chest of drawers with a mirror against another wall and a sofa and chair at the end of the room. There were two more doors, one to a bathroom and one to a walk-in closet. The bed was unmade.

Chuck carried his drink to the bed and sat down. His father had thrown back these covers last Thursday, a week ago, gotten up, walked into that bathroom and then dressed. It was hard to imagine. He looked down at Bear. The dog's head rested on a pair of slippers. Chuck, feeling his eyes moistening, patted the dog's head.

He stood and went to the chest of drawers. There were several framed pictures of Vivian, Josh and their mother, whom he'd seen in the portrait. The lid of a wooden box was open and inside were cufflinks, tie clips, an old Elgin wristwatch with no band and several foreign coins of small denomination.

He looked again at the thrown-back sheet and blanket and decided he was not going to sleep in that bed. Too close to his father. The thought made him shiver. He picked up his scotch from the chest and went out into the hall.

"Come on, Bear. Let's go exploring." The dog groaned, got up and followed him.

Turning left around the balcony, they passed the hall that went to the right. The first two doors were to bedrooms no longer used as such. Probably they were Josh's and Vivian's when they were growing up. The next door led to a bathroom. Beyond that, at the end of the balcony, was yet another bedroom.

This was obviously a guest room. The bed was an antique four-poster with a canopy, and the rest of the furniture matched it. There was a table with a lamp—an electric light hidden in the chimney of a lantern—two straight chairs, a tall chest of drawers and a vanity. The bed was too short for Chuck, but he decided it would do for one night.

Bear watched him look around, then followed him as he went back into the hall.

"What's next, Bear?" The dog looked at him but didn't move. "Let's go down the hallway." They crossed the balcony to the hall leading to the other side of the house, where he found a stairway to the third level and another door to what was obviously a study. He flipped the wall switch and the desk light came on. The desk was an old gray metal, government-issue desk that Chuck dimly remembered. In fact, the whole room tugged at his mind. On the walls were framed pictures of World War II fighter planes and bombers. He looked at a picture over the desk and knew what it was before he drew near. He had seen it before. His dad, in leather cap and goggles, dressed in a flying suit, standing beside a P-47 Thunderbolt.

He let his eyes drift shut and saw a young child come into the study and climb up on his father's lap.

"What's that one, Daddy?"

"That's the P-47. What an airplane. We won the war with that one. It'd go four hundred and fifty miles an hour and fly higher and faster than anything the Germans had."

"And that one?" the boy asked.

"That's my wing."

The boy laughed. "It doesn't look like a wing. It looks like a bunch of men." It was a game they played.

"Not that kind of wing, silly. Those were the guys I flew with."

The boy smiled. He knew.

Chuck opened his eyes and looked at the picture of several pilots standing in a semicircle, arms around each other's shoulders, his father on the end. A pained expression crossed his face. Was this the man he hated, the man he'd grown up fearing?

He sat down at the desk. Papers were placed in two neat piles at the back on either side of the desk lamp, a dull bronze affair with a long green shade under which were two lightbulbs. The base had a tray that was filled with pencils and pens. Beside the desk was a Remington portable typewriter, not electric, sitting on a movable typing table. Chuck knew he would have to go through all this stuff on the desk, but not tonight.

He looked down at Bear, who raised his head as if to say, "Okay, let's go." This time Chuck followed Bear into the hall. He was taking him back downstairs.

"Wait," Chuck said. "I want to look at the attic level."

Bear remained where he was while Chuck climbed the stairs across from the study. At the top were three doors. One opened to an unfinished section of the attic and another to a bathroom. The third was locked. My room, Chuck thought, the one Josh said was kept locked. I can't deal with that tonight.

Back downstairs, Bear led the way to the kitchen, where Chuck added a little more scotch to his glass and more ice, then sipped at it while making a salad. He took the chicken out of its bag and put it on a plate, then into a microwave above the stove for two minutes. When dinner was ready, he put it all on a tray and carried it into the living room. A chair was placed so a person could watch the TV from across the room. He turned it on, found some news and sat down.

He was ravenous. Tearing the chicken leg free, he ate the meat and licked his fingers. Bear had positioned himself in front of the TV so that Chuck had to lean his head to the side to see. If he leaned right, Bear moved to his left. If left, then Bear moved right.

There was no way Chuck could escape the penetrating stare of the big dog's eyes.

"All right," Chuck said, giving in to the intense begging. "Here's a piece of skin." He tossed it to the dog, who caught it deftly in his large mouth. Bear moved closer. Chuck ate some more, finished the salad and tossed a piece of meat to the dog. When the food was gone, Bear lost interest, lay down and let him finish watching the news.

"You love me when I feed you," he said. "You're almost human."

When he finished cleaning up, Chuck decided to call his mother. He dialed the area code for Rochester, and then his mother's number.

Harriet Carver answered on the third ring.

"Hi Mom. It's Chuck. How's it going?"

"Oh, Chuck. Things are fine here." But her voice sounded tired. "It rained yesterday but it's nice today. Cold, though. I can hardly wait for warmer weather."

He could imagine her sitting at the phone, probably still in her nurse's uniform on which was pinned her name badge and title, Director of Nursing. Her hair was pure white, like his would soon be, and she had a full figure but not one you'd call fat. She was attractive and disguised the loose skin on her neck by holding her head high.

"How are things in Virginia? Warmer, I'll bet."

"I'm not in Virginia. I'm in Marblehead."

There was a long silence.

"Mom? You still there?"

"Yes. What are you doing there?"

"You don't know, then?"

"Know what?"

"Dad died last Friday. They had the funeral on Monday."

Again, silence.

"Mom. You okay?"

"Yes. So he's gone. I don't know why it should be such a shock. He's been gone for me for the last thirty-two years." Chuck could hear her voice catch. She was fighting back tears.

"I know. For me, too."

"Were you there for the funeral?"

"No. I came a day later. His lawyer called and asked me to be present for the reading of the will. I wouldn't have come otherwise." He realized he'd said this out of loyalty to his mother.

"And?"

"And he left me the house."

"He did, huh?" Chuck could hear her sudden anger. "So he finally got you to go back to Marblehead."

"Yeah. I'm not staying, though. As soon as I can put it on the market, I'm going back to Alexandria."

There was a long pause. "How does it look? Do you remember any of it?"

"Bits and pieces. Not much." He wasn't going to tell her about his locked room that hadn't been changed since they left.

"What kind of shape is it in? It ought to bring a pretty good price."

"It's not bad. I haven't had a chance to look it all over."

"Chuck, I really feel funny about this. I haven't thought about your father in years."

"It's strange for me, too." Then he had to say it. "Mom, I met my half-brother and half-sister. They were here for the reading of the will. Did you know about them? Did you know he remarried and had a family?"

When she finally spoke, he could hardly hear her. "Yes."

"How? When did you find out?"

"I'd hear from him occasionally. He told me when they were born."

"He wrote you? I thought he never contacted you, that you hated him so much you didn't want to hear from him."

"It got that way. At first I wanted us to get back together. You didn't know that. But he wasn't interested. He had somebody else. And then he started fighting to get you away from me. That's when I really got mad. But I don't want to talk about it. It was a long time ago. The memories hurt too much."

"No," Chuck insisted. "I'm down here sitting in his kitchen. I'm having a hell of time trying to figure this all out. I grew up hating him and everybody here loves him. What's going on?"

There was another long silence. He could hear her breathing.

Then she spoke. "He came up here and tried to take you away." Chuck didn't interrupt. He waited and she went on. "He got so violent the judge ruled him unfit to even have visiting rights. That's why you never saw him."

"I don't remember any of this. If you listen to the people around here, he was anything but violent."

"I guess anyone can be driven to violence if he's pushed far enough."

Now it was Chuck who paused. "But why didn't you tell me about my half-brother and sister?"

"I wanted to put all of it out of my mind. I figured you and I would never see him again, so why tell you about his other family?"

"Well, I felt like a fool when I walked into the lawyer's office and there they sat."

"Okay. I'm sorry. I should have told you."

"Is there anything else you haven't told me?"

There was a split-second pause before she said, "No, why should there be?" Chuck was suspicious.

"I don't know. You didn't tell me about my brother and sister, so how do I now there isn't more?"

"Well, there isn't." The finality of this was pretty clear.

"Okay." He waited for a moment, then, changing the subject, asked, "Any more thought about retirement?"

"Only that I'm planning to when I reach sixty-five."

"Good for you. Just over a year away."

"Chuck . . . I'm glad you got the house. At least he did that much."

"Thanks, Mom."

Chuck hung up, troubled. She had known about Vivian and Josh, but hadn't told him. He had the distinct feeling that she was holding other things to herself, maybe more important things.

EIGHT

Chuck locked up, turned off the lights and went upstairs. Bear was at his heels. At the top of the stairs, Chuck turned toward the guest room. Bear watched him go, then went the other way into his former master's bedroom. Chuck heard him clomp down on the floor and utter his long groan that sounded like thunder resonating through a canyon.

Chuck undressed and got into bed. In the silence of the big house, he could hear Bear cry softly as each breath of air was expelled.

Sometime in the middle of the night, Chuck awoke rigid with terror. A familiar terror, a terror he knew so well he called it his dragon. Whatever this dragon was, it was hiding in the shadows of this strange room and hadn't yet seized him. He lay flat on his back, stretched out on the bed, covered by the sheet and blanket. Exposed and vulnerable, he moved his hands down his sweat-covered chest, across his stomach, and cupped his genitals protectively. His eyes darted from ceiling to corner to door, on guard, ready, waiting for the dragon.

Not knowing what it was or when it would strike made the terror worse.

Gradually, in time, his breathing became regular. He let go of himself and his hands dropped to his sides. The tension in his body gave way to a slight feeling of nausea, as if something from his stomach was crawling up his throat. The chair, chest of drawers, closet door that moments before had grown grotesquely, ballooning until they pressed in upon him, had once again become objects in the room. It was over. The terror, the dragon, was gone.

It had long been a part of his life, ever since he'd moved to Rochester. At least once a month, for reasons he could not determine, the dragon would steal upon him in the night or early morning and grip his soul with fear. Sometimes it happened more often. He never told anyone, not even his mother. When he was married, his wife, Michelle, had suffered through his nightmares, so he couldn't hide them from her. They frightened her and she pleaded with him to get professional help, but he never would. "They're not that important," he'd tell her. She continued to insist, but he remained steadfast in refusing. He later realized their disagreement over his need for help was partly responsible for the end of their marriage. That and their sexual problems, but he didn't want to think about those.

When will it stop? he wondered. How much longer do I have to put up with being scared out of my mind? Maybe Michelle was right. Maybe I do need help.

Angry and still nauseous, he got up to go to the bathroom. When he opened the bedroom door, he stumbled over Bear, who was sprawled across the floor just outside the guest room.

"Goddamn dog!" he grumbled as he fumbled for the bathroom light.

Bear got up, walked to the bathroom door and watched Chuck as he stood over the toilet. Then he followed him back into the bedroom and lay down next to the bed. Chuck sat on it. "Next time, don't lie in a doorway." Bear eyed him for a moment, then laid his head down.

Immediately Chuck felt guilty. Why did I shout at him like that? I lost my temper just like I used to do with Michelle after I'd had a nightmare. It could be the same thing, or it could be that I'm just upset with being here. I didn't need to come. I would have gotten the house anyway. It was in the will. That attorney, Constanza, could have sold it for me. Why the hell did I come and get mixed up with these people I've never seen before?

He thought about Vivian, looking at him like a long-lost brother.

The prodigal brother returns. And Josh! Gay, for God's sake. Now he and his lover wanted him to come for dinner. Fat chance.

But remembering the tenderness Vivian and Josh had shown each other, his anger faded. He wished that he too might be able to know such tenderness. Thinking this, his mind leapfrogged to Dawn Ireland as she rested her head against his chest. Dawn Ireland, whose blond hair smelled like springtime. Dawn Ireland with a tear in her jeans just above her left knee. "Forget it," he said aloud. His terrible nightmares, his dragon, would always get in the way. Love me, love my dragon, he thought, laughing to himself. We come as a set. Not funny, he told himself. Why even think about finding someone? Why hurt them and hurt myself? Better just keep to myself. Me and my dragon.

He turned on the light and looked at his watch. 7:10. It seemed like five. He went to the window and looked out around the edge of the shade. A thick fog hung in the air, blocking the sun and obscuring his view of the side yard.

"Time to get moving," he said aloud. "Get this place sold and get out of here." Bear watched him come around the bed. Chuck stopped beside him and the two stared at each other. Finally, Chuck reached out his hand and scratched Bear's right ear. "See," he said, "I'm not such a bad guy."

It was eight o'clock when Chuck put the breakfast dishes, including Bear's bowl, into the dishwasher.

Now for some exercise, he thought. There's been too much sitting around worrying about other people taking over my life. He put on his sweats and hiking shoes, grabbed his jacket and headed for the front door. A brisk four-mile walk was just what he needed.

As he put his hand on the doorknob, Bear shouldered his way in front of him, then looked up wide-eyed and excited.

"Shit!" Chuck said. "I suppose you want to come." Then, resigned, "All right, but we're not going to poke along stopping at every bush. This is *my* walk."

He hooked up the leash and they started down the front walk at a rapid pace, Chuck pleased that Bear understood there'd be no dawdling. At the road, Chuck turned right and the dog turned left, practically jerking Chuck's arm out of its socket.

"Come on!" he ordered. The dog dropped his head and planted his feet firmly in front of him.

Chuck pulled hard on the leash. "Damn it! This is my walk." Bear set his 142-pound body down, looked up at him and gestured with his head in the direction he wanted to go.

Chuck sighed. "All right, we'll go that way."

The dog, apparently pleased with his new master's sudden burst of intelligence, got up and charged in the direction of Dawn's house.

"Oh no," Chuck called, trying to put the brakes on. "It's just you and me this morning."

Too late. Dawn was standing on her porch. "Hi. I was just heading out, too."

It's a conspiracy, Chuck thought, two against one. Just then, Clara shot off the porch and ran up to Bear, growling hello and chewing his neck. Wrong, he decided. It's three against one.

Dawn was dressed in a shiny blue running outfit plus a yellow scarf and mittens. She jogged down the walk holding Clara's leash, which she hooked onto the dog's collar.

"Hope I'm not barging in. If I am, just say so."

"Oh no, it's okay." Why didn't I say no? She gave me my chance and I blew it.

"They love the swamp. It's up the road a short way. They can run free there if we keep an eye on them."

Now that Bear had picked up Clara, he had no trouble turning right at the end of the walk. When it was clear they were going in the direction of the swamp, the dogs quickened their pace, pulling on their chains. At least I'm stretching my legs, Chuck thought.

Entering the forest trail that led into the swamp, they unhooked the dogs and watched them charge ahead. Two hundred feet along the path, Dawn and Chuck climbed a small hill and onto a huge granite rock from which they could observe the swamp.

"The wet part's down there," Dawn said, pointing at clumps of brown reeds and matted grass interspersed with pools of black water. "The trail runs along these hills above the swamp. It'll be pretty in a few weeks when the leaves and flowers come out."

Chuck stood beside her. "It's nice now, in the fog."

They stood quietly for several moments absorbing the bleak

landscape of the swamp and the shaded outlines of trees barely visible through the mist. Somewhere in the grayness a mourning dove cooed its plaintive call. Chuck was glad that Dawn seemed to like the silence of the fog as much as he.

Clara ran back up the trail to see where they were, then, reassured they'd not run off, whirled and ran back to find Bear somewhere ahead. Dawn turned to follow, and Chuck took her arm to help her down from the rock.

"Thanks," she said pleasantly, then glanced quickly into his eyes as if she were trying to read his mind.

The trail made a steep drop down a hill between rock outcroppings until it came to a swollen stream at the bottom. Chuck picked his way across some stones and then tightroped a log to the other side.

"I'll take that hand again," Dawn said when she got to the log. "I've got terrible balance." Barely touching his fingers, she inched her way across, then jumped beside him, gripping his arm.

"Thanks," she said again and smiled. The anguish of yesterday seemed to be gone.

She continued to stand beside him, looking into the fog. "We often walked here, your dad and I," she said wistfully. Then, lifting her head to look at him, "I want to apologize about last night. I lost control." She paused for a moment, then went on. "You see, Charlie was like a father to me. I mean that literally. I was fourteen when my dad was killed and Mom and I moved here to Marblehead next door to Charlie. That was twenty years ago. He took me under his wing and treated me like one of his own, like Vivian's sister. When I was eighteen and got married, he gave me away. My husband and I got an apartment in town for a couple of years, then Mom remarried and moved to the West Coast. She gave us the house. So there I was, next door to Charlie again. In a way he was better than a dad because he didn't tell me what to do, or force his values on me. I'm afraid I do that with Brian, my son. I try not to, but I know if he doesn't turn out all right, I'll feel it's my fault. Charlie was never like that with me." Her voice caught and she brought her hand up to her mouth to stifle a cry. Then, gaining control, she squared her shoulders and started down the path.

Chuck followed without speaking. She walked with a determined gait, yet graceful as a deer. She had tied her long hair back into a ponytail and it swung from one side to the other like a pendulum as she walked.

"It just occurred to me that when I was little I spent a lot of time in your house. A friend of mine used to live there—Bruce McIntyre."

"When did you leave Marblehead?"

"Nineteen sixty-five."

"We didn't move there until nineteen seventy-eight. I don't remember who Mom bought the house from."

"Does your husband travel? I haven't seen him around." Now why the hell did I ask that, he said to himself. It sounds like I'm checking her out.

"No, he doesn't travel, and he's not my husband anymore. We were divorced three years ago. Now it's just Brian and me and he's away at Brighton Academy."

"That's a big house for one person."

"Yes, especially when it's time to do the cleaning. But Brian's home some weekends and I love being near the water. Charlie used to look in on me every day to be sure I was okay." She stopped to stare at nothing in particular.

The dogs came panting up the trail to check in, then off they went again.

Dawn and Chuck continued along the path in silence. He was beginning to feel less uncomfortable with her nearness.

The fog was lifting and the sun was beginning to break through. "Look," Dawn said pointing at the ground. There were several blue and yellow crocuses braving the still cold weather.

Chuck stooped to pick one.

"Oh, don't pick it," she said touching his shoulder. "If we leave it there we can see it again tomorrow."

"I might be busy," he said, assuring himself of an excuse should he need it. "Do you walk every morning?"

"When I can. I need the exercise and Clara has to get out for a while."

"What do you do when you're not cleaning the house and walking the dog?"

"My job? I buy and sell art and set up exhibits for museums."

"Is that what you were doing when you were away last week?"

Dawn, in the lead, was picking her way along the edge of the path, avoiding the muddy center and trying to escape wild raspberry thorns on one side. When she was past the mud she said, "I was in Germany buying posters."

"Posters? You mean like travel posters?"

"No. Political posters from before the second world war."

"I guess I never thought of posters as art," he said, squishing through the mud Dawn had so carefully avoided.

"Really? I'm doing a show at the Boston Museum of Art. You'll have to visit the show when it opens."

"When's that?"

"September second."

"I'm afraid I'll be long gone by then."

"So you're not planning to stay in the house?"

"No. I'll be talking to a real estate agent today."

"It'll be strange not having a Carver in the house," she said with a sad smile. "With Charlie gone I hoped you'd be staying on."

"Thanks, but I've got to get back to Alexandria."

The fog and low clouds had completely disappeared and now the sun reflected on patches of water in the swamp. With the dogs leading the way, they followed the path up a steep hill to the crest of a barren rock from which they could see the smokestacks of the power plant in Salem.

Chuck was breathing hard when he arrived beside Dawn. "I'm more out of shape than I thought. A couple of years ago I could walk all day in the mountains and not get winded."

"I noticed the hiking boots. Do you still hike?"

"When I can, but generally I'm too busy."

Gazing into the distance, Dawn asked, "Doing what?"

"I design computer programs for banks."

"Do you like it?"

He thought for a minute. "Never really thought about whether I like it or not. I just do it. It's a good job and I do it well, so there's satisfaction in that. And I like being my own boss."

"Same here. I couldn't imagine working for someone else." She paused for a moment, then continued, "I had a partner for the last five years, but that was different. We were a team." She turned away from Chuck so he couldn't see her face. "He died five months ago."

Hearing her voice waver, he said, "And now Charlie. I'm sorry."

"Yes, and now Charlie." Then after a pause, "When Gareth died, that was my partner's name, Charlie was the one who got me through it."

She glanced at Chuck. In the split second that their eyes met, he could see the question on her face—Who will get me through this time?

NINE

As soon as he got home he looked up real estate companies in the Yellow Pages and selected the one with the most prestigious ad. He told the woman who answered that he wanted to put his house on the market and was looking for a company that could sell it in a hurry. The woman assured him he'd come to the right place.

"When can you come by?" he asked.

"Two o'clock, if that's convenient."

"Fine. My name's Carver and it's number 9 Cove Road."

"Oh my," she said. "I know the house. It's lovely. I'll bring comparables of houses that have sold nearby so you'll have some idea about the market value of your house."

Chuck hung up feeling a return of confidence in his ability to take control of his life.

At two on the dot an attractive woman in a tailored rust-colored suit stepped from her BMW and started up the walk, stopping along the way to look at the house and grounds. Seeing Chuck on the porch, she waved.

"Lovely day, isn't it?" she called.

"Yes. Almost springlike."

Carrying a briefcase in her left hand, she extended her right to Chuck.

"Hello, I'm Charlotte Grisom from Harkens Realty."

"Thanks for coming, Ms. Grisom. I'm Chuck Carver."

"I'm sorry to hear about your father's death. I had a chance to meet him three years ago when he was considering selling the house. He talked to Mr. Harkens, my broker, and two or three other companies, then decided not to put it on the market."

"I'll probably interview a couple of other companies myself," he said, turning toward the house. "Shall we get started?"

"I'd like to take a tour of the house to refresh my memory. Would you lead the way?"

He held the front door for her, but she stopped to look disapprovingly at the porch flooring. The paint was flaking and some of the boards were warped.

"We'll be refreshing both our memories," Chuck said. "I arrived two days ago and have been in only a few of the rooms myself."

The agent set her briefcase on the hall table and removed a notebook, then followed Chuck into the living room.

"Oh," she said, "the portrait of Mrs. Carver is gone."

"Yes. That was left to Vivian, the second Mrs. Carver's daughter."

"Pity. It shows the walls need cleaning or repapering." She made a note in her book.

In the dining room, Chuck turned on the lights for the first time, revealing walls as dingy as the living room's. In both rooms there were large rugs over varnished floors. She knelt and lifted the corner of the dining room rug.

"The floors are nice, Mr. Carver, hardwood, but notice how badly worn the varnish is. Nothing sells a house like newly refinished hardwood floors."

In the kitchen she said, "I see your father took our advice and had the kitchen redone. They did a good job." Moving to the door to the garage, she said, "I've forgotten where the circuit breaker box is."

"You've got me, but let's look in the basement off the garage."

They went down the steps and through the garage to the basement. The electrical box was next to a workbench and across from a large oil furnace.

"Uh-huh, just what I was afraid of. They put in circuit breakers for the kitchen when they remodeled but left the old fuse box for the rest of the house. It means the entire house probably needs rewiring and you'll need to bring in additional service. You'd better have an electrician look at that."

With each of her comments about the house, Chuck grimaced. He knew she was right if he wanted to make the house salable, but he could see himself getting bogged down in endless repairs.

They returned to the first floor and had started up to the second when Ms. Grisom stopped. She drew the toe of her shoe over the worn carpet treads and wiggled the loose banister. Shaking her head disapprovingly, she made notes in her book.

They started with his father's bedroom. Still untouched, the bedclothes were thrown back and the pillow dented where Charlie's head had been. Charlotte didn't seem to notice, making a professional sweep of the room and going into the adjoining bathroom.

"This bathroom's pretty old. He probably put it in when he bought the house in the fifties. For a property as nice as this, a buyer will expect a modern bathroom." She turned on the hot water in the tub and it ran with only moderate pressure. She let it flow for some time, then felt the temperature of the water. "Hmm. Not very hot. You'd better have a plumber check the water heater and the piping. Something's not right here."

From there they visited the two bedrooms, probably Vivian's and Josh's, the bathroom and the guest room, where Chuck had slept. She continued her note-taking. In the other direction they went down the hall to Charlie's study, giving it only a cursory glance.

At the doorway to the third floor, she asked, "What's up there?"

"Another bedroom, bathroom and the attic. The bedroom's locked and I don't have a key."

"We'll look at it some other time when you've found it. Is the attic still unfinished?"

"Yes. Do you want to see it?"

"Not now. Let's go downstairs and look at the comparables."

In the kitchen she spread out listings of homes of comparable size that had sold nearby.

"It's a wonderful location, Mr. Carver, and basically a good house, but it's very much in need of refurbishing. If you want a quick sale, that is, selling it as is, I recommend a list price of six hundred and fifty thousand."

Chuck flinched. "That seems low. Mr. Constanza, my father's lawyer, said it was appraised at one point two million."

"I don't know where he got that figure. If you look at the comparables, you'll see they're not selling in that range. Of course, I did say a quick sale. If you're interested in putting some money into the house—painting, repairing the porch, refinishing the floors, repapering the rooms, upgrading the bathroom, rewiring and so forth—oh yes, and the plumbing—the house would probably draw close to a million. You've got the location, but this house was built before the war and if you leave it as is, you'll be trying to sell a nineteen-thirties house in a nineties market."

Chuck sighed. "Nothing's easy, is it? That's not what I wanted to hear."

"I know, but I think I'm right. Talk to some other companies, although I think they'll say the same thing."

"This is a bit of a shock. I'd hoped we'd settle on the appraised price and I could be out of here and on my way to Alexandria." He rose. "Let me think about it, maybe get some estimates on the work you mentioned, and get back to you."

The real estate agent left and Chuck made a list of the projects she'd outlined. He called two plumbers who said they'd come by the next day, a carpenter about the bathroom who couldn't make it until the weekend, an electrician with an answering machine and a wallpaperer whose wife said he'd come the next morning at nine.

Depressed, he whistled for Bear and the two of them went outside to walk around the property. It was a large lot, about two acres, and at the back, with a separate driveway of its own, was a boat shed. The door was padlocked. Through the window Chuck could see a sailboat on a trailer. He'd have to find the key. Probably somewhere in the kitchen.

At the side of the house were three apple trees in need of pruning and in back, what had once been a garden plot but was now strewn with rotting weeds.

Continuing his trek, he passed between his house and Dawn's, careful not to look in that direction in case she might be looking out the window. He had enjoyed their walk through the swamp and could feel himself drawn to her, but there was no sense in trying to get something going there. He'd be leaving soon, and anyway, a relationship was too risky. Then he noticed her car was gone.

Back in the kitchen, he found the boat shed key on a hook by the stairs to the garage. That was where he would have put it and that was just what his father had done. He'd look at the boat later. Undoubtedly it was one more thing that needed work.

He opened a bottle of Sam Adams ale from the refrigerator and sat down. This was not fitting his picture. He'd planned to be back in Alexandria by now, completing a project.

Taking his beer, he collected his briefcase from the hall and went to his father's study, where he turned on the hooded desk lamp and sat down. Leaning back, he surveyed the papers stacked neatly at the back of the desk and gazed at the pictures on the walls.

He considered his situation. If there really was a chance he could sell the house for more than a million dollars, he'd be damned if he'd give it away for six hundred and fifty thousand or less. That would be throwing away almost a half-million bucks. Probably it would cost a couple hundred thousand to put it in shape. He'd have no trouble covering the cost because he could borrow against the house. But the problem was time. Contractors could take forever to get work done.

No matter what he did, even if he decided to sell the house as is, he was going to be stuck here for several days.

He had no choice. He'd have to drive back to Alexandria and move his office, computers and all, to Marblehead. Fortunately, it didn't matter where he was located as long as he had a good modem and good phone service. He decided to talk with the contractors, then go to Virginia and pick up his stuff.

He let his eyes wander over the papers at the back of the desk. One pile was paid bills and the other unpaid. That was another thing. Sometime he'd have to look over his dad's bills.

Leaning back, he crossed his legs and bumped the bottom of the desk drawer. It opened slightly, so he pulled it out the rest of the way. There were the usual paper clips, typewriter ribbons, ruler, letter opener and so forth.

Then his eyes fell on an envelope sitting squarely in the middle of the drawer. Printed across the front were the words,

TO BE OPENED ONLY BY CHARLES CARVER, JR.

His hands trembled as he lifted it from the drawer.

"Go ahead, Chucky, open it."
The box was large and heavy, wrapped in fancy paper and tied with a bow. Chucky looked up at his dad, who was beaming down at him.
"Happy Birthday, ten-year-old."
Chucky lifted the box, weighing it in his hands, his eyes widening excitedly. "It's the hockey skates, isn't it?"
"Well, go ahead, open it."

He shook himself free from the memory and found a letter opener in the drawer. He took it and slit open the envelope, removing two sheets of paper undated and written in longhand.

Dear Chuck,

I hope that what I failed to do in life I have been able to accomplish in death—to bring you home.

I'm not expecting to die anytime soon but last week I had a scare with the kind of pains that might indicate a heart problem, so I'm writing this just in case. Anyway, who knows? We all go sometime and what I have to say to you can be said now or ten years from now.

So, if you find this and if you read it, I'll be gone.

First I want to tell you how sorry I am my marriage with your mother didn't work out. Not sorry that it ended, but sorry for the pain and trouble it must have caused you. Whether it's better for a couple to get divorced when their lives are going in different directions or to stick it out and live unhappily, I don't know. I'm sure it's hard on the children either way.

What I regret most is having lost you. I wanted desperately to be a father to you but that wasn't to be. When I came to Rochester to talk with your mother about visitation rights, I lost my head and got a little too rough.

Chuck looked up from the letter. That's the violence Mom was talking about. He searched his memory for some recollection of what had happened. Drawing a blank, he continued reading.

That's when I lost the right not only to have you with me part-time, but to visit you.

Later I married a wonderful girl named Jacqueline and we had two children, Vivian and Josh. They're grown now and Vivian has three children of her own. I wonder if your mother ever told you. Jacqueline and I had a good life together until she died in 1989, the year I retired from TWA. We had looked forward to those retirement years, to gardening, sailing and traveling around the world. I had to do it alone and it wasn't the same.

I followed your growing up and your business career. When you graduated *summa cum laude* from Syracuse University, I was standing at the back of the auditorium, afraid to make myself known. Afraid you wouldn't want to see me.

He's right about that, Chuck thought.

When you went to work for Riggs Bank and later the computer company, I asked a friend of mine in D.C. to keep an eye on you and let me know how you were doing. I was proud of you. He also sent me the announcement of your marriage to Michelle and later the news of your divorce.

Chuck squinted. Sounds like he was tracking me. I wonder if he paid someone.

Maybe, being divorced yourself, you can understand why certain people can't make it together and not blame me too much for leaving your mother.

"Shit!" Chuck said aloud, growing angry. "Not blame you for uprooting our lives and making us move to a place where I didn't know anybody?" He shook the folds of the letter so hard the paper almost ripped. He read on.

Now you're in business for yourself. I think of you down there in Alexandria, in that little apartment, and wish you could be here in this big house. Well, it's yours now.

After you and Harriet left, I went into your bedroom. The bed was unmade and the room a mess. I straightened things up, and closed the door thinking it would only be a matter of days and I'd have you back with me. Days became weeks and weeks stretched into months. Sometimes I'd go into your room and sit on your bed, thinking about you. Sometimes I'd cry.

"Christ! This is too much," Chuck said into the stillness of the room. Bear, who had come into the study to lie at his feet, raised his head for a moment, then laid it back down.

When Vivian and Josh were born I locked the door so they couldn't play in there. I'd let them in sometimes to look around, but I wouldn't let them touch anything. It was your room and I was saving it for you. As they grew up they thought I was a little crazy about that. Vivian used the word "obsessive." Maybe so, but by that time I'd kept the room locked for years. Unlocking it would have been an admission I'd been wrong.

Wrong about what? Chuck thought. Hoping I'd come back here? Hoping I'd beg you to love me? Not on your life.

If you're reading this, you have come back. I only wish I was here to greet you.
I love you, Chucky. Your room is there, waiting for you.

A picture of a tired old man came into Chuck's mind, a man hunched over this very desk, scratching out a letter as he wiped tears from his eyes. The image filled him with disgust. One more line to go.

The key to your room is in the envelope. Welcome home, son.

Your Loving Dad

Chuck picked up the envelope and turned it upside-down. A key dropped onto the desk.
"Well, let's get this over with," he said. Bear decided he was talking to him, so he followed Chuck up to the third floor and the room at the top of stairs.
The door opened easily and Chuck walked in, stopping in the middle of the room. A subdued light from the double windows in the dormer across from the door allowed him to look about the room. In front of him, built into the recess of the dormer, was a bench covered with pillows. Beneath it were two large wooden

boxes on rollers that he knew he could pull out to find a collection of toys and games.

To the left was his chest of drawers and a worktable. A fluorescent light on a movable arm was attached to a corner of the table. Without thinking, he reached directly to the switch part on the cord and turned it on. Spread out on the table were plans for a model P-47. Carefully cut pieces of balsa wood were still pinned to a layout of the right wing, just as he had left it that morning years ago. Beside the table was the door to his closet.

On the other side of the room, to the right as he entered, was his bed, with turned maple posts and headboard. A heavy black spread with a huge *Bruins* logo in yellow letters covered the bed. Chuck smiled and leaned over to touch the coarse fabric.

On the left side of the bed was a bookcase jammed to overflowing with children's books. He glanced at the titles and a flood of memories came rushing back. He remembered every one, from the Dr. Seuss stories to the Narnia series. He'd never thrown a book away.

On the other side of the bed was a small table and a reading lamp with a ceramic base in the shape of Bugs Bunny. Chuck sat on the bed and grinned at his old bedside companion. Twisting the switch at the base of the stand, the light came on and he noticed that Bugs's hand that held a carrot was missing, broken off. He looked at the ceramic stand more carefully and noticed cracks where it had been glued back together. Poor Bugs, he thought. Someone gave you a bashing and then repaired you.

When he tried to look away, he couldn't. His gaze was fixed on the jagged lines of the cracks, which drew him closer and closer into their web until his vision blurred. Suddenly a flash of memory erupted into consciousness.

The light from the hall pierced the darkness of his room as his door was flung open.

Shouting.

The lamp was raised and came crashing down against . . . against . . .

As quickly as it had come upon him, it was gone. Shaken, he sat back on the bed, bracing his arms behind him. He realized he was sweating and his hands were shaking. The room, his place of refuge until he was ten, had become an instant nightmare. He remained sitting on the bed with his eyes closed until the tremors in his hands subsided and his breathing returned to normal.

Slowly he opened his eyes and looked around the room, his room. Everything was as it had been moments before. The pale afternoon light shone through the windows. The lamp over the worktable was still on. Nothing had been touched. He stood and walked to the windows. Bear, who had slept through the episode, now raised his head. When Chuck sat on the bench in the alcove, he joined him, placing his head in his lap. Looking out at the left edge of Quiet Cove and the island beyond, Chuck dropped his hand to the thick fur of the dog's neck and petted him.

He thought about what had happened. Had he imagined it? Was his mind playing tricks on him? Or was it a fragmentary memory that burst upon him with the force of present reality? It seemed like a memory, a flash of something that had happened long ago. A memory of something horrible.

There was something about this house, about his father, that was churning up the past. He'd felt it when he heard his father's voice on the answering machine and when this thing happened with the broken lamp. In each case the experience was terrifying. He shuddered, then realized it was the same terror he'd felt when he awoke that morning, the same undefined, undirected terror he had experienced so many other times upon wakening or, what was worse, in dreams.

Something, he thought, must have happened in this house, in this room. Something I don't want to remember.

Again he let his eyes rove about the room: his bed, the lamp, the door to the hall.

"This is it," he said aloud. "This is where my dragon lives."

For several moments he sat quietly, expecting the terror to strike, but, surprisingly, he didn't feel afraid. Instead, he seemed to take courage from his discovery.

"What the hell!" he said aloud. "I've got to face it sooner or later."

He went down to the guest room, picked up his overnight bag and toilet articles from the bathroom and brought them up to his old room.

"I'm sleeping here tonight, Bear, and you're welcome to join me. In fact, I insist."

TEN

"So, Dawn, you've got yourself a problem," her editor, Joel Rabinowitz, said over the phone. "If you go ahead with that picture of the poster in the book without permission, you could be sued for copyright violation."

Dawn was sitting in her kitchen, a second cup of coffee beside the open briefcase. She frowned. "It isn't that I haven't tried to reach the owner. I've called information in both Moscow and St. Petersburg, but he's not listed. I've written three letters to his old address, asking that they be forwarded if he's moved, but there's no reply. And when Gareth was in Moscow in December, he was going to try to find Krubinski. That's the man's name. Now, of course, with Gareth . . . with Gareth gone, we don't know if he found him or not."

"Maybe he'd dead," Joel said in his usual gruff manner. "Then the only thing you'd have to worry about would be his heirs suing you."

"What would be the worst they could do?" she asked.

"Well, if the book makes a lot of money—and I guess that includes the exhibit, too—they could burn you pretty bad."

"At least I've tried. Doesn't that count for something?"

"It might satisfy your conscience, but it won't mean much to a judge. Maybe you should go to Moscow and see if you can find him?"

"As if I've got time to do that. Thanks a lot, Joel."

"It's your lawsuit, not mine." He thought for a moment, then asked, "Haven't you got another copyright permission to settle?"

"Yes. With Monsieur Proudhomme. I'm going to Paris this weekend. There's no problem there. We just have to agree on the fee."

"I've got an idea. After Gareth died, didn't the police ship all his stuff back to his office at the university in Cardiff?"

"As far as I know," Dawn said.

"Why not stop off there on your way to Paris and see what you can find? Maybe Gareth did get to see Krubinski. Maybe the permission is sitting there in his briefcase."

"You could be right, Joel. It's just . . ."

"I know, Dawn. It'd be hard to go back there."

After a few more exchanges, Dawn thanked him for his advice and hung up.

Her appointment with the curator at the BMA was at eleven-thirty, and she had just time enough to make the one-hour trip into Boston. She and Christopher Jackson, the curator in charge of the Drawing, Print and Photograph Department, had played telephone tag before she left on her last trip. In spite of his insistence on needing to talk with her, he had never been available when she called. So she had phoned him from Berlin. That was when Jackson became hysterical.

She met him in his office, itself a miniature museum of wall hangings and sculptures. He sat rigidly behind a polished mahogany desk, clicking his ballpoint pen as he talked.

"You realize, Dawn, major shows like this are scheduled months, even years, in advance. You can't just juggle dates around. If there's the slightest possibility your book and the permissions for some of the posters will not be ready on time, we must cancel the whole thing right now."

"Dr. Jackson," she said with a serenity she didn't feel, "I've just talked with my editor and I can tell you everything is on track. Please feel free to call him if you'd like."

"No," he blurted nervously. "I want to hear it from you. Where do we stand on Alexander Apsit's poster, *The International*? It is the centerpiece of the show. Do you have it yet?"

"No, I don't, but . . ."

"Oh, Gaaahd! I knew it was something like this."

"I'm going to Cardiff this weekend, to Professor Gareth Davies's office. I have every reason to believe I'll find the poster there, along with the permission for its use. The police sent all of Gareth's personal effects back to his office after he died. If it's not there, I'll be able to find some lead that will direct me to the owner of the poster. Then I'll go to Moscow myself and get the permission and pick up the poster."

"It's too shaky. You've got to give me more than that. There's too much at stake."

"I know. For me, too. Just hold on until I let you know what I find in Cardiff."

Finishing the meeting, Dawn ran to her car and started her drive to Manchester, New Hampshire, and Brighton Academy.

Pulling onto Storrow Drive going toward I-93, her worries concerning the missing copyright permission began eating away at her excitement about seeing Brian. Joel was right. She had to go to Cardiff. But the thought of walking into Gareth's office terrified her. It had taken months for her to recover from his death. Was she strong enough to sit at the desk where the two of them had spent so many hours, to go through the briefcase his hands had so recently held, to smell the aroma of his pipes that sat at the back of the desk? The thought filled her with apprehension, but at the same time drew her back into memories of the time they had together. Memories, she told herself, are all that I have left. As traffic inched forward toward the ramp for I-93, she let herself remember.

It was late afternoon when she and Gareth returned from his office to Triskin Manor, where she had taken a room. It was a special night because they were going to celebrate the completion of the manuscript. Low clouds rolled over the rounded crests of nearby hills and turned the December sky to night. Clutching their unbuttoned coats against the first drops of rain, they ran from Gareth's Peugeot across the courtyard to the large oak door of the manor.

"We followed your request, Professor Davies," the desk clerk said as she handed Dawn her key.

"What request?" Dawn asked as they started up the wide staircase to her room on the second floor.

Gareth smiled broadly. "You'll see."

Dawn unlocked the door and they entered. *"Violà!"* Gareth said with a wave of his hand.

A fire was burning in the fireplace and a bottle of champagne was cooling in an ice bucket next to the table beneath the tall casement windows.

"Gareth, it's perfect." She threw her arms around him and they kissed.

"Let me help you out of that coat."

Gareth removed her coat, then his, and hung them in the closet. As he returned, she held out her hands to him. He still looked like a professor, but during the five years they had known each other, he'd evolved from a quiet, conservative scholar to an adventurous, witty companion. Traveling together around Europe, they had found it harder and harder to say good night at the door of her hotel room. Then, one night in Paris, they resisted no longer and from then on took only one room.

"Warm yourself by the fire, luv, while I open the champagne."

"No. I want to help." She followed him across the large high-ceilinged room. Before World War II, Triskin Manor had been the home of a Welsh coal exporter, and before that, the manor house of an English lord. Now it was a hotel and the place Dawn called home when she was in Cardiff.

POP! The champagne cork ricocheted against one of the tall casement windows that overlooked the garden. "Ah-ah-ah!" Dawn said, holding a glass under the foaming neck of the bottle.

"Let it go," Gareth laughed. "We've got plenty."

"Easy now," she said. "It'll overflow." Gareth filled hers, then his, topping off each glass as the bubbles receded.

"A toast." He raised his glass. "To the completed manuscript."

"To a job well done," Dawn added. They drained their glasses.

"Another?"

"Sure." When her glass was filled, she said, "And here's to us, one hell of a team."

"Hear, hear!" They drank.

They helped each other undress and, putting on their robes, sat on the couch in front of the fire.

"Five years ago when we started," Gareth asked, "did you ever think we'd finish?"

Dawn smiled and snuggled against him. "Did you ever think we'd be drinking champagne, sitting in our bathrobes in front of a fire?"

He turned toward her. "I never thought an old professor like me would be sitting next to a beautiful Norse goddess."

She kissed him. "I love you."

Gareth turned so he could look directly at her. He cleared his throat, started to speak, then stopped. He tried it again. "Would . . . would you be willing to marry an old guy like me?"

Dawn froze, then drew in a quick breath. Eyes opened wide, smiling broadly, she said, "You're not so old." Then she pulled herself up on the couch and threw her arms around him. "Yes, of course I'll marry you."

"And we'll be together for the rest of our lives."

"Forever."

"Finish your champagne," he said, taking his down in one gulp. Dawn finished hers. "Now, do what I do."

He threw his glass into the fire. Dawn, delighted, threw hers, too, smashing it against the andirons. She didn't stop laughing as she pulled his robe from his shoulders and ran her hand over his chest. He eased her back onto the soft cushions of the couch and brought his lips to her breasts.

Two weeks later he was found dead, lying on a sidewalk in Moscow.

North of Boston on I-93 the traffic eased and she increased her speed. She'd make Manchester with time to spare.

"Gareth, dear Gareth," she whispered. Tears began to cloud her vision and she wiped them away with the back of her hand.

Two hours later she drove through the stone gate of Brighton Academy and up the winding drive beneath huge maples that were just beginning to bud. The school, located about three miles from Manchester on a country road, was housed in a cluster of two- and three-story brick buildings that enclosed a large central courtyard. Dawn parked and went into the administration building, where she made arrangements for Brian to be off campus for the balance of the day.

The sun was shining and there was a hint of warmth in the air, so she strolled out onto the walks that criss-crossed the yard. Somewhere a muffled bell rang the end of the period, and immediately a stream of boys and girls emerged onto the square. Then she saw him, half a head taller than the others, his blond hair catching the sunlight.

Don't run to him, she told herself, though she wanted to. Be calm and smile, though she wanted to shout.

Casually, with long loping strides, he approached. He stopped twenty feet away to say goodbye to the two boys beside him, then walked to her.

"Hi!" He smiled. His fingers touched hers. Her son. His mother.

ELEVEN

Morning. Chuck lay on his back, eyes toward the window. The sun, still below the horizon, was turning the eastern sky a pastel pink. It was going to be a beautiful day.

He'd awakened peacefully, with none of the terror of the previous day. Maybe it was being in his old bedroom rather than the guest room.

Feeling chilled, he tugged at the blanket. It didn't move. Bear lay diagonally across the lower left side of the bed.

"You again," Chuck said, sitting up.

Just as he started to push him out of bed, Bear raised a sleepy eyelid, groaned, and rolled onto his back. His front legs stuck up awkwardly around his enormous chest and his back legs around his hairy penis and de-balled scrotum.

Chuck looked down. "Poor guy. They cut the life out of you."

Bear looked longingly at Chuck.

"I know what you want." Chuck smiled and knelt over him. "A belly rub."

Vigorously he kneaded the huge chest and the dog's sides. Bear's back leg immediately started a scratching motion. After a minute, Chuck took a deep breath.

"Whew! There's so much of you."

Downstairs, over two soft-boiled eggs, three strips of bacon and toast, Chuck tried to decide whether to invite Dawn to accompany them on the morning walk. He thought about what she'd said the day before and about the sadness in her voice, and knew there was nothing he could do to help her pick up the pieces of her life. But then, she hadn't asked him to help.

This is ridiculous, he said to himself. This is just a simple walk, not a proposal of marriage. He looked down at Bear, who looked up at him. "I've still got to ask her to take care of you for a couple of days when I go to Alexandria. Let's ask her to join us."

He got up, rinsed his dishes and Bear's bowl and put them in the dishwasher.

Dawn was ready to go, as if she'd been expecting them.

"The swamp?" she asked.

"Okay by me." The dogs seconded the motion by heading off in that direction.

Dawn was dressed as she had been the day before, in her blue running outfit, but looked different. Then Chuck noticed she was smiling. He returned the smile.

"I told you about my son, Brian. I saw him yesterday afternoon."

"How is he?"

"He's taking Charlie's death pretty hard. I'm glad I went up there."

Another person who loved his father, Chuck thought.

"We drove to Freeport, to L.L. Bean, and I bought him a pair of pants." She looked at Chuck and smiled. "I felt like a mother again."

As they left the road and entered the swamp, the dogs darted ahead and soon were out of sight. Then Dawn touched his arm.

"Wait," she whispered. Surprised, he looked at her. Still as a statue, she gazed into the woods that opened before them. "It's like a forest primeval, like the beginning of life on earth." She turned to him and smiled. "Listen. Do you hear it?"

"I hear birds."

"Yes, but more than that. You can hear the earth being reborn."

Chuck waffled, a little embarrassed by Dawn's imagination. "I can almost hear it, but not quite."

"Follow me. I'll show you."

They headed into the swamp, past the rock on which they'd stood the day before, then down a different path to the marshy bottom next to the water.

"There." Dawn pointed toward the ground. "Do you see it, hear it?"

The mud, like primordial ooze, seeped through last year's fallen leaves. It was alive with tiny fiddleback ferns and splitting seeds sitting like hats on the heads of tender maple shoots. Large nascent green leaves, like sharp lances, shot upright through black pools of water and seemed to unfurl before their eyes. The air was heavy with the dank smell of rotting logs and wet humus, and the fecund odor of fungus and spores. Through naked trees the sun shone on sprouting weeds and tiny buds that hungrily drank its life-giving energy. Above them birds and squirrels darted from limb to limb, performing their passionate rite of spring. Dawn, her hand still on his arm, cocked her head to one side and listened. A smile of excitement was on her lips. Chuck let his eyes sink into the strands of her blond hair, let the scent of her body fill his soul. He felt like he was floating in time, as if Dawn were earth's first woman and he, first man. Or was she a wood nymph who had addled his brain? He gazed at her, mesmerized, until the sun's brilliant reflection off the standing water blurred his vision.

Her voice drew him back to the present.

"This swamp is one of the reasons I love living here in Marblehead," she said. "Each season is different. I don't know which I like best. On April Fools' Day we had a freak storm. Your dad and I and the dogs waded through two feet of snow right where we're walking now." She looked at Chuck with a can-you-believe-it expression. He grunted. She continued, "And this summer it'll be like a jungle with vines and trees and all kinds of plants." They walked for a while in silence until they stood high on a rock from which they could look across the tops of the trees. "It's the fall, though, that's the most beautiful. Out there," she said pointing at the now barren limbs, "it'll be afire with colors. I hope you'll be here to see it."

"I'll be here for a while, but probably not that long," he said, slipping free of Dawn's bucolic mood. "I saw the real estate agent yesterday and she pointed out what I needed to do to get the house in shape to sell. It's more rundown than you'd think and needs some updating."

"I'm not surprised. Charlie let it go the last couple of years. I think it got to be too much for him."

"I'm going to Alexandria tomorrow to get my computers and move my office here. I was wondering if you'd mind taking care of Bear for a couple of days."

"I wouldn't mind, but I won't be here either. I'm leaving for Cardiff this afternoon. I'll be gone for at least a week."

"You just got home."

"I know. That's what happens when you're planning an exhibition in Boston and buying posters in Europe."

"I'm impressed," Chuck said.

"Thanks," she said, tipping her head slightly

"Well, it looks like another trip for Bear to Kendall Kennels."

"Oh, no. Take Bear with you. He loves to ride in the truck."

"Two days in the truck with Bear? I'm not sure I could take it. What do you do with Clara when you're away?"

"Paul takes care of her."

"Paul?"

"My ex-husband."

"Oh. Yeah."

Bear and Clara barked that it was time to move on.

Partway down the slope, Dawn asked, "How's it going in your new house?"

"New? You forget it was my house thirty years ago."

"Well, you know what I mean."

Without turning to look at her, he muttered, "It's strange."

"Did you say strange?"

He stopped but didn't address her directly. "Yes, strange." Squinting, he seemed to be searching for what to say next. "Coming here and discovering I have a half-brother and sister, for one thing. And then the other day when the kennel called, I heard my father's voice on the answering machine, as if he were still in the house."

"Oh."

"Then yesterday I found a letter he'd written to me in his desk drawer. He put it there knowing I'd eventually find it. 'To be opened only by Charles Carver Junior,' it said."

Dawn looked up at him, capturing his eyes with hers. She waited for him to continue.

"It's not as if I dropped in on him every so often. I hadn't seen him nor heard from him since he chased us out the door thirty-two years ago. But there was this letter waiting for me. How did he know I'd come back?"

"Maybe he knew there was something here in Marblehead, something in the house that would draw you back."

There is, Chuck thought. Bad memories that need resolving.

They started walking again.

After a minute, Chuck spoke. "What you don't know is, I grew up hating my father. Whether it was stories my mother told me or actual memories, I saw him as the mean man who drove us away. That's why I have so much trouble understanding that you liked him. And Vivian and Josh, too."

"Yes, we loved him." Then, after a moment's pause, "For what it's worth, I think if he wanted you to come back it must have been because he loved you."

"Three days ago I would have laughed at that. Now I'm not so sure. Maybe he did love me. I can remember sitting on his lap in his study and looking at his war pictures." Chuck shook his head. "I just can't put it all together." Then, feeling it was time to change the subject, he asked, "Any chance Paul might be willing to take care of Bear while he's seeing to Clara?"

"Hah! I can hardly get him to take Brian for a weekend, much less feed and walk Clara."

"You're not too fond of him, I take it?"

"Oh, he's all right, I guess. I'm just glad I don't have to deal with him full-time. It's not so bad now. He puts up with what I'm doing, but he sure fought it for a while. He didn't want me out running around the world meeting all kinds of people and starting a business he didn't think I was capable of running. I don't think he's ever understood that it was more than just setting up a business. I was making a life for myself."

"And he got in the way."

"Actually, no. He fell behind. Then, four years ago, he just gave up." Chuck said nothing. "Well? Do you think I'm a horrible person?"

"No. I'm divorced too, and I know Michelle, my ex-wife, is not a horrible person."

"And what about you?"

"I'm working on that one."

They were back by five after nine to find the wallpaper man standing by his truck. Chuck said good-bye to Dawn, wishing her success on her trip, and led the man into the house. He took some measurements and gave him a price, then suggested a place to buy the wallpaper. He explained apologetically that it would be two or three weeks before he could get to it. That long? Chuck thought, but then he realized Dawn would be back by then. Maybe she'd help him pick out the wallpaper.

One of the plumbers arrived as the wallpaperer was leaving. Chuck took him to the basement to see the water heater. He shook his head hopelessly.

"It's pretty old. Doesn't have the capacity for this house. I can put in a new one that'll do the job and it'll be a lot more efficient. Save you money in the long run."

That means it's expensive, Chuck figured.

In the bathroom off his dad's bedroom the plumber shook his head again. More money, Chuck thought.

"Put this in in the fifties?" Chuck nodded. "Looks like whoever did it used about the cheapest stuff they could find. But there's enough room here to upgrade with a top-quality built-in fiberglass tub and shower and matching sink and commode. I'd have to coordinate with the carpenter to rough it in, then put in the new fixtures. There's a bath and plumbing store in Salem where you can pick out what you want."

Another plumber came that afternoon, as well as the electrician on whose answering machine Chuck had left a message. The plumber's estimate was close to that of the guy who'd come in the morning, both costly, but the electrician said the job didn't look too big.

"I'll just run in additional service, change over to circuit breakers, replace the old knob and tube wiring, run a few new circuits and you'll be in business for another fifty years." He then sat at the kitchen table and figured an estimate that stunned Chuck.

"I'll let you know," Chuck said.

Between visiting contractors, Chuck called other companies and made appointments for additional estimates at the beginning of the week.

He was beginning to think about dinner when he heard a scratching at the front door. Bear heard it too and ran to the front hall. When Chuck opened the door, Clara charged in and began her growling greeting with Bear. At that point a man ran onto the porch carrying a leash.

"I'm sorry," he said to Chuck. Then, "Clara, come out here this instant." Back to Chuck, "Hi, I'm Paul Ireland."

"I'm Chuck Carver. I've met Clara. Don't worry, she's not upsetting me."

"The minute she gets out of the house, she races over here to see Bear. You'd think she lives here." Paul, in his late forties, partially bald and wearing glasses, was dressed in a brown three-piece suit. Apparently he'd come straight from work. He stalked awkwardly into the hall and grabbed Clara's collar. Holding her away from his pants leg, he secured the leash and dragged her onto the porch. Bear followed casually, expecting this to be the beginning of a walk. Clara delightedly picked up on Bear's presumption and circled Paul's legs, binding them in her chain. She commenced her barking howl that sounded like a human voice and lunged toward Bear's neck. Paul, hobbled by her leash, teetered precariously on the top step, then fell down the stairs. Chuck rushed to his aid.

He lay on the cement walkway, his feet on the lower steps, his right arm pinned under his body, and his glasses askew on the side of his head. Clara, excited beyond measure, continued jumping this way and that, yanking at the leash wrapped around Paul's legs.

"Ahhh!" Paul's moan was only barely audible.

"Are you okay?" Chuck grabbed the leash and unwound it from his legs. "Don't move until you're sure you haven't broken something."

He lifted his face from the cement. There was blood on his cheek. "That goddamned dog. I swear I'll kill her one of these days." He rolled onto his back and brought his feet and legs down to the walk, then closed his eyes in pain. "My elbow. I think it's broken." He laid his right arm across his chest. The sleeve of his coat was torn at the elbow, and blood was staining the exposed white shirt.

"We'd better get you to the emergency room. Stay here while I put the dogs in the house." Paul, dazed, lifted himself off the walk and sat on the steps.

"I guess you're right." Then, "Goddamn! Look at this suit, brand new this spring."

Meanwhile, the dogs had raced down to the beach, Clara dragging her leash, and were playing at the water's edge. Chuck called and called, but the dogs ignored him.

"You're going to have to get the truck. That's the only way you'll get them. I've seen Charlie do it. Drive down there and they'll think you're taking them for a ride. Ohh, Christ! This hurts."

Chuck ran into the house and got the truck keys, then drove the pickup to the end of the drive by the cove. One toot of the horn and both dogs came running, Bear trailing a stream of water from his thick coat. Chuck opened the door and pulled the seat forward and the dogs jumped into the extended cab behind the front seat.

He parked as close as he could to Paul, who sat on the front steps. Chuck said to himself, Why am I smiling? Then he went to help Dawn's ex-husband.

The rear seat had been lowered to make a floor and both dogs sat up with their heads above the back of the men's seats, Bear looking like a sea captain guiding his helmsman, and Clara sticking her large pointed ears upward like a radar antenna. Between painful groans, Paul gave directions, and Chuck drove to Salem Hospital.

"Now what am I going to do?" Paul began. "I can't walk Clara if I've got my arm in a cast." Chuck thought of telling him he still had his other arm, but didn't.

"I'll take her out when I get home, but I'm afraid I'm leaving tomorrow for the weekend."

Then, out of the blue, "Are you married?"

"No, but I was."

"Well, I might as well be. You've met Dawn, I take it. She's my ex-wife."

"She mentioned you."

"Well, we might as well still be married with all she expects of me. Away for two weeks, home for three days and then off again for another trip. And I'm supposed to take care of Clara." He looked at Chuck for pity and, receiving none, went on. "Brian will just have to come home this weekend whether he wants to or not and take care of the dog."

He sat in silence, speaking only to give directions while he grimaced with pain.

"Turn in here. The emergency entrance is down to the left."

Chuck turned in.

"Thanks for the ride." Then, looking at Chuck in a last attempt to gain his sympathy, he said, "After all I do for her, you'd think I'd get something in return."

Clara looked at him sympathetically, then shot out her nose and licked him on the lips.

"Ugh!"

"I think she loves you, Paul."

"Yuck!" He reached with his left hand to open the door. "I'll get a cab home. Thanks again."

Back at his house, Chuck fed the two dogs and took them out for their evening walk. He turned left at the end of the drive and walked out Cove Road to the point. In the fading light he could see several islands, ones he must have looked at as a child but could no longer remember.

It seemed strange to be with Clara and not have Dawn there, too. He missed her. Standing with her that morning at the edge of the swamp had so burned itself into his memory, he could recall it vividly: the sun in her hair, the touch of her hand on his arm, the scent of her warm breath. Something about her reminded him of Michelle, maybe their love of nature. No, it was more than that. Then he realized what it was. He felt himself drawn to Dawn in the same way he had been drawn to Michelle when they first met. And the knowledge that he could not risk falling in love again filled him with sadness.

TWELVE

There is a silence in vastness. Chuck looked out across the Shenandoah Valley from an opening in the trees along the Appalachian Trail. It was June 1986. Far below, a truck crept along a highway. Smoke climbed skyward through still air from a controlled fire at the corner of a wood lot. A tractor made geometric patterns as it inched its way around a green field. Cows like tiny ants grazed on a hillside. And far beyond, mountains from another range rose and fell along the horizon. He had come here to be alone, to hike the trails and to listen to the silence.

The silence was interrupted by the snap of a twig and the crunch of stones on the trail. He turned to see a young woman approaching. She stopped beside him to share the view of the valley and said, "Beautiful, isn't it?"

"It surely is," he replied, hardly looking at her.

Then she was gone.

Farther down the trail, he surprised her as she rested on a rock promontory, knapsack at her feet. She was running her fingers through her short brown hair, then shaking her head vigorously to let her hair fall into place. The scene was so intimate he was afraid he'd violated her privacy. Yet she nodded when she saw him and he returned her nod.

An hour later he sat on a fallen log taking a drink from his canteen and she strode past without reducing her pace, but they did exchange glances.

He watched her disappear into the trees. She looked to be in her mid-twenties, and was tall, perhaps six feet. She wore a flannel shirt and carried a backpack strapped to her broad shoulders.

The first night they pitched their tents within shouting distance, but neither shouted. The next day, farther down the trail, they exchanged greetings and talked about the weather when they met. That night, they got water from the same stream.

By the third day they were hiking together and that night pitched their tents side by side. Chuck learned her name, Michelle Mitchell. He repeated it silently again and again. It sounded like the rustle of dry leaves blown by the wind. He learned also that she had just graduated from UVA and worked in D.C. at NASDAQ. On the fourth day they decided it didn't make sense to fix two separate meals, so they built one fire and began sharing their dehydrated trail mix. The night of the fifth day, as they sat together watching the embers of their campfire slowly die, Chuck put his arm around her and pulled her close. At first she resisted, then cautiously placed her head in the hollow of his neck.

Just as Chuck was about to suggest they share the same tent, Michelle said, "Good night Chuck. This has been great," and crawled into her own tent, zipping it shut.

The next day they packed up their equipment and went their separate ways. Better luck next time, Chuck sighed to himself. A week later Michelle telephoned and invited him for dinner. He was quick to accept and arrived with a bottle of wine and flowers. There were more dinners at his condo and at her apartment on Capitol Hill and more hikes in the mountains. Good night kisses became more and more ardent and gradually she let Chuck's eager hands wander over her body, but never inside her clothes. He admired her self-control, yet did his best to break it down.

The third weekend of August they drove to the National Seashore on Assateague Island and set up their tent in the remote area. It was a two-person tent they had mutually agreed on and purchased together. Chuck took this as a hopeful sign. Then they went walking on the beach.

"Take your boots off," Michelle said. "Let's wade." She sat down and undid her laces, then tied them together and hung the boots over her shoulder. Chuck did the same. The wide beach between the dunes and the ocean stretched as far as the eye could see. Michelle ran ahead of him, chasing each retreating wave and dodging back as the next breaker crashed. He ran after her, finally catching hold of her hand and pulling her into the water.

"Far enough," she called. "My jeans are getting wet."

He let go of her hand and immediately she scooped up water and threw it at the back of his head. Laughing, she ran back to the beach. He pursued her across the sand until he ran out of breath, then bent over with his hands on his knees.

"You win," he yelled to her.

Laughing, she came back to him and patted his back as he leaned over panting. Suddenly he grabbed her and began tickling her until she rolled onto the sand.

"Stooooop. Ooooh, please stop."

He took his hands from the bare skin of her stomach and suddenly she was on him, pinning his arms against the sand.

"Say uncle!" she demanded. He just smiled.

"Come on, say uncle!"

"I love you."

"No, say uncle."

"I love you."

She shook her head as if disgusted, then collapsed on him, covering his face with kisses. "I love you, too."

They lay in each other's arms for several minutes until Chuck noticed storm clouds rolling in from the southwest.

"Looks like a downpour's coming. We'd better head back."

They hadn't gone two hundred yards before the heavens opened. By the time they reached camp, they were soaked to the bone. They crawled into their new tent, filled with the steamy heat of an August afternoon.

"We'd better get out of these wet clothes," Chuck suggested.

She didn't answer but, sitting with her back to him, cautiously began removing her shirt and jeans. He did the same, then slid across the tent floor toward her. Stiffening at the touch of Chuck's towel against her back and neck, she made no move to resist. He hardly touched her skin as he drew the towel across her bare shoulders and along her arms, then down her back to her waist. Michelle dropped her head forward and closed her eyes as he knelt against her, his knees straddling her hips, his naked chest pressed against her back. As he brought the towel beneath her right arm and gently dried her breasts, she shivered.

No words were spoken as he eased her back onto the sleeping bag and leaned on one elbow to gaze upon her body for the first time and to touch it tenderly. Again she tensed, locking her eyes tightly shut, and Chuck realized that it wasn't self-control or strength of will that had held him at bay, but shyness and inexperience. If he loved her before, he now worshipped her.

Slowly, patiently, Chuck made love to Michelle, although she hardly responded to his kisses and shivered as he touched her breasts and moved his hand between her legs. When he put on the condom her eyes filled with fear, and as he parted her legs the muscles in her strong thighs grew taut as iron. She winced with pain as he entered her, but made no sound. Moving slowly, he spoke softly about his love for her, but she remained tense. Finally his own passion took control of his body and he moved heatedly to climax.

"I'm sorry," he said. "I tried to go slow for you, but . . ."

"That's okay." The words came quickly. "It's all right."

"Do you want me to . . ."

"No. No, it's okay, just hold me."

And he did. He took her in his arms and brought her head onto his chest while he massaged her temples and neck and rubbed her back.

"I love you, Michelle. I've never loved anyone before."

"I know," she whispered. "That's why I wanted you to make love to me." She lay there quietly for a minute. "It was my first time, Chuck. I'm glad it was you."

As darkness came upon them and rain continued to beat against the tent, Michelle told him that she had seldom dated in college. She thought men found her unattractive because she was so tall and didn't have a slim waist or slender legs.

"No, no, no," he whispered in her ear, "you are beautiful and lovely and I'm lucky to be the one who found you."

They were married two months later and Chuck began the two happiest years of his life. He and Michelle worked hard at their jobs, she at NASDAQ and he at Riggs Bank. Living together in his condo in Alexandria was like playing house. Together they shopped, cooked and redecorated their living space. To add to their fun, they bought bikes and, after work, rode bike trails along the Potomac to Mount Vernon or the other way into the District and along Rock Creek. Weekends they hiked. They were happily married.

Michelle's continued shyness about sex offered Chuck the chance to become a gentle, patient teacher. Instead of the lusty sex he'd known with other women, they made love to each other with a purity that he considered almost holy.

When they felt the time had come to have a baby and Michelle went off the Pill, the inhibitions she had felt around sex began to drop away. The change was gradual and at first Chuck was pleased to see her take more pleasure in their lovemaking. Sometimes she would even take the initiative, making the first moves and telling Chuck what she wanted. Orgasms that had been occasional now became a regular thing, and Michelle made sure Chuck satisfied her before he rolled over to go to sleep. As the months passed and she didn't get pregnant, they made love more frequently, and the more they did, the more she enjoyed sex.

And the more Chuck began to feel intimidated.

Nightmares that had tormented him from youth returned. At first Michelle was unconcerned. But as they continued and became more frequent, she suggested he see a doctor. Chuck brushed the suggestion aside.

Meanwhile, Michelle read books that explained in detail how joyful sex could be and soon the student was becoming the teacher. Chuck began to wonder who was in control. Their love-making, which had been so pure and beautiful, was, in his mind, becoming a dirty thing, and the woman he had thought to be above bodily passions was beginning to ooze lust. Instead of making love, they were fucking.

And then it happened.

He was lying between Michelle's legs while she groaned with ecstasy, urging him on with sexy talk.

Chuck lost his erection.

The first time, frustrating as it was, they attributed it to a cold from which he was recovering. The second time, it was too much beer during the evening.

The third time, as Chuck rolled to his side of the bed, angry, Michelle began to cry.

"It's my fault, isn't it? Tell me. What am I doing wrong?"

Immediately Chuck's anger evaporated and he pulled Michelle to him so her head rested on his chest. "There, there, it's nobody's fault." Gradually her crying became a series of jerky sobs as he stroked her back and hips. Then, like the legendary phoenix, his penis came to life and pressed hard against her leg. They made love again, this time with Chuck taking the lead. It was one of the last times.

Each night as they went to bed, Michelle could feel Chuck's tension as he lay beside her. She was afraid to touch him and afraid to ask what was wrong. But she was sure it was her fault.

The nightmares were becoming a weekly occurrence.

One Sunday morning as they lay in bed reading the *Washington Post*, she gathered her courage and said, "Darling, I'm sorry things aren't going right for us." She waited for a response, but Chuck only gripped the Business Section more tightly. "I love you," she touched his arm, "and I want to do whatever I can to make it right for us, but I don't know what to do." Still he refused to lower his paper. "I think we need some help. Some outside help, like counseling."

That did it. Down came the paper.

"If you think I'm going to talk to some crackpot about our sex life, you're crazy. It's nobody's business but ours."

"But we've got a problem," she said with an insistence that surprised him, "and it's not going away."

"Forget it," he said angrily. "We'll handle it."

The next week, without telling Michelle, Chuck went to a doctor to see if there was a physiological reason for his inability to maintain an erection. There was none.

So, he began to believe, it must be her fault. She doesn't want to make love, just to have sex.

The strain of their sexual dysfunction plus Michelle's urging that Chuck get professional help for his nightmares erupted one night when they were trying yet again to make love. When his erection dwindled away, he rolled off her and jumped up from the bed. Then, standing over her, he growled, "If you'd stop acting like a goddamned whore, maybe we could make love."

Michelle looked at him with disbelief as tears filled her eyes. Seeing her sobbing, he immediately knelt down on the bed, stricken with grief.

"No!" she cried. "No more. I can't take it anymore."

She threw back the covers and ran to the bathroom. Chuck fell on the bed weeping. Later he heard her dressing and throwing things into an overnight bag. But he never looked up.

She left.

THIRTEEN

Dawn looked for Chuck, hoping she might wave good-bye to him, as she got into the airport limousine. But she didn't see him. Two hours later she was on the night flight to London, arriving Saturday morning as the sun was coming up. After an hour's wait, she caught a plane to Cardiff, then rented a car and drove the short distance to Triskin Manor.

"Mrs. Ireland," the desk clerk said, "it's nice to see you again. Traveling alone this time?" She was about Dawn's age and wore a tan jacket to which a name plate was attached.

"Yes." Dawn glanced at her name. "I'm alone, Sylvia."

"I'll put you in twenty-seven, then. It's smaller than your usual room but has a lovely view of the garden."

Dawn climbed the wide, winding stairs of the converted manor home, found twenty-seven and, without noticing the garden, fell onto the bed. She was asleep as soon as she closed her eyes.

It was late afternoon when she awoke with a rancid, dry taste in her mouth and an ache throbbing in her temples. Slowly she pulled herself up from the bed, took off her traveling clothes and stepped into the shower. The hot water streaming over her washed away some of her sleepiness and began to ease the pounding in her head.

There was only one thing she had to do that afternoon, and that was to confirm with Rhian Evans, the woman who had been Gareth's secretary, their appointment in his office the next morning.

Putting on the heavy terrycloth bathrobe provided by the Manor, she settled herself next to the phone by the window.

As she reached for the phone, a flicker of movement caught her eye at the edge of the hedgerow on the far side of the garden. Two rabbits hopped onto the lawn and leisurely began hop-stepping from one hidden clump of clover to the next. Then, on the other side of the garden, a swish of rust-brown and red drew her attention to a pheasant darting from the hedgerow to hide behind the trunk of a huge beech tree. Was it the same pheasant she and Gareth had watched from their window the last time they were here? Gradually the view of the garden became blurred with tears.

She was still for a few moments, then wiped her eyes on the sleeve of her robe and picked up the phone, dialing Miss Evans's number.

Early Sunday she met Rhian Evans at the door to the history department and they climbed the stairs to what had been Gareth's office. Rhian had been Gareth's secretary for ten years and had come to know Dawn during her many visits to the university. She was an attractive woman, in her late forties, single and an avid soccer fan. She was dressed in a brown wool skirt and a buttoned sweater over a white blouse.

"I appreciate your taking time on Sunday to come here."

"I'm glad to do it, Dawn. It's been a long time since I've seen you." She took keys from her purse and unlocked the door. "Professor Settle is using the office now, but Gareth's things are still stored here in the closet." She brought out a briefcase and set it on a worktable. "There are several other boxes. I've gone through them and I don't think they'd be of interest to you, mainly files relating to his classes here."

Dawn gazed at the briefcase that was so familiar to her. She could picture Gareth tucking it under his arm as he walked to his car. Her eyes grew moist. "The briefcase is what I'd like to go through."

Rhian looked up in time to see Dawn wipe her eye. "I don't see why you can't take it back to the manor, look through it at your leisure, and bring in back tomorrow morning on your way to the airport."

"I'd appreciate that."

"It's so sad," Rhian said, placing her hand on Dawn's arm. "He was a dear man."

Dawn returned to Triskin Manor and spread the contents of the briefcase on the bed. Her eyes fell on an envelope containing photographs. She carried them to the table by the window and sat down. One by one she lifted them like precious jewels, studying them carefully and smiling through her tears. Most of the pictures were of her standing next to a waterfall or in front of Notre Dame or seated at a cafe in Prague. She could remember Gareth telling her to smile as he took each picture. A few were of the two of them at the beach in France or on the deck of a riverboat on the Danube or sitting in a heated pool at Baden-Baden. Finally she sighed, put the photos back in the envelope and returned to the bed.

There were several folders containing notes related to the seminar Gareth had been leading as a visiting professor at Moscow University. These she set aside. Another was marked "Correspondence," and here she found letters from Nikolai Neleginski, the Russian professor who had arranged for Gareth to come to Moscow. She noticed one in which Neleginski invited Gareth to stay with him when he came to Moscow. Then she came upon a copy of a letter Gareth had sent to him asking for help in contacting Demitri Krubinski. ". . . My partner with whom I am writing the book *European Poster Politics: 1910–1940* has asked me to arrange with Krubinski for the use of a poster he owns. We believe he is still living somewhere in Moscow. Apparently he has moved and left no forwarding address. If you have any idea how we might locate him, I'll try when I arrive."

When she spotted a folder marked "Krubinski," she opened it excitedly. Inside she found her letter to Gareth asking his help in contacting Krubinski. There was also a scratch pad with notes on it. Krubinski's name was written at the top, followed by a telephone number. The rest of the pad contained directions on how to take the Metro from the Cosmos Hotel to the Ukraina Hotel.

A year had passed since she'd seen Krubinski. They'd met in his apartment in Moscow and he'd shown her the Alexander Apsit poster *The International*. It was a magnificent piece and Dawn decided it would be perfect for the exhibit. Tentatively they agreed on a fee for the use of the poster and its inclusion in the book. Dawn said she would draw up a contract and send it with the fee in November, and he agreed to ship her the poster the week after that. Based on their tentative agreement, Dawn included a picture of the poster in the book and set aside a place for the poster in the exhibit.

That was the last she heard from him. Repeated attempts by phone and mail to contact him had brought no results.

Now, at long last, she had a telephone number and an address. Elated, she took Gareth's notepad to the phone and dialed the international operator, asking for an English-speaking operator in Moscow. Dawn gave her the number and the phone began to ring. Finally, someone answered and the operator asked for Demitri Krubinski. Some Russian words were exchanged and the operator said there was no one there by that name. Before she could disconnect, Dawn asked her to dial the Ukraina Hotel and ask for an English-speaking desk clerk.

"Do you have a Demitri Krubinski staying there?" Dawn asked when the clerk came on the line.

"No, there is no guest by that name."

Discouraged, Dawn hung up. Sighing, she leaned on her elbows and rubbed her temples with her fingers. The throbbing had returned. She was no closer to finding the owner of *The International* than she'd been six months before.

At least having Gareth's briefcase had given her a chance to see their pictures again. Returning to the bed, she scooped up the papers and the folders and put them in the briefcase. When she came to the envelope containing the photos, she thought for moment, then put them in her suitcase.

FOURTEEN

Saturday morning and the eastern sky was just beginning to grow light as Chuck turned off Interstate 95 onto the Mass Pike west of Boston. He figured it would take nine or ten hours to get to Alexandria. He'd be there around three o'clock. Traffic was light, being a Saturday morning, so he'd encountered no backups on 95. One of his dad's CDs, a Jimmy Buffet recording, was beating out a Caribbean rhythm and he was sipping coffee from a mug. Beside him Bear sat looking out the front window, happy to be riding in the pickup.

The night before, when he returned from his walk with Clara and Bear, he locked Clara in her house using a key Paul had given him. Then he checked the fluid levels in the truck and examined the maintenance record he found in the glove compartment. His father had kept everything in good shape and up to date, as one might expect of an ex-pilot.

When they left, he had tried to get Bear to sit on the folded-down backseat, but to no avail. He'd climbed into the passenger side of the front, obviously his seat, and there he was going to stay.

As the miles rolled by, Chuck thought again about Dawn and Michelle. Michelle was younger than Dawn, less worldly, taller and probably thirty pounds heavier. At least that was how he remembered her. He'd heard she'd remarried about a year and a half after the divorce and now had two children. He pictured her on the hiking trails full of life and energy, her laughing face devoid of dissemblance and pretense. With Michelle, what you saw was what you got.

Then why did their lovemaking go bad? Was it his fault or hers? How many times in the last decade had he asked himself that question?

Whatever it was that made him unable to keep an erection, he was sure of one thing. Never again would he put himself through such a humiliating ordeal.

Bear began turning in circles on the seat beside him and finally lay down, putting his head in Chuck's lap. Chuck rubbed his ears and dug his fingers into the thick fur at the nape of the big dog's neck. Bear was a good companion.

They had driven two and a half hours and were on the other side of Hartford when he saw the sign for food at the next exit. He was ready for breakfast.

Stopping at a McDonald's, Chuck went in and ordered a ham and egg McMuffin, which he brought back to the truck. Bear stared at him.

"You ate before we left, big guy. This is mine."

Bear stared at him intently, a long string of drool forming at the side of his mouth and running down to the seat.

"Oh, all right." Chuck tore off a small piece of muffin and Bear snapped it up, cascading his drool onto Chuck's leg. Quickly Chuck finished the rest of his McMuffin and started the car. Bear refused even to look at him.

They rounded New York City with relative ease and made a lunch stop on the New Jersey Turnpike. After walking Bear, Chuck bought a fish sandwich for himself and a hamburger for Bear. He broke off small pieces and fed them to him while he finished his own sandwich. This worked pretty well, but he had to use five napkins to clean off the seat.

They arrived in Alexandria at three-thirty. Chuck led Bear around the parking lot so he could relieve himself, then sneaked him into the elevator and up to his fifth-floor condo. Dogs were not allowed in the condominium.

Home again, Chuck thought as he walked to the picture window in his living room and looked down on the Potomac River. Bear checked the two bedrooms, the smaller of which had been turned into an office, the kitchen and the dining area off the living room. In the bathroom he had a drink from the toilet.

Chuck turned from the window and let his eyes wander over

the bare walls of the room. It didn't feel much like home. No longer were there any traces of Michelle. She had come back a week after she left to pick up her things and collect most of the furnishings and pictures they had bought together. That was nine years ago, and Chuck had replaced nothing but a sofa, chair and table, which he bought at the Salvation Army resale center. The condo was little more than an office with sleeping and eating quarters attached.

He removed a meatloaf dinner from the freezer to thaw, and commenced unplugging his equipment and gathering his files. It didn't take long. He put all his spring and summer clothes in two suitcases and found a box for his favorite CDs and books. These he stacked by the door, then stood back and looked at it.

"Two suitcases, computers and a couple of boxes," he said aloud, "the measure of my life."

Suddenly the condo seemed cold and barren. He realized he was longing for the house on Cove Road and Dawn's voice calling, "Hey, Chuck, let's take the dogs for a walk."

He left at four in the morning because he couldn't go back to sleep after two-thirty. Bear escorted him down the elevator along with the first box, then remained in the cab of the truck guarding it while Chuck brought down the rest of the stuff. They stopped twice along the way, for breakfast and for lunch.

At one-fifteen they pulled into the driveway of 9 Cove Road.

Bear jumped down from the cab and circled the front of the house toward Dawn's house. He probably needs a walk, Chuck thought, and I might as well take Clara, too.

Clara, who had been sitting on the front lawn, bounded over to meet Bear. She nipped his tail and chewed his ears until he began chasing her.

A boy was standing between the two houses. In each hand he held a bracket from which strings rose to a bird-like kite with a long colorful strip of Mylar for a tail. As he moved his hands this way and that, the kite did acrobatics, trailing its tail in loops and corkscrews.

"Hi," Chuck called.

"Hi," the boy said, not taking his eyes off his kite.

"Are you Brian?"

"Uh-huh." The boy wore baggy pants and a Boston Bruins sweatshirt that was several sizes too big. His blond hair crept out from beneath his baseball cap, which was turned forward, its visor rounded into a perfect arc that reflected hours of careful shaping. His face was smooth, with only one or two pimples, and his eyelashes would have been the envy of any woman.

Chuck walked up to him.

"You're pretty good."

"Thanks." They watched the kite pirouette and dive for several moments. Without looking away from the kite, Brian asked, "Are you Charlie's son?"

"Yes."

"Sorry about your dad."

"Thanks." A minute later Chuck asked, "Did you know him well?"

"I did." Still concentrating on his kite, he added, "He was my best friend."

Chuck remained beside him, oddly moved by what he'd said about his father. "I was going to take Bear for a little walk. I'll take Clara, too, if you'd like."

"Gimme a minute and I'll come with you."

"Sure. I'll get Bear's leash."

Chuck stopped by the bathroom, got the leash from the truck and returned to the front yard. Brian was bringing in the kite.

Chuck said, "Your dad told me he was going to ask you to come home for the weekend and take care of Clara. How's his elbow?"

"He's got it in a cast and a sling. I'm going back tonight," Brian said with a certain defiance in his voice, "so he'd better find a way to get Clara taken care of."

"Maybe I can help." Chuck waited for Brian to put the kite on his porch. "You lead the way. I'm new here."

"How about Fort Sewall?" Chuck recalled the name when he heard it, but couldn't remember where it was. Brian said, "Follow me."

They circled Little Harbor and walked along some of the roads Chuck had used when he'd come from the Harbor Light Inn.

"How do you like Brighton Academy?"

"It's all right."

"What grade are you in?"

"Sophomore."

"Sports?"

"Hockey."

Chuck looked at his Bruins jacket. "That would have been my choice too if I'd stayed here. I was a big Bruins fan."

Brian smiled for the first time. "Me too. How come you left? I don't remember seeing you when Viv and Josh were here."

"Actually, they're my half-brother and sister from my dad's second marriage. I left with my mom when I was ten. We moved to Rochester, New York."

"Didn't they have a hockey team?"

"Yeah, but you had to pay to belong and we didn't have the money."

"Too bad. It's fun."

As they approached the earthwork fort at the mouth of Marblehead Harbor, Chuck remembered it.

"Do you come home often?"

"Not much. Mom travels a lot and Dad's busy with work he brings home on the weekends. This year's easier than last. I've made some friends now and I'm on the junior varsity hockey team."

The kid's lonely, Chuck thought. I know about that. "How're you getting to school tonight? Can your dad drive?"

"Same way as I got here. Northshore Limo. Dad's got a stick shift."

"I see." Poor kid, he thought. I'd love to drive him up there, but Paul might think I was trying to make advances on his son. What a shitty world we live in! I think I'll ask Paul anyway.

When they got back, he called Paul Ireland. Chuck said it would be no extra work taking care of Clara the next week because he had to feed and walk Bear anyway. Paul said, with no note of gratitude in his voice, that that was all right with him.

"I met your son. We took the dogs for a walk."

"Yeah, that's what he was supposed to do."

"Would you like me to drive him back to school tonight?"

"Hmm." Paul hesitated.

Here it comes, Chuck thought. He doesn't trust me and he'll make up some excuse.

"That'd be fine by me. That damned limo costs seventy-five bucks." Christ, thought Chuck, it's the money he was worried about. Paul continued, "Come by here before five and get his stuff. I'll be out after that."

Chuck asked Brian if he wanted a ride back to school and he accepted eagerly. "We'll take the truck so the two dogs can come, too."

On the drive to Manchester, Brian said, "Have you met Mom?"

"Yes. She's quite a person."

"What do you mean?"

"Well, she's setting up this exhibition and publishing a book to go with it."

They drove in silence for maybe five minutes.

"Do you like her?"

Where did that come from? Chuck wondered. What's going on in this kid's mind?

"I've only just met her. Like I said, she's quite something."

"So, you like her?"

"Yeah, I like her."

That seemed to satisfy him for a while, then he spoke. "The man who was writing the book with Mom, Gareth Davies, did she mention him?"

"Not by name. Only that he'd died and it'd been a hard time for her."

"Yeah. He died about five months ago." A minute's silence. "He was a good guy. Welsh." Brian turned to look at Chuck, who kept his eyes on the road. "When he died Mom stayed at home for two months, didn't work. Charlie took care of her. It was a bad time."

"Your mom and Mr. Davies must have been close friends."

"He was Professor Davies and, yeah, they were close. He liked her a lot."

Chuck didn't answer, didn't know what to say.

"And she liked him," Brian added.

It was growing dark as they neared Manchester. They'd driven in silence for fifteen minutes when the boy said, his voice sad, "And now Charlie's gone, too."

FIFTEEN

On Tuesday morning Vivian called.

"How's it going, Chuck?"

"Not bad. I'm getting organized. Went to Alexandria this last weekend and brought my computer back so I can work out of the house here."

"So you're staying for a while?"

"It looks like I'll have to. It's going to take time to put the house in shape to sell."

She hesitated for a moment, then said, "The reason I called, Chuck, is to ask if I could help you with this month's bills for the house. The last few years I took over the bill paying for Dad, and it might help you if you knew what I've been doing. I'm not trying to interfere, and if you don't want me to, just say so."

"It's the end of the month already, isn't it? That means I've got bills to pay in Alexandria, too. Sure, come on by."

"There's something else, too." Again she paused. "I think Dad kept all Mom's costume jewelry. If it's still there, I know it belongs to you along with everything in the house, but I thought if you didn't want it, I'd like it. I think he intended to give it to my daughters someday and then forgot."

"Sure, of course."

"I really appreciate that. Would tomorrow be okay?"

"Fine. I'm going to be here all day every day for a while."

Chuck hung up and leaned back in his chair. He was in the

study, where he'd been working on the computer. He wondered if he'd been too quick in agreeing to let her have the jewelry. What if there was a diamond brooch worth thousands of dollars in that jewelry box? But the thought melted away. Instead, he was touched that she wanted to help him. He'd forgotten about the bills. And as for jewelry, he didn't care if there *was* a diamond brooch. She could have it.

The morning was going fine for Chuck. He'd set up his office in the study, had the phone company run two more lines for the modem and fax, and worked two hours on an accounting system for the Watertown Bank, one of his clients. The only interruptions had been an electrician and a carpenter who had come by to give estimates on rewiring and upgrading the bathroom. His new life in Marblehead was going well.

As he started back to work he realized how dark the study was, so he found an old floor lamp with a large three-way bulb. He brought it from the basement to the study and inserted the battered plug into the wall outlet. Suddenly there was a blue flash. Immediately the desk light went out and the computer screen went black.

"Nuts!" he said. "A blown fuse." Then the full impact of what he'd done hit him. "Shit, shit, shit. I just lost an hour's work on the Watertown program."

Infuriated, he stomped down the stairs, got a flashlight from the kitchen and went to the fuse box in the basement, where he unscrewed the burned-out fuse. It was fifteen amps. He realized that if he hadn't blown it out with the faulty plug, he probably would have with an overload.

Chuck called the electrician who had given him the lowest bid and left word with his wife for him to call. Frustrated, and with the computer dead, he decided to take out his anger on the front porch. He grabbed a crowbar and attacked the decking with a vengeance.

The dogs followed him outside and began playing tag on the lawn with an old tennis ball while Chuck pried up boards, adding them to the pile on the lawn he had started the day before.

After an hour or so, the sound of the dogs had become background noise, so he didn't notice that he no longer could hear them. Suddenly there was the sound of ferocious growling and barking. He jumped up and saw Bear at the end of the driveway in what looked like a fight to the death with a large black lab, while Clara kept a safe distance and barked. A woman standing by helplessly was yelling at the dogs and whipping them with the end of the leash attached to her dog. Chuck rushed down to the driveway still carrying the crowbar.

He caught hold of Bear's collar with the curved end of the bar and dragged him off, the woman pulling on her dog's leash. The snarling continued, but the dogs were separated.

"That dog should be on a leash," the woman shouted.

"Why didn't you keep your dog off my driveway? Bear was just defending his property."

"No he wasn't. He charged into the road and attacked my dog."

Chuck hadn't seen it, so he couldn't argue the point. "Well, it's over now." He caught hold of Bear's collar with his hand and pulled him toward the house.

"It is *not* over. I'm taking Thor to the vet and if he's hurt you'll pay. And if I ever see that dog of yours not on a leash, I'm calling the police." She stalked off toward the main road.

Clara wasn't giving up, though. She chased after the dog barking at the top of her voice.

"Clara!" Chuck yelled so threateningly that she stopped in her tracks and ran back to him.

"Up to the house, both of you." But he wasn't mad at them. He was furious with the woman and her dog. "What the hell was she doing coming up our road anyway?" he said to Bear. "It's a private road. Now, you two, get in the house." He slammed the door and sat on the steps fuming.

The electrician called at a little after one.

"What's up?" he asked.

Chuck explained about the blown fuse. "Can I replace it with one of higher amperage?"

"Might be dangerous. Until I can run another circuit up there, the safest thing would be to move your office to the kitchen. That's all been rewired. Plenty of juice there."

"This is really inconvenient. I've got my phone lines for my

modem and fax in the study. How soon can you get out here and
do the rewiring?"

"It's a major job. It'll take two men at least half a day to get it
done. Right now I'm tied up on a big job and I can't get to you for
three or four weeks. If you can wait that long we can do the circuit
to the study with all the other stuff."

Chuck swore silently at all contractors, asked the electrician to
get to him as soon as he could, then lugged his computer to the
kitchen table.

He managed to reproduce the work he'd done earlier that morning, remembering to save it as he went along, but he couldn't put
his mind in gear to accomplish anything else. He was glad when
the day was over.

The next morning, Vivian arrived at a little after nine and came
in through the garage. She stopped short when she saw him working on his computer in the kitchen.

"Don't even ask," Chuck said. "Yesterday was not a good day."

Bear and Clara, however, gave her a cheerful greeting with
much tail-wagging and whiny "hello" barks.

Vivian, in a pair of snug jeans and a khaki shirt, was dressed for
going through closets and digging through boxes. She looked ten
years younger than she had in Constanza's office the week before,
and Chuck couldn't help but notice her trim figure. Her brunette
hair was pulled back and tied in a bun that emphasized her oval
face and large brown eyes. Chuck reminded himself that this was
his sister. Then he noticed the strain and sadness in her face.

"You okay?" he said, standing.

"I guess." She slumped into a chair at the end of the table.

"Coffee?" Chuck offered.

"Love a cup. Just black."

He poured two mugs and brought them to the table.

"I started out fine this morning," she said, "but the closer I got
to Marblehead the more depressed I felt."

"Hope it's not me."

"No." She forced a smile. "Every month for the last two years,
this is the time I came by to see Dad. We'd go over the bills together and then we'd sit and talk. Sometimes we'd go out for
lunch." She was holding back tears. "It was a favorite time."

He tried to think about himself and his occasional visits with his mom, but it wasn't the same.

"Dad missed Mom terribly. He never got over losing her. When I came he'd talk about the things they'd done together and I'd encourage him to go on. Sometimes he'd tear up, but more often he'd laugh and smile. I think I helped to fill the gap in his life."

"And what was it like for you?"

She thought for moment. "Oh, it was hard, but I was so busy holding Dad together and consoling Josh that I didn't notice what I was feeling."

"You weren't very old then, were you?"

"Twenty-three. But I grew up quickly that year."

"That's a lot for someone so young."

"I managed." Some of the confidence Chuck had seen in the lawyer's office returned to her face. "Well, enough of this sad talk. Shall we get to the bills?"

They went to the study, where Chuck, having replaced the fifteen-amp fuse, turned on the desk lamp. His dad had stacked envelopes having to do with money on the right side of the lamp, and Chuck had added more recent bills to the pile. They began looking through the unopened envelopes: bills for electricity, water, heating oil, car and life insurance and credit cards. There were also statements from his HMO and his dental insurance company.

"Would you like me to cancel the dental and HMO insurance? I expect Constanza contacted the life insurance company. Also, I could have Dad's name changed to yours on all the other stuff."

"There's so much. I didn't figure on all this detail." He sighed, and she put her hand on his arm.

"Let me do the bills this time and you can start with them next month."

"I'd appreciate that." He looked at her and smiled. "Do you want to look for the jewelry now?"

"Yes. I'll come back to this later."

They went to their father's room, and as they entered she looked at the unmade bed. "Are you sleeping here now?"

"No. I've hardly been in here since I arrived. That's just how he left it."

Her hand went to her mouth and she caught her breath. After a moment she went to the bed and sat on the edge. Slowly she reached out with her left hand and caressed the indentation in the pillow. Chuck said nothing, just waited by the chest of drawers.

"When I'd come by each month, I'd check his linens. They always needed washing. I don't think he changed them from one month to the next."

With that, she stood and pulled the blankets from the bed, then removed the sheets and pillowcases. She put them in a clothes hamper in the closet, which was half filled with underwear and socks.

"Go ahead and start looking for the jewelry." Her voice had regained its efficient manner. "I'll just run these to the basement and put them in the machine."

When she returned, Chuck was in the walk-in closet looking at the racks of hanging clothes. "Could Josh use any of these clothes? There's some nice winter coats and leather boots."

"None of them would fit Josh. He was smaller than Dad by at least three sizes. But I'll tell you what I would like to do with them. Our church has a thrift shop and I could take all of them there."

"That's fine with me," Chuck said.

"See that metal box up there? Would you hand it to me?"

When he brought it down, they could hear the objects inside shifting. Vivian took it to the stripped-down bed and sat on the mattress.

"This is it. I remember the box." She opened it and dumped the contents onto the bed. "I remember this brooch. Mom had one particular blouse that she wore it with, pinned at the neck. And these pearls, they're just costume, but they looked so pretty against her sweaters. Ahh!" She held up a clip for a scarf. "Mom had so many scarves, all colors, silk and wool. They were beautiful. Dad bought them for her for every occasion: birthdays, Christmas, anniversaries. And she'd wear them with such flair around her neck or waist, even braided into her hair." Tears were forming at the edge of her eyes. "Scarves were Mom's signature." Then she looked up, wide-eyed. "I never saw her scarves again after she died. I'll bet Dad saved them. They were so much a part of her."

She jumped up and went back to the closet. "Chuck. Help me with this box on the top shelf. I can't reach it."

He brought it down for her and carried it to the bed. It was a coat box about five inches deep. She lifted the lid. Inside were all the scarves of which she'd spoken. Vivian dug her hands into the colorful mass of silk and wool and raised it above the box, letting it fall back scarf by scarf. She began to cry softly as she chose a red, white and blue scarf and laid it around her shoulders.

"The colors of France," she said through her tears. "Did you know Mom was French? She always wore it on Bastille Day." She gripped the ends of the scarf tightly and began sobbing. Once she straightened up in an attempt to gain control, only to explode again in wracking sobs.

Chuck sat down beside her and took her bent body into his arms, turning her so she rested her head against his chest. Her crying turned into a sorrowful wail and she squeezed his chest so tightly he could hardly breathe. He'd held Michelle this same way when she'd received word of her mother's death. He hadn't known what to say then either, so he just continued to hold his sister the same way. Soon tears were forming in his own eyes.

After several minutes, Vivian began to gain control herself. She relaxed her arms and let her body lean against him as he gently patted and massaged her back. His shirt was wet from her tears. He handed her his handkerchief and she wiped her eyes, then slowly sat up.

"I didn't cry at the funeral or afterwards. I was too busy taking care of everybody else. I didn't realize how much I missed her."

They sat side by side. She held his hand. "With Dad, I bawled and bawled at the funeral and it was Josh and Cliff who took care of me." She raised her lips to Chuck's cheek and kissed him.

"Thanks, big brother."

"You're welcome." He paused, then added, "How about we have lunch together when you finish the bills?"

SIXTEEN

Dawn left Triskin Manor Monday morning, dropped off the briefcase at the university and got to the Cardiff airport in plenty of time, only to find her flight to Heathrow delayed an hour. She sat in the departure lounge, thinking as she frowned at the flight information board. It was clear she would have to go to Moscow, and soon. Still, there was no sense going until she had some way of finding Krubinski. She'd copied Professor Neleginski's address and phone number from one of his letters to Gareth and would call him Tuesday morning from Paris. Apparently he had helped Gareth and maybe he could help her.

Because of the delay, it was late afternoon when she arrived at the Hotel Vendôme in Paris.

Hotel Vendôme had been Gareth's and her favorite when they stayed in Paris, especially the room on the top floor nestled beneath the sloping roof. When registering, she marshaled her courage and asked if that room was available. It was.

Dawn took the narrow elevator to the top floor and unlocked the door to the room. Wondering if she would be greeted by memories of the nights they had spent there, she found instead just another hotel room. For a moment she let her eyes wander over the room, waiting for something, some feeling, but nothing happened. She dropped her bag on the bed and began to unpack. Fifteen minutes later she was in the bathtub submerged in hot water up to her neck, her eyes closed.

She awoke not knowing how long she'd dozed, but aware that the water in the tub had cooled. She got out, dried herself and put on her robe.

Her room had one window placed in a dormer projecting out from the sloping roof. She went to the large round window that looked out like a huge eye on the Place Vendôme. It was dark now and raining. The plaza, as big as a city block, was square, with streetlights around its perimeter that glistened on the wet paving stones. Cars raced back and forth across the center of the plaza, around the tall, slender column memorializing Napoleon's victory at Austerlitz. People hunched under umbrellas hurried around the edge of the plaza beneath the lampposts.

A memory of Gareth and her standing at this same window last summer came to mind. They were looking down on the buildings surrounding the plaza, craning their necks as far as possible out the open window, searching for the apartment that had belonged to George Sand, the one in which she had lived with her lover, Frédéric Chopin.

"There it is," Gareth said, "in the center."

"Where the plaque is?"

"Yes. Just above it." Then he kissed her cheek. "Lovers like us."

"Not quite. Chopin died there."

"Don't worry, luv," he smiled confidently, "I'm not planning to die."

The memory had come upon her so quickly she wasn't prepared to defend herself. Shaken, she crossed to the bed and sat for several minutes looking into space, conscious only of her loneliness. Then she took a deep breath, reached for the phone and called Brighton Academy. Eventually Brian came on the line, pleased to have been pulled from class and to have a chance to tell his mom about his weekend taking care of Clara.

Dawn smiled. She was a mother again.

The next morning, before her first appointment, she telephoned Professor Neleginski, but no one answered. She would try again later that day. To play it safe, she wrote him a letter and left it with the hotel desk clerk to be mailed.

Her first appointment was with Felix Proudhomme, owner of the Galerie d'Art de l'Affiche on the Rue des Écoles. It was a beautiful April day, so she decided to walk through the Jardin des Tuileries, past the Louvre and across the Seine to the Left Bank. The meeting concerned *La Victoire du Communisme*, a huge original poster measuring three by two meters that was to have a prominent place in the exhibit at the BMA. And Monsieur Proudhomme, knowing the poster would also occupy an important place in the book, was expecting a permission fee higher than she planned to pay.

Proudhomme rose when she entered his office, smiling warmly. He looked the same as he had the year before, when she and Gareth had first talked with him: the same black suit, tiny round glasses, and black hair slicked back to cover the beginnings of baldness.

Leaning across his desk, he took her hand. "Madame Ireland, I'm very sorry to hear about the death of your partner, Professor Davies. He was a fine man and I enjoyed doing business with him."

"Thank you, Monsieur Proudhomme," she said sincerely. Then, returning to business, "But I'm pleased to say the exhibit and book are still on track."

Dawn opened her briefcase and set it on the chair beside her. 'Monsieur Proudhomme, I'm afraid there may be some misunderstanding about what is covered in the fee that we agreed on for the loan of the poster. It was our understanding that it would cover reproductions for promotional purposes."

"I have no problem with that, Madame Ireland. You can use reproductions of the poster for the exhibit's informational pamphlet and ads in newspapers."

"We also intend to use a reproduction in the book we are writing. As I'm sure you know, the purpose of the book is to help promote the exhibit. So there should be no additional cost for that reproduction."

"I am afraid that is not the case," he said, shaking his head. "No, the fee for use of a reproduction in the book is an additional one thousand five hundred dollars."

"But, Monsieur," Dawn said, "we are promoting not only the

exhibit, but your gallery as well. The first printing of five thousand will bring the name of Galerie d'Art de l'Affiche to five thousand prospective customers."

He dropped his head and looked at her over the top of his glasses. Smiling, he said, "And thousands of dollars to you and your publishers. It is only fair that a portion of those dollars come to me for allowing you to use the reproduction."

"But, Monsieur . . ."

"No," he said. "You are a forceful negotiator, but a promotional pamphlet is simply not the same thing as a book."

Dawn leaned back in her chair and sighed. She knew he was right, but fifteen hundred dollars was beyond her budget. A plan began to form in her head.

Smiling, she said, "Okay, a pamphlet is a pamphlet and a book is a book. So let's discuss the fee for using a reproduction in the book. I want to be reasonable, but the amount you're asking is more than I am able to pay." Proudhomme rocked his head from side to side equivocally. Dawn continued, "The publisher plans ultimately to print fifteen thousand books. We are willing to pay your fee of fifteen hundred dollars for a printing of fifteen thousand books"—a smile crept out from the edges of his mouth—"and to begin by paying you five hundred dollars for the printing of the first five thousand books." His smile faded. "Remember the publicity you'll receive. Then, with each successive printing of five thousand books, we'll pay an additional five hundred dollars."

Shaking his head, but smiling, he agreed. "You are a remarkable young lady, Madame Ireland. And very crafty."

"Thank you, sir. I'm sure both of us will benefit from our agreement."

Pleased with herself, she decided to enjoy the spring day and walk back to the hotel. Her only regret was not having someone with whom to share her victory.

If Charlie were still alive she'd have called him, as she had done so many times before. Distance had never been a problem in their friendship. She thought about calling Chuck, but decided not to.

Walking down the street in the warm sunshine, she surrendered to a sudden feeling of lightheartedness and began swinging her briefcase like a schoolgirl swinging her bookbag. She listened to the sounds of Paris and smelled the rich coffee brewing in the sidewalk cafes. Then she stopped. Something caught her eye in the window of a travel agency. It was an old poster for Air France's Concorde. Faded and somewhat dusty, she could still make out the graceful droop-nosed jet climbing into the sky and the Eiffel Tower in the background.

If I could find a few hundred copies of that poster, she told herself, I could sell them in a minute.

Back at the hotel, she set up appointments for the next day with the two remaining art dealers who would be providing posters for the book and the exhibit, then telephoned Air France's marketing department to see if they had copies of early Concorde posters she could buy. They agreed to talk with her the following day.

Keeping busy was Dawn's defense against loneliness, so with the business of the day completed, she set out for the Printemps department store to browse the latest fashions.

The next day she negotiated reasonable permission fees with the two art dealers and found Air France receptive to the idea of her purchasing several hundred old posters that were collecting dust on their storage shelves.

But as the afternoon waned, loneliness came upon her like an evening chill. Longing for someone to talk with, she decided to ignore her misgivings and call Chuck. Anyway, she figured, it's almost like dialing Charlie. It's the same number.

"Hi, Chuck, it's Dawn."

"Dawn! Are you back?"

"No, I'm in Paris."

"You sound like you're next door." The excitement in his voice turned to disappointment.

"Is this a bad time to call?"

"No. Vivian's here and we're looking through some of her mother's things."

"Give her my love. By the way, I talked to Brian Monday night. He said he'd met you and that you'd driven him back to school. Thanks for doing that."

"I enjoyed it. He's a nice kid."

"He also told me why he was home. Sounds like Clara got her revenge on Paul."

"She didn't do it intentionally. She was just excited. Paul had a pretty bad fall."

"Brian said his arm's in a cast."

"Yeah. Broken elbow."

"He'll milk *that* for weeks to come. Is he taking care of Clara?"

"No, she's moved in with us."

"See?"

"It's okay. No harder to take care of two dogs than one."

"Well, I thank you."

"How's your trip going?"

"Great." It was right to call him, she thought. That's just what Charlie would have asked. "If I sound like I'm boasting, it's because I am."

"Go ahead. I can tell you're excited about something."

"Well, I think I'm going to be able to buy hundreds of old Air France travel posters that I can sell to several of my clients. It's not part of the book or exhibit, but it'll help the cash reserve."

"That's great, Dawn. When will you be coming home?"

"I've got to finalize the deal with Air France, but I should be home sometime on Saturday."

"Come over for a drink when you get here and tell me all the details."

"I'll do that. Oh, and Chuck, give Clara a kiss for me and tell her I miss her."

"Kiss a dog? How about if I just hug her?"

Dawn laughed.

"Bear misses you, too," he said, "and . . . and sends his love."

SEVENTEEN

May Day morning and spring was in the air, riding in on a brisk south wind. Chuck piled the dogs into the pickup and drove to Marblehead's Devereux Beach. When he turned onto Ocean Avenue, the dogs sensed their destination and began to whine with anticipation. He drove into the parking lot, opened the truck door, and Bear and Clara bolted through the opening. Frantically, he grabbed their leashes, and off they raced toward the water like two horses pulling a wagon.

Down the beach to his right three people were walking, and far to the left, there was one person with a dog. It looked safe enough, so Chuck unhooked the leashes. Bear ran to the line of seaweed left by the last high tide and took care of his business, while Clara began digging for rocks. Chuck cleaned up after Bear and began walking slowly toward the water. He stopped for a moment to enjoy the expanse of ocean and the way the sun shone through green water just before the waves broke onto the beach. The sound of jets taking off at Logan Airport thirteen miles to the south was picked up by the warm southerly breeze and carried across the water as if the airplanes were much closer.

He started down the beach to the left, the breakers on his right and the concrete wall of the causeway leading to Marblehead Neck on his left. Overhead, seagulls soared like kites, wings motionless, riding the south wind's updraft as it lifted over the causeway. He removed his leather jacket and tossed it over one shoulder. The sun warmed his body and he felt, for the first time that year, the dreamy serenity of spring fever.

The dogs were about a hundred yards ahead when he realized they were running to meet the dog he'd seen earlier. Oh, God, he thought, another dog fight. He took off after them. The owner of the dog, a young woman, seemed unconcerned when Bear and Clara came charging up. In fact, she called them by name. Her dog, a small black lab, darted in circles around Clara, initiating a game of tag. Bear gave the dog a whiff, then sauntered into the surf and lay down. The woman was doing a combination of Yoga and stretching exercises.

"Hi," she said without stopping her movements. "I haven't seen Bear and Clara for a while."

Chuck sat on a large boulder beneath the wall of the causeway and rolled up the sleeves of his khaki shirt. The woman wore loose-fitting nylon shorts and a black running bra. Her firm abdominal muscles showed she was in good shape. The long dark hair of her ponytail swung from side to side as she moved her upper body first to the left, then to the right.

"You know them?"

"Uh-huh, but they're usually with a couple, a woman and an older man."

"That's Dawn Ireland. She owns Clara. Bear belonged to my dad, Charlie Carver. He died suddenly a couple of weeks ago."

"Sorry to hear that." She stopped for a moment, tipping her head to the side sympathetically, then added, "I didn't know his name. We know each other by our dogs."

"What's your dog's name?"

"Seaweed," she said, resuming her regimen, this time spreading her feet far apart and gracefully arching her right arm over her head while bending her torso to the left. She repeated the motion in the reverse direction.

The dogs were happy, so Chuck leaned back against the rock and watched the woman. It would have been like watching ballet had she not grunted "Ah!" each time she strained to bend her body a little further.

"Do you come to the beach often?" Chuck asked.

"No. It's just that today is so beautiful." She spoke with a seemingly unending supply of breath. "When I finish here, I'll take Seaweed for a run around the Neck."

"Watching you, I feel like a slacker." He raised himself from the comfort of his rock seat and stood.

She looked him up and down. "You don't look like a slacker." Chuck noticed she wasn't wearing a wedding ring.

"I'm not much of a runner, but I like hiking."

"That's good, too." She stopped, raised her arms in a circle over her head, took a deep breath and dropped her arms behind her. Chuck noticed how the motion lifted her breasts in spite of the running bra. "Well, time for my run. Nice talking to you." She smiled warmly, then called, "Come on, Seaweed. Time to run."

Chuck's eyes followed her up the beach until her bouncing ponytail disappeared around the end of the causeway wall.

How long has it been? Chuck asked himself. Six, no, eight months. When I was in San Francisco.

He whistled for the dogs and started up the beach in the direction the woman had gone. Maybe he'd pass her on her return run. But soon his thoughts had shifted from her to Dawn, and he smiled as he thought about her returning home on Saturday. Two more days.

By night the south wind had brought heavy cumulus thunderheads and rain began falling. For the first time that year, Chuck heard thunder rolling in the distance. At ten o'clock he locked up and climbed the stairs to his bedroom on the third floor, Bear and Clara trudging behind him.

He remembered one of the things he liked best about his room: being on the top floor, he could hear the rain on the roof. He opened the window just enough to add to the sound of the storm without letting in too much rain, and got ready for bed. Halfway through brushing his teeth in the small bathroom next to his room, he began to think about the woman he'd seen on the beach. A few minutes later, as he climbed into bed, he replayed the whole scene, from his running toward her fearing a dog fight to watching her and Seaweed depart. As he stretched out on his back, his mind returned to the graceful movements of her body. He remembered that her shiny nylon shorts were cut up the sides about three inches, revealing the rounded edge of her buttocks. He saw her smiling at him invitingly when she said he didn't look like a slacker. But when he tried to imagine her coming toward him, removing her running bra and her shorts, the vision of the woman vanished, dissolving into a fog, leaving only sadness.

Footsteps on the stairs? He pulled the blanket over his head and turned away from the door. He began to shiver. His eyes opened wide in the blackness beneath the blanket. Terrified, he waited.

The knob turned and the door squeaked ever so slightly as it slowly opened. A floorboard groaned under the weight of a footstep. Why aren't the dogs barking? he asked himself. But he knew there were no dogs to save him, and he knew that what was going to happen would happen no matter what he did.

A hand touched his shoulder and turned him onto his back. Then it pulled the blanket off his face, and he opened his eyes.

There, only inches from him, was the shadowed outline of a woman with a long ponytail. She was whispering softly, "Shhh. Shhh." Why am I afraid? he thought. It's the woman from the beach. But he was afraid, rigid with fear. He felt her cheek on his chest, her hand against his forehead gently rubbing, and the fingers of her other hand caressing his stomach. She began kissing his chest and moving her hand below his stomach. In spite of his fear, a voice in his head was asking her, pleading with her, to do it. But it was wrong. He tried to lift himself, to get up, but the hand that had been on his forehead now pressed down hard on his chest. As she moved her head down his stomach, licking and kissing his skin, she continued to whisper, "Shhh. Shhh."

He could feel her hand enfold him. *Stop, but don't stop.* Was he saying it out loud, or was he thinking it? It's wrong, he called out in his mind, it's dirty. But do it and get it over with.

Suddenly she was on top of him, covering him, pressing him down into the mattress. He touched her naked body, but instead of supple smoothness his fingers slid over coarse, slimy skin. The woman was gone, transformed into his dragon. "Don't stop, do it," he said to the dragon as it took him into its huge warm mouth.

"Ahhhh!" Chuck gasped, sitting upright in the bed. He was breathing rapidly, irregularly, his eyes open wide, darting about the room. His body was wet with sweat and semen, yet he was shivering with cold. Falling back onto his pillow, he was filled with self-loathing.

Immediately, Bear and Clara were beside the bed, black shadows peering at him. Chuck brought his knees against his chest, curled into a ball and rolled over to stare out the window.

Bear circled the bed so his head was next to Chuck's. A huge black shape silhouetted against the window, he waited quietly for some response from his new master. When none came, he placed his paw on the bed and whined softly. Gradually, Chuck's shivering stopped and his breathing became regular. He reached out and touched Bear's paw.

"It's still there, big guy, my dragon."

Instead of the usual anger that followed his nightmares, Chuck felt sadness, a deep profound sadness, that brought tears to his eyes. "It's still there," he said aloud.

Bear, waiting no longer for an invitation, climbed onto the bed, and with one of his deep groans, plopped down so his face was next to Chuck's. Stretched out on the bed, he was almost as long as his new master, who moved over slightly to give the dog more room. Clara watched from the window seat.

EIGHTEEN

When Vivian called inviting Chuck to dinner on Friday night, he thanked her but declined. Too much work, he said. What he actually planned to do Friday evening was be by himself with a glass of scotch, a thick steak and the latest video release. Too much had inundated his life too quickly, and he wanted to be alone. His new brother and sister, Dawn, the dogs, even his house on Quiet Cove were sucking the life out of him. He craved solitude in which to restore his sense of personhood. But Vivian persisted, reminding him how much she appreciated his understanding when they had gone through her mother's things. Finally he gave in. "Oh," she said, "and Bear's invited, too."

Now he was sitting in Vivian's living room in Weston, thumbing through a copy of *Smithsonian* while three children played peek-a-boo around the corner of the dining room. He could hear Vivian preparing dinner in the kitchen. By the occasional banging of pots and pans, he concluded she was upset with Carl, her husband, for being late. Bear was with Vivian in the kitchen—where the food was.

The house was an old Victorian with high ceilings and tall windows. Between the living room and dining room was a wide arch with dark maple trim. The floor was also polished maple, covered for the most part with an oriental rug. Three windows faced the street. On the opposite wall a fireplace with an ornate cast-iron grate and grill work was swept so clean that Chuck wondered if they'd ever had a fire in it. He sat in a wingback chair facing the arch to the dining room.

"Go ahead," a child's voice urged.

"No. You go first." It was a younger voice.

Chuck looked up from his magazine just in time to see a bundle of long curls disappear around the corner. There was more mumbling.

"Mom said," the older voice declared.

"Not until you go," said the younger voice.

At that moment, a little girl on unsteady legs ran a few feet into the living room and stopped short. She looked back at her brother and sister around the corner and then at Chuck. A mischievous smile played on her lips as she clasped her hands together and rocked from side to side. Her short brown hair was uncombed and her yellow dress bulged over her diapers. She gazed at Chuck for a moment until her attention was drawn to the leg of a doll sticking out from under the chair across from him. Cautiously she walked to the doll, extracted it and ran laughing back to the dining room.

Vivian appeared at the archway.

"Are they bothering you?"

"Not at all."

"Come on and meet your uncle," she said, drawing the three children into view, the baby first, followed by her sister and brother. "When they finished eating, I told them to go into the living room and meet you, but I guess they need some help." She touched the head of her son and said, "This is Jeremy. He's six. And this is Jackie." Jackie had squeezed behind her mother's apron. "Don't be shy," Vivian said, tugging her daughter to the front. The baby had once again ventured into the living room. "And my brave little girl is Joslynn. She's two and Jackie's four."

"Hello," Chuck said uncertainly, having had little experience with children.

"This is Uncle Chuck, kids. You didn't know you had an Uncle Chuck, but you do. Go on," she said, gently pushing on Jeremy's and Jackie's backs. "Talk to him. I've got to go back to the kitchen." She turned to go, then stopped, "I'm sorry about Carl. He should have been here an hour ago." She disappeared.

Chuck looked at the three blank faces staring at him and offered another feeble, "Hello."

Jeremy studied him. The boy's hair was straight and looked like it had been cut with a bowl on his head. Then Chuck saw it was neatly trimmed around the bottom and figured it must be the latest style. He wore a pair of baggy pants and a T-shirt bearing a menagerie of wild animals. Lifting his chin with a trace of defiance, he took three steps toward Chuck.

"Uncle Josh is our uncle."

"You can have more than one."

Jeremy thought about that, but said nothing.

Jackie, wearing a frilly rose-colored dress, stared intently at her new uncle for several moments, then ran to her brother and whispered in his ear.

Jeremy spoke. "You have whiskers."

"Uh-huh."

Jackie giggled and whispered again to Jeremy.

"She wants to touch your wishers."

With a shrug, Chuck said, "Okay." He set the magazine aside.

Jackie, her head down, the tip of her finger in her mouth and her eyes fixed on Chuck, moved coquettishly toward him. He leaned forward and stuck out his chin. One little finger rose, touched his beard and then pulled quickly back. Again her hand went to his face, and this time all the fingers dug into the tight graying curls around his chin. She looked at her brother and laughed, then both hands went to his cheeks.

"Like Sanna Claus," she proclaimed.

The front door opened and Carl rushed into the foyer, his briefcase swinging from one arm as he slammed the door with the other.

"Hi, Viv," he called. "Sorry I'm late." Then seeing Chuck and his three children in the living room, he said, "Oh, hello." He crossed quickly into the room and extended his hand. "I'm Carl." Chuck rose to meet him.

He was a few inches shorter than Chuck and, like Vivian, in his early thirties. Well built, and with coarse dark hair and a day's growth of beard, he had a rugged look. His tie was loosened and the top button of his white shirt unbuttoned. He wore a brown tweed sport coat and dark brown pleated pants well wrinkled from a day on the job.

"And I'm Chuck."

"I'm really sorry to be so late. We had an office thing that I couldn't miss. You know."

It wasn't a question, so Chuck didn't bother to answer.

"Didn't Vivian offer you a drink?"

"It's okay. I'm in no hurry."

"Well, I need one. What'll it be?"

"Scotch on the rocks?"

"Sure. Hi, kids. Gimme a kiss." He bent down and touched his lips to Jeremy's and Jackie's foreheads, but little Joslynn ran toward the dining room. "You little devil," her father said and took off after her, scooping her up in his arms and giving her a hug. Suddenly he held her at arm's length. "Ugh. You stink." She laughed as he set her down. "Stay away from this one, Chuck. She'll asphyxiate you." Heading through the dining room to the kitchen, he called, "I'll be back in a minute with your drink."

The children returned their attention to Chuck, who was sitting down.

"Let's see now," he said, "you're Jeremy." The boy nodded. "And you're Jackie."

"Not really," Jeremy said. "Her real name is Jacqueline, for Gramma."

"But they call me Jackie," she announced proudly.

"Okay. Jackie it is." She smiled. "And this one's . . ." The baby ran to him. "Whew! And this one's Stinky." They all laughed.

As the laughter subsided, Vivian's voice was heard from the kitchen. "One night was all I asked. Be home by seven."

"I said I was sorry. It couldn't be helped. Sharon closed the deal with Top Flight Shoes and all of us went out to celebrate."

The children's eyes turned toward the archway. Jackie said, "Mommy's mad." Jeremy shushed her. "Well, she is."

"They're just having a discussion," Chuck said.

Joslynn decided she wanted to sit on Chuck's lap. He drew back and wrinkled his nose, but the baby was insistent.

"Is it safe?" Chuck asked Jeremy.

"Uh-huh. She won't leak."

Chuck picked her up and set her on the ends of his knees.

More voices from the kitchen. "You could have called. I feel like an idiot here in the kitchen while Chuck's stuck in the living room."

"She didn't get the contract signed until six o'clock. I only stayed for one drink."

"See?" Jackie said. "They *are* fighting."

Jeremy, looking annoyed with his sister, changed the subject. "Why do you have whiskers?"

Chuck thought for a moment. "I like the way they feel."

"Well," Jeremy stated, "they look funny."

"*I* like the way they feel," said Jackie coming to his defense.

Voices exploded in the kitchen. "I've about had it with all these celebrations with Sharon. Is she the only one getting new business?"

"Oh, for Christ's sake, Viv." A cabinet door slammed shut. Immediately, Bear, the caretaker of the world, began barking and didn't stop for half a minute. The four people in the living room listened in stunned silence. When Bear stopped, all was quiet.

Moments later, Carl bounded through the archway, smiling. "One scotch on the rocks." He handed Chuck his drink.

"Ah, thanks."

"Okay, kids, say good night. Time for bed."

A chorus of moans was soon silenced and the children were marched up to bed. Chuck picked up his drink and wandered into the kitchen. Vivian, looking harried, was wiping her brow with the end of her apron. A strand of hair had fallen across her cheek. She looked at Chuck and smiled wanly.

"Great children, Viv."

"Do you want them? You can have them. Right now they're a pain in the you know what. Dinner's about ready. As soon as Carl comes down."

"Anything I can do?"

She looked as if she was about to unload her troubles, then changed her mind. "Yes. You can uncork that bottle of wine. It needs to breathe a little before dinner."

Fifteen minutes later they were seated around the dining room table eating prime rib, baked potatoes with sour cream, asparagus and a tossed salad. Chuck noticed Vivian and Carl talked only with him and hardly ever with each other. Tension hung heavy over the table.

Carl gave a sigh of relief. "Ahhh, Friday night, the beginning of the weekend. For you, though, working at home," he said to Chuck, "it must be just another day."

"No," Chuck said, "I take weekends off, usually. There's no one at the other end of my modem."

"Viv tells me you're renovating the house."

"Yes, and it's a bigger job than I thought."

"Doing it yourself?"

"Oh Lord, no. Just the porch. I've got contractors for the rest."

"Has Dawn called again?" Vivian had been at the house when she called from Paris.

"No. I'll be seeing her tomorrow, though, when she gets home."

"Oh?" Eyebrows raised and surprise in her voice. "That's nice. She's a wonderful person. I think she misses Dad almost as much as I do."

"And on top of losing her partner, too," Chuck said.

"She had a tough time for a while," Vivian said. "I think it was Dad who pulled her through."

"More wine, Chuck?" Carl got up and topped off Chuck's glass.

"Thanks."

Carl continued to stand beside him, looking at him. "It's strange seeing you sitting there in Charlie's place."

"I expect it is. And in his house, too?"

"I've got to admit that I was pretty upset when Viv came home from Constanza's office and told me you'd inherited it."

"Carl!" Vivian broke in. "Why bring that up?"

"Well, it's true. Just let me finish, will you? I *was* upset, but then I realized it was for the best. We didn't need the house anyway."

Chuck could feel their anger toward each other boiling over onto him and was tempted to turn it back on them, especially Carl.

"Josh said he'd hoped to get the house someday too, and I offered to give him the right of first refusal when I sell it. I'll do the same for you, Carl, if you'd like."

"No. Like I said, we're happy here. Aren't we, Viv?"

She glared at him.

"In a way," Carl went on, "it's strange meeting you. I've heard about you from Viv. Especially about that locked bedroom on the third floor. Have you gone in there yet?"

"Yup. I'm sleeping there."

"No kidding. It's a child's room, isn't it?"

"You forget, it *is* my room."

"Yes," Vivian asserted, and to her husband, "and it's his house, too."

That seemed to shut Carl up for a while and everybody took advantage of the silence to eat some prime rib.

Bear, sitting quietly, followed Chuck's fork as it moved from the plate to his mouth and back to his plate.

"If you want to feed Bear some scraps," Vivian said, "go ahead. Dad always did and he expects it." Chuck cut off a piece of juicy fat and dropped it in Bear's mouth. It was gone in an instant, and he looked up at Chuck hoping for more.

"How are the kids taking Dad's death?" Chuck asked.

"I really don't think it's sunk in. Jeremy understands that he died and has gone to heaven to be with Gramma. Jackie says that too, but she really doesn't comprehend the dying part. And Joslynn's too young."

"He was a great guy," Carl put in. "I'll miss sailing with him this summer."

Chuck took a sip of his wine, then asked, "How did Dad meet your mother?"

Vivian leaned back in her chair and set her fork down. "Let's see. I remember asking them when I was a teenager. We were sitting on the porch on a summer afternoon. Dad said that he knew her father before she was born, which gives you an idea of their age difference. You know he was a fighter pilot in World War Two."

"Yes, the pictures on the study wall."

"Well, Mom's dad, Grandfather Chambier, we called him *Grandpère*, escaped the Nazi invasion of France and went to England, where he joined the RAF as a fighter pilot. Somewhere along the line, the two met and became friends. Then years later, when Dad was flying the TWA run to Paris, he looked up his old friend and found him. Whenever Dad had a layover, the two of them would get together. Well, Grandpère had a daughter named Jacqueline. At first she used to follow along with Dad and Grandpère when they'd go sightseeing. Mom must have been seventeen: long brunette hair, a wispy figure—she was beautiful. And Dad, he was Grandpère's age. You should see the pictures of them, the way she looks at Dad. Well, pretty soon, when Dad would go over, it was just Dad and Mom seeing each other. There's pictures of them at the Eiffel Tower, with Notre-Dame in the background, at Versailles and some at Cannes and the Riviera." Vivian stopped, noticing Chuck's pensive look.

"I was trying to figure out," Chuck said, "when this was taking place."

"Well, if Mom was seventeen when they met and was born in nineteen forty-five, it must have been, let's see, nineteen sixty-two."

"Uh-huh."

"Oh," Vivian uttered when she realized what he was thinking.

"Uh-huh," Chuck said bitterly. "So he was playing around in France with a girl half his age while he was still married to Mom."

"It wasn't like that, I'm sure," Vivian said.

"Those pictures you mention taken in Cannes, do you think they had separate rooms?"

"Get off it, Chuck," Carl said. "Hell, it was over thirty years ago."

"I knew there must be something like this," Chuck said, ignoring Carl. "I remember now, the night before Mom and I left, they had an awful fight." There was a distant, pained look in his eyes. "They were yelling and screaming. Mom must have discovered he was playing around."

"You make my mom sound cheap," Vivian said, sitting up straight. "It wasn't like that at all."

Chuck, remembering the argument he'd heard from the kitchen, looked at Carl, then at Vivian and back to Carl. Carl, apparently sensing he was on dangerous ground, dropped his eyes.

"And what would you call it?" Chuck asked Vivian.

She stared at her half-brother, her eyes flaming, then gradually relaxed and leaned back in her chair.

When she finally spoke, her voice was calm and even. "I'd call it true love." She paused. "I knew Mom, and I grew up knowing how much she loved Dad and how much Dad loved her. I'm sorry about your mom and I'm sorry about the dates. It was simply a case of bad chronology."

NINETEEN

Chuck and the two dogs were coming back from a walk when the airport limo pulled into the driveway. The dogs sensed it was Dawn and pulled so hard on their leashes that Chuck had to let go. They raced to the limo, arriving there just as Dawn was getting out. Clara stood on her hind legs and pushed her head into Dawn's stomach, howl-whining her joyful hello. Bear approached from the rear, shoving his head between her legs, and received a knuckle-rub on both ears.

The dogs were still barking and dancing around Dawn as Chuck ran up. God, but she's stunning, he thought as he took both her hands in his. "Welcome home." Her blue eyes were tired and there were strain lines around her mouth, but her fair skin and long hair seemed to radiate freshness. She wore beige slacks and a hip-length knit sweater in shades of yellow and soft brown.

Dawn laughed, "What a welcome! You'd think I'd been gone a year."

The driver got Dawn's bags from the trunk and she handed him some bills. Chuck undid the leashes and put them over his shoulder. "May I help with the bags?"

"Thanks."

The dogs led the way to her house. At the door Chuck asked if she'd like to drop by for a drink.

"Clara too?"

"Of course."

120

"Give us about an hour."

"See you then." Chuck and Bear went to their house. The emptiness and coldness he'd felt there during the last week vanished in anticipation of Dawn's visit. He fed Bear and put some cheese and crackers on a plate.

It was six o'clock when they arrived.

"Exhausted?" Chuck said.

"A little tired, that's all. It's not so bad crossing the Atlantic this way and I slept some on the plane. If I were still in Paris it'd only be midnight."

"And you'd just be heading out for a night on the town."

"Right." Dawn had changed into Levi's and a sweatshirt.

"Here," she said, handing Chuck a small, brightly colored box. "A gift from Paris."

"*Pâté foie du canard?*" He struggled with the French.

"Duck liver pâté, a cholesterol blockbuster. And I've got some crackers to put it on."

"Well, I just happen to have a cold bottle of chardonnay *du* California. Have a seat. I'll be right back."

Dawn sat on the sofa and both dogs put their heads in her lap. Clara licked her hand and Bear rumbled his pleasure as she rubbed under his chin. In a couple of minutes Chuck returned carrying a bottle of wine, two glasses and the tray of cheese and crackers.

He filled the glasses and they toasted her return.

"I'm glad you're back."

"Has Clara been a bother?" she said, concerned.

"Not at all. It's just that the dogs aren't much on conversation."

They sat on the sofa with the tray in front of them on the coffee table. Chuck spread some pâté on a cracker and took a bite. "This is delicious."

"And duty-free, too. I had a bunch of francs left over when I got to the airport."

"Try the cheese."

"I will." Dawn peeled a shaving with a cheese knife. "I see the pile of wood in the front yard's bigger."

"Yup. A few more days and I'll have all the old porch ripped away. The carpenter's coming next week to start tearing up the bathroom and he's ordered a big Dumpster. I'll put the old boards in it and get the yard cleaned up. More wine?"

"The pâté makes me thirsty, I guess." He filled both glasses.

"So, how was the trip? You said you'd fill me in."

"Good and not so good," she said. "In Paris I arranged for the use of some posters for the exhibit and the book, but I ran into a dead end concerning a poster I need from Moscow."

"Will you be home now for a while?"

"For a while, but I'm going to have to make a trip to Moscow soon. In the meantime, I'll be here, busy with the exhibit."

The pâté and crackers were disappearing fast.

"I'm hungrier than I thought," Chuck said, cutting some cheese.

"Maybe you need to eat dinner."

"No. I can eat anytime. Say, I've got some smoked oysters in the pantry and some more crackers. Fill the glasses and I'll be right back."

When Chuck returned, Dawn said, "I forgot the most important thing."

"What's that?"

"I'm going to make some money." She pretended a serious look. "And I need to."

"Doing what?"

"I found hundreds of old Air France posters at their headquarters in Paris and I got them for a song. I'm having them shipped here."

"And you'll sell them?"

"At a nice profit."

Chuck took a drink of wine. "I guess I don't understand about posters. I see them in framing stores and bookstores and they're about five or six bucks. Wholesale they can't be much more than two or three."

"Those are reprints. Originals, especially old ones, go for a lot more."

"Like how much more?"

"The Air France posters I got are the ones they used to introduce the Concorde about thirty years ago. They're striking. I'll sell them through wholesale poster catalogs."

"Roughly, how much would one cost me?"

"Oh, about a hundred dollars."

"You're kidding."

"No. If they were scarce and a little older, they'd cost more."

Chuck was dumbfounded. "Well, what would a prewar poster cost?"

"If it's from a famous designer and there's only a few left, about ten to fifteen thousand dollars. A really rare one could go for as much as a hundred thousand."

"My God! I had no idea."

"Right. A few of those and you're talking big business."

Chuck, shaking his head, poured the remaining wine into their glasses and Dawn fed the last two crackers to the dogs.

"I'd better let you eat." She finished her wine.

"Don't go. Unless you're too tired."

"Actually, I feel pretty good. I've been dying to tell somebody about the Air France posters."

Chuck turned toward her. "Stay, then. This is too much fun. I'll open another bottle of wine."

"You're on." She grinned.

He returned with the bottle plus chips and dip. "From French crackers and pâté *de* duck liver to potato chips and onion dip."

Dawn laughed, "It's the company that counts."

Three-quarters of an hour later, the dogs were curled up on the floor and Chuck and Dawn were slumped down in the sofa, legs stretched out and their shoulders touching. The second bottle was two-thirds gone.

Dawn's head leaned slightly toward Chuck's. "The truth is, the trip wasn't all that great. Oh, the poster part was okay, but the rest of it was tough."

The touch of Dawn's shoulder against his was like a bare electrical wire. Even the strands of her hair that had fallen against his neck were igniting the nerves along his spine. Out of the corner of his eye he could see the outline of her breasts beneath the sweatshirt rise and fall as she breathed. Does she know what she's doing, he thought, or is it the wine?

"Tough, huh?"

"Yeah." She was silent for so long, Chuck thought she might

have dozed off. She took a deep breath and went on, "Did I tell you that a partner and I were writing the book to accompany the exhibit?"

"Yes. You said he died."

"Oh, that's right. I think I told you his name was Gareth, Gareth Davies. He lived in Cardiff, was a professor at the university there. The first couple of years we were working on the book we'd get together occasionally, compare notes, plan what we were going to do, and that was all. After a while we knew we were falling in love and tried to pretend nothing was happening. Then, one night in Paris, we stopped pretending."

Her head leaned further until it was touching his. Their glasses were empty, but he didn't want to get up to refill them.

"What I didn't tell you was, Gareth had gone to Russia, to Moscow, to teach a seminar. I'd asked him to see if he could locate a man who owned a poster I needed for the exhibit. I know he tried, because of notes he'd left in his briefcase." She was quiet for a moment. "If he succeeded, I don't know. They found Gareth on a Moscow sidewalk. Dead."

Chuck, realizing the mood was broken, sat up and poured the rest of the wine. When he sat back he slipped his arm under Dawn's head and she laid it on his shoulder. After a minute or two, she went on.

"I know this sounds crazy, but I can't help thinking there may have been some connection between Gareth looking for this guy and his getting killed. If there is, I'll never forgive myself. Finding Krubinski, that's the guy's name, was my job, not Gareth's. He was doing it for me."

She stopped talking and leaned her head against Chuck. After a minute or so, he started rubbing her temples and running his fingers through her hair.

"That feels good," she said, burrowing her head into Chuck's neck, his beard catching in her hair. "In Paris, I stayed in the same hotel Gareth and I used to stayed in." He could feel her breath catch. "Same room we'd made love in the first time." She was sobbing quietly. He could feel her tears against his skin.

"Damn it, Charlie, I love him so much."

"Chuck. I'm Chuck, Dawn." He raised the cheek that had been pressing against her forehead.

"Oh, hell. I'm sorry. I know. I meant to say Chuck."

"That's okay."

She sat up and looked at him. "Please forgive me."

"Honest, it's okay. There's nothing to forgive."

She opened her eyes wide, clearing her head. "I've been doing all the talking. Tell me, what's happened to you this week?" She took another sip of her wine. "Wish I coulda seen Clara trip up old Paul. That musta been a sight."

"It was, and then at the hospital, she kissed him good-bye."

"Sounds like you had a pretty good week."

"Uh-huh." He thought for a minute. "Actually, it wasn't all that great, especially last night."

Chuck leaned back. Dawn looked at him, drained her glass and set it down, then snuggled back onto his shoulder where she'd been before.

"Tell me 'bout it. What happened last night?"

"Well, I was at Vivian's. She invited me over for dinner. Carl was late getting home and that made her mad and then Carl got mad at her."

"Too bad." Pause. "But not *so* bad."

"That's not the bad part. We were talkin' about Dad and how he met Jacqueline and we figured out he'd been playin' 'round with this little girl half his age at least two years before Mom left him. I got mad about that and, more or less, said Vivian's mom was a little hussy or somethin' like that. Vivian got mad. Carl was already mad. And I left pissed. It was a bad scene."

He waited for Dawn to say something. She didn't. He could feel her head weighing heavily on his shoulder and hear her long and even breathing. She was asleep.

He sat for several minutes, afraid if he moved she'd awaken. His arm was around her shoulder and he gently pulled her closer, enjoying the warmth of her body next to his. Eventually, he eased up from beneath her and gently laid her down on the sofa, bringing her legs up onto the cushions. Then he went to the guest room, found two blankets and a pillow and brought them downstairs.

Carefully he slipped the pillow under her head and covered her with the blankets.

Clara watched the whole proceeding, sitting like the Egyptian Sphinx adorned with huge pointed ears. When Chuck tapped Bear on the head and motioned toward the stairs, the big dog pulled himself upright and, with eyes half-closed and head down, followed Chuck to the bedroom. Clara watched them go, then looked at her mistress. Putting her head back down, she remained at Dawn's side.

TWENTY

The knocking penetrated Chuck's sleep, insinuating itself into his dream and filling him with terror. "Oh, God! Not again!"

More knocking. The dream began to evaporate. His eyes opened slowly. He was looking at the wall.

Knock, knock.

He rolled over. There was Dawn standing at his open door, Clara beside her. She was carrying a tray.

"Good morning," she said cheerfully.

The dog pushed past her into the room and began licking Bear's ears.

Chuck rubbed his eyes and propped his arms behind his head.

"Hi." He yawned.

"Thanks for taking care of me last night."

"You fell asleep. I couldn't bear to wake you." Another yawn. "How was the sofa?"

"Not bad. I woke up on France time, though—about three—then drifted off again until six. So I got up and made your breakfast."

"Have a seat." He slid over in the bed, shoving two pillows behind his head, and she sat down, placing the tray on his lap. The dogs lined up on the other side of the bed, alert to the prospects of food. On the tray was a plate of eggs, bacon, toast and jam, a cup of steaming coffee, orange juice, a bottle of Advil and a narrow vase containing a jonquil. She must have picked it from the side yard.

"Thought you might need the Advil. I did."

Chuck opened his eyes wide, arching his brows. "See what you mean." He unscrewed the cap and shook two pills into his hand, swallowing them with orange juice. "The last time someone made me breakfast in bed was when I was home from school, sick. Mom brought it to me before she left for work. Never with a jonquil, though. Have you eaten?"

"I had coffee and a piece of toast. That's all the breakfast I ever eat."

She sat near the foot of the bed facing Chuck. When he glanced at her, he could see she was studying him. Her eyes moved from his head, resting against the headboard, down the length of his body to the little tent his feet made under the blankets at the end of the bed.

She smiled. "You surely are big." He smiled back as he scooped up some egg yolk on a piece of toast. When her eyes fixed on the few inches of bare skin exposed below his navel, he tugged self-consciously at the blanket.

She was grinning again. "What's so funny?" he asked. "Do I look that bad in the morning?"

"No. I was just wondering how you can fit in this bed."

"You should see it when Bear's in here with me."

"You're kidding."

"Ask him. He'll tell you."

Chuck went back to eating. Dawn became pensive.

"I fixed meals for Charlie a few times when he was sick in bed with the flu."

"You're welcome to fix mine anytime. By the way, you called me Charlie once last night."

"I know. I hoped you'd forgotten." She was silent for a few moments, then, "I talked a lot, didn't I?"

"Uh-huh. A lot about Gareth. You still love him, don't you?"

She took a deep breath, exhaling slowly. "Yeah. I'm doing better, though. At least now I can work. At first I couldn't do that. And last night, the wine didn't help. Sorry I got so maudlin."

"That's all right." He looked at her. The morning sun had come into the room, touching her blond hair, lighting her face. She was dressed in the same sweatshirt and Levi's. When she saw him gazing at her, she averted her eyes.

"I must be a mess. No makeup and I haven't combed my hair."

He wanted to say she was the loveliest woman he had ever seen, but instead settled for, "You look fine."

She ran both hands through her hair, combing it back over her shoulders. Chuck watched her until she noticed what he was doing, then she stopped. Nodding toward the dogs, she said, "You've got some admirers there."

Chuck broke off two pieces of toast. "Here, but you're not getting any bacon." He tossed one piece to Bear, who caught it in midair, then handed one to Clara, who cautiously sniffed it before accepting it.

"Did I ever let you talk last night?" she asked.

"Eventually." He smiled. "And you immediately fell asleep."

"That wasn't very nice of me, but then you plied me with all that wine."

"Yeah, for all the good it did me." They laughed.

"Tell me what you said."

"I said I had a hell of time at Vivian's Friday night. They got mad at me and I got mad at them."

"Really. What about?"

"About Charlie playing around with her mother while he was still married to my mom."

"Hmm. And you rushed to your mom's defense."

"Well, yes." There was a trace of Friday night's anger in his voice.

"That's kind of absurd, isn't it?" She gave him a moment to think about that. "It happened thirty years ago. Right?" He nodded. "And your mom took care of it."

"Yes. She divorced him."

"So why are you getting upset?"

Chuck thought some more. He drank some coffee and looked out the window. Finally he turned toward Dawn and said, "You're right, it doesn't make sense. I don't know why I got so mad."

"I'm divorced. You're divorced. Things that start out good sometimes go bad."

"I know."

She got up, walked to the window and looked out. Without turning back to him, she added, "Don't be too quick to point the finger. There may be more than one side to it."

He wanted it to be settled. She was right, and he'd acted like a child. But he couldn't let go of it. What was it that bothered him so much?

She faced him. "You don't look convinced."

"No. There's more. It's got something to do with being in this house after thirty-two years. Like suddenly I'm back here again, ten years old." He thought for a minute, but came up with nothing. "Well, at least I can understand why Mom and Dad had that terrible fight the night before we left."

"What was that?"

"I remember their yelling and screaming. It was awful." He shook his head. "Mom must have found out what Dad was doing."

"Sounds reasonable." She turned back to the window. Chuck realized it was time to drop the subject.

When a minute had passed, she looked at him. "I've wondered about this room. It was always locked."

"I didn't tell you. Charlie wrote me a letter. I found it in his desk drawer. It contained the key to this room. He said he was saving my room for me, keeping it just as I'd left it when Mom and I pulled out. He locked it, I guess, so his kids and later his grandchildren wouldn't play in here."

Dawn let her eyes wander over the room. "Hmm. Books, toys, model airplane, everything, just like it was thirty-two years ago?"

"Uh-huh."

"No wonder it's a time warp for you." She reached behind the curtains hanging at the window. "What's this?" She picked up two shiny tin cans around which was wound a long string.

Chuck looked at them for a moment. "Oh my God! You found my tin can telephone. Bruce—I told you about Bruce McIntyre—we used to talk to each other with that. His room was right over there."

"That's Brian's room."

"Oh. It was Bruce's then. The string goes in the hole on the bottom of the can. Turn it over. See the button it's tied to? Well, we'd pull the string tight between the two cans, and we'd be able to talk to each other. Your voice vibrated the button and the string carried the vibration to the button in the other can. We used to signal each other with flashlights when we were supposed to be in bed, and then we'd talk on our tin can phone."

"Sounds like fun."

"Yeah. We'd talk about our parents and the kids at school. We'd tell each other our darkest secrets, things we'd never mention in the daytime." Chuck smiled as he thought about his friend.

"How times change. Brian has his own phone line with a different ring." She replaced the tin can phone and sat down again on the end of the bed.

"Speaking of Brian, I'm driving up there to see him today."

"Oh, I've been meaning to ask you. When does his school year end?"

"He's got three more weeks."

"I was thinking I'd ask him to help me get the sailboat ready. I'd pay him."

"He'd probably do it for nothing, but he'd love the money. I'll ask him when I see him today." As she leaned forward to take the tray, which Chuck had set on the bed beside him, she noticed the Bugs Bunny lamp on the bedstand.

"Who smashed poor old Bugs? He's lost his carrot." She touched the lamp and felt the cracks where it had been glued back together. "Did you get mad at your lamp one night?"

Laughing, she turned to look at Chuck. He was sitting up, staring at the lamp, his face frozen with fear.

"Chuck? Are you all right?"

He said nothing, his eyes fixed on the cracked body of Bugs Bunny. Dawn reached across the tray and placed her hand over his.

"Chuck. What is it?"

"It . . . it happened here, in this room. The fight. I can see them. The light from the hall was shining into the room. Mom was screaming. She grabbed the lamp and smashed it down on Dad's head. Again and again until it shattered. He ran to the hall. Mom dropped what was left of the lamp and chased him. I could hear them downstairs, still yelling. Then I buried my head under the pillow."

Chuck took a deep breath and fell back against the pillows. Dawn moved the tray to the floor and sat against the headboard next to him. With her left hand she wiped a trace of sweat from his forehead. For several moments they said nothing, she stroking his forehead and temples, and he leaning back against the head-board next to her.

"So that's why you've been sleeping in your old room. You knew there was something here you wanted to remember."

"I only hope that was all of it."

TWENTY-ONE

I think I remember what to do," Brian said. "I helped Charlie get the boat ready last spring."

"I hope so, because I don't know much about boats."

Chuck got the key to the boat shed from the hook at the top of the stairs and started down the steps to the garage with Brian and Bear following. It was Memorial Day and the spring term had ended at Brighton Academy the previous week. Dawn had told her son that Chuck wanted him to help with the boat, and he'd jumped at the chance.

When Chuck pressed the button and the garage door opened, Bear trotted ahead to the boat shed as if he knew where they were going.

"Now, how did he know where to go?" Chuck asked, puzzled.

Brian answered matter-of-factly, "He saw you pick up the key. Last spring he'd wait in the kitchen for Charlie to get the key and then follow us down to the boat shed."

"Go on!"

"Yup." He grinned. "Then he'd lie in the shade and keep his eye on us—make sure we kept busy."

When they caught up with Bear, he was prancing in front of the boat shed, barking to get in. Chuck unlocked the padlock and pulled open the two big doors and the dog dashed inside, circling the trailer on which the boat rested.

"Must be a squirrel or something in here."

"Nope," Brian said sadly.

Bear, standing on his back legs with his front paws against the hull, was trying to look into the boat. He cried softly, then ran to the other side of the boat and stood up against its side. Chuck now realized what he was doing.

"This is the only place he hasn't looked for Charlie, isn't it?"

"Yeah."

The two of them watched Bear until he gave up his search.

"Here, Bear," Brian said.

He knelt on the dirt floor and Bear, head down, came over to press against him. The boy put his arms around him and whispered in his ear, "I miss him, too."

Standing by the door, Chuck sighed, but not from sadness. He was getting tired of people and dogs grieving for his father.

Pretty soon Bear went outside and lay down in the shade.

"So this is it," Chuck said, moving their attention to the boat. The sailboat was an older-model O'Day 22 with a small cabin. The mast had been removed and was set on brackets attached to the outside wall of the boat shed. "Have a look around," he said to Brian, "and see what we need to do to put it in shape. I'll bring the truck down and we'll pull the trailer out into the open."

A few minutes later they had the trailer parked on the short driveway. "I'm glad you know what to do, because I've never had a boat before."

"I think I remember," the boy said. They stood together looking up at the bow. "First, we sand off the old varnish from the wood trim and the flaky paint on the bottom of the hull and then we varnish and paint it."

"You mean, *you* sand and paint. I'm hiring you for the job."

Only a trace of a smile crossed the boy's lips, but he stood a little taller when he said, "Oh, that *is* what I meant." Then, pointing to the hull, he added, "I'll need varnish and bottom paint."

"Sounds to me like you know what you're talking about. Let's go to the workshop and see what's left over from last year."

The two of them headed toward the house. Bear watched them go, then, groaning, pulled himself up and trudged after them. They went through the garage and into the basement workshop.

Brian opened the paint cabinet and found what was left of the paint.

"It's not enough," he said lifting the cans. "We'll have to buy more." He looked in another cabinet and found the sandpaper and the orbital sander. "There's plenty of sandpaper and we've got both the fine stuff for the hull and the coarser stuff for the wood trim."

"Can you operate one of these?" Chuck had visions of the electric sander cutting a deep gouge in the fiberglass hull.

"Did it last year."

"I'd still like to check you out on it."

"Sure."

"What about brushes?"

"They're up there hanging on those pins."

Chuck took down three of them of different sizes and felt the bristles. "Look okay to me. Let's go buy the paint."

Carrying the sander, sandpaper and brushes, they returned to the boat shed. Brian pointed at an outboard engine hanging on a rack at the rear of the shed. "Charlie took care of the outboard himself. I didn't learn that part."

"Oh. Did you see what he did?"

"Something about changing spark plugs and draining oil, but that's all I know."

"I think I'll get someone else to do it," Chuck said as he unhooked the truck from the trailer. Bear climbed into the back of the truck behind the seat just as Clara came sailing around the corner. A moment later Dawn appeared.

"Hi, fellas," she said, catching her breath as she jogged to a stop. Her fair skin was flushed from running, and there was perspiration on her forehead. Chuck let his eyes cruise the curves of her body beneath her bright blue spandex shorts and a matching athletic halter. Her figure was as good as he had imagined.

"Morning," Chuck said.

"Hi, Mom."

"What are you guys up to?" As she spoke she took a stance about three feet from the truck and, leaning forward, put both hands on the fender. She began stretching her legs, first bending her right knee and extending her left leg back as far as it would go, then reversing legs. Does she do this on purpose to drive me nuts, Chuck wondered, or is she totally unaware? His eyes were locked on the firm swell first of her right buttock and then her left—right and left, right and left. When she stood up and turned toward him, there was only an expression of having enjoyed a good stretch. He decided she was unaware.

"What're we doing? Ask my partner."

Brian raised his head proudly. "Going to buy paint for the boat."

"And where do you do that?" Dawn asked.

"Don't worry, Mom, I know."

Chuck shrugged a don't-ask-me gesture and got in the truck.

"Wait!" Dawn came to the window and leaned in. "It's a holiday. What say we three have a cookout tonight?"

"Great," Chuck said, thinking maybe he'd misjudged her indifference—her face was so close he could smell the warmth of her breath.

"I'm going shopping and I'll get three steaks," she said. "Let's do it at my house."

"Yeah, Chuck," Brian said, "our house. I'll build a fire in the grill and you can cook the meat, just like Charlie did last year."

"It's kind of a Memorial Day tradition," Dawn said.

Chuck shrugged. *Won't that man ever go away?*

Dawn watched Chuck, Brian and Bear drive away, then, with Clara, headed for the house. He seemed upset, she thought. Hope I wasn't the cause. She picked up a stick and threw it far into her yard. Clara took off like a shot and was on top of the stick the instant it hit the ground. He's a hard guy to figure out. One minute he's easy to be around, like Charlie. The next, he closes a door. At least Brian's taking to him, and that's good.

The dog returned, proudly carrying the stick, and began dancing around Dawn until she grabbed the stick for a tug-of-war.

I wonder if I was too forward inviting him for dinner? She thought about that as she and Clara entered her house and headed upstairs. That couldn't be it, she said to herself. He had me over for drinks the night I got back. She laughed to herself, I even spent the night, sort of. In her bedroom she took the rubber band from her ponytail and peeled off her running outfit. As Clara helped herself to a drink from the toilet, Dawn turned on the shower and stepped in.

Shampooing her hair, she reminisced about the morning she'd brought breakfast to Chuck when he was still in bed. He was obviously nude beneath the blanket, she thought with a smile. And here I was sitting on the bed beside him. The more she thought about it, the more she realized how intimate a scene it was. I may have brought Charlie meals when he was sick, but clearly Chuck's breakfast in bed had another element to it.

She squeezed a dollop of Dove body lotion onto the netted applicator and vigorously scrubbed a deep lather onto her arms, shoulders, breasts and down her body. The slippery, cool lotion soothed her hot skin. Closing her eyes, she saw Chuck's broad shoulders and strong arms as he lay in the bed. Her mind's vision moved from his chest to his beard, and she wrinkled her nose. Wish he'd shave it off, she said to herself. On the other hand, it goes with his big lumbering body.

The warm water and creamy lotion felt so good, she resoaped the applicator. Slowly moving it in small circles, she caressed her breasts and stomach. She and Gareth sometimes showered together, each massaging the other with soapy hands that left not one part of the body untouched. She imagined him standing there beside her, his body slippery with soap, hot to the touch. She could almost hear his voice speaking softly, "Don't ever leave me, Dawn. Be mine forever." Then he seemed to appear and disappear, in and out of the steamy vapor. She shut her eyes and caught hold of him, pulling him against her. "I'll never leave you," she said aloud. Gradually, through the mist, his face took shape.

The face was Chuck's.

She shook her head, confused.

Later, she sat in front of her mirror slowly, pensively drawing a brush through her damp hair. She hadn't realized how much her new neighbor had aroused her. Setting down her brush, she rested her chin on her folded fingers and stared at herself in the mirror.

"There's nothing wrong with having a good friend," she said, trying to convince the image in the mirror. "After all, he's Charlie's son and it's good to have someone to talk to. So he's got a sexy body. It's nice to know I still notice such things. Doesn't mean I have to sleep with him."

Gradually a smile began to flicker in her eyes. Of course she still loved Gareth, but certainly there was room in her life for a good friend. She gave her reflection an approving nod, picked up her brush and vigorously stroked her hair.

TWENTY-TWO

Dawn, Chuck and Brian were standing on her deck off the kitchen on a perfect spring evening, the adults with glasses of scotch and Brian with a can of Coke. Dawn wore a flowered blouse with long full sleeves and a straight brown skirt. Chuck had changed from his usual Levi's to a gray polo shirt and black pleated pants. Brian was dressed in a T-shirt and baggy shorts. The steaks, rubbed with garlic and pepper, were on the porch table under an iron lid of sufficient weight that Clara wouldn't be likely to move it. They were looking at Chuck's house.

"It's coming along," Chuck said. "The carpenter's roughed in the new bathroom off the master bedroom and now I'm waiting for the plumber to do his part. He's also putting in a new water heater and replacing some of the old pipes. And I've decided to put in a Jacuzzi."

"May I come over and try it out?" Dawn smiled.

"You bet. It ought to be ready by the end of August."

Dawn looked at the neatly stacked pile of new lumber sitting under a plastic covering beside the front walk. "Is that the decking for the porch?"

"Uh-huh. I guess you've noticed it's been there for a week. I haven't had a chance to get to it."

"Well," Brian piped in, "you won't have to worry about the boat. I'll get that done for you."

"I'm counting on that," Chuck said.

"Will you take us sailing when it's done?" Dawn asked Chuck.

"On one condition." He looked at Brian. "You've got to teach me how to sail."

"I can do that, too."

"I'm sure you can."

The boy beamed.

"Brian," Dawn asked, "would you bring out the dip and the chips? Dip's in the fridge and the chips are in the pantry."

When he left, Dawn came to Chuck's side. "The dogs have missed our walks together."

"I know. Our schedules don't seem to be meshing. What's happening with the exhibit?"

"Right now the biggest job is arranging for the pieces to be shipped here. You'd be surprised at the red tape: each piece has to be inspected for any damage before packing and then wrapped and crated. And there's the insurance and freight handlers. And that's just at the other end."

"What about this end?"

"Dr. Jackson, the curator at the BMA, is really on my case. Calls every other day. 'Where is that Russian poster?' I'm so sick of it, but there's nothing I can do until I reach Professor Neleginski in Moscow. He's the man Gareth was staying with when he was . . ." she took a breath, "when he was killed. I think he can give me a lead on where to find the man who owns the poster. I've telephoned and written him, but as yet haven't reached him."

"Does this mean a trip to Moscow?"

"I'm afraid so," she said, resigned.

Chuck looked at her, concerned. "Be careful. It sounds like a dangerous place."

"Not really, but I will be careful."

Chuck walked over to the grill. There were three potatoes wrapped in aluminum foil baking over the coals. As cook, he took a knife and poked one of the potatoes. "Not quite done. Time for another drink?"

"Sure."

They walked into the kitchen, where Brian was placing the dip and chips on a tray. "You did a good job today," Chuck told him.

"You handle tools well." Dawn beamed at Chuck's praise of her son.

"Thanks." He paused, and without looking up said, "I like working with you. You tell me what you want and then let me do it."

"That's 'cause you know what you're doing." Chuck added ice to the glasses and poured some more scotch.

"And . . . I like having you over." The boy looked up and they smiled.

By the time the potatoes were done and the steaks briefly singed on each side, a cool east wind was up, so they moved inside to eat at the kitchen table. Brian sat at the end and Dawn and Chuck across from each other while the dogs placed themselves strategically next to the person they thought would slip them the most scraps.

After dinner, Dawn cajoled Brian into cleaning up in exchange for letting him stay up to watch a late-night show on HBO, and she and Chuck took the dogs for a walk. They headed out to the point on the road that skirted Quiet Cove. The sun had set, leaving the sky a pale iridescent blue and the ocean almost white. Bear plodded along on his leash while Clara tugged ahead on her chain, which she always did until she found a place to poop. After that, she slowed down.

"Thanks for working with Brian," Dawn said.

"Don't thank me, I like him. He seems older than fifteen, especially the way he handles tools."

"I've put him through a lot, what with the divorce and my traveling. He's had to grow up in hurry."

"He must have been just a little older than I was when my folks divorced."

"Then you know what it's like."

He nodded. "It's funny. I don't remember much about the divorce, only that I was afraid of Dad and just as glad he wasn't around. What stands out for me was how hard it was in the new school and how I had no friends. I'd come home after school— Mom was working—and I'd go to my room, shut the door and read. It took me two years before I made any friends."

"At least Brian didn't have to move away from his friends, that is, until he went to Brighton last year. But he seems to be adjusting better this year."

"I'm glad he'll be around this summer. When he finishes the boat, if it's all right with you, I'll ask him to help with the porch."

"Please do." She paused for a moment. "Have you told him you're planning to sell the house and leave at the end of the summer?"

"No."

"You know, he thinks you've moved here permanently."

Chuck winced. "I hadn't thought about that."

"It'll be tough on him when you go." They walked a ways, then she said, "I'll miss you, too."

"Yeah." There was a slight edge to his voice. "I guess I've become Charlie's replacement."

"Ah-hah!" She stopped and faced him. "That's it, isn't it?"

"That's what?"

"That's what I'm doing that's bothering you. I keep treating you like you're Charlie."

"You're not bothering me," Chuck said, surprised by her comment.

"Oh, sure. How about this morning when I invited you over for our *traditional* Memorial Day dinner that Charlie always came to?"

"Well, it did sound like I was his stand-in."

They moved on, and she put her arm through his. "The truth is, I have been trying to make you into Charlie."

"Yeah, I thought maybe you were."

"And it's not working." She looked up at him. "No, I like you better as Chuck."

They walked on down the road without speaking, eventually reaching the point. No one was around, so they unhooked the dogs. Then Chuck put his arm around Dawn's waist and looked out toward the open water.

"I'm glad," he said.

"So am I." She put her arm around his waist and leaned her head against his shoulder.

TWENTY-THREE

Chuck stood on a plywood sheet he had laid across the exposed beams of his porch, pulled his ratty bathrobe tightly around him and breathed in the morning air. A mist hanging over the island at the mouth of Quiet Cove captured the morning sunlight, illuminating the trees and rocks with a soft golden hue.

Bear sauntered onto the porch, looked to the right, then the left, and, seeing nothing exciting, sat down beside his master.

"Isn't that beautiful?" Chuck said.

Bear raised his eyes to him.

"I never had a view like this in Alexandria."

The dog moved his gaze to the cove and followed the long glide path of a cormorant as it landed on the smooth water.

Chuck took a deep breath, filling his lungs, and exhaled slowly. "What a wonderful day." There was a buoyancy in his voice.

Since the morning Dawn brought him breakfast and sat on the edge of his bed, things had begun to look up. For one thing, he hadn't had a nightmare in almost a month and he was beginning to think—at least, to hope—that his dragon had departed. And for another thing, he was seeing Dawn every so often, if only to wave hello.

His thoughts drifted to last night, when he and Dawn had walked the dogs to the point. He smiled. What was it she'd said? That she liked me as Chuck. Something like that. And she put her arm around me and leaned her head against my shoulder. That part he remembered perfectly.

"Hi there." Dawn's voice was as clear and crisp as the morning. She waved to him from her porch, and the motion of her arm parted the top of her bathrobe just enough so he could see that the robe was all she had on. Even her feet were bare.

"Good morning!" He waved back.

"Did you get your paper?" she called.

"I don't know. I'm still looking for it."

"He usually throws mine on the porch, but it's not here."

Chuck looked through the beam supports to the dirt beneath the porch. If it's down there, he thought, I'll never find it. "No, I don't see mine."

"That's funny. He's never missed us before."

"Maybe he's sick."

"Could be," she said, nodding. "Wanna walk to town and buy a paper? We could take the dogs."

"Sure. Okay to go like this?"

"Oh yeah," she laughed. "I'll meet you out here in ten minutes."

Ten minutes later, Chuck, in a blue sweatshirt and jeans, and Dawn, in black sweats, were walking the dogs along the waterfront, then up the road past the sawmill, the boatyard and Redd's Pond. Bear woofed at several mallards near the edge of the pond and set them flapping across the water to the other side.

As they walked along Pond Street toward Christy's Market, Dawn said, "It's nice to be walking the dogs again."

"What's nice is walking them together."

She gave him a quick look and smiled. "That's what I meant."

They bought two *Boston Globes* at Christy's and started back. "What's up for you today?" she asked.

"Well, I'll get Brian started on the boat and then I'll spend about six hours on the computer. How about you?"

"Into Boston again, to the BMA. I'll be back about five."

"Want to come by for dinner?"

"Isn't that a lot for you to do?"

"I'd be doing it for myself anyway," he said with a wave of the folded newspaper he was carrying.

Suddenly Clara yanked on her chain, cowering away from him. She folded her ears back and put her tail between her legs.

"What wrong with her?" Chuck asked.

"It's the newspaper. She thinks you're going to hit her."

Chuck knelt down to pet her, and again she pulled away.

"Hand me the paper," Dawn said.

He did, then called to Clara. "I'm sorry, little girl. I didn't mean to scare you." The dog turned away from him. Chuck looked up at Dawn. "She's terrified."

"I know. She was about three months old when I got her at the animal rescue shelter. I think she was badly abused by her first owners."

"Poor thing." He stroked her back. It was as taut as a spring. "They must have beat the living daylights out of her."

"She does this if I'm carrying an umbrella or, like last night, when I took out a box of aluminum foil to wrap the potatoes for the grill. I try to be careful, but sometimes I forget." Chuck stood and they began walking down the street, Clara following but looking anxious. "Toilet training her was a problem. Threatening just didn't work. I had to guess when she needed to go and then I put her outside before it was too late. I had papers by the door for the times I guessed wrong."

"She certainly doesn't want for loving now," he said. "While you were gone she'd curl up next to me on the sofa and I'd rub her belly. She must know I love her."

"That just shows the power of early experiences. I show her love all the time, but one accidental threatening gesture and she's right back there, a puppy again, being beaten by some bastard with a newspaper."

Chuck was halfway through the morning, sitting at his computer, when he made the connection—Clara's early beatings and the fight his mom and dad had when he was ten. He leaned back in his chair and looked out his kitchen window. It wasn't exactly the same, but there were parallels. Both he and Clara had had bad experiences when they were young, Clara being punished with a newspaper and he having his parents yelling and smashing a lamp right next to his bed. Now, rolled-up newspapers made Clara cringe, and something made him have nightmares. Was it that fight his mom and dad had had?

He wished he knew Dawn well enough to talk to her about it.

He tried to return to the computer, but he'd lost his concentration. Instead he got up and took two cans of Coke from the fridge and went down to the boat shed. Brian, his nose and mouth covered with a dust mask, was half-kneeling under the hull, moving the orbital sander back and forth over the fiberglass. Chuck watched him for a while. The boy's shirt was off, and his shoulders, chest and arms were covered with the red dust of old bottom paint.

"Hi," Chuck called over the noise of the sander.

Brian turned off the machine. He came out from under the hull, straightened up and stretched. "Ahh, that feels good."

"Wanna Coke?"

"Sure." He popped the top and looked up at the boat. "What do you think? Looks pretty good, doesn't it?"

"It does. You'll be ready to paint soon."

"I should have the hull done tomorrow. The wood trim is all finished."

"Good for you," Chuck said. "When I finish the project I'm working on, I'll come help you."

"Okay."

"When do you think we'll have it in the water?"

"If the weather holds so I can do the painting," Brian said, glancing at the sky like a mariner, "I'd say weekend after this."

"That long, huh?"

"I don't know, maybe less."

Chuck looked at the smooth hull. The boy was doing a good job, no gouges and no parts missed. "I've invited your mom and you for dinner tonight. I'm going over to Marblehead Lobster and pick up lobsters."

"Oh." There was disappointment in his voice.

"What's wrong? Don't you like lobsters?"

"It's not that. A friend of mine came by a little while ago. We were going to go to a show when I get off work. If Mom says it's okay."

"That's fine. I'll give you a rain check on the dinner."

"Thanks."

* * *

That evening, Chuck and Dawn were standing in his kitchen by a pot of water heating on the stove. The two dogs lay in the doorway to the dining room watching every move the humans made. The dogs' noses knew there were lobsters in the brown bag sitting on the counter.

Chuck was wearing an apron over his work shirt and jeans. He handed another apron to Dawn. "That blouse is too pretty to get slopped with lobster juice."

She set down her glass and put the apron on. "I'm glad Brian met up with Mike. They were good friends before Brian started Brighton. Mike goes to Winston Academy, so he's in the same boat as Brian when he comes home from school. They'll be able to hang out together this summer."

"It'd be nice to have him here tonight, but it's even better without him."

"Hmm." She smiled. "You mean not having a chaperon?"

"Something like that." He grinned.

"I'd feel a little more relaxed if the two of them had ridden their bikes down to the Warwick Theater here in town, like they used to. Now Mike's sixteen and has a driver's license. He's driving Brian to the mall."

"That sounds terrifying."

"Thanks a lot. That's all I need. I called Mike's mom and she assured me he's very careful and they let him drive to the mall. They're supposed to be home by ten."

"Sometimes I wish I had kids, but I wonder if I could handle things like their first time out driving."

"It's easy," Dawn said. "You just have another glass of wine and keep talking as fast as you can about any nonsense that comes to mind."

"More wine?"

"Just kidding. Maybe later." She paused. "Seriously, I wonder sometimes if I travel as much as I do so I won't have to face all these passages in Brian's life. A few more months and he'll be getting a license himself."

Chuck turned toward her. "I haven't known you long, but I

don't think you're one to avoid facing things. Look how you took care of that fellow in Paris who wanted to charge you too much."

She sighed. "Yeah, but this is family."

"Guilt, huh?"

"It's always there."

The water was boiling, so Dawn reached into the bag and caught hold of a lobster's back just above its tail. The creature's claws, held closed by a rubber band, wandered aimlessly about as she pulled it out of the bag. Both dogs raised their heads.

"Watch this," she said. With her left hand she began stroking the back of the lobster's head as if she were petting it. Pretty soon the wandering claws relaxed, and Dawn placed the lobster head-down on the floor, tail in the air, braced upright by its subdued claws. The dogs got up and cautiously approached.

"How'd you do that?"

"It's hypnotized," Dawn said. "Here, I'll do it to the other one. Just keep your eye on the dogs."

In a minute there were two lobsters standing on their heads on the kitchen floor.

"That's remarkable," Chuck said.

Quick as a flash, Clara's long snout shot out and hit one of the lobsters, knocking it over.

"Show's over," Dawn said and picked up both lobsters. "Open the top of the pot." Chuck did as ordered, and Dawn plopped in the two lobsters. "Get 'em there while they're still hypnotized," she said. Chuck brought the top down, sealing the poor creatures to their fate.

"Now I'll have that next glass of wine," Dawn said.

After dinner they took the dogs down to the cove and let them run. The tide was out, leaving a wide beach with stones for Clara to dig up and smelly mussels for Bear to rout through. Chuck and Dawn sat side by side on the concrete culvert that brought water from the storm sewers to the cove. Dawn looked at her watch.

"Nine-thirty," she said. "They should be getting in the car pretty soon and starting home."

"Worried?"

"Yes. If I worry, I feel like I'm doing something. It's like telling him to be careful when he leaves the house."

"It is?"

"Absolutely. If I'm doing something, then I don't feel so guilty."

Chuck shook his head. "That's a great rationalization."

"I know, and it makes as much sense as feeling guilty." She looked at him. "But it doesn't hurt as much."

"You're serious, aren't you?"

"Yes. I feel guilty about those poor lobsters we dropped into the boiling water. I feel guilty for sending Brian off to a prep school so I can spend more time working, and I feel guilty every time I take off for Europe."

He wanted to say something to ease her burden, but couldn't think of anything.

Looking down at the stony beach below the culvert, she continued in a soft voice, "And I feel guilty about Gareth's death." She looked up at Chuck. "When he was killed, if he was on his way to meet Krubinski—he's the man who owns the poster—then his death *is* my fault. It was my job to get it from Krubinski. We'd agreed on that. But I couldn't locate him, so I asked Gareth to do it for me."

"But you don't know if he was on his way to see Krubinski."

"No. That's the other reason I'm going to Moscow. First to find Krubinski and then to find out if he had already signed the agreement with Gareth for the loan of the poster."

"And if he had, then you're free and clear."

"Maybe, but what if his seeing Krubinski shifted his time schedule just enough so he wound up being in the place where he was attacked?"

"Do you want to know what I think of that idea?"

"I think I already know."

"Yeah. That it's pretty farfetched."

"That's what I thought you'd say." After a pause, she added, "Maybe I just like to feel guilty."

Chuck shook his head. "Nobody *likes* to feel guilty."

She leaned her head against his shoulder. "You're right, of course. I don't like it."

Chuck put his arm around her shoulders and pulled her to him. For several minutes they sat there, not speaking, watching the darkening sky.

"There's something I want your opinion on," Chuck said quietly. "Something that's bothered me for a long time." She put her hand on his knee and looked at him. "I've had nightmares for years, fairly frequently. When I was married, they really scared my wife. I've had them a couple of times since I've been here. Well, today, when that thing happened with Clara, how she cringed at my newspaper, it got me thinking. Maybe I had some bad experience when I was young, just like Clara did, that's causing the bad dreams."

"I guess that can happen."

"Well, after all these years, I think I know what it was. I think it was that fight my parents had beside my bed, the one I remembered that day you brought me breakfast in bed."

"I'll never forget that. You scared me. You froze up like you were having an attack."

"I did. The whole scene was happening all over again." He turned his head so he could face her. "Now that I know what might be causing the nightmares, do you think I won't have them anymore?"

"I'm not a shrink, but it sounds reasonable."

"I hope you're right. Since that morning, I haven't had any." He paused for a moment, then added, "Maybe they're gone because I've met you."

"Please don't say that." He felt her shiver. "It sounds like you mean more than friendship."

He nodded his head. "I know. I did."

"That scares me. I don't know if I can handle more than friendship."

"I'm sorry," he sighed. "I should have kept it to myself."

"No. I'm beginning to have feelings about you, too. That's what really scares me."

"Then, I don't understand," he said, confused.

"Don't you see?" Her face was contorted with pain. "The people I love—I lose them. They . . . they die. Like Gareth died. And your father." Now she was crying. "And I'm terrified I'll lose Brian because I love him so much."

Chuck stood and pulled her into his arms. At first she tried to resist, but then fell against his chest, weeping.

"I need you, Chuck," she said between sobs, "and I don't want to lose you."

Stars began to appear in the dark sky and still she clung to him. Holding her, stroking her head tenderly, filled him with a sense of completeness he hadn't known since he held Michelle in the same way. Immediately his joy was derailed by the memory of how badly he had hurt Michelle. *I can't let that happen to Dawn.*

The headlights of a car turning into Dawn's driveway caught their attention. The door opened, then slammed shut.

"Thanks, Mike," they could hear Brian call back to the car as he ran up the porch steps. Then the car backed out and drove away.

"He's home," Dawn said with a long sigh.

"Safe and sound," Chuck added, smiling.

"All right. Don't tease me." They began to walk toward their houses. "Come on, Clara. Time for bed." Both dogs arrived, panting, and followed them across the beach to the road.

She took his arm and looked up at him. "You see, it worked."

"What worked?"

"My worrying. It got him home safely."

"I think you halfway believe that."

She laughed. "More than halfway, I'm afraid." Then she stopped and, taking both his hands in hers, looked him in the eye. "Chuck Carver," she announced, "if you're going to live next door, and wave at me in the morning when I get my paper, and take walks with me, and hold me when I cry, and look at me the way you're doing right now, I'm not sure I'm going to be able to control what I do."

"That makes two of us, but I'll try."

"Agreed. So will I," she said, dropping his hands and heading toward her house. Then, over her shoulder, "I'll worry about it. That always works."

TWENTY-FOUR

The following Thursday a downcast Brian stood in Chuck's kitchen looking out the window at a steady drizzle. He'd finished the sanding the day before and was ready to start painting the boat, but now he'd have to postpone it.

"How about the inside of the cabin?" Chuck asked. "Does it need some work?"

"Oh, yeah." His face brightened. "I could haul the two mattresses into the shed to air and give the cabin a good cleaning."

"Good idea. Get the 409 from under the sink. There're some rags there, too." Brian immediately started pulling stuff from the sink cabinet. "You'll need a bucket. There's one in the basement next to the sink." In a flash, the boy was racing down the steps.

Chuck returned to his computer, which was still sitting on the kitchen table for want of a dedicated circuit to the study. As soon as he sat down, the doorbell rang. He was crossing through the living room when the front door opened and a head poked in.

"Anybody home?" Then, seeing Chuck, "Oh, hi, Mr. Carver."

"Come on in, Francis, and for God's sake call me Chuck. You make me sound like I'm my father."

Francis Carney, dressed in work clothes and wearing a leather belt with pockets and slots crammed with screwdrivers, pliers, electrical tape, circuit tester, flashlight and wire cutters, stopped at the door and called back to the van parked in the driveway.

Painted on the side of the van were the words,

Carney Electric

No Shock Connections
With
No Shocking Bills

LICENSED AND INSURED

A young man stood by the van, cupping his ear to hear Francis.

"He's here. Bring up the tools." Turning back to Chuck, he said, "Here we are."

Chuck wanted to say, finally, but instead said, "Good. Can you run the circuit to the study today?"

"We'll have it in by lunchtime."

Francis was of medium build, about five-ten and in his early thirties. You could spot his Irish heritage in his round face and ruddy complexion. Dark curls crept out from beneath his Greek fisherman's hat, and in his left ear was an earring shaped like a marlin breaking the surface.

His partner arrived carrying a coiled extension cord, an electric drill with a two-foot bit and an electric saber saw.

"This is Mort, Chuck. He's my apprentice." Mort was about twenty, as tall as Chuck but slender. He nodded to Chuck, but said nothing.

"Hi," Chuck said.

Francis headed for the kitchen. "We won't interrupt the kitchen circuit, so you can keep working." He looked around the room. "The electrician that wired up this kitchen sure did a good job."

"I thought you said you did it?" Chuck asked.

"I did," he said proudly. "Good job, wouldn't you say?"

Chuck laughed. Mort's dour expression remained unchanged. Chuck figured he'd heard the joke before. Francis and Mort descended the basement steps and Chuck returned to his computer.

Halfway through the morning, they came back into the kitchen. "Coffee break," Francis announced. "Want to join us?" They each pulled out kitchen chairs and sat down.

"Do I have a choice?" Chuck said.

"Course. Have tea if you want," Francis said without cracking a smile. Then, after a pause, "We're not bothering you, are we?"

"Oh no. The wheels of international finance may grind to a stop, but don't let that concern you."

"Good." Francis and Mort opened their thermoses and poured coffee into the cups. "What do you do, anyway?"

"I help banks develop computer programs to keep their records straight."

"From your kitchen?" Francis asked. Even Mort raised his eyes with a trace of disbelief.

"Sure. I'm plugged into their computers."

"Amazing." He picked up the phone cable that ran from the computer to the wall outlet and held it in his hand. "Are you saying that through this line you've got access to the bank's accounts?"

"Yup, more or less."

"So, if I did all your rewiring for free, you could push a few buttons and transfer money from the bank at the end of this line into my account at my bank?"

Chuck sighed and looked at the ceiling. "Would you come visit me in jail?"

"Sure, if you don't tell 'em about my savings account."

Chuck got up and poured himself a cup of coffee.

"How's your sister, Vivian?"

Chuck, surprised, said, "You know her?"

"Yeah. We used to date some in high school. Nice girl. Just when I was getting serious, your old man put a stop to it. Guess he figured the son of a fisherman wouldn't be able to provide for his daughter in the manner to which she was accustomed." The last was said mimicking a cultured accent.

"She's fine. Married, living in Weston. She's got three kids."

"I'm glad. I like her and I wish her the best. Probably wouldn't have worked out for us anyway." He sipped his coffee. "How about you?"

Chuck was beginning to like Francis, and the break from work was a relief. "How about me, what?"

"Married?"

"No. Was, though."

"That's too bad, or maybe not. Which?"

Chuck didn't answer, just looked at him and shook his head. Undaunted, Francis carried on.

"Your brother, Josh. He was younger than Viv, but I'd see him when I came to pick her up. He's gay, isn't he?"

"What makes you say that?"

"Oh, nothing. I heard he was living in Boston with some guy." Then, quickly, "Don't get me wrong. I'm not interested. I'm married. Great woman, too. We've got two little girls."

"How long do you take for coffee breaks?" Chuck asked.

"Hmm. Too many questions, huh?"

"Well, I do want to get back in the study today."

"Like I said—" he stood and Mort got up also "—we'll have you in there by lunchtime."

He's a character, Chuck thought. I like him.

At noon, Chuck walked down to the boat. The drizzle had stopped, but the air was heavy with humidity and the sky still overcast. He could hear Brian inside the cabin.

"How's it going in there?"

"Hey, come on in."

Chuck climbed the stepladder standing next to the trailer and stepped into the cockpit of the sailboat. Brian's head popped out of the hatch.

"Look inside here," he said excitedly.

Chuck squatted and stuck his head into the hatch. The smell of 409 hit his nostrils and the beam of a flashlight his eyes. Brian then directed the light to the far reaches of the little cabin, showing two bunks in the bow, a small galley and a head.

"The mattresses are in the shed. It's neat, isn't it?"

"You've really been working."

"Actually, I finished scrubbing it out about an hour ago. I found one of Charlie's boating magazines and I've been reading that." Two life preservers were set up against the end of the bunk where he'd made a headrest. "It was fun, being in here with the rain on the roof. When we get it in the water I'd like to spend a night on the boat. Would that be okay?"

"Sure."

"I'll ask Mike."

"Maybe we can take it out for an overnight cruise sometime," Chuck suggested.

"Can we? Charlie said he wanted to do that, too, but we never did."

Gee! Chuck thought. One up on my dad. "What are you going to do this afternoon?"

"There's not much more I can do here. Would you mind if I took off? Mike came by and asked me to come over."

"Sure. Maybe the weather'll be better tomorrow and you can paint."

Chuck returned to the house and Brian left to find his friend. It was twelve-thirty, a half-hour into his usual lunchtime, and he was hungry. He made a sliced turkey sandwich, opened the *Globe* to the editorial page and sat down to eat. Just as he was finishing, Francis and Mort came down the steps from the study.

"Lunchtime's over," Chuck said as they came into the kitchen, "and you haven't got me hooked up yet, like you promised."

"It's not over. Yours may be, but ours is just starting, and you *are* hooked up."

"Congratulations."

"You're welcome. Have another cup of coffee and keep us company while we eat. Then we'll help you move this stuff up to the study. Won't we, Mort?" Mort answered with an acquiescent toss of his head. Chuck rolled his eyes and got another cup of coffee. When he returned to the table, Francis had spread out an elaborate lunch consisting of hot soup and what looked like leftover tuna casserole. There was also a slice of buttered bread and a salad. "See, Chuck, the advantages of having a loving wife." He gestured with open palms to the feast before him. "See how she takes care of me?"

"You're a lucky man, Francis."

"Now Mort, here, is not married and all he's got is a sub he bought from Mino's this morning." It looked pretty good to Chuck, and Mort was putting it away with gusto.

"How about you?" Francis asked. "Going to get married again?"

"I haven't thought much about it," Chuck answered, which was true. "Guess I'd have to find the right woman."

Francis leaned back, looking pleased with himself. "I know just the one." Chuck laughed, shaking his head. "Right next door. Dawn Ireland. Put in a garbage disposal for her last year. I could hardly concentrate on my work when she'd come into the kitchen. Christ, what a beautiful woman. Long blond hair and a figure like a movie star."

"I've seen her."

"Then you know what I mean. Marry her and you'll be a happy man."

"You're right, she is beautiful."

"Want me to introduce you? I saw her car there, so I know she's home."

"Relax. I've met her. We walk our dogs together."

"Good. That's a first step."

"When will you start on the rest of the wiring?" Chuck asked, obviously changing the subject.

"Okay," Francis said. "I get the message." He paused for an instant, then said, "We'll start this afternoon. It'll take about a week. Hey! Tell you what. Do you like to fish? We could celebrate the completion of the job by going fishing. I've got an Aquasport, Osprey with a two-hundred-horse Evinrude. You'd love it. And the bluefish are running."

Chuck closed his eyes and rubbed his forehead. He was having trouble keeping up with the deluge of words.

"I'll bet you work all the time," Francis said. Then, looking directly at him, "What do you do for fun?"

The question jarred Chuck. What did he do for fun? He hadn't been hiking in months. He no longer rode his bike. He liked working on the porch, but he hadn't done that in over a week.

"I walk the dog."

"Wow! Hey, Mort. He walks the dog." Francis tipped his head to the side and looked Chuck in the eye. "I'm talking fun," his voice serious. "Real fun. Like getting in my twenty-foot Aquasport and heading out into the ocean, opening up that two-hundred horsepower engine and feeling the wind and spray in your face as you skip over the tops of the waves. I'm talking about hooking a twelve-pound bluefish and getting the fight of your life. Now, that's fun."

Chuck stared at him, captured by the image Francis had

painted. Chuck had seen boats heading out in the morning when he was walking Bear, boats with three or four men in them, talking and laughing as they made ready their fishing poles. He'd envied their companionship, and wondered what it would be like to venture out far beyond the island at the mouth of Quiet Cove.

"I haven't got any fishing tackle."

"That's okay. I've got plenty."

"When would we go?"

"Saturday after next. I pick you up at five and we'll be out there when the sun's coming up."

Chuck looked at him. "Let's do it."

"Great. You won't be sorry."

A few minutes later they were taking the computer equipment up to the study. Chuck was first with the printer, Francis behind him with the monitor. Partway up the steps, Francis let his foot slip and bang down against the stair.

"Oops!" he cried.

"You all right?" Chuck called, terrified.

"Hah. Just kidding."

I'm spending a day on a boat with this nut? Chuck wondered, shaking his head.

When the computer, printer, fax and copy machine were hooked up on his father's desk, Francis said, "I found this metal file box in the back of the closet when we were bringing in the line." Slapping his right hand over his heart and raising his left, he said, "I didn't look in it, but I just thought you ought to know about it."

"Thanks, I'll look at it later. And thanks for your help."

"Anytime. Don't forget, a week from Saturday."

Francis and Mort left to begin the larger task of stripping out the old knob and tube wiring and rewiring the entire house. They would also be putting in the wiring for the new bathroom off the master bedroom. The last job would be installing a new circuit breaker box that could handle the additional service.

Chuck moved things around on the desk until it felt right to him. Just as he was settling down to work, his eyes fell on the metal box Francis had found. The box was about a foot cubed and had a keyed latch and a handle on top. He set it on his desk and examined the lock, then went downstairs and got a screwdriver.

One pry and the latch popped open. Inside were several files. He looked through them and pulled out one entitled "Restraining Orders."

There were two, both issued by the Rochester Municipal Court and dated March 10 and March 12, 1965, respectively. That was a month after he and his mother had fled to her family home in Rochester. Chuck scanned through them quickly. The first ordered Charles Carver Senior to stay at least five hundred feet away from 10 Elm Drive, Rochester, New York, and the second the same distance away from the James Fenimore Cooper Elementary School. There was also correspondence with an attorney in Rochester in which his father attempted to explain to a Mr. Clarence Haggerty the circumstances that apparently resulted in the court orders. Chuck skipped through the first few sentences that had to do with retaining Haggerty's services.

> . . . It's not at all like her lawyer described it. I was not irrational or violent. I simply came to her house, knocked on the door with the intention of talking to her about the custody of our son. Chucky answered the door and we began talking. I think he was glad to see me. I asked him how he was and if he wouldn't like to come live with me. He said he didn't know. I then asked him if he'd like to go with me and get a chocolate sundae and he stepped outside the door. I was just going to take him to the drugstore and then bring him home again. At that point, Harriet came running into the kitchen and caught hold of Chucky's arm and started pulling him back into the kitchen. I tried to tell her I was just taking him to the drugstore but she wouldn't listen and started screaming at me. She pulled my son into the kitchen and slammed the screen door, hooking the latch. I guess by this time I was outraged at her hysterics and started kicking at the door. There was a baseball bat sitting by the door and she picked it up and held it in a threatening manner. I broke through the screen and was attempting to unlatch the hook when she brought the bat down on my hand injuring two fingers. That was when I left. While there were some angry words exchanged, as you can see, the only violence was committed by her.

"That bastard," Chuck said aloud. Then, like leaves caught in a whirlwind, forgotten memories of that day swirled up into his consciousness. He could hear them yelling at each other, see his father throwing his shoulder against the door and pushing his hand through the screen. He could hear the crash of the bat as his mother swung it against the intruding hand, his father's screams of pain. Then the silence when it was over. She took him onto her lap and told him that she'd never let his father have him, that that other woman would never be his mother.

Still feeling the fury of that day, he continued reading the next paragraph.

> The next day I waited for Chucky at the school. When he came down the walk I asked him if I could drive him home. I was sitting in the driver's seat and had opened the door on the passenger side. Chucky stood by the open door. We talked for a while, I pleading with him to let me take him home. I moved to the passenger side and gently took him by the hand. When I tried to bring him into the car, I noticed the crossing guard coming in my direction. It may have been a wrong decision, but I realized it was now or never, so I pulled on his arm. He started crying as I tried to get him in the car before the guard got there. Well, as you know, I was too late. The guard got there and wrenched Chucky free. She must have called the police because I was arrested at the motel when I went there to get my bag and check out. The rest you know.

As he read, he became that little boy, torn with confusion about this man whom he had loved and trusted who was forcing him into a car, and frozen with terror at being kidnapped. Then it passed and he remembered sitting in the nurse's office and drinking a glass of apple juice.

Chuck looked again at the letter.

> I admit I got carried away at the school, but I knew she intended to keep Chucky and to deny me my rights as his father.

> Before we can even begin to talk about joint custody, you have got to get the attempted kidnapping charges dropped. He's my son, for God's sake. It's preposterous to think I was trying to kidnap him.

Chuck scoffed at those words, returning the letter to the file and taking out another, a letter from Clarence Haggerty to his father dated four weeks later.

> . . . Unfortunately, Mr. Carver, the attempted kidnapping case against you is very strong. The District Attorney is determined to take it to trial, knowing that the testimony of the crossing guard would be incontrovertible. I have therefore met with Harriet's attorney and we are suggesting a compromise which I hope you will find acceptable. Harriet

does not want Chucky brought into court as a witness against his father and is therefore willing to drop the charges of attempted kidnapping in return for a divorce settlement that denies you the right to see your son again. While this is a terrible loss to you, I'm sure you will see that it is far better than years in jail for attempted kidnapping, which I am sure the District Attorney would be able to prove.

Chuck had read enough. Feeling heartsick, he put the letter back in the file and was at the point of closing the lid when he noticed the heading on another folder: "Record of Child Support Payments." He removed the file and found it filled with a stack of canceled checks that dated from 1965 to 1973. There was another file entitled "College Support," and there he found checks to his mother for hundreds of dollars during the time he was attending Syracuse University.

"What the hell is this?" he said, feeling the foundation of his life shift. "It wasn't Mom. Dad put me through college. And all those years I was growing up, she took money from this guy she taught me to hate."

TWENTY-FIVE

Chuck waited a day before he called his mother. He wanted to calm down. If he exploded on the phone, he was afraid she'd hang up. Stay cool, he told himself, and dialed her number.

After the hellos, he said, "I was going through Dad's file box last night and found the correspondence he had with a lawyer in Rochester. It was right after he went there and tried to kidnap me. Copies of the restraining orders were there, too."

"I thought I told you about that." Her voice was tired after a day's work, but not defensive or antagonistic.

"You did, but this was his side of the story. He claims he just wanted to take me out for a sundae. What a liar. I can still feel him pulling on my arm and trying to force me into his car."

"It was awful, wasn't it."

"I'll say." He paused for a moment, then went on. "I also found the canceled checks for his child support and for my college tuition."

"Sounds like he kept everything."

Struggling to keep his voice on an even keel, he said, "You never told me he paid child support or paid my way at Syracuse."

"Of course he did. I certainly couldn't have done it on a nurse's salary."

"But you let me think you were doing it all on your own." His voice was angry.

"I never said one way or another, and you didn't ask. So let's stop the accusations right now. We can't settle stuff like this on the phone." For a moment neither said anything. "Look, it just so happens I'm coming to Boston next week for our national association meeting. Why don't you come down and meet me? We'll talk about this at lunch."

"You're coming to Boston and didn't tell me?" Immediately, he wanted to kick himself for sounding like a hurt teenager.

"Hmm. Seems like I can't do anything right today. I don't suppose you'd believe me if I told you I was planning to call you when I got there and found out what your schedule was?"

"Okay." Still there was annoyance in his voice. "When will you know?"

"I get there Monday morning. I'll call you after I register."

"Why don't you come out to Marblehead?" And with a cautious note of pride, "I could show you what I'm doing on the house."

"Nooo, I don't think so. Too many memories I don't want to face. You come to Boston."

"Well, give me call on Monday."

She called at eleven on Monday and said that except for some preliminary meetings she didn't have to attend, the convention proper didn't started until five o'clock.

"Should I meet you for lunch?" he asked.

"Well, I've been thinking. I've got the whole afternoon. Maybe I'll come out there to Marblehead."

"I'd like that. There's a few demons left, but I've got them in cages."

"Okay. I've checked around and I can take the Blue Line north to Wonderland. That'd save you driving into Boston."

He agreed, and they settled on an approximate time of twelve-thirty.

Chuck was waiting at the Wonderland Station at the appointed time. When her train pulled in she was the first out the door. It had been almost a year since he'd seen her, and he noticed the skin at her neck was a little looser and her shoulders slightly bent forward. Still, she maintained her rigid posture, extending her hand to her son and smiling. There would be no hugs or kisses, Chuck knew that. There seldom had been. Her white hair was tied in a bun, and she looked at him through the top of her trifocal glasses.

"It wasn't too bad, you coming down here?" she said by way of greeting. She was dressed casually in a green cotton sweater and tan slacks.

"No. I see you found your way to the Blue Line."

When they were in the car, he asked, "What caused you to change your mind?"

"I didn't want to sit around the hotel all afternoon, and anyway, I was curious."

"Yeah. I'll bet the town has changed a lot."

"Actually, I was more curious about how I would feel. Living there with you and your dad were some of the best years of my life. Then having them end so abruptly and with so much hate was awful. I'm wondering if I can walk into the house and remember the good times without getting mad."

Twenty minutes later, they pulled into the driveway of 9 Cove Road. He looked over at Dawn's house and was glad to see that her car was gone. He wanted to be alone with his mother.

Well, almost alone. When he slammed the car door, he could hear Bear barking.

Harriet stopped on the front lawn and gazed at the house. Chuck studied her face but couldn't read her reaction. She passed the pile of discarded porch flooring and went up the stairs.

"You're doing a good job on the porch."

"Thanks."

Inside, Bear met her as if she were a long-lost friend. He wagged his tale and waited for her to pet him.

"Big, isn't he? Yours, or was he Charlie's?"

When she didn't give him any pats on the head, Bear went to Chuck, who rubbed his ears and petted his back. "He was Dad's."

Harriet, ignoring the dog, went into the living room, giving it only a passing glance, and walked through the dining room toward the kitchen. There her eyes opened with surprise. "This is all new," she said, looking at the cabinets and new appliances.

"He did this two or three years ago." His mom continued to move about the room, touching the countertops. She stopped at the window and looked out at the boat shed.

"We used to have a little sailboat. Is it still in the shed?"

"There's one in there, but it's not little." Then he added, "How about some lunch?"

"Sure."

Together they made lettuce and cheese sandwiches and Chuck opened a couple of beers. They sat at the kitchen table.

Halfway through her sandwich, Harriet said, "I don't see why you got so upset about his child support and college tuition."

Chuck said nothing for a full minute. She let him think about his answer. "I wish I could love him like everybody else around here. If I'd known that he'd done those things for me, it would have helped. Instead, I grew up hating him like you did."

"I did hate him for a while. He'd left me for a kid half my age and then tried to take you away from me so she could be your mother. After three or four years, when I was sure he wasn't going to get you, I gave up hating. It took too much energy."

"I wish you'd told me, so *I* could have given it up."

"I doubt you would have. You were a teenager and hated both of us for getting divorced. It was easier for me to let you vent that anger on your dad instead of me. I know now I shouldn't have done that." She took a sip of beer. "You should be damned glad you and Michelle didn't have a kid. You'd know what I mean about taking the easy path. There's only so much stress a person can bear."

He wanted to continue trying to make her wrong, but instead changed the subject.

"When did you know that Dad was playing around?"

She sighed, then a sad smile crossed her lips. "About a year before the divorce."

"I was talking to Vivian a few weeks ago and we figured out that Dad started his affair with Jacqueline three years before the divorce." His mother winced, and he wondered if he'd said this to hurt her.

"That could be. I knew she existed, because the wartime flying buddy he visited in Paris had a daughter. He even showed me pictures of her and her father. I became suspicious when he visited them every time he flew the Paris route. Once I said something like, 'Who are you visiting, her or her father?' and he flew off the handle. That's when I knew."

"What did you do?"

"Nothing at first. Then, after a few months with him hardly looking at me when he came home, I started seeing one of the doctors at the hospital. I was lonely and angry. It was so easy. Charlie was away most of the time and there was nothing to get in the way of my new friend dropping by."

"Where was I?"

"Asleep, I hope."

This was not what Chuck wanted to hear, especially after having accused Vivian's mother of being a homewrecker. He twisted in his chair, then got up and took the dishes to the sink.

He was beginning to think having his mother come to the house wasn't such a good idea, but he decided to try to redeem what was left of the visit. "Want to see the rest of the house?"

His mother seemed to be ready to drop the subject, too. Laughing, she asked, "Have you got those demons locked up?"

"God, I hope so." Chuck was thinking about the dragon that stalked him in his dreams.

At the top of the stairs, when they turned toward his father's bedroom, his mother held back for a moment, then followed him into the room. Bear came in, too, and lay down near the bed. Harriet said nothing for a while, just looked around.

"Thank God, it's all changed. New furniture, new curtains. I was afraid I was going to walk into my old bedroom with all its memories."

"Let me show you what I'm doing in here." He led her into the bathroom. The floor and walls were ripped up. There were exposed pipes, studs and wires and, where the commode should be, a rag jammed into a hole in the floor. "It's kind of hard to visualize, but the Jacuzzi will go here and a new sink and toilet there."

"Jacuzzi, huh? Pretty nice." She looked at the bare pipes and two-by-fours for another second, then said, "I'll take your word for it." That seemed to be the extent of her interest in a carpentry project, so he took her down the hall to the study.

"This is pretty much as Dad left it, so there might be a small demon in here." He turned on the lights and she looked in the door.

Her eyes rested on Charlie's wartime pictures hanging on the walls. Warily she approached them. Tilting back her head to see the detail through the bottom of her trifocals, she said, "I never saw him when he was old. This is closer to how I remember him, young and dashing." Then she turned her attention to the computer equipment on the desk. "These can't be Charlie's."

"No. They're mine. I've made this my office until I move back to Alexandria."

"You're not staying here? It is yours, isn't it?"

"It's mine. I'm not sure what I'm going to do. Sometimes I think about staying here. I don't know." He walked to the desk and pulled out the drawer. "This is where I found Charlie's letter to me."

She looked up, surprised. "What letter?"

"He'd written it months ago, I guess, and put it in the drawer in case he died. The house was left to me in the will, so he assumed I would come here one day. And there it was. He said he was sorry that he couldn't be a father to me and that he'd kept close touch on what I was doing. He said he was even at the back of the auditorium when I graduated from Syracuse. He knew about Michelle, the wedding *and* the divorce, and about my work. Then he said he loved me."

As he spoke, Harriet continued to stare into the empty drawer as if the letter were still there. "Yes, I think he really did love you."

"There was also a key in the envelope. It was for my old bedroom at the top of the stairs next to the attic." She was nodding, apparently remembering the room. "He said he'd kept it locked so it would always be just as I left it if I ever returned. I'm using it now."

"Could I see it?"

"Sure."

They climbed to the third floor, Bear plodding behind, and Harriet stepped into the room. Immediately she caught her breath. With one hand to her throat, she moved about the room, touching the worktable on which the model plane was still laid out, going to the window where she sat on the cushioned bench, then to the bookcase where she ran her finger along the titles of the books.

"I remember every one of these. I'd sit on the edge of your bed and read to you each night." She sat down on the still unmade bed and looked down at the pillow. "It's like yesterday." When she looked up at Chuck, he could see tears in her eyes. "I haven't let myself think about this for thirty-two years, about the good times. It makes the bad times harder to bear."

Chuck came to her side and put his hand on her shoulder. He had never seen her cry in all the years he'd known her. He was embarrassed for her, knowing she was letting down her defenses, letting him see a part of her that she always kept locked up. And he felt awkward, wanting to comfort her, but afraid to embrace her. Mainly, he wanted her to stop crying. He was relieved when she straightened up.

She wiped her eyes and turned on the bed so she was facing the nightstand. "And here is old Bugs Bunny," she said with a smile of recognition. Instantly the smile froze on her face. She jerked her head toward her son, her mouth open, her eyes filled with terror.

"That's the lamp, all right," Chuck said. "The one you smashed over his head the night before we left." He stared at her. The compassion he'd felt moments before had vanished. Christ, he thought suddenly. Did I set this up, too, so I could get her for what they did to me that night? But he couldn't stop himself.

"Why did you smash him on the head? Why did you have to bring your fight into my bedroom?"

She was breathing in quick gasps. Her head was shaking. "No! No! No!"

"And what was Dad doing in here? Something was wrong about it. It was more than saying good night. What had you done? Tell him you were leaving him so that he came here to my room weeping? I remember him with his head on my shoulder. Then the door flew open. You came in and hit him with the lamp again and again until it broke. Why couldn't you keep your fucking problems out of my bedroom?"

He stopped to catch his breath. His jaw was clinched. She looked up at him. Her appeal for mercy only ignited another outburst. "You don't know the nightmares I've had about that night.

The yelling, the crashing, the violence. And it didn't end when you went downstairs. I could still hear you."

She stood and, brushing past him, walked to the window. Looking out at a corner of the cove, she took several deep breaths.

He came up behind her. "And what was Dad doing? Why was he lying across my chest?"

Harriet swung around and faced her son. "Nothing. Your dad did nothing wrong. Whatever it seemed like to you, your dad did nothing wrong."

He returned her stare, then slowly shook his head. "Something was wrong. I don't know what it was, but something was not right that night and it wasn't just your fighting."

TWENTY-SIX

The sun was warm on his bare back as he bent over the decking, driving nails into the tongued and grooved boards. From his neck and chest sweat fell in drops, making dark brown spots on the fir strips. He wore only work boots and a pair of shorts, over which he'd tied his tool belt containing a supply of stainless steel ringed nails. It was midafternoon, the first Wednesday of June, and the unseasonable temperature was climbing into the lower eighties.

As he worked, he thought about his mother's visit. It had raised more questions than it had answered and left him feeling angrier and more confused than he was before she came. He was convinced something had happened that night in his bedroom that was the cause of his nightmares and probably had something to do with his parents' divorce. In spite of his continued questioning, his mother insisted that his father had done nothing wrong. Finally she yelled at him to shut up and refused to discuss it further. On the drive to Wonderland, where she caught her train into Boston, she kept her eyes glued to the passenger window, hardly speaking to him.

Chuck stood, stretched his back and looked at the lines of new boards covering the joists he'd already replaced. Slowly, the porch was taking shape, but at the rate he was going, it'd take another four weeks. He'd worked all morning on the computer, not stopping until one-thirty for lunch. Now he was repaying himself for

his morning's diligence by being out of doors in the warm spring
sunshine doing work he liked. Every time he lifted a stack of lumber or hammered a nail, he could feel the hardness returning to
the muscles in his shoulders, arms and hands. It was a good feeling,
and he could see the difference when he looked in the mirror
while shaving errant whiskers from his neck and cheekbones. Now
those same muscles, covered with sweat, reflected the afternoon
sun.

Somewhere inside the house, Francis and Mort were pulling BX
wires through old walls and connecting them to the new circuit
breaker box. They had completed the wiring for the new bathroom, but the carpenter was still waiting for the plumber to install
the fixtures before he could do the finishing touches.

Bear and Clara had found a cool spot in the shade at the side of
the house and were taking their afternoon naps.

Chuck glanced at Dawn's house, knowing she was sunning herself on the back deck, concealed from view by the bushes that
circled the deck. He knew because he'd seen her from his third-
floor window when he'd gone to his bedroom to change clothes
after lunch. He hadn't been looking for her, simply staring blankly
out the window while he unbuttoned his shirt. Motion on the deck
below caught his attention, and he looked down to see her coming
onto the porch wearing a bikini. He couldn't help but watch. She
spread out an exercise mat and sat down, then removed the top of
the bathing suit and, leaning back, stretched out her legs. She
closed her eyes and turned her face toward the sun, her breasts
white against her tanned body. He started to turn away out of re-
spect for her privacy, but was unable to move. Entranced, he
slowly unbuttoned his shirt and tossed it on the bed without turning his head. When she lay back and began rubbing suntan lotion
on her body, he quickly walked to the other side of the bed, put
on his shorts and workboots and went down the stairs.

Dawn lay on her back, letting the warm sun relax her body. She
wished she dared to strip completely nude, as she had done with
Gareth on the beach in the south of France. Peeling off the last
shred of confinement was an exhilarating feeling, knowing there
was nothing between your body and the eyes of the other people

lying nude on the beach beside you. But Marblehead wasn't the south of France. She noticed she was in full view of Chuck's bedroom window and wondered if he was looking down at her. No, he's probably in his study banging away on his computer. Then she heard him dump an armload of lumber on the porch and begin to hammer. So much for a nap. She lay there for several minutes listening to the erratic rhythm of the hammer, enjoying the fact that only a few leaves separated her from Chuck, like Eve's strategically placed fig leaves. Smiling, she raised herself on one elbow and peered through the bushes. There he was, bent over the deck, his hand gripping a hammer and bringing it down hard against the head of a nail. Every so often he would stand and stretch his back—too much time at the computer, she thought—but before returning to his work, he would look in her direction. Could he see her through the bushes? A part of her hoped he could.

He'd been working on the porch for an hour and a half, struggling to keep his attention on fitting tongues into grooves and hammering nails without bending them, but knowing all the time that Dawn was lying topless on her deck only yards away behind the shrubs.

Last night she'd asked him if he would take care of Clara for the night so she could attend a party in Boston. Brian wasn't available because he was in Maine with Mike and his mother opening their summer cottage. Chuck had agreed, of course. She explained that the PR company for the Boston Museum of Art was having a big pre-exhibit promotional affair and she had to attend. It might last late into the night, because the people would probably stay until the food and liquor ran out. Chuck said it sounded like fun and not to worry about Clara. No wonder she was taking a nap. She'd probably gotten in late.

He walked to his stack of lumber, picked up an armload of fir strips and returned to the porch, glancing at the bushes around her deck. She was well shielded from view.

He let his mind drift to the other night when she said she might be falling in love with him. Probably just the strain of worrying about Brian, he thought. How can I even imagine she could like me, he wondered. She's beautiful and smart. She has her own company and travels all over the world. And the circles she moves in—I would be considered a computer nerd or dweeb or whatever it is they call people like me. But she did put her arm around me. Forget it, he said to himself. It won't last when she gets to know me. What chance have I got with a woman as beautiful and appealing as Dawn Ireland?

The silence awakened Dawn. The hammering had stopped. She realized she'd been asleep. Rolling onto her side, she found a small gap in the bushes through which she could see Chuck. He was coming back onto the porch carrying more boards. The sweat on his broad shoulders and back glistened in the sun. She imagined touching his chest with the tip of her tongue and tasting the saltiness. When he knelt to set the boards down, she wondered what it would be like to press her hand against the hard muscles that stood out in his thighs.

What a guy, she thought.

A truck turned around and backed into Dawn's driveway. On its side was the name Spaulding Air Freight. The driver parked as close to the house as he could without crossing the lawn, then got out. He went to the rear of the truck, where he moved a wooden crate onto a hydraulic tailgate, then lowered it to the ground. Chuck walked to the truck.

"For Dawn Ireland?" Chuck asked.

"Yup."

"I'll get her," Chuck said. "She's around back."

He walked to the deck, but stopped before he could see her and called, "Dawn, you've got a delivery."

"Chuck?"

"It's me."

"Come on up."

As he climbed the steps, she looked up and smiled, then reached for her bathing suit top and began slipping it on. He stopped dead in his tracks and, for an instant, stared at the graceful upward curve of her breasts, then averted his eyes. Dawn didn't seem to mind his seeing her. When the top was in place, she stood and walked to him.

"Thanks for taking care of Clara last night. Some of us went for dinner after the party and I didn't get home until two. She would have been howling to get out."

"Glad I could do it." Then, turning to leave, "I think he's got something for you to sign."

Chuck returned to his porch and began laying fir strips across the joists in preparation for nailing, but he continued to monitor the events next door. He saw Dawn, now in her robe, come onto her front porch. The driver of the truck was attempting to pull a dolly up the steps with a heavy box strapped to it. They exchanged a few words and soon Dawn was heading toward his porch.

Halfway there, she called to him, "Could you help us? We need to get this box up the steps and into the house."

"Sure." He set his hammer down and returned with Dawn to her house.

With Chuck pushing from the bottom and the man pulling from the top, the dolly and box were wrestled up the steps and into the house. "Where do you want it?" the man asked.

"In here would be fine," Dawn said, leading them into the dining room, which she'd converted to a workroom. This was Chuck's first time in the room. The door had always been closed before. Instead of a dining room table, there were two worktables side by side, each about eight feet by three. Another table of the same size was against one wall, and several boxes and large mailing tubes were placed around the room. On the table by the wall were brown wrapping paper and tape, scissors and a long ruler. Every available wall space was hung with posters, filling the room with vivid colors.

The man stood the box upright and eased it off the dolly, then gave Dawn a metal clipboard and a pen. "Sign right here." Dawn gave him a five-dollar tip for his extra help and he left. Chuck came over to examine the box.

"What is it?"

"My posters from Air France. Want to see them?"

Her smile was so genuine that Chuck began to feel she really wanted him to be there with her. "Sure. May I help uncrate them?"

"I'd appreciate that."

"Give me about ten minutes to put my tools away," he said.

"I might even have a cool drink ready for you. Gin and tonic?"

"That'd be great."

"Come as you are. It'll be hot in here and I don't want to get the fans out yet."

When he returned, two tall drinks were sitting on coasters on the side table and Dawn, wearing only her bikini, was prying at one end of the crate with a screwdriver.

"I don't think you'll get far with a screwdriver. I brought my crowbar and hammer. Let me see what I can do." He'd taken her at her word and was still dressed only in his shorts and work boots.

"Watch my toes with those boots," Dawn said. "I'm barefoot."

He was standing beside her, their bodies almost touching. "I'll be careful."

Chuck drove the crowbar beneath an end of a board and pried it up a quarter-inch. "Let's do this together. Put your screwdriver into the gap where I've raised the board." When she shoved it in, he slipped the bar out and moved it down into the space where the two boards came together. Wiggling the bar back and forth, he eased it into the slit between the boards and forced them apart. "Now, put your screwdriver in this hole and I'll move my bar further down." She did, and Chuck repeated what he'd done before. Then, leaning on the bar, he lifted the board free of the crate.

"Wow," Dawn laughed, "I didn't know uncrating a box could be so sensual."

Chuck looked at her. "Well, then, let's do it again."

They did. Another board. More prying and lifting. Then ripping it free. Covered with sweat and working side by side, they felt their shoulders and upper arms touch and slip, touch and slip. Chuck fought to keep a serious face, afraid that if he let her see how aroused he was getting, she would move away or put on her robe.

"How about a break?" she said, exhaling a deep breath. "We'd better have some of those drinks before all the ice melts."

"Uh, it *is* hot in here." They went to the table and picked up the glasses. Chuck began looking at the posters on the walls. "I never realized a poster could be so dramatic. And they're huge."

"Don't you like this one?" She pointed to a poster of a young girl holding the handlebars of a bicycle but floating above it as if caught in a rushing wind. Her hair, blowing in the wind, flowed over her nude body, which was perfectly arched to show her breasts and bottom to their fullest advantage.

"Fetching, isn't it," Chuck said. "What's it about?"

"It's a turn-of-the-century ad for a bicycle."

"Hmm. Sex in advertising, even back then?"

"It's been around awhile."

He moved to a different poster. "How about this one?" It showed the naked backs of two men crouched on the front of a locomotive just behind its headlight as it emerged from a dark tunnel into the brilliant light of day. The men wore the winged helmet of Mercury and their backs reflected the deep red glow of the locomotive's fire box.

"It's a poster for an Italian exposition in 1906 for the opening of a railroad tunnel. I think it's one of the most dramatic posters ever printed."

They continued around the room looking at posters, then Chuck asked, "What do you do here in your workroom?"

"I receive the posters I've bought overseas and keep them here until I eventually repack them and ship them off to customers. That's what all this packing material's for."

"So these posters aren't part of the exhibit at the BMA?"

"Oh no. Those posters are far too valuable to have here in the house. They'll be shipped directly to the museum."

"Fascinating," Chuck said. "It's another world I didn't know existed. Well, let's finish the uncrating."

"First," Dawn said, "we need to lay the box flat and remove the boards on the top and sides. You'll see why later."

"Okay." They pulled the box toward its flat side and then, straining under its weight, let it come down onto the floor.

Piece by piece, they carefully removed all the boards and set them aside. With the crate flat on the floor, they found themselves on their hands and knees reaching across each other to wedge boards free and pressing their hips and legs together as they lifted boards. Chuck tried to remain calm, but at each touch of her body, his breath caught in his throat. Occasionally Dawn would lean against him. He wondered if it was intentional.

When the last board was removed, what was left was a large package wrapped in brown paper sitting on the remaining wooden side.

"Now you see why I leave it on the floor. It's too heavy and floppy to lift onto the table. I just take a few at a time, what I need for a shipment." She began unwrapping the paper, being careful not to tear it. Folding back the last piece, she lifted one of the posters out and set it on the table.

"Have a look."

Chuck got up and came to the table. On the poster was a white Concorde rising into a blue sky like a rocket ship taking off. In the background was the Eiffel Tower.

"Exciting, isn't it?" she said.

"Very." His arm was touching hers.

"Look here at the clouds." She pointed. "See how the artist shaded the blue of the sky into the white base of the clouds and then repeated it again in the fuselage of the plane?"

As Chuck leaned over the poster, some drops of sweat fell from his chest.

"Wait a minute," Dawn said, picking up a towel. "Let me dry you off."

Chuck stood before her as she reached up to dry his forehead and eyes. With each dab of the towel, she slowed the movement of her hand until each touch became a delicate operation. Lowering the towel to his neck, she smiled as she rubbed his beard beneath his chin. Then, keeping her eyes fixed on his, she brought the towel to his shoulders and chest and lazily stroked it up and down. Next she reached to his sides, first one side and then the other, each time bringing the towel across his stomach in slow circular motions. In order to dry his back, she pressed her body tightly against his and, holding the towel in both hands behind him, moved it up and down, up and down.

He could stand it no longer. Chuck pulled her into his arms and they kissed. Parting momentarily, they looked into each other's eyes and smiled softly. Then they kissed again.

Dawn stepped back and took his hands in hers. Walking backward, she began leading him to the door of the workroom, then across the entranceway to the stairs. He followed, lost in a dream.

They heard the kitchen door open and a backpack drop to the floor, followed by several welcoming yelps from Clara.

"Hi, Mom," Brian's call echoed through the house. "What's for dinner?"

TWENTY-SEVEN

H ello."
"Hi."
Dawn was standing at his front door. An early morning rain was falling, turning the leaves to glistening reflectors for the street-lights, which had not yet gone off. The hood of her yellow rain slicker was pulled over her head and buttoned beneath her chin, puffing her cheeks slightly and creating an oval frame for her face. Raindrops dripped from her eyebrows, and strands of blond hair that crept out of the left side of the hood were clinging to her wet cheek. She looked up at Chuck, her blue eyes catching the light from the hall, and smiled.

"It's raining," her voice dreamy.

"So I see." Chuck was dressed in his gray sweats. "Come inside."

"Oh, that's all right. I was going to walk Clara and I saw your light. Thought you might like to come."

"Bear!" he called in a loud voice, but the dog was standing right behind him. "Want to go for a walk?" Bear pushed past him and out into the rain to receive Clara's good morning chew on the neck. "Lemme get my slicker."

"I'll wait on the porch."

A minute later they were walking down the front walk, her arm through his, and each holding a leash. Every so often they'd look at each other and smile tentatively, not sure how to begin a conversation. Finally Chuck spoke.

"Did yesterday really happen or was I dreaming?"

"If it was a dream, I dreamed it too."

Again they walked in silence, the only people on the road as they circled Quiet Cove. Their arms locked together, they followed Clara, who was following Bear.

"Maybe it was the gin and tonic?" he said.

"No. It started before we'd touched a drop."

"Or the heat."

"Hmm. That's possible," she said thoughtfully. "It was awfully hot." After a long silence, she said, "I think it was your shorts."

"You mean my muscular body," he laughed.

"That's what I meant."

"I think it was your bikini."

"That piece of string?"

"That's what *I* meant."

He turned her toward him and they kissed. Then he looked into her upturned face and watched the rain fall on her forehead and cheeks. "Then I wasn't dreaming?"

"No." She lifted her lips toward his and kissed him.

The dogs had stopped at the end of their leashes and looked back at the humans, granting them a reasonable time to embrace. Then they commenced walking again, pulling the humans along behind them.

"When Gareth died," Dawn said, "I decided I'd never let myself feel this way again. And look at me, hanging on you, waiting for the next kiss." He kissed her.

The dogs took them along the road next to Little Harbor, then past the boatyard toward Fort Sewall.

"I didn't believe that someone like you would be interested in me," Chuck said.

"What do you mean, like me?"

"Someone beautiful, outgoing."

"Thanks. But don't sell yourself short." She glanced at him and wondered if he walked with his head down because of the rain or because of the way he felt about himself. "Yesterday, when you came to get me on my deck, why did you leave so abruptly?"

"You said you'd gone out for dinner after the party and," with a shrug of his shoulders, "it hit me. I wouldn't fit in with the kind of men you know."

"Whew! I thought it was something else."

"What?"

"I was afraid you'd left because I'd taken so long to get the top of my bathing suit on." She glanced at him. "Maybe you thought I was being forward."

He smiled. "I didn't mind that part."

"I'm going to tell you a secret." She pulled him to a stop. "While you were working on the porch, I peeked at you through the hedge." Chuck drew his head back skeptically. Dawn continued, "And do you know what I was thinking?" He shook his head. "That there wasn't a man at the party who could hold a candle to you."

She waited for a reaction. What she saw was pain. Then he turned away so she couldn't see his face.

"Chuck?" She caught his arm and turned him back toward her. "What is it?"

"I'm not the big strong guy you think I am." He looked away. "I found that out when I was married to Michelle. There were times when . . . when it didn't go too well."

He took her arm and they started walking again. Soon they found themselves on the earthen wall of the old fort above the waves that dashed on the rocks fifty feet below. Dark clouds hung over the water, and sheets of rain blurred the horizon. They unhooked the dogs, who walked about ten feet down the bank, then returned almost immediately to sit beside them and blink their eyes against the rain.

Dawn put her arms around him. "I don't know what's going on with you, but I do know this. You're a good person and I'm beginning to care a lot about you."

"I feel the same way," he said. "I want it to be right, and I'm so afraid it won't be."

"Let's not worry," she said, leaning back so she could see his face. "I want it to be right, too. So we're both scared. Let's just take it easy and see what happens, give it time."

"Okay." He forced a smile.

"And while we're doing that, let's enjoy how much we like each other."

Dawn spent the rest of the morning in her workroom. She began with a long phone call to the insurance company that was covering the shipments of posters to the BMA. Then there were several calls to the shipping companies in Europe to be sure everything was on schedule. Finally, she telephoned an appraiser in Milan who was evaluating the condition of the posters before they were boxed up. He was complaining about the freight company she had chosen, a company he considered incompetent and sure to damage the shipment. As the man droned on, her mind flip-flopped between thinking about Chuck and listening to the appraiser. Eventually she managed to reassure him and hung up, but she couldn't get Chuck out of her mind.

Something must have happened in his marriage, she thought, that burned him so badly he hasn't recovered. Well, if it's going to take him time to work it through, maybe that's a good thing for both of us.

Sitting there, staring blankly at the phone, pictures drifted through her mind: walking with Chuck in the rain, watching him dressed in his shorts and working on the porch, eating lobsters together, being held in his arms. "Dawn Ireland," she said aloud, "are you falling in love?"

From her window she saw the mailman walking back down her front walk. She went to her mailbox and removed several envelopes—first-of-the-month bills, some circulars, a letter for Brian from someone she figured was a Brighton Academy friend, and a letter for her from Russia.

"This is it," she said excitedly and ran to her workroom. Standing by her table, she tore open the envelope.

Dear Mrs. Ireland:

I apologize for not sending my condolences after the death of your partner, Professor Davies, but I did not know how to reach you. I am pleased you wrote me, giving me your address, so that I can extend to you my deepest sympathies. Gareth was a good friend and a fine scholar. During the two weeks he was here for the seminar he spoke of you often, so I almost feel I know you.

You say you must come to Moscow and would like to see me. And I would like to see you and share memories of our dear friend. Unfortunately, I will be in Vladivostok on a government project until the second week in July. I have been working there for the last three months, and would be there now had I not returned home for my brother's funeral. I found your letter waiting for me.

If you can come to Moscow in July, I can see you in my office at the university sometime after the eighth.

You asked if I was able to help Gareth find a man named Krubinski who deals in historic posters. I did try, making several telephone calls which produced no results. For some reason, Mr. Krubinski is very elusive. I suggested to Gareth that he go to a shop on New Arbat Street that sells posters and ask if they know the man. I don't know what, if anything, he found out.

I look forward to meeting you. Please confirm your coming by writing me in Vladivostok at Hotel Amursky Zaliv, 9 Naberezhnaya Ulitsa.

Warm Regards,
Nikolai Neleginski

"Well," she said aloud, "it's a start." She walked to the window and gazed out at Quiet Cove as she pondered the letter. So, she said to herself, he'd gone to a shop on New Arbat Street to get information about Krubinski. She pictured Gareth at the counter jotting down the same notes she'd found in his briefcase. If they helped Gareth, maybe they would help me, too. And she liked what the professor said about sharing memories of Gareth. He sounds like a nice man. Then it occurred to her that Neleginski probably knew what Gareth was doing the night he was killed. This she had to know, and yet she was afraid of what she might learn.

TWENTY-EIGHT

"A re you ready?" the off-the-wall electrician said, one hand on
the wheel, one on the throttle. They were in Francis's boat
and had just finished maneuvering through Marblehead Harbor,
reaching the end of the restricted speed zone.

"Yeah," Chuck replied, not sure what he was ready for.

"Here we go!" Francis pushed forward on the throttle, the engine roared and the boat leaped forward.

They rounded Lighthouse Point and he turned the Aquasport
20 toward the open ocean. Waves slapped with quickening rapidity
at the sleek hull as the boat gained speed. The bow wave unfolded
before it like the wings of a bird taking flight, and behind, the
wake carved a white, foaming V through the dark water. With the
increasing speed the aquadynamic hull lifted out of the water and
the bow wave disappeared. The boat began planing the crest of
the waves.

Francis looked at Chuck with the pride of a schoolboy present-
ing an all-A report card. He said something that was lost in the roar
of the engine, but his smile delivered the message. Chuck grinned
back at him.

The eastern sky was brightening behind a cloud bank reclining
on the horizon, the air was chilly and a sliver of translucent moon
was setting in the west. They flew past lobster boats as if they
were standing still in the water, Francis waving to the lobstermen
and they waving back. Distant islands, coal black and rising out of

the ocean, began to take on color and definition as they neared them. High overhead, the rising sun transformed a jet liner's vapor trail into a golden javelin and sent it sailing across the sky.

They sat in two chairs mounted on posts just behind the central console with its stainless steel steering wheel, accelerator lever, compass and various gauges. It was an open boat with no cabin but lots of room for moving about and storage space for gear. Their fishing poles stuck out of holders on the gunwales just aft of their seats, and at the stern was the powerful two-hundred–horsepower Evinrude. Secured to the console was a device that looked like the monitor of a small computer. They'd been under way for ten minutes when Francis turned it on and began adjusting a dial. Chuck pointed at it and mouthed, "What's this?"

Francis put his mouth next to Chuck's ear and yelled, "It's a fish finder." Chuck looked at him as if he were putting him on. "No. It really is," he said.

Francis throttled down and the boat settled into the water, the engine's roar being replaced by a muffled rumbling. He pointed at the multicolored lines that etched a jagged pattern across the screen.

"See this line? It tells us the bottom is hard, probably sand and gravel. If there was a school of fish down there, it'd show up as a cloudy line above the bottom. But there's no fish there now."

"Like sonar," Chuck said, reaching into his meager supply of nautical knowledge.

"You got it." Francis slipped off his seat and begin opening his fishing box just behind them. "Let's get fitted up. You use the pole on the port side—yeah, that's it. This one's mine." He rummaged through the trash in his box until he found a silver spoon with a vicious-looking hook extending from its underside. "Attach this to the steel leader on the end of your line."

Chuck took it and found the task relatively easy because the leader had a safety pin–like catch on the end of it. Francis watched him, then smiled.

"You've never been fishing before, have you?"

"No. First time."

Francis shook his head. "How can a guy get to be, what, forty years old, and never been fishing?"

"Nobody ever took me."

"Didn't your dad? I know he was a fisherman because I've seen him out on the water."

"Not while I lived here."

Francis attached a lure to his line and slowly let it out. "What we're gonna do is troll. We'll let lines run out the stern and go along at about five knots." A glance at Chuck showed him his partner didn't know what to do next. "Lift that. It's called a bailer, and let the forward motion of the boat pull your line out." Chuck complied and his line began to spool out. After a short while, "That's about enough. Now close the bailer like this"—Chuck watched him—"and that's all there is to it. Hold the pole and wait for a fish to strike your lure."

"What do I do then?"

"Give it a jerk to set the hook in its mouth and start reeling in."

Both men returned to their seats. "Now that I think of it," Francis said, "I don't remember seeing you when I was dating Vivian. You're about ten years older, right?"

"I guess you don't know that she and Josh are my half-sister and brother. Mom left Dad when I was ten and this is the first time I've been back to Marblehead."

"That's too bad. Your dad was a good guy. I told you I did the electrical work for the kitchen. I was having a hard time financially back then and your dad paid me up front. That was the first time, and last, that anybody's ever done that."

A seagull floated above them for a while until it was convinced there were no fish aboard, then sailed away. From time to time, Francis glanced at the fish-finder, checking the depth and looking for signs of a school.

"I guess you inherited the house when he died."

"That's right."

"Well, it'll be a good place to live when you finish fixing it up."

"Marblehead's a nice town, isn't it?"

"The best. It's good for tradespeople like me. There's always new building going on or renovations. It's a bit pricey for us, but you get by, barely. The schools are good, too, when my kids get to that age. And the fishing's great, or at least it used to be. The big commercial fishing companies have just about ruined it for us sports fishermen, and for themselves, for that matter."

"And you got me up at four-thirty to come out here fishing and there's no more fish?" For a moment Francis looked hurt. "Just kidding," Chuck said quickly. "I wouldn't have missed this for anything."

At that instant, a fish hit Chuck's line with the force of falling bricks, almost pulling the pole out of his hand. "My God!" he shouted, "I've got one."

"Start winding it in. Keep the line taut and bring it in slow and steady."

As the fish neared the boat, it shot to the right, then the left, then dove for the bottom. Chuck was standing at the stern reeling in and Francis was by his side with a gaff hook.

"I think I've got a whale," Chuck said, laughing with delight. "Jeez, but it's strong."

As he brought it up to the boat, Francis warned, "Don't let him hit the side. He might get free. Bring it up here so I can gaff it." The end of the bent pole switched this way and that as Chuck continued his steady winding. When the head of the fish just broke the water, Francis reached over the side and caught it in the gill with the big hook, whipping it up and onto the deck.

"Wow!" Chuck shouted. "Look at that. I caught a fish."

A bluefish, about thirty inches long lay on the deck, its body flopping under Francis's boot. "Now there's a real fish," Francis exclaimed. "Good going." He unhooked Chuck's line and put the fish in the livewell. "Now it's my turn."

They continued trolling. Chuck gripped the pole tightly, every nerve in his body ready for the next strike. After twenty minutes without a hit, he began to relax. Two seagulls had picked up surveillance over their stern as if they sensed the presence of the big blue in the livewell. The sun was up and a glorious day was beginning.

"Thanks for bringing me, Francis. I haven't had this much fun in I don't know how long." He thought briefly about last Wednesday when Dawn had wiped the sweat from his chest and kissed him, but he wasn't going to tell Francis about that.

"My pleasure. Seeing you catch your first fish made it all worth-while." He turned to look at the fish-finder. Still no fish visible.

Chuck let out a little more line. "You said the house will be nice when I get it finished. Do you know that when I first got here, all I wanted to do was sell it and go back to Alexandria? Then I started working on the porch and getting you guys to renovate the inside. Now I'm beginning to change my mind. Maybe I should stay here."

"I've told you, if you'd just let me help you get acquainted with your neighbor, I'm sure you'd stay. She's divorced, or didn't you know?"

"I know," Chuck said.

Francis, immediately picking up on Chuck's smile, said, "Hmm. Maybe you know her better than I realized."

"The truth is, she's one of the reasons I'd like to stay."

"Now you're talking. And another reason?—don't tell me—you want to take up fishing."

"Hah. You could be right. . . . Wait. . . . I think. . . . *I got another one!*"

Late that afternoon, Dawn, Brian and Chuck were standing in his kitchen looking at the bluefish lying on aluminum foil on the table. Chuck, under Brian's supervision, had scaled and gutted it, then cut off the head and tail. About twenty inches of fish remained, and Chuck was putting salt, pepper and pieces of fresh basil on it.

"For someone who's never been fishing until this morning," Dawn said, "how come you're so good at cooking them?"

"They sell fish in stores, you know."

"Oh."

"Actually, Francis told me how he does it."

Dawn smiled. "Sounds like you've found a fishing buddy."

"He's a lot of fun, if he doesn't drive you crazy."

Chuck wore a white apron over a clean pair of slacks and a polo shirt. As he worked on the fish, he and Dawn sipped gin and tonics and she made a salad. Because Chuck had invited her to dinner for a *very* special occasion, she had dressed in a dark blue, ankle-length cotton shift.

"Where's the other one?" Brian asked. "I thought you caught

two." He was dressed in knee-length baggy shorts and an over-sized T-shirt heralding a musical group called Coughing Up Blood.

"I gave it to Francis," Chuck declared with a hint of pride. "He didn't catch any."

"Will we be eating soon?" the boy asked.

"Brian! We're guests."

"Sorry. We're together so much I forgot. Anyway, I'm meeting Mike pretty soon."

"It won't be long," Chuck said, opening the fridge. "Now for the *pièce de résistance.*" He brought out six slices of bacon and angled them across the side of the fish, then wrapped it all in the aluminum foil. *Dum-dumming* the notes of the funeral dirge, he solemnly carried the fish to the oven, preheated to 350 degrees. "Brian, can you wait about forty minutes?"

"He'll wait," Dawn declared. Brian sighed and looked at the floor.

After twenty minutes, Chuck opened the oven door and tore back the aluminum foil, exposing the fish, then pushed it back into the oven. "Twenty more minutes to brown the top."

When he took it out, the bacon was crisp and the fish golden brown. "Now, isn't that beautiful?" he exclaimed.

"Your talent as a fisherman," Dawn announced, "is exceeded only by your ability as a cook." She and Chuck clicked their gin and tonic glasses against Brian's raised Coke can, and Bear and Clara joined the excitement, their noses as close to the table as dog etiquette would allow.

After dinner, the kitchen cleaned up, the dogs walked and Brian off with Mike, Dawn curled up on the sofa next to Chuck. She put her head against his chest. He drew his fingers through her hair, combing it down over her shoulder.

"You had fun today," Dawn said.

"Yup. It *was* fun—doing something just for the hell of it. Working on the porch is okay, but being out there today with Francis was something else. I felt free, miles away from everything."

She hunched up further into his lap, turning around so she was cradled in his arms and looking up at him.

"From me, too?"

"No, not you." He smiled, shaking his head slightly. "I can't believe you're here with me, wanting to be here."

"Well, I am."

She slipped an arm around his neck and pulled his face toward hers. They kissed.

"Today Francis said I should get to know you."

"So you did talk about me."

"Of course. I told him I was getting acquainted with you."

"Getting acquainted, huh? Is that what we were doing the other day in my workroom?"

"Well, I didn't go into detail. He said that if I got to know you I might decide to stay."

"And you said?"

"And I said you were one of the reasons I was thinking about staying."

"What would I have to do to make me the main reason?"

He waited several moments before answering. "Give me just a little more time."

She placed her hand against his cheek. "I will, but . . ."

Answering before she could ask her question, he said, "I need to know I can love you without making a mess of it. I don't want to hurt you—or me."

TWENTY-NINE

Vivian, this is Chuck." He was at his desk in the study. It was Monday morning. Vivian hadn't come by on the first of June to work on the bills, so he knew it was time to make amends.

There was a pause, then Vivian spoke. "Hello, Chuck."

"First, I want to apologize for the things I said at your house."

"It wasn't a very good evening, was it?"

"I shouldn't have talked that way about your mother and our dad. It happened a long time ago, and who can tell what the circumstances were?"

"It hit me pretty hard. You didn't seem like the same person who helped me go through Mom's old jewelry."

"It's been a strange time for me these last few weeks, being in the house after all these years and running into Dad's old records. It's like one day I'm back in the sixties and the next in the present."

She paused again and said, "I need to apologize, too. I was in a bad mood, with Carl being late and the kids fussing. I think we were all on edge."

"Thanks, but I was the one out of line." He waited a moment, then said, "I'd like to invite you, Carl and the kids over next Saturday. I've asked Josh and Cliff and they're coming. We're putting the sailboat in the water. Afterwards, we'll have lunch on the porch if it's nice weather. Otherwise, inside."

"Hmm. That sounds like fun. The kids love to come to the house. It'll be hard for them not seeing Gramps there, but it has to happen sometime. Isn't that a lot for you to do, fixing lunch for so many people?"

"Oh, Dawn is helping me."

"Hmm. Sounds like you're getting to know her."

"I'm working on it."

Vivian laughed. "I'll have to check with Carl and let you know. What time do you want us to come?"

"Josh and Cliff are coming at eleven to get the boat in the water. If you want to help, come then. Otherwise, about one. We'll eat and then go for rides on the sailboat or just take it easy."

"I'll call you tomorrow."

Thunderbolt was ready for launching Saturday morning. After two days of rain at the beginning of the week, which delayed Brian putting the finishing touches on the bottom paint, it cleared up on Wednesday and he completed the boat on Thursday. Vivian had called saying the whole family would be there, but not until one o'clock. Josh and Cliff arrived early, at ten-thirty, and were standing with Chuck and Brian next to the boat. Josh was dressed in jeans and Cliff in cutoffs, and both wore short-sleeved sport shirts. Chuck was in his work shorts and a T-shirt and Brian in his baggy shorts and a sleeveless sweatshirt.

"Brian did the whole thing," Chuck said, pointing at the boat as he spoke. "Sanded the teak and revarnished it, compounded the hull, put on the bottom paint and painted the waterline."

"Don't forget cleaning out the cabin," Brian added.

"That too."

"You've done well," Josh said. "Used to be my job, when I was your age."

"All I did," Chuck said, "was take the outboard over to Fair Winds Outboard to be tuned up. And it was Brian's idea to ask you to help launch it. He said you'd done it before."

"A few times. There's not much to it."

Cliff was admiring the straight, neat edge of the waterline. "Good job, Brian."

"Thanks. I used masking tape to get the edge straight."

"Well, shall we?" Chuck asked.

"One thing first," Josh interrupted. "We need to put the dinghy in the water or we'll have no way to get to shore when we hook up to the mooring out in the cove."

"See why we asked your help?" Chuck laughed.

Chuck brought the pickup around while the other three hauled the dinghy out of the shed. Then they put it in the truck and took it to the water's edge.

"Whoever drives the truck back can row out to the buoy and pick us up," Josh said.

"I'll do that," Cliff volunteered. "Let the new owner get the first ride of the season."

They returned to the boat shed, and as they were attaching the trailer to the truck, Dawn and the two dogs, on leashes, walked down from the house.

"If you're later than twelve-thirty," she said to Chuck, "I'll start the fire in the grill."

"Oh, I won't be late."

"Uh-huh. Tell me another one. I know about men and their boats." Then, turning to leave, "Good luck with the launching."

"How are you at backing up a trailer?" Josh asked Chuck.

"Not very good."

"Want me to drive?"

"I think you'd better."

Slowly, with Josh at the wheel, they made their way through town to Parker's Boat Yard and down the circuitous road to the quay between sailboats still on their winter cradles.

"I'm glad you're driving," Chuck said.

While they were waiting for another boat to be launched, they put the mast in position and secured its rigging. Then Josh backed the trailer beneath the crane and he and Chuck climbed into the cockpit of the boat. He showed Chuck how to attach the cable from the crane to the steel ring fixed to the deck at the center of gravity, then they got out of the boat. With Cliff on a bow line, Chuck on a stern line and Brian with a boat hook to keep the hull away from the stone quay, Josh pushed the UP button on the electric controls for the crane and the boat lifted off the trailer. Slowly they swung the crane arm and boat over the water, with Josh giving commands.

"Ease in on the stern line. Watch those rocks, Brian. Okay, now pull in on the bow line, Cliff. Chuck, let yours out some."

And *Thunderbolt* was in the water.

Brian tightened the turnbuckles on the stays while Josh showed Chuck how to attach the sail to the boom and mast and how to run up the jib. In half an hour they were ready to leave the dock. Cliff said goodbye and returned to the truck. The boat crew pushed off, Josh at the tiller.

A fifteen-knot northwest wind took them smartly through the harbor, past dozens of other sailboats rocking at their moorings, and out into the open water. At Lighthouse Point, Chuck remembered that this was where Francis had given his boat full throttle, causing it to rise out of the water with a deafening roar. The sailboat, on the other hand, slipped smoothly and quietly over the water with only the sound of the wind and waves—a different kind of power.

"Want to give it a try?" Josh said. "It *is* yours."

"Okay," Chuck said warily, "but tell me what to do."

He took the tiller and, with Josh talking him through the various operations, soon got the feel of synchronizing the rudder with the sail. They practiced changing course, by coming about into the wind, and where to hold the sail for different wind directions. Chuck was like a child with a new toy, laughing excitedly with the successful completion of each new maneuver. Once, when bow spray caught them in the face, giving them a good soaking, he shouted for joy.

"Hey, Skipper," Brian called. "It's quarter to one."

"Oh my god! We better head in. Take over, Josh."

From the completed section of porch on Chuck's house, Dawn, Vivian, Carl and Cliff watched the sailboat coming into Quiet Cove. Cliff excused himself and headed for the dinghy.

"Not bad," Dawn said. "Only forty minutes late."

"You can't be too particular when it comes to sailing," Vivian said, retying the tail of her shirt across her midriff. "I learned that with Dad. It's not the boats—it's the sailors. They lose track of time. Anyway, the kids are happy."

The three children, Jeremy, Jackie and Joslynn, were playing with Bear and Clara on the front lawn. Six-year-old Jeremy was trying to place two-year-old Joslynn on Bear's back while the big dog waited patiently. Four-year-old Jackie was hugging Clara so she wouldn't feel left out.

Dawn, dressed in shorts, halter and sandals, asked, "Did they say anything about Gramps when they arrived?"

"No. Whatever they were feeling they kept to themselves, but I noticed Jeremy looking around as if he expected to see Dad walk out to meet us."

"Kids get over things in a hurry," Carl said. He wore light blue slacks and a collarless dark blue shirt buttoned to the top. A bottle of Sam Adams ale was in his hand.

"Maybe," Dawn said, "but I think sometimes they keep it inside."

"Can I help you get lunch ready?" Vivian offered.

"It's all set. Chuck and I made the hamburger patties and potato salad this morning before the boys came."

"Sounds like you two are getting to know each other."

Dawn smiled. "It seems that way." Then changing the subject, "Let's go down and meet them?"

Carl gathered the children and dogs while Vivian walked with Dawn. In the cove, Cliff was rowing the dinghy out to the mooring.

Across the water, Dawn could hear Chuck calling to Cliff, telling him he'd missed a great sail. She smiled to see him so happy. Fishing last week, sailing this week, she thought, he's like a different person.

Because of the small size of the dinghy, Cliff had to make two trips to get the boating party ashore. Bear waded into the water following the dinghy on its first trip, but turned back after fifty feet. Meanwhile, the children threw stones into the water for Clara to chase and laughed when she couldn't find them. Soon everyone was ashore, with the dinghy secured to a long line looped between a ring embedded in a rock on shore and the anchor for the sailboat's mooring. By pulling on this line, the next person to go sailing could shuttle between the shore and the sailboat.

"We'll go ahead and get lunch started," Chuck said to the others as he and Dawn started toward the house. "Take your time."

When the two were some distance up the road, Dawn took Chuck's hand. "Think you'll like sailing?"

"I love it already. I can hardly wait to take you out. Maybe we could even take a trip in it someday. It's got a little galley and two bunks."

"Sounds romantic." She smiled.

"Hmm. It does, doesn't it?" He walked a few paces. "I said that, didn't I?" Then, with a smile of realization, "And I don't feel scared."

"I'd hate to think I scare you."

"Not you. Me. I'm the one I'm afraid of, but it's gone. Puff!" He put his arm around her and pulled her closer. "It feels great." Then he leaned down and whispered in her ear. "Let's go right now. Grab some grub, a bottle of wine and ditch the rest of 'em."

Dawn laughed, "Let's do it."

When the others arrived back at the house, Dawn was in the kitchen slicing pickles and tomatoes for the hamburgers and Chuck was at the grill cooking. Vivian, holding a glass of wine, stood beside him.

"I watched you and Dawn walking up to the house. It looks like you've found a friend."

"Well, because you're my sister, I'll tell you." He looked at her and smiled. "Viv, I haven't felt this way about anybody for years. She's really great, isn't she?"

"She is that. I was twelve when she moved next door. She was only two years older than I. Marblehead was her mother's home town, so they moved back here after her father was killed. They bought the house Dawn has now."

"What happened to Dawn's mother?" Chuck asked. "She's never mentioned her."

"They don't get along. It's been that way as long as I've known her. I think Dawn got married right after high school just to get away from her mother. Then, two years later, her mother married another naval officer and moved to California. She gave the house to Dawn and Paul."

"She thinks a lot of you," Chuck said, giving the hamburgers a flip.

"It's mutual. When she first came to Marblehead, she was over here all the time—I think Dad took the place of her father—and we got to be as close as sisters. When Mom died, she was a life support for our family, especially Dad. And then when her friend Gareth was killed last December, we did what we could for her. I think it was Dad that pulled her through."

"She hasn't gotten over Gareth's death yet. She still feels guilty about it."

"Well, I haven't seen her this happy in months. I think you two are good for each other."

"Hope so. I know she's good for me."

"Sounds serious. What are you going to do when you sell the house?"

He looked at her. "Maybe I won't sell it. Maybe I'll just stay here."

She reached up and kissed his cheek. "I'd like that."

After lunch, Josh, with Brian's help, organized a game of Wiffle ball with his nephew and two nieces, while Dawn took Vivian and Carl to her house to show them the Air France posters. Chuck and Cliff were drinking coffee on the porch.

Cliff looked closely at Chuck. "Thanks for including me today."

"Of course you're included."

"It hasn't always been that way here in this house. I came with Josh a couple of times when we first got together. Charlie didn't like me much but didn't say anything because I was Josh's friend. I think he had some idea Josh might be gay, but he wouldn't let himself believe it. When we decided to make a lifelong commitment, Josh finally told his dad. At first Charlie wouldn't even talk to him. Later he came around. He figured Josh needed help, that he had some kind of mental problem. Charlie offered to pay for a psychologist to get him cured. But he never wanted to see me." Cliff paused. "Chuck, I hope my being gay doesn't bother you."

Chuck thought for a moment. "It doesn't bother me. I guess I don't understand it, two guys loving each other, but I don't see anything wrong with it."

"I appreciate your honesty." Then he laughed, "For that mat-

ter, I don't understand your feelings for a woman, but I guess
you've got them. It's the same thing." He drank some coffee.
"What upset his father the most was Josh not getting married. He
wanted a grandson to pass on the family name. So he tried to drive
a wedge between us whenever he could, hoping I'd disappear and
Josh would see the error of his ways and fall in love with a woman."

"He must have come to terms with Josh being gay. He provided
for him in the will."

"I know. Eight hundred thousand dollars. But he never accepted me."

"Well, I'm glad you're here and I'm glad you and Josh have each
other."

"Thanks. I wanted you to know about us. You're Josh's brother.
You're family." He looked away. "Josh, you and Viv's family are
the closest thing to a family I have. I'm from Tennessee, Baptist.
My family says they don't even know me."

Chuck shook his head. "I'm sorry."

They heard voices and looked up to see Dawn, Carl and Vivian
coming across the yard. Carl was calling to Josh, "What inning
is it?"

"Top of the ninth," Josh yelled.

"We're ahead," Brian said. "Jackie and Joslynn are on my team
and Jeremy's on Josh's."

Jackie swung the plastic bat and missed the Wiffle ball. Joslynn
ran, picked it up and started pumping her little legs toward the
paper plate that was first base.

Carl came up on the porch. "Chuck, you know what I'd really
like to see?"

"No."

"Your room. In all the years we've been married, every time I've
come to the house, the door's been locked. Are there skeletons up
there or nude pictures on the ceiling?"

"Hardly. It's just the way it was when I was ten years old, except
the bed's not made. I'll show it to you."

The ballplayers had given up and were coming up the steps.
"I'd like to see it again, too," Josh said.

"So would I," Vivian joined in.

"Well, let's all go up," Chuck said. And to the children, "Want to see the mystery room?"

"Yeah! Yeah!"

So with Chuck in the lead, followed by Bear and Clara, the entire group made their way to the third floor.

When they entered the room, Vivian said to her kids, "Now, don't touch things."

"I don't think they can hurt anything," Chuck said.

Bear sprawled across the floor at the end of the bed, making it impossible for people to move about the room without stepping over him, and Clara watched the proceedings from the door.

"Gee," Carl said, "it's just a kid's room."

"I told you," Chuck laughed.

Brian was standing at the window. "Hey, you can see my room from here."

"Right," Chuck said, "and when I lived here, Bruce McIntyre, my best friend, had your room."

Brian picked up the tin can telephone that sat on the ledge. "What's this?"

"Bruce and I used to talk through that."

Brian looked puzzled. "Through this?"

"Yup. I had one can here in my bedroom and Bruce had the other. The string connected the cans. At night, when we wanted to talk, one of us would signal the other with a flashlight. Want to try it out?"

"Sure."

"Unroll one of the cans and drop it out the window on its string. Then go down and pick it up. I'll be at this end."

Brian opened the screen and let the can bobble and twist as it unrolled itself down to the ground. In a minute he was outside holding the can.

Chuck picked up the other can and called down, "Now walk back until the sting is taut. Keep going." Brian moved backward across the lawn. "That's good. Now hold it up to your ear." He turned sideways and pressed the can over his ear.

Chuck spoke into the other can. "How much do I owe you for getting the boat ready?"

Immediately, Brian switched the can to his mouth and said,

"Eighty-two dollars and fifty cents." Then, beaming, he called up to the window, "Hey, this thing really works."

"Sure it does."

Behind him there was a crash, and he turned to see the top row of books in his bookcase strewn across the floor.

"I told you kids to be careful when you got the books out," Vivian said with a sigh. "Now look what you've done."

"Don't worry," Chuck said. "I'll just stack them up and put them away later."

He scooped up twenty or thirty of his old children's books and set them on top of the bookshelf. Glancing down, he noticed the book on top of the pile. Hmm, he thought, *Gingerbread Boy*, my old favorite. He smiled as he thought about the refrain—*Run, run as fast as you can. You can't catch me, I'm the Gingerbread Man.*

Instantly, time stopped. He felt dazed. The rhyme echoed through his brain, bouncing off past memories, searching for a connection. It was only weeks ago that he'd heard those words. They had tumbled in upon him like a ton of bricks, but why? Then he remembered what had triggered them—his father's voice on the answering machine the second day he was in the house.

"Catch you later," his father had said.

And his mind had fought back with, *You can't catch me, I'm the Gingerbread Man.*

THIRTY

Eleven o'clock Sunday night Dawn turned off her computer, leaned back in her chair and rubbed her eyes. She'd written a letter to Professor Neleginski in Vladivostok, telling him she would like to meet with him on July 9 when he returned to Moscow. Then she finished extracting sections of the book for use in the exhibit brochure, material she needed for a meeting the next morning at the BMA. Usually she didn't leave things to the last minute, but Chuck had taken her sailing that afternoon. Actually, it was she who had taken Chuck sailing. After she helped him rig the sails and maneuver out of the cove, he took over in the open water. They'd had a good time until he noticed clouds rolling in and the wind picking up. Then he handed the tiller to her and she brought them into the mooring. It was just as well. She had to get to work on the extracts.

Now she was done and could go to bed.

She turned out the light in her workroom and, with Clara at her side, crossed through the darkened hall to the kitchen. The house felt hollow and cold, and her footsteps on the wooden floor seemed to echo through the empty rooms. Except for Clara, she was alone. Brian had left that morning to spend a week with Mike's family in Maine. Outside a steady rain was falling.

She poured herself a glass of wine and stood for a few minutes at her kitchen sink looking out the window. Through tree branches whipped by the wind, she could see Chuck's house, dark except

201

for one light coming from his bedroom on the third floor. She imagined him lying in his bed, propped up on his pillow, reading. Maybe he had a glass of scotch by the bed that he sipped as he turned the pages. He'd be listening to the rain on the roof just above him, one of the reasons he said he liked being on the top floor. She was sure he slept nude, as she did. She remembered again the day she'd brought him breakfast in bed. The covers were well below his navel and no pajama bottoms were visible.

"Clara," she said. The dog pricked up her ears and looked at her. "I'll bet he's up there right now, stretched out on that little bed without a stitch on. And here I am, cold and lonely and . . . dammit, in love with him." She drank some wine. "Don't tell him I said that, Clara. It might scare him away." She turned off the kitchen light and headed for her bedroom.

Climbing the stairs, she said aloud, "God, if you really are a woman, you'll understand and send me a miracle."

The wind shifted and rain began coming in Chuck's window. He got up, stepped over Bear and closed it most of the way, leaving it open just enough to hear the wind howling through the pines on the hill behind his house. He looked over at Dawn's house in time to see the kitchen light go out. A minute later, the upstairs hall light came on. He wished he could see Dawn's bedroom, but it was at the front of the house.

Right about now she'd be walking into her room, he thought, turning on her light, taking off her clothes and getting ready for bed. That afternoon when they were sailing she wore a loose blouse with no bra, and the movement of her breasts beneath the fabric had gotten him so aroused he was sure she could tell. He'd noticed it with pleasure, considering it a second affirmation that his old problem was over. The absence of nightmares was the first.

The upstairs hall light in Dawn's house went out.

"Bear," he said. Bear raised the eyelid of one sleepy eye halfway and looked at his master, then let it drift closed. "She's there and I'm here, less than a hundred feet away. Why can't I be there, crawling into bed beside her?"

* * *

Dawn didn't see it as much as she felt it. Lying there in the dark with the covers pulled up to her neck, she popped open her eyes and stared at the ceiling. Nothing but blackness. Suddenly, another *whoosh* of wind like the air blown by one stroke of a hand fan. Was she imagining it? The window was open slightly. It must have been a gust of wind from the storm. She waited. Nothing. Still, she kept her eyes open wide and her ears on alert. Nothing.

Then, *whoosh.*

Enough! She reached for the light on the bedstand and turned it on, then quickly huddled back under the sheet and blanket with only her eyes and the top of her head exposed. She waited. Then she saw it, a flapping flash of dark brown, like wadded-up paper, darting through her room, its course erratic, bouncing off air, just missing the walls.

"Oh, God! It's a bat." Instantly she submerged beneath the covers. She heard Clara jump up. Then the dog began barking and tore from the room. Seconds later she was back, on top of the bed, then off the bed and out of the room. Maybe she'll get it, Dawn hoped. But Clara continued racing in and out of the room. If only Brian were here, Dawn thought. She waited in the partial darkness beneath the sheet and blanket, then something heavy jumped onto the bed. It was Clara returning from the hunt.

"Did you get it, girl?" Dawn asked. Clara groaned and put her head down. Dawn peeked out, hoping against hope she wouldn't see the bat in Clara's mouth. It wasn't. Clara's head rested against Dawn's stomach, but her ears stood straight up like radar beacons and her eyes searched the corners of the room. Before Dawn saw anything, Clara shot into the air and off the bed. The bat was making another sortie through the room.

Dawn reached for the phone and pulled it under the covers. Dialing, she let it ring several times, knowing that Chuck had to run from his bedroom on the third floor down to his study on the second floor. On the seventh ring, he answered.

"Chuck! Oh, thank God you're there."

"Dawn? What's wrong?"

"It's awful. It's flying around my room."

"What is?"

"It's going to get in my hair."

"What is?"

"A bat, and it's flying around my bedroom."

"I'll be right over."

"How can you get in? I don't want to get out from under these covers."

"I've still got a key."

"Hurry."

"I'll just throw on my bathrobe."

Seconds later Chuck was running up the stairs, with Bear charging behind. Clara greeted them at the door with loud barks. Chuck entered and sat on the edge of the bed.

"Is that you under there?"

"Yes," her voice like a little girl's. "Is it gone?"

"For now." He turned back the covers. Dawn's arms shot out, circling his neck and pulling him down.

"It was awful," she whimpered. "Like some evil thing."

"It was only a bat, a little flying mouse."

"Ugh! I hate mice."

Chuck slipped his arms beneath her shoulders, his hand feeling the bare skin of her back.

Dawn, cradled in Chuck's arms, moved her fingers to his hair. "Poor darling. You're all wet." She dropped one hand to his robe, moving it inside to his bare chest. "You're wet through to the skin."

"Yeah, I know. It's raining outside." They held each other, her hands warm against his chest, his hands cold against her back. "Do you have any tennis racquets?"

"Yes. Why?"

"That's how we used to take care of bats up in Rochester."

"I think there're a couple in Brian's closet."

"I'll get them."

He left with both dogs. Dawn got up quickly, put on her robe and tied a bandana around her hair. Chuck returned with the tennis racquets.

"Here's the game plan," he said, handing her a racquet. "We'll turn on the lights and see if we can stir it up. As it flies by, we whack it."

"*You* whack it. I duck."

"Come on." Like hunters with their trusty dogs, they stole out of the bedroom and into the hall, turning on lights as they went, holding their racquets at the ready should the flying beast counter-attack.

The second and third bedroom lights came on and still no bat. Stealthily they crept into Brian's bathroom. Instantly, the dogs became agitated, sniffing behind the toilet, and under the sink and pushing their noses against the drawn shower curtain. Chuck clutched the edge of the curtain and whipped it back. The bat shot out, flashing once around the small room and out into the hall.

Clara was first out of the bathroom, careening into the hall. Bear was next, almost knocking over Dawn, who was crouching by the door.

"Let's get him," Chuck shouted. Into the hall they raced, the dogs leaping into the air, the humans swinging their racquets. Dawn's bandana flew off. Robe sashes fell away and robes flew open as Chuck and Dawn flailed at empty air. The bat disappeared into another room and the four hunters stopped like children playing statues. Heads still, their eyes roved the ceiling, the corners, the doorways. Clara's radar ears twitched this way and that.

Whoosh! It was back, sailing directly between Dawn and Chuck. Their racquets swung, colliding in midair with a crack. Dawn dropped hers and fell against Chuck. His racquet clattered down the stairs, followed by the dogs, who acted as if the bat was caught up in the strings. Chuck braced Dawn, who leaned against him, putting her arms around him beneath the robe. Pressed together, robes open, they could feel the entire length of their bodies touching, her breasts just below his chest, his groin against her stomach, her right thigh squeezed between his thighs, his right knee finding its way between her legs. In concert, their hands eased the bathrobes from their shoulders. Slippery with sweat from the chase, they began moving in a kind of slow dance, rubbing their bodies together. She raised her head to his and they kissed, open-mouthed, their tongues darting, circling, exploring. Dawn locked her left leg around his buttocks, cinching him toward her, as she pulled herself up until she was riding his hard penis. Chuck groaned, then scooped her into his arms and carried her to her bed.

She was on him, over him, every part of her body writhing against him.

"I want you," she breathed. "Oh, yes."

His mouth closed over hers, and his hands grasped her firm bottom, pulling her over his penis. She raised herself onto it and rocked back and forth, her eyes dreamy, her voice low and hot. "Yes, yes." Chuck's hands moved to her breasts, massaging them, letting her taut nipples excite the palms of his hands.

Then she came down onto him again, sliding off to the side, her tongue sneaking through the hair on his chest. She moved her mouth down his body to his stomach, drilling his navel with the tip of her tongue. Chuck's breathing came in quick gasps, his hands at one moment on her shoulders holding her back, and the next pushing her further down. Her head rolled back and forth across his stomach, her long hair sweeping his body. Then her lips found him and she took him into her mouth, slathering him with her tongue.

Chuck groaned and, clutching her shoulders, pulled her around and onto him. Then, rolling her over, his mouth fixed on hers, his body between her open legs, he entered her. His movements were strong and insistent. Despite the weight of his body, she responded with equal fervor.

Then he sensed it, but he didn't want to believe it. Fighting to stay with her, in her, his rhythm changed from uncontrolled passion to frantic determination. He was losing his erection.

What moments before had been a high-flying ride on the crest of passion became a steep dive into humiliation. His mind took over from his emotions. If only she hadn't gone down on me, he said to himself. I never should have let her do that. Then he tried to regenerate his passion by looking down at the rolling movement of her breasts, by feeling her hips coming up to meet him. Nothing worked. *He* didn't work. It was over. He crashed.

Dropping upon her, he rolled to the side. She turned to him, putting her face next to his.

"It's okay," she whispered. "I love you. It'll be all right. This is only one time and we have a whole lifetime for loving."

He turned on his side facing her and buried his face in her neck. "I love you." He couldn't talk straight. "Oh, God, I wanted it to be right. I wanted it to work for us. But it's not. I thought maybe it would. The nightmares are gone and I love you so much. I don't know what's wrong with me."

"Darling, listen to me." She turned his face so she could see him. "We can make it work. We have time and we have each other. Being here with you, having you hold me, is wonderful."

Abruptly, he sat up. "I love you too much to put you through this. If you want to know, this is what happened to my first marriage and I won't let it happen to you or to me. It's more than I can stand."

"Chuck, please listen."

"There's nothing to talk about. It's not you and it's not us. It's me, for Christ's sake." He looked around the room for his robe and remembered they'd dropped them in the hall. "I'm sorry, Dawn. Oh, God, I'm sorry, but I just can't stand to go through it again."

He went into the hall and found his robe. He could hear Dawn begin to cry, softly at first, then harder and harder until she was wailing. Bear watched him from the doorway, then ran after him.

It was two o'clock and Chuck was still awake. Neither the drumming of the rain on the roof nor the howling of the wind in the pines could calm his thoughts. The agony of his brutal treatment of Michelle and the sadness of her leaving came back to him as if it were yesterday. He couldn't inflict such sorrow on Dawn, and he couldn't endure it himself.

His mind drifted back to the passion he had just experienced with Dawn and again he found himself aroused. He saw her riding on top of him, her breasts bouncing as he reached for them.

"No! Goddamnit, no!" He rolled over and beat his fists against his pillow. "It's over," he cried. "It's over."

Finally he sank into a troubled sleep.

The room was dark. It was already there, standing in the darkened doorway. Slowly, cautiously, it approached his bed and knelt beside it. "Shhh. Shhh." Its voice was low and nurturing.

"No," Chucky said. "Don't, please."

"Shhh. Shhh." It was the deep voice of a man.

A heavy hand was placed over his chest, pressing him down,

hurting him. A shadowed face loomed over the edge of the bed and came down against his stomach.

"No, go away, please."

"Shhh. Shhh."

Something wet, rough, touched his skin.

"Please, no."

The tongue moved down in long strokes.

"Please, no, please," Chucky breathed. His body and legs began to twitch.

Chuck awoke, wrung out. It was the nightmare again. The dream he hoped would never return. The same one, but this time with one difference. The dragon had come without disguise. It was a man.

He lay there for several moments, exhausted. Then he moved his hand down to his stomach. It was wet and sticky.

He felt sick.

THIRTY-ONE

Chuck had hoped to sleep until eight, when Francis and the carpenter would arrive, but at six o'clock he was wide awake, staring at the ceiling. He got up and closed the window. The rain had ended, but clouds hung heavy in the sky.

Standing by the window, he looked down and saw Dawn and Clara coming out of her kitchen door. She was dressed for her morning jog and held Clara on a retractable leash. Together they stopped on the porch and gazed over at his house. When her eyes turned upward toward his bedroom, he ducked back around the corner of the window. After a moment he peered out again and saw her walking down her front walk, stopping every so often to look at his house. When she reached the road, she began jogging off toward the point, with Clara running ahead to chase a blowing leaf or dropping behind to sniff a rock, then catching up again.

Exhaustion pressed on Chuck's head like a vise. His eyes felt swollen and grainy with gunk. Through an emotional fog, he watched Dawn as she disappeared around a curve in the road. He tried to muster a sense of longing, but none came.

He showered and went to the kitchen, keeping the lights off so Dawn wouldn't know he was up. There was enough light from outside to feed Bear and fix his own breakfast.

"You'll just have to wait awhile, big guy, then I'll take you out." Bear looked at him. His master was deviating from the usual routine. Chuck puttered around the kitchen until he heard Francis's panel truck pull into the driveway, then went to the door to meet him.

"Morning!" Francis said.

"Hi."

"We ought to be out there right now," Francis said enthusiastically as he entered. He was followed by Mort, who greeted Chuck with one quick nod of his head. "When I came around the cove I could see seagulls working over the water. That's a sure sign of blues. How 'bout it, Chuck? Want to knock off for the morning and go fishing?"

"You're serious, aren't you?"

"Hell, yes, I'm serious. Work should never interfere with fishing."

"What about the wiring inspector? You said he was coming this morning to check your work so you can tie into the new service."

"Oh, shit. That's right. Well, maybe some other time."

"Yeah—maybe. I want to get this house finished. I'm tired of the clutter and worrying about contractors not showing up."

Francis reacted to the tone of Chuck's voice. "You saying I don't show up when I say I will?"

"No, you do, but some of these other guys . . ."

"Well, I'm outta here today, just as soon as the inspection's over and the service is tied in." Annoyed with Chuck's attitude, he headed for the basement with Mort close behind.

Another truck pulled into the drive. The carpenter got out and headed up the walk. When he saw Chuck standing in the doorway, he called to him. "Hey, Mr. Carver."

"Hello, Sam."

"Did the plumber get the fixtures installed?"

"No. He was here last Friday and said he couldn't do it until you did something with the bracing for the Jacuzzi."

Sam shook his head disgustedly. "He doesn't know what he's talking about. That bracing's all in place. I'll bet the fixtures haven't come in yet." He shrugged. "Well, there's nothing I can do here today."

"Isn't there something else you can work on?"

"Not until the tub's in and the sink and toilet. You better get ahold of that plumber and tell him to get the fixtures in."

"That won't work. You've got to explain the bracing, that it's in place like you said."

"Okay. If I see his truck today, I'll talk to him."

"If you don't see him, then call him. Let's get this damn job done."

The carpenter left.

Dawn came out of her house carrying her briefcase and headed for her car. When she saw Chuck, she stopped. For a moment they looked at each other, then she waved.

"Hi," she called.

"Hi," Chuck said, his hands in his pockets.

They continued looking at each other, Chuck impassive, Dawn hesitantly hopeful. Moments passed. Her smile melted away. Then, blinking sadly, she walked quickly to her car, got in and drove away. Chuck gazed at the empty driveway for a few seconds, then went inside to find Bear and his leash.

Dawn spent the morning at the BMA, and returned to Marblehead after lunch to fill orders for the Air France posters. Several times during the afternoon, she stepped out onto her porch hoping to see Chuck. She could hear him hammering, but he was around on the other side of the house. Once she called to him. The hammering stopped momentarily, then started again. He was purposely ignoring her.

Damn him, she said to herself. So he lost it. So what! Why do men have such a thing about that? Freud surely was wrong when he talked about penis envy. Who wants one? Then, for the first time that day, she laughed to herself. Well, if it's attached to Chuck, that'd be okay.

By evening she decided he'd had enough time to himself. With Clara in tow, she marched up to his front door and knocked. She had to knock three times before he opened the door.

"Come on," she said, "we're going for a walk." Bear was ready. He pitched onto the porch and received a chewing on the neck by Clara.

"I'm pretty busy now. Right in the middle of . . ."

"No. We're going for a walk." She stood squarely in front of him, her hands on her hips.

Chuck shrugged. "I'll get Bear's leash."

They were halfway down the walk when Dawn said, "I appreciate you're having a tough time, but goddamnit, so am I." She whipped him around so he was facing her. "Do you think I was making love to you just because you were handy, the closest guy around? Do you think I'm that kind of woman? Well, I'm not." He looked away. She reached up and pulled his chin back so he was looking at her. "No, you're not getting away. You're going to hear this. Chuck Carver, I love you. I don't make love to someone I don't love."

Bear and Clara sat down and watched the humans.

Chuck looked down at the ground. "I never said you were that kind of a person, and I'm not doing this to hurt you. It's just the opposite. I love you and the best way to show it is to end this right now before I say something that really does hurt you."

"Bullshit. You're acting like a little kid who's embarrassed so you're going to your room and hide."

"Okay, if that's how you feel, then take your dog that way," he gestured with his head toward the point, "and I'll go this way."

"There. You're doing it again."

Bear had had enough sitting. He barked and, together with Clara, began pulling the humans toward the swamp. Chuck trudged along beside Dawn in silence. When they reached the entrance to the swamp and headed down the trail into the woods, they unhooked the dogs. Finally Chuck spoke.

"I don't know how to handle this. When it happened with Michelle I made a mess of it. I said things I didn't mean, cruel things. She left and had every right to do so. I can see it happening all over again."

Dawn said nothing. They came to the rock that overlooked the marsh below, where weeks before they had gazed at pools of water. Now it was a jungle collage of elephant-ear leaves and spear-pointed rushes.

"I should have stopped right at the beginning, but I let it drift along, telling myself I was over my old problem." Then, hopelessly, "It's still there." He turned and, not waiting for Dawn, climbed off the rock and walked down the path.

She caught up to him and took hold of his arm. "Will you please stop and listen." He stopped. "That time in my workroom and last night in my bedroom I gave myself to you, my whole being, and you gave yourself to me. So you took a chance. What do you think I was doing? I was risking falling in love with you and then losing you in the same way I lost Gareth." Her voice broke. "I don't want to lose what we found in each other."

Bear and Clara stood quietly beside them, their heads cocked to one side as they listened. Dawn began sobbing and Chuck pulled her to him, burying her face in his chest. She could feel him crying, too. After a while he eased her back so he could look into her eyes.

"It's because I love you that I've got to do this." Then, abruptly, his face distorted with pain, he grabbed hold of Bear's collar and attached the leash. Chuck turned and marched back toward the road with long strides, pulling Bear so hard his choke collar looked like a hangman's noose. Clara followed for a few feet, then, confused, ran back to her mistress.

"Chuck," Dawn called. "Please. Don't go."

He didn't answer. Dragging Bear behind him, he disappeared around a bend in the trail.

Dawn gazed at the empty path for several seconds until the view was blurred by her tears. She slumped to the ground and pulled up her knees, resting her forehead against them. Clara circled her, whining softly, and began licking her cheek.

"It's okay, little girl," Dawn said, reaching out and cuddling her friend. "I've just lost another man." She sat up and began petting the dog, drawing her hand down Clara's back in long strokes. The dog half-closed her eyes with enjoyment. Finally Dawn stood and looked at the trail Chuck had taken, then, decisively, turned and walked in the opposite direction.

By the time she reached the high point on the other side of the swamp, her tears had dried and her sadness had turned to resentment. In the spring when they had stood together on this spot, the trees were bare. Now she looked out across a gently swaying carpet of green leaves. She wished Charlie were still alive. If he were, she'd tell him a thing or two about his son.

"Charlie," she said under her breath, "your son's a jerk, an idiot. Why is he throwing me over just because he has a problem? Whatever it is, we could solve it together. Why does he have to run off and hide?" Was it something I did? she asked herself. She thought about how he'd carried her into the bedroom, about the intensity of their kisses and the passion of their lovemaking. It was going so well and then, wham, it ended, like someone slamming a door. Whatever it is, she thought, he's got to get it out of his system.

I'll give him a few days, she thought, starting down the path toward home. Let him cool down, then see if he's willing to talk.

THIRTY-TWO

On Saturday morning Chuck called Carl.

"Hi, Chuck. Did you want Viv?"

"No. Actually, I wanted you."

"Oh," he said, surprised.

"Remember when I was at your house for dinner and I talked about selling the house? And I said I'd give you a chance to buy it before I put it on the market?"

"Are you thinking of selling?"

"Maybe."

"Hmm. I thought you were staying. Change your mind?"

"Thinking about it. I've still got my condo in Alexandria. I was pretty well settled there before Charlie left me the house. I think I might like to go back."

"I expect life would be easier without such a big place to take care of."

"That, and I've got lots of my business connections down there."

"When you mentioned the house that night, we said we weren't interested. I think that's still the case, but I'll mention it again to Viv and see what she says."

Fifteen minutes later Chuck's phone rang.

"Chuck, this is Vivian," her voice insistent. "What's going on?"

"You talked to Carl."

"Yes. He said you're planning to sell the house and go back to Alexandria. Is that right?"

"I'm strongly considering it."

"What's happened? Last week you said you were staying."

"I said I was thinking about staying."

"Okay, big brother, tell me what's really going on. Did you and Dawn have a fight?"

"No. Nothing like that."

"But it's got something to do with her, hasn't it? Last week you were on top of the world. You and Dawn both. Now you sound like you've hit bottom."

After a moment's quiet, Chuck said, "It's not working out."

"How can you be so sure? It couldn't have gone bad in a week."

"Viv, I appreciate your concern, but there's a lot more to this than you know. It's stuff I've got to work out myself and I've got no right to burden Dawn with it."

"And how does she feel about that? Have you asked her if she's willing to share the burden?"

Again he was quiet. "No. I didn't need to ask. She already said she was."

"Was?" Vivian snapped. "Was what?"

"She's willing to help me work through this."

Vivian sighed. "Chuck, I haven't known you very long, but in the course of the last two months you've become a real brother to me and Josh and an uncle to my children. Now, in a matter of days, you're willing to throw all of that over?"

"Look, Viv, if it were as simple as you make it sound, I would be an idiot to throw it away. But it's not that simple."

"And you're not going to tell me what it's about, are you?"

"No, not now, anyway."

Vivian was silent. Finally she spoke. "Do me one favor, Chuck. Don't do anything in a hurry. Give it some time. Things have a way of working out."

"The real estate agent was by yesterday. She says the house will be ready to show in a couple of weeks when the papering and painting are done and the floors refinished. I'll have the porch done by then and the master bathroom will be finished this week."

"Have you signed a listing agreement yet?"

"No, I'm waiting until it's ready to be shown."

"Good. Please don't rush into it."

"Okay, I'll agree to that."

"And Chuck, don't leave. I always wanted a big brother and now that I've found one, I don't want to lose you."

"That's what Dawn said—she doesn't want to lose me."

"Yeah, you big jerk. It's because we both love you."

Sunday afternoon Chuck decided to go sailing. He'd done nothing but work at the computer or on the porch decking for six straight days and was fed up with both. He realized he'd had enough when he hit his finger with the hammer and got so mad he threw the hammer across the yard. As fate would have it, he made a direct hit on the boat shed window. Disgusted with himself, he went down to the shed to retrieve his hammer and pick up shards of broken glass. That was when he cut his hand. "Fuck!" he said and returned to the house for a bandage.

With a Band-Aid affixed to his wound, he made a sandwich and opened a bottle of Sam Adams, then went to the front porch to eat his lunch. *Thunderbolt* was rocking gently at its mooring, its mast swaying back and forth as if beckoning him to go sailing. He accepted. Wearing a Red Sox ball cap, a polo shirt with the sleeves cut off and his shorts, he jogged down to the dinghy before he had a chance to change his mind.

The tide was in, so the dinghy was afloat and bobbing in the water below the ring embedded in the rock wall. He released the boat and pulled himself out to the sailboat on the continuous loop between the ring and the mooring. So far so good. He attached the dinghy to the mooring and climbed into the sailboat. Taking a seat on the stern bench, he contemplated his task. He was fairly sure he could handle the boat once he was under way, but putting up the sail and leaving the mooring was something he hadn't done on his own. First off, he thought, I'll remove the bungee cords and the sail covers.

"Hi!" a voice said from shore. He turned to see Brian standing on the rock by the ring.

"Hi," Chuck called across the water. "I thought you were up in Maine."

"I was. Got back this morning. Going sailing?"

"Yeah." Damnit, he said to himself, I wanted to go out alone. Oh well. "Want to come along?"

"Sure."

Chuck untied the dinghy's painter from the mooring and Brian began pulling the line to get the little boat to shore. In a couple of minutes the dinghy was back and Brian was boarding the sailboat.

"Thanks for asking me. I was getting bored."

"Have you sailed this before?" Chuck asked.

"A lot of times."

"Alone?"

"Never alone, but I've taken it out with a friend when Charlie wasn't with us."

"I may need your help," Chuck said, "but I want to try to do it alone so I'll learn how."

"Okay, I'll keep my mouth shut." Brian sat on the bench and watched Chuck finish uncovering the sail. That completed, he went to the mast and sorted out the halyard that raised the mainsail. Finding it, he uncleated it and began tentatively raising the main. When all seemed to be in order, he pulled the halyard rapidly hand over hand until the sail was all the way up. A fair breeze immediately billowed the sail and the boat began moving off on a close-haul tack until it reached the end of its painter, which was tied to the mooring. With a sudden jerk, the boat came to a halt, spun around and started off on the opposite tack.

"What the hell's happening?" Chuck yelled.

Brian sat calmly in the stern gripping the gunwale as the boat veered first to one side, then to the other.

"I give up," Chuck shouted. "Help me."

As the boat crossed into the wind, the instant the sail luffed, Brian reached behind him and unclipped the boom from the back stay. Then he uncleated the sheet. Immediately the boom swung outward, spilling the wind from the sail, and the boat stopped dancing on its mooring.

"Thanks," Chuck exclaimed. "Guess I don't know as much as I thought I did."

"I'll bet you never forget to unclip the boom and release the sheet, though."

Chuck laughed. "You're right about that. What's next?"

"Take the jib sheet and unspool the jib, then unhook your painter from the mooring."

Chuck performed these tasks, then ran back to the stern, pulled in the mainsheet and they were under way.

Beyond the island at the head of the cove, they entered open water. While Chuck practiced various maneuvers, Brian sat on the bench by the cabin hatch and watched the lobster buoys pass by.

"How was Maine?" Chuck asked without taking his eyes from the sail.

"Okay."

"I thought your mom said you were staying longer."

"I was supposed to, but Mike's cousins arrived unannounced. Not enough beds. Mom came up yesterday and drove me home this morning."

At the mention of his mother, Chuck felt a stab of pain.

Brian continued, "She said she'd seen a real estate person going into your house."

Chuck avoided looking at Brian. "Uh-huh. Harkens Realty."

"So, are you gonna sell it?"

"Probably."

"And move away?"

"Uh-huh."

Brian said nothing, just looked out across the water. Several minutes later he asked, "When?"

"Moving?"

"Yeah."

"It takes two or three months at the earliest to sell a house, so it won't be soon."

"That's still pretty soon." He was quiet for a moment, then said, "I had this idea." He looked back at Chuck. "I was thinking that if you stayed on here, I was going to ask Mom if I could transfer back to Marblehead High School and live here. Then when Mom was away on trips, you could look in on me or maybe I could even," he hesitated, "bunk in with you."

Chuck closed his eyes and took a deep breath. "If I were going to be here I wouldn't mind at all having you stay with me. I don't think it's in the cards, though."

Brian leaned back against the edge of the cockpit and, stretching out his legs, stared at his feet. He didn't speak again until Chuck said it was time to go in.

"Before we do," Brian asked, "do you know how to come up to a mooring?"

"I haven't done it myself, but I watched Josh and your mom do it."

"Okay. See that lobster buoy over there?" Chuck nodded. "Let's pretend it's the mooring. Get downwind of it and tack toward it."

"Okay." Moments later he was approaching the buoy.

"Now just before you get there, head directly into the wind, luff the sail and let the momentum of the boat carry you up to the buoy."

Chuck gave it a try and shot past the buoy, missing it by ten feet. "This is harder than I thought. I'll try again."

It took him six attempts before he nosed *Thunderbolt* up to the buoy.

"Good," Brian said. "Now try it again."

"Tell you what. Why don't you take it in this time and when I go out again, I'll practice on lobster buoys?"

Brian took the tiller and brought the boat smartly up to the mooring. Together they furled the sails and put on the covers.

"Don't forget to clip the boom to the back stay," Brian said, "and cleat the sheet."

"Aye, aye, sir." Chuck laughed.

They pulled the dinghy to shore and tied the painter to the ring. On the way to their houses, Brian said, "I hope you change your mind about moving."

"Thanks, Brian, but I'm afraid I've got to go." He put his hand on Brian's shoulder. "Can we still be friends, though?"

"Yeah, but it won't be like it was."

All day Wednesday the house was filled with the sound of floor sanders and the fine dust of powdered oak. It was after two o'clock when Chuck came down from the study, picked up his mail from the porch mailbox and went to the kitchen. He heated some left-over beef stroganoff that he'd bought in a family-sized frozen package for yesterday's meal, and took his lunch and the mail to the relative peace and quiet of the back porch. Flipping through the mail while he ate he removed a letter from Harkens Realty. Charlotte Grisom was thanking him for his interest in listing the house with Harkens and would call him for an appointment to finalize the listing. As he read the letter, he realized he'd dreamed about the agent the night before, except it was somebody else, a face he couldn't place. She'd come to the house to show it to a prospective buyer. He couldn't remember the rest of the dream, only that it left a bad feeling in his stomach. Maybe it was the double portion of beef stroganoff he'd eaten for last night's dinner.

As he ate, he flipped through the rest of mail, mostly circulars, until he came to a letter addressed to Dawn Ireland. The envelope had French stamps and a Paris return address. Mailman made a mistake, he said to himself.

Chuck hadn't talked to Dawn for a week and a half. They'd nodded to each other and waved as they picked up their morning newspapers or when they were heading to their cars, but there'd been no conversation. Each occasion was a test of his will to end the relationship or at least cool it down. And each time required him to cauterize yet another level of the love he felt for her. He looked at the letter and decided the safest thing to do was slip it into her mailbox for her to find the next day.

It didn't work out that way. As he was crossing the lawn to her house, she saw him from her back deck and waved. Taking a deep breath and resolving to hand her the letter and depart, he headed in her direction.

"The mailman left this letter at my house," he said, climbing the steps to the deck. Dawn was sitting at a table beneath a large sun umbrella reading her mail. "It's addressed to you."

"Thanks." She was dressed in a loose-fitting blouse and shorts and had her hair tied in a bun. "How about a glass of lemonade?"

"I ought to be getting back," he stammered.

"Chuck," she said, shaking her head, "you're making a federal case out of this. I know you want to cool things off between us, but it's getting to be an obsession for you. Look, we're neighbors. We live side by side and we're going to run into each other a lot. I promise I won't bite." She reached out her hand to him. "Let's be friends."

He took her hand, touching it lightly for only an instant. He wanted to tell her that the wall he was building was against his own emotions, not her. But she knew this. He'd told her already and the subject was getting boring. Maybe this whole charade of avoidance was boring. It certainly was for him. He slumped his shoulders, sighed and sat in a chair across the table from Dawn.

"Good," she smiled reassuringly. "Relax. I'll be right back with the lemonade."

While she was gone he tried to ease the muscles in his jaw and around his mouth, but couldn't. Dawn returned with a pitcher and another glass that she filled with the pink liquid.

"Thanks for taking Brian sailing last Sunday," she said cheerfully. "He was disappointed his stay with Mike was cut short."

"Actually, he saved my neck." Chuck managed to squeeze out a smile. "Did he tell you?"

"He mentioned you tried to sail the boat while it was still tied to the mooring."

"Then he told you. But that's not all. He taught me how to come up to mooring. We practiced on a lobster buoy that I missed by ten feet. He brought us in. Imagine. If I'd managed to get out there alone, I'd probably still be out there sailing forever, like the Flying Dutchman."

They laughed, and some of the tension in Chuck's face gave way.

Is it possible we can be just friends? Chuck wondered. Dawn broke the silence.

"Brian said you're going to move."

Chuck dropped his eyes to the table. "We talked about it. I said I was putting the house up for sale."

"He was pretty upset when he told me."

Chuck thought about telling her that Brian had had hopes of transferring back to Marblehead High and staying with him when Dawn was traveling, but decided not to. It would open up subjects he wanted kept closed.

"I saw the Harkens real estate agent come by again last week."

"Yeah. She wants to put it on the market as soon as the painting and wallpapering are done." Then, trying to lighten the conversation, he went on, "If dreams mean anything, I don't think I'll have much luck with Harkens Realty. Last night I dreamed the agent came by with someone to see the house." He grinned and Dawn smiled slightly, joining him in his attempt to change the subject. "We went into the front hall, and," he hesitated as more and more of the dream came back to him, "and there was this big door leading from the entrance hall to the rest of the house." As he spoke, his grin became twisted. "I opened it and we went into this room that was dark. We could feel the boards crumbling under our feet. There were cobwebs hanging from the ceiling and the walls were caving in." He wanted to stop, but the memories of the dream pulled him on. "It stank, like something had died." He stopped and blinked his eyes.

"God, Chuck, what an awful dream," Dawn said sympathetically.

Chuck leaned back in his chair and forced a laugh. "Must have been something I ate last night."

He could tell by the look in her eyes that she didn't think so.

By Friday of that week the floor refinishers had completed their work in both the living and dining rooms. The furniture remained stacked in the entrance hall and kitchen while the polyurethane was drying. Around two that afternoon, Francis carried his tools down from the master bathroom, squeezing past the chairs and sofa piled near the entrance, and met Chuck on the porch.

"That's it. All finished," he said. "Jacuzzi's hooked up."

"You've done a good job."

"Thanks."

"I'm sorry I got a little hot under the collar last week."

"That's okay," Francis said with a shrug. "Figured you had a lot on your mind."

"I do. I've been thinking I might go ahead and put the house on the market."

"Move?"

"Yup. Back to Alexandria."

"Leaving paradise, huh?"

Chuck laughed. "You could say that."

"I can see selling the house if it's too big for you, but leaving Marblehead—big mistake."

They were standing at the top of the steps looking across Quiet Cove. Overhead, dark clouds were rolling in from the northeast on a freshening breeze and the air was heavy with humidity.

"A person's gotta do what he's gotta do," Chuck said.

"Uh-huh, and a lotta people have missed out on a lotta fun because of bullshit sayings like that. No offense, of course."

"You do speak your mind, don't you."

"It's only because I like you, and if you leave I'll be losing a fishing buddy."

"That's right," Chuck grinned, "you wouldn't have had a fish to take home if I hadn't given you one of mine."

"See why I want you to stay." He grew quiet as he studied the sky. "Have you checked your mooring for the sailboat? They're calling for a real nor'easter tonight."

"No. I hooked up the painter to the mooring when I came in, but what else should I check?"

"I'd check to be sure your lines are well attached on both the boat and the buoy, and then I'd check the chain beneath the mooring that goes down to the anchor."

"Never thought of that."

"This is going to be some storm. They're saying gusts of maybe sixty knots."

"Thanks for the tip. And Francis, I really appreciate the job you did."

"Just put your thanks on a check when you get my bill," he laughed and headed for his truck.

THIRTY-THREE

Like a giant waterwheel, the counterclockwise wind of the low-pressure area centered two hundred miles off the coast of New England scooped moisture from the ocean and dumped it in buckets on the coast of Massachusetts. Dark cumulonimbus clouds as low as seven hundred feet tumbled inland as winds increased to forty knots. Ocean waves shouldered their way into Quiet Cove between the point and the island and broke against the rock wall next to the road. A hundred feet from shore *Thunderbolt* rode the waves, its bow pointed valiantly into the wind.

After Francis left, Chuck had gone through the house closing windows, then returned to his study to finish a project he'd started that morning. His plan was to check on the sailboat later that evening. At five o'clock, when he looked out his window, he was shocked at how quickly the storm had materialized. He ran from the house to the beach, not bothering about a rain jacket, and began untying the dinghy.

"Can I help?" Brian shouted as he ran across the lawn toward the road.

Chuck looked up and smiled. He liked Brian's willingness to face challenge. "Hop in." In two seconds the boy was there and they were shuttling the little craft through the waves toward the sailboat. When they reached the mooring the dinghy bumped and banged against the sailboat as each vessel fought for a place amidst the waves. Chuck held the rail while Brian climbed aboard, then

225

he followed. They sat on the bench, catching their breath and laughing at their soaking wet clothes.

"I'm going to tie the dinghy to the stern of the sailboat so it won't hit the boat," Chuck said.

"Good idea."

With that accomplished, the banging stopped and they were able to consider what needed to be done to prepare *Thunderbolt* for the storm.

"Francis said to check the line from the boat to the mooring and also the chain from the mooring to the anchor."

"While you're doing that," Brian shouted against the wind, "I'll make sure the cabin vents are closed."

Brain disappeared through the hatch into the cabin, then immediately reappeared. "Here," he called, holding a life vest. "Put this on. I've got one for me, too."

"Thanks." Chuck donned the vest and began inching his way to the bow. It was like riding a bucking bronco. Four-foot waves pitched the bow upward, instantly dropping it back down into the trough. He found the painter securely cleated to the bow and passing through the guide. Then, lying flat, he leaned over the bow, catching wave after wave in the face, and pulled on the line until he could reach the ring on the mooring. That line was reefed through a stainless steel clip that was hooked to the ring. Everything seemed to be in order. As for the chain from the mooring to the anchor, there was no way he was going to be able to check it in this sea.

Brian emerged from the cabin and replaced the hatch as Chuck started back across the forward deck. Feeling more at ease with the boat's pitching, Chuck stood up and steadied himself on the forestay. Anticipating the rise and fall of the deck, he reached for the shroud on the port side of the mast. A sudden roll of the boat to port caused his hand to miss the shroud, and he fell into the water. Immediately his head bobbed to the surface, his body buoyed by the life vest.

Brian grabbed the rail with his right hand and leaned over the side, reaching for his shipmate. He caught Chuck's hand and pulled him up to the side, where he was able to climb in.

Chuck rolled into the cockpit, shaking his head to get the water out of his eyes. "Thanks for the hand." Then, laughing, "Hey, that was fun."

"Can I do it now?" Brian shouted.

"It wasn't that much fun. Let's finish up here and go back. What else should we do?"

"If you'll make sure the boom is secure and the halyard cleated, I'll check the turnbuckles."

"Aye, aye, sir!" Chuck said, pleased with the way Brian took charge.

Five minutes later they were climbing aboard the dinghy and shuttling to shore. That was when they noticed Dawn, wearing her yellow slicker and sou'wester hat, standing on the rock wall. Ten feet from shore, they could hear her.

"You idiots. You could have gotten yourselves killed out there."

"Naw," Brian called from the boat, "we got our life vests on."

"I saw you fall in, Chuck. You could have hit your head and been knocked unconscious."

They got out and tied up the dinghy. Chuck said, "Actually, it was fun."

Dawn shook her head, disgusted. "Well, come up to the house and get out of those wet clothes." In spite of the warm air, both were shivering from the cold water.

Back at the house, Dawn gave Chuck a cotton blanket and sent him into the bathroom to change out of his wet clothes. Brian went up to his room and returned five minutes later wearing slippers and a bathrobe. Chuck was sitting at the kitchen table wrapped in the blanket, his graying hair and beard tightly curled and his cheeks still red from the cold water.

"You should have been with us, Mom," Brian declared excitedly. "You'd have loved it."

"I couldn't have done it without Brian." The boy smiled and went up to Chuck. They exchanged a high-five. "He saved my life."

"You see?" Dawn said. "It was dangerous."

"Naw," Brain laughed, "he's just kidding."

Dawn poured three fingers of rum into a glass for Chuck and took some for herself, then made a cup of cocoa for her son. She watched the two of them go on about their adventure as if it had been a mid-ocean rescue from a sinking ship.

"You guys must be starved," Dawn said. "How about some dinner?"

Chuck stood, pulling the blanket around him. "Thanks, but I'd better head home and feed Bear."

Dawn wasn't going to argue. Just getting him into the house for a drink was an accomplishment.

"Mind if I wear your blanket home?"

"Be my guest, but don't forget your wet clothes."

At the door when Chuck said good-bye he longed to fold Dawn inside his blanket and whisk her through the storm to his house. In his mind he could feel her body pressed against his, smell the freshness of her hair, kiss her eyes, taste her tongue. But even before he reached his house the fantasy began to dissolve, as all his good fantasies did, transforming itself into a vile, dirty picture.

He reached his porch and, rushing inside, slammed the door against the evil thoughts that pursued him.

Bear met him with tail wagging, pushing against his legs with one hundred and forty pounds of love. Chuck petted him gratefully. "I'll bet you're hungry." Still in the blanket, he went directly to the kitchen and prepared the dog's dinner. He took Bear's dinner bowl down the steps to the garage and opened the garage door.

"Eat your dinner, then go out and take care of your business. I'm not going out again tonight."

Chuck went to his bedroom, put on a bathrobe and came back downstairs. With the TV tuned to the Weather Channel, he heated up a can of clam chowder and warmed a loaf of sourdough bread, then ate his dinner. Bear joined him just in case there was a scrap for him. The weatherperson said to expect sixty-knot winds and coastal flooding especially in the early morning hours when it was high tide. Chuck wondered what that would mean for him, but decided the house had been there for decades and hadn't been washed away yet. At ten o'clock, he and Bear went up to his third-floor bedroom. Bear stretched out on the floor and Chuck climbed into bed.

It was a perfect night for sleeping. The rain hammered against the window and the wind howled through the trees. His only regret was that he couldn't open the window even a crack because it was on the northeast side of the house. It wasn't long before he fell asleep.

He was awakened suddenly by a brilliant flash of lightning and an instantaneous crash of thunder. He ran to the window to see one of his maples in the front yard split down the middle as if cleaved by a giant ax. The ground around the trunk was smoking. It had been hit by lightning. Bear, who had been asleep on the bed, was now standing by his master at the window. From the streetlight where the road met the beach, Chuck could see breakers roaring over the stone wall, sweeping across the road and into his yard. Already there was a sizable pool of water at the southeast side of his lot next to the road. To the left, the yard in front of Dawn's house, situated on a rise, had no standing water. The limbs of trees were whipping so violently in the wind that he wondered how they stayed attached. In fact, several had been ripped free and were blowing across his lawn.

"So this is what a sixty-knot wind looks like," he said to Bear. "We're lucky to be inside."

Chuck strained his eyes to see if *Thunderbolt* was holding fast to its mooring, but the rain was so heavy he could see only blurred objects pitching wildly in the rough waters. He hoped one of them was his boat.

Wide awake, he returned to his bed and twisted on the switch at the base on his Bugs Bunny lamp. The sassy little creature with the broken arm grinned a bucktooth grin from beneath the shade. Chuck smiled back at his old friend, then pulled himself up, leaned against the headboard and listened to the storm. He looked around for the book he'd been reading, then remembered he'd left it downstairs. Well, he certainly wasn't going to go down two flights of stairs to get it. Letting his eyes roam around the room, he noticed the stack of children's books that he'd piled on the bookcase after Vivian's kids had knocked them to the floor. He picked up the one on top.

"*The Gingerbread Boy*," he said to Bear. "My favorite book when I was a kid." Smiling, he quoted the line, "Run! run! as fast as you can! You can't catch me, I'm the Gingerbread Man!" As he spoke the rhyme, a sense of uneasiness came over him. Again he heard

his father's voice on the answering machine say, "Catch you later."
Chuck shivered.

He began turning the pages of the book. The colorful pictures
had been indelibly printed in his memory: the farmer and his wife
baking the gingerbread boy, the boy coming to life and racing from
the farmhouse shouting, "You can't catch me." Even before he
turned the next page, he knew what was coming: first it was the
cow who wanted to eat him, then the horse. The cocky little gingerbread boy strutted his naked two-dimensional body in front of
them, teasing them to eat him. Then, just in time, he'd dash away
shouting the familiar couplet.

Chuck stopped reading. He looked down at his own naked
body. Suddenly a memory popped into his mind. His friend Bruce
was showing him pictures from one of his dad's magazines, dirty
pictures of a man and a woman doing it. He knew he was being
bad and wondered if his mother would be able to read his dirty
thoughts when she looked into his eyes. The memory faded, and
he picked up the book again.

He turned the page. The little cookie boy was enticing the farmhands with tantalizing gestures. Opened-mouthed and leering,
they jumped and tumbled over each other to catch him and eat
him. But the gingerbread boy laughed in their faces and ran down
the road. "You can't catch me," he shouted, "I'm the Gingerbread
Man!"

Chuck closed his eyes. He could feel the book again carrying
him back to his childhood. Rising out of the drumming of the rain
on the roof and the howling of the wind, he could hear voices.
Two groups of boys were yelling at each other in a corner of the
playground. "Suck my dick, you fairy!" a member of one group
shouted. And then someone in his crowd grabbed his crotch and
pumped it lasciviously. "Eat me! Eat me, you cocksucker!"

Chuck pulled the sheet up to cover his nakedness.

Disgusted with the images the book was arousing, he closed it
and started to put it back on the shelf. His hand reached for the
bookcase but stopped halfway, not wanting to let go of the book.
He tried to push it further, but his hand resisted. Despairing,
Chuck dropped back against the headboard and opened the book

to the page where the farmhands are lusting to eat the gingerbread boy.

He turned that page.

Now the saucy little boy was meeting the fox and trying to tempt him to join the chase. But Mr. Fox says he's not interested in chasing him and assures him he has no intention of hurting him. In the background, the people and animals are closing in. The sly fox offers to help him. "Climb upon my back and I'll take you to the other side of the river." The naked boy, trusting Mr. Fox, climbs first on his back and then onto his head.

Chuck raised his eyes from the book and gazed into the shadows on the opposite wall. He was covered with sweat. Throwing back the sheet, he took a deep breath and tried to relax.

A gust of wind hit the side of the house like a wrecking ball, strong enough that he felt the jolt as he lay on the bed. The house creaked and creaked again as the powerful winds beat and battered the shingled single.

Or was it the creaking of the stairs outside his door, the stairs that led up from the second floor, where his father's bedroom was? He could always tell when someone was coming. The stairs would let him know. Like they did each time his father had come to his room those last few weeks before his mom and dad had the fight in his room.

He was near the end of the book. Two more pages to go. Why did he hesitate to turn the page? Why was his vision beginning to blur? Why was he shaking?

He turned the page.

Mr. Fox, with a flip of his head, is throwing the boy into the air. The fox's mouth is open wide and his eyes are longing to eat the boy. Above him, the gingerbread boy's naked arms and legs are spread out wide.

Between his legs was a penis, large and hard, penciled in and smudged by an attempt to erase it.

Chuck looked at the drawing. Remarkably, his agitation subsided. For over thirty years his mind had fought to block the memory. But the memory had won. It was a relief to surrender.

"There it is," Chuck said calmly, "right where I drew it."

Suddenly, everything went black.

Chuck lay in darkness for a moment, then got up and went to the rain-streaked window. The streetlight was out. A power failure.

He returned to his bed and stretched out.

He didn't need the light. He stared into the blackness and saw it all. Scenes so dirty, so terrifying, that he had hid them from himself, blotted them from his memory, for all these years.

It started a few weeks before I drew the penis. Dad had come home from a trip, one of his flights to France. It was very late. He and Mom had come into my room. There was a crack of light as the hall light shone into my room. I closed my eyes and pretended to be asleep.

"Isn't he handsome?" Mom said.

"He's beautiful," Dad responded in a voice so low I could hardly hear him.

They left.

Later that night I heard the stairs creaking. The door opened. There was no light now from the hall, only a dim glow coming from outside the window. He crossed to my bed. Mom wasn't there. With my eyes tightly shut, I could feel his hand stroking my hair. He whispered, "Shhh, shhh," and for several minutes traced the lines of my face and neck with his fingers. He'd been drinking. I could smell it on his breath. He'd never done this before. It was scary, but also oddly enticing.

A few days later when Dad arrived home, he came into my room again in the middle of the night. Again I could smell liquor. Pretending to be asleep, I let him stroke my hair and face as he'd done the first night. But his fingers continued down my chest to my stomach. "Shhh, shhh," he said softly. I tried to keep my breathing even, like I was still asleep. Why was he doing this? He'd never touched me this way before. It felt wrong. But I kept quiet. His hand made wider and wider circles on my stomach until his fingers brushed my penis. I gasped and all he said was, "Shhh." After a while, he left.

Each time he returned home, he came into my room. On nights when he was due back, I would lie awake in bed, terrified. I waited for the sound of the creaking stairs and when I heard them I shivered with fear. Now he didn't bother with stroking my hair and face. He'd begin at my chest, then untie my pajama bottoms and play with me. "Shhh," he would say, pressing down with his right hand on my chest so I couldn't get up if I wanted to. I gave up pretending I was asleep because I couldn't stop gasping when he touched me. He'd keep it up until I got hard. When I did, I could hear him breathing heavily. Then he'd leave.

One night, holding me down with his right hand, he played with me with his left until I was hard. Then I could feel him take me in his mouth. I didn't dare say a word. I was too terrified. I wanted him to stop, but it felt so good I wanted him to keep doing it. He moved his hand from my chest, and I could tell from the shaking of the bed that he was jacking off. He let go of me with his mouth and groaned. Then he left.

In the morning, when' I'd go to school, he was still asleep. I was thankful for that. I didn't want to face my father for fear he would punish me or say something to Mom. When I'd come home from school, if he was there, he'd say hello as if he'd just gotten back. I'd say hello and run to my room.

The last night, the night I drew the penis on the gingerbread boy, I heard the stairs creak for the last time. He came to the bed and didn't waste time with a lot of stomach rubbing. He bent over me and began sucking me while his hand pumped hard on himself.

Suddenly the hall light came on and the door flew open. Mom rushed into the room yelling and screaming. I turned away feeling guilty and afraid because she saw me there and saw what Dad was doing. I heard the lamp crash down on Dad's head and heard her struggling with him, pulling him toward the door. She kept on hitting him and pushing him all the way down the stairs. I rolled over. The hall light was still on and I could see Bugs Bunny lying in pieces on the floor. Downstairs I could hear them fighting and shouting. I pressed my hands over my ears and put my head under the pillow, but I could still hear them.

That was when I picked up The Gingerbread Boy and started reading to see if that would shut them out. When I came to the last page, I took a pencil and drew a penis on the boy, just before he was about to fall into the fox's mouth and be eaten. Suddenly it was quiet. The fighting stopped. I looked at the book and, feeling guilty, tried to erase what I'd drawn.

But I made a mess of it.

THIRTY-FOUR

C huck lay on his back, the bed sheet askew. He felt something heavy on his left arm. Opening one eye, he gazed directly into Bear's brown eyes. The dog's paw lay across his left arm. Chuck had learned that when Bear gave you the paw, he was serious.

"What's up, big guy? Hungry?" Chuck said as he raised his head to look at the clock. The blank face of the digital clock informed him the electricity was still off. He flopped back on his pillow and raised his right arm to look at his wrist watch. "Eight-thirty. No wonder you're hungry."

He got out of bed feeling distraught and uneasy, but unable to put his finger on what was bothering him. He recalled listening to the storm and the explosive lightning strike, but there was something else from last night. He tried to focus, to remember, but his mind felt encased in a lead shroud. "It'll probably come to me," he said to Bear. He put on his bathrobe, and let Bear lead him down the stairs.

At the front door they stopped and Chuck looked out. It was still raining and the wind was blowing. Whitecaps churned across the cove. And there it was, *Thunderbolt*, still tugging at its mooring. Thank God, he thought. Scanning the rest of the cove he saw a sailboat on its side, sitting high and dry atop the rock wall, its mast bent. And, in the middle of the road, a fiberglass dinghy wrenched in two like a piece of torn cardboard. Unbelievable, he thought, and headed for the kitchen.

He put two cups of dry dog food into Bear's bowl and began to open a can of Alpo. The electric can opener was buzzless. "Oh, yeah," he said aloud.

"Dry food it is, my friend."

He carried Bear's bowl down to the garage and noticed he'd left the door open the night before. A large puddle covered the floor, but the electric door was open, which meant he could get the car out.

"Eat your breakfast and take a walk around the yard, then come on upstairs."

Chuck felt numb, his brain shut down from overload. He dressed grudgingly, then came downstairs and rounded up Bear.

"Come on. Get in the truck. I gotta get some breakfast." As he drove down the driveway to the road he noticed that the pool of seawater in the southeast corner of his yard had receded, but gravel and debris covered the lawn and road. The maple that had been hit by lightning lay forlornly across the wet grass. He looked back at his and Dawn's houses. They appeared to have survived the storm. Driving slowly past the marooned sailboat and the wrecked dinghy, he marveled at the power of the storm.

He passed two Marblehead Electric trucks, the crews of which were busy removing fallen tree branches and restringing wires. By the time he reached downtown, he noticed lights on in the houses he passed. The outage must have occurred only in his part of town.

Chuck stopped for breakfast at the Shipyard Galley on Atlantic Street, patronized by fishermen, town employees, tradespeople, and other locals who'd discovered its good food. Chuck listened to the conversations going on around him. Was it bigger than the No Name storm of 1992? How much longer will it last? Is the road across the causeway to the Neck still closed? He ordered blueberry pancakes with a side of bacon and saved half the bacon for Bear. Back in the car, the dog ate his share of the breakfast and Chuck started the engine. He began driving, not knowing nor caring where he was going.

Gradually, snatches of the buried memories he'd uncovered the night before began to bubble to the surface of his consciousness. He recalled hearing the stairs creaking and remembered the fear he'd felt. He'd catch a picture of the man in the shadows, his father, coming into his bedroom and . . . touching him. Then he'd lose it for a while.

For no particular reason, he drove through Salem on highway 1-A heading toward Beverly. When he got to Route 127, he followed the coast road, stopping occasionally along the way to look at storm damage. There was only one thing of which he was certain: he didn't want to go home.

In Gloucester he parked by the Gloucester Fisherman statue, put up the hood on his slicker and took Bear for a walk down the quay.

Was I imagining all that last night? he asked himself. When I was ten, did Dad really come into my room and do those things to me? Chuck wrestled with that thought for a while, feeling his stomach turn with disgust.

How could a father do that to a son? How could any adult do that to a child? But it must have happened. I knew I drew that penis on the gingerbread boy. I can remember doing it. And the broken lamp Mom smashed over Dad's head. No, I'm sure I'm not making it up.

His pants were soaking wet from the penetrating rain, so he turned and headed back toward the car. They drove through Gloucester, following Route 133 back to highway 1-A. Still not ready to go home, he turned north and drove to Newburyport, then out to Plum Island. The waves should be huge out there, he thought. He parked near the mouth of the Merrimack River and trudged across the sand to the ocean's edge. Here, with no obstructions to diminish the power of the storm, waves twelve feet high crashed onto the beach. Even Bear, who loved the surf, wouldn't venture near those waves. Chuck stood there letting the driving rain hit his face like a cleansing shower, but it couldn't dissolve the revulsion he felt inside.

Other thoughts came to mind. He'd read that sometimes when a father abuses one of his children, the mother is a silent accomplice, not for what she does, but for ignoring what's going on. Chuck shook his head. That didn't apply to Mom, he decided. She bashed Dad on the head and took me to Rochester.

Bear grew tired of standing in one spot and woofed. "Okay," Chuck said, "let's go back to the car." As they returned across the sand, another thought came to him. The newspapers and TV were filled with stories of people accused of child abuse who tried to excuse their actions by claiming they themselves had been abused as children. Did that mean Dad had been abused when he was a boy? Chuck shrugged. Who knows, or cares, for that matter?

Suddenly, he stopped dead in his tracks. "Christ!" he said aloud, "Does that mean that I might someday abuse a child?" He tried to laugh it off, but the thought had gripped his brain and wouldn't let go. Frantically his mind began to run wild. Was this why he liked Brian, why he liked to have him around, why he liked to sail with him? The idea of touching Brian as his father had touched him filled Chuck with so much revulsion he felt nauseous. He stood there, bent over, holding his stomach with the rain beating against his back. Finally, the blessed numbness returned and the possibility of that particular degradation faded. They reached the car and got in. Both were wet through, and quarts of water ran from Bear's thick fur onto the car seat.

"Let's see if we can find a McDonald's. I think we could both use a Big Mac."

Chuck drove through Newburyport and headed for I-95. Just before he reached the interstate there was a McDonald's on the left. He pulled in and parked. "Stay here. I'll be right back."

As he waited in line at the counter, still another thought came to him: What about Josh?

His turn came at the counter. "Two Big Macs, please."

The next question hung in the air like the menu board over the counter. *Had Dad abused Josh as he had me?*

Dawn and Brian had cereal and cold bagels for breakfast. When they finished, she carried the dishes to the sink and happened to glance out the window to see Chuck and Bear drive away in the pickup truck. Bet he's off to buy a hot breakfast, she thought. I wish I were going with him.

"How long is this cruddy weather going to last?" Brian moaned.

"Well, it's a nor'easter and they can last as long as three days.

It'll probably start clearing up tonight or tomorrow." She turned to look at her son. "What are you doing today?"

"In this weather?" he said dismally. "Nothing. Maybe get a movie and watch it."

"Better wait for the electricity to come back on."

"Oh. Yeah."

"I was going to write letters today and now I can't. I've got an idea," she said. "Let's walk to Fort Sewall. It'll be high tide in about two hours. I'd like to see the waves."

Brian agreed the waves would be "phat," so they put on their rain gear, hooked up Clara and started out. Brian had been out earlier to check on *Thunderbolt,* so he was eager to show his mom the derelict sailboat and the smashed dinghy. Dawn was saddened to see all the destruction.

"We must have done a good job securing Chuck's boat," he said.

"You usually do a good job."

Ahead they could see the twirling yellow lights of the Marble-head Electric trucks. A man in a bucket was working high over-head on a transformer and two other men and a woman were standing by a huge spool of wire, feeding it into a pulley connected to the pole.

Dawn asked them, "How long before we'll have power again?"

"We're about done here," said one of the men. "Would of been done sooner if there hadn't been so many tree limbs across the wires."

"Some storm, isn't it?" Dawn said.

"It's a good one, all right, but I've seen worse."

Soon they came to the road leading over to Love's Cove just below the fort. The road was flooded and a crowd of people were watching the huge waves crash into the seawall, sending geysers of spray as high as the light poles. Each time the wave erupted the people oohed and ahhed like spectators at a fireworks display.

"Wow!" Brian exclaimed. "Did you see that one?"

"That was something," Dawn agreed.

Clara, however, was rigid with fear. There was too much excite-ment and too many people. Tugging at the end of her leash, she'd dart first one way and then another.

"I'd better take her home," Dawn said. "Poor thing. She scares so easily."

"I want to see what's going on over there," Brian said. Another group of people had gathered halfway up the block. "Can Clara stand just a little more?"

"We'll give it a try."

They circled through a parking lot and came out on the street across from a house and a large condominium building situated above the harbor. Each time a wave crashed against them, tons of water shot through the three-foot gap separating the two buildings and exploded onto the street with a shaft of water fifteen feet high. Brian was out there in a minute, challenging the wave and dashing back to safety just in time.

After a while he ran back to his mother. "Let's get Chuck. He should see this."

"I saw him drive away earlier. Anyway," Dawn said uneasily, "I think he wants to keep his distance."

Brian thought about that for a second and said, "Yeah, maybe you're right. Like last night when he left suddenly."

"Uh-huh. We'd better take Clara home." They'd walked about two blocks when Dawn added, "He's going through a hard time. I'm not sure what it's about."

"Like you did last winter?"

"That was hard, all right, but it's not the same thing."

"Is that why he's talking about selling the house and moving?"

"I think so."

"You like him, don't you?"

Her voice wavered. "Yes, I do."

"So do I."

Walking up their driveway, they could see that their kitchen light was on.

"Oh, good!" Dawn said. "We've got electricity." She went inside and immediately made herself a cup of coffee. Brian hopped on his bike and headed for Chet's Video.

The rain had slackened to a drizzle and the wind had calmed to about twenty knots when Chuck and Bear returned home in the middle of the afternoon. Chuck parked in the drive so he could sweep the puddle of water out of the garage, then went upstairs and reset clocks and timers.

The house was dark and musty, much like his mood. He'd spent the entire day thinking about last night's realizations and their possible consequences, and he was tired of it. But try as he might, he couldn't put the matter out of his mind. There was something still buried in his memory, some horror so disgusting that his conscious mind refused to look at it.

That night when he went to bed, the rain had stopped, so he opened his window wide. Looking out, he could see stars peeking through gaps in the clouds. The nor'easter had passed, but the storm was not over for Chuck.

THIRTY-FIVE

Chuck slept fitfully, dreaming again about the house with rotting rooms that smelled of putrid flesh. Frantically he tried to free himself from the dream by raising his head and fixing his eyes on the window. When the rectangle of dim light skewed into the shape of a grotesque funhouse mirror, he threw back the sheet and went to the window. The moon peeked in and out of broken clouds that scudded the sky and reflected off the can that was half of the tin can telephone. Was this a dream, or was he awake?

He stared at the can. *If I can pick it up, I must be awake.* He touched it. The metal was cool to his fingers. Cautiously he lifted the can. The white string trailed down the side of the house and arched into the yard where his friend Bruce McIntyre lived. No, he thought, I mean where Brian lives. Was it Bruce or was it Brian? It must have been Bruce. He's the one I talk to. With his left hand steadying himself on the sill, his right hand brought the can to his mouth.

"Bruce!" he called into the can-phone. He began to sob. "Bruce. Are you there?"

"I'm here, Chucky. Why're you crying?"

He took a deep breath, trying to stop. "I've done something bad." His voice caught in his throat.

"Mom catch you skinning the weeny?"

"Worse'n that."

"What's worse'n that?"

"If I tell you, you won't like me anymore."

"You can tell me. Didn't I show you my dad's dirty magazines?"

"Yeah. This is worse." Again he paused. "Okay, I'll tell you. Dad comes into my bedroom at night. He touches me."

"Touches you?"

"You know, plays with my dick."

"No kidding?"

"Uh-huh."

"Naw. Dads don't do that."

"That's what I thought. But he does."

"Does he do it often?"

"Maybe five, six times."

"Plays with your dick? . . . What do you do?"

"I just lie there, pretend I'm asleep. I couldn't do anything if I wanted to. He holds me down."

"Do you get a hard-on?"

"Course I get a hard-on. You would, too."

"And he sees it?"

"He's touching it . . . and there's more." Chucky waited so long he heard Bruce asking if he was still there. "I'm here."

"Well?"

"He sucks me."

"Your dad?"

"My dad. And then I can feel the bed shaking 'cause he's jacking off."

"Jesus!"

"When he finishes he says, 'Shhh' and leaves."

"What's he do in the morning?"

"He's not up when I leave. After school he talks to me like nothing's happened."

"Does your mom know?"

"I don't think so."

"Does it hurt when he sucks you?"

"No."

"What's it feel like?"

"Scary. Wrong. I want him to stop. But . . ."

"Yeah?"

"It feels sorta good, like jacking off, only ten times better."

"Gosh!"

"That's what scares me, that it feels so good. Mom'd kill me if she found out. But it's Dad who's doing it, so maybe I'm suppose to let him. I get so mixed up. It's wrong. I want him to stop, but it feels so good I want him to do it."

"Yeah, I see."

"And there's more. Maybe . . . maybe it's my fault he's doin' it."

"Your fault?"

"It started when he'd come in to say good night after he got back from a trip. I musta done something that made him want to touch me, play with me."

"What'd you do?"

"I don't know. Maybe he can tell I want him to do it, and he can't stop himself."

"Oh."

"If I didn't want him to do it, he wouldn't. That's the really bad part. I make him do it."

"Oh."

"Bruce?" Chucky hesitated. "Are you still my friend?"

Silence.

"Bruce?"

Nothing. The string was slack.

Warm rays from the morning sun touched Chuck's forehead. Slowly he opened his eyes, then immediately blinked them shut against the brilliance of the sun. He was stretched out on the bench beneath the window, with his head resting on his left arm on the windowsill. His arm was asleep. The tips of his fingers on his right hand just touched the can, which sat upright on the sill. He let his feet drop to the floor and raised his body to a sitting position, holding his head in his hands. He stood and looked down at the can and the string that extended out the window. It had been so real, holding the can in his hand and talking into it, talking to his old friend Bruce. Not like a dream at all. Now, awake, he could look out the window and see Dawn's house, not Bruce McIntyre's.

Chuck stretched and filled his lungs with the cool morning air.

He tried to shake off the distress left by the dream, but it lay in the bottom of his mind like slime in a stagnant pool. Bruce had listened to him, he remembered that. That was good. But he hadn't said he was still his friend.

"Oh God!" Chuck said aloud, snapping his head back. "I'm arguing with a fucking dream!"

The hot water streaming over his head in the shower gradually washed away the dream, but thoughts about Bruce lingered. As he dried himself, an idea formed in his mind. I wonder if I can find Bruce. Maybe he still lives around here.

He dressed and went downstairs. When he finished feeding Bear and eating his own breakfast, he looked up McIntyre in the phone book. "What was his father's name?" he said aloud. Then he remembered that Bruce was a junior. "Here it is, Mrs. B. McIntyre." He dialed the number and waited through several rings. Just when he was about to hang up, someone answered.

"Hello." The voice was that of an older woman.

"Hello, Mrs. McIntyre?"

"Yes. Who's this?"

"It's Chuck Carver. Are you the Mrs. McIntyre that used to live on Cove Road?"

"Yes, I am."

"Well, I'm Chuck, ah, Chucky, that is. I lived next door to you. Bruce and I were best friends."

"Oh, Chucky. I remember you. You and your mom. Harriet, wasn't that her name?"

"That's right."

"You moved away and then your father remarried. Where do you live now?"

"Right here in Marblehead. Dad died and left me the house."

"I saw in the paper that he'd died. I'm sorry."

"Where do you live, Mrs. McIntyre?"

"In a condominium at Glover Landing. Mr. McIntyre passed away, let's see, it's been twenty years now. The house on Cove Road was too much for me to handle, so I moved in here."

"I remember your voice now that I'm talking to you. You sound just the same."

"Well, I'm a lot older. You must come by and pay me a visit. I'd love to talk to you."

"I'll do that, but I wonder if you could tell me where Bruce is now. I'd like to give him a call and say hello."

"Oh, Chucky, didn't you know? Bruce was killed right at the end of the Vietnam War."

THIRTY-SIX

Sunday afternoon, Vivian called. It was time, she said, to plan the family gathering for the Fourth of July. "We always get together at the house on Quiet Cove."

"I don't know, Viv. I've got painters and wallpaperers coming in this week and the yard is full of branches and gravel from the storm."

"You don't have to worry about a thing. If you can just set up the chairs and the lawn tables on your new porch, which I'm dying to see, I'll bring all the food. We'll have an old-fashioned picnic. And Josh'll bring the drinks."

"You're not going to let me get out of this, are you?"

" 'Fraid not, big brother. It's a family thing. Every year we come there for the Fourth. The kids would be heartbroken if we didn't. There's the Horribles Parade in the morning and the fireworks in the evening. We make a day of it."

"The Horribles Parade? What's that?"

"You'll see. It's fun."

"The truth is, I was thinking of going up to Rochester to see Mom over the Fourth. Why don't all of you just come out here to Quiet Cove and take over the house, have your celebration like you always do? I don't need to be here."

"I wouldn't think of it. The house on Quiet Cove is yours, and anyway, I miss you. See your mother next weekend."

"I give up, but if the house isn't all put back together after the painters leave, you'll just have to live with it."

"That won't be a problem. Oh, and Chuck. We always ask Dawn and Brian to come. I'll give her a call."

The painters and wallpaperers did finish, and Chuck hired a landscaping company to clean up the yard. He tried to tell himself that the house looked so nice it would sell in a week, but what he really wanted to do was to show it off to the family.

Dawn waved from her porch as Vivian's van and Josh's car pulled into the driveway, one behind the other. The day was sunny, with a slight breeze off the water. Both women wore brightly colored cotton dresses. Carl had on dark blue slacks and a white pullover, while Josh and Cliff were more casual in shorts and T-shirts. Brian had his baggy shorts with a T-shirt so long it almost covered his shorts, and the children were dressed in play clothes. Chuck came out of his door wearing a loose-knit polo shirt and slacks plus a new pair of Converse walking shoes—his old ones had paint on them. Dawn called to Bear and Clara and tied red, white and blue bandanas around their necks.

Vivian arranged the transportation downtown: Chuck, Dawn, Brian and the two dogs in the pickup truck and the rest in their van. When Dawn got into the truck, she made sure Brian got in first as a buffer between her and Chuck. She'd seen Chuck's expression when Vivian directed her to ride in the truck, and she felt more comfortable with a little distance between them.

They parked three blocks from the parade route and walked to Pleasant Street. With the three children waving small flags, the ten people and two dogs were a parade all by themselves. They joined other families at curbside and soon the Marblehead Police motorcycles, with sirens blaring, lead the Horribles Parade up the street from the town square. Then came members of the Glover Regiment dressed in Revolutionary War costumes and marching to the music of a fife and drum. While they were still a block away, they stopped and fired their flintlock rifles with a thunderous roar.

Clara, already terrified by the crowd and the sirens, bolted in three directions at once.

"What's wrong with her?" Cliff asked.

"She freaks out when there's too much noise and excitement."

"Pretty high-strung, huh?"

"We think she was abused when she was a puppy. In spite of all the love we give her, she's never gotten over it."

"Here," Chuck said, "let me take her. You hold Bear and I'll walk her up this side street."

"That's not fair," Dawn insisted. "You haven't seen the Horribles yet. I'll do it."

"I don't mind. I've seen parades before." With that, Chuck took the leash and he and Clara started up the street away from the crowd.

"He won't see the best part," Dawn said to Cliff.

"Yeah?" Cliff asked. "What are the Horribles, anyway?"

"Here they come now."

Down the street came children, singly and in groups, some dressed as local selectmen to spoof an issue before the town board, others in outlandish school uniforms to ridicule a proposed dress code, and still others made up to be rocket ships, birds or animals. One child's costume, composed of seaweed taken off the beach, covered her from head to foot. The crowd cheered, laughed and applauded.

He's missing all the fun, Dawn thought. She stepped back from the curb and looked up the street. There, half a block away, she saw him sitting on a stone wall in front of a house. Clara was by his side, held in the crook of his arm. He was petting her head and she was licking his chin. Two scared children, she thought, shaking her head sadly.

After the parade they returned to the house. Vivian produced a selection of cold-cut sandwiches and potato chips and Josh brought a cooler from his car filled with beer and soft drinks. Dawn and Brian helped arrange chairs on the porch around two tables with umbrellas.

"You've done a wonderful job on the house, Chuck," Vivian said. "I hadn't realized how tired the old place had become."

"You're a pretty good carpenter, too," Carl said as he stomped the new decking on the porch. "Nice and solid."

"Thanks."

"Show us what you've done inside," Josh asked.

"Okay." Then, with a trace of pride in his voice, Chuck announced, "Who wants a tour?"

Dawn followed in the rear as the entire gathering crossed newly refinished floors to gaze with admiration at the bright new wallpaper and freshly painted woodwork. Then, up the stairs to the master bedroom to see the new bathroom.

"Hey," Josh said, "a Jacuzzi. Not bad."

Vivian approached Chuck and took his arm. "Dad would love it. You've done a wonderful job." Dawn could see by the look in her eyes that Vivian didn't want him to move away.

During the afternoon the group split up. Josh, Cliff and Dawn went back into town to visit the art displays in the various churches, all part of the Marblehead Festival of Arts. Brian and Carl were heading out to go sailing, while Vivian remained to watch the children, who were playing with the dogs on the lawn.

"You first, Carl," Vivian said, "but come back in a couple of hours. It'll be your turn to watch the kids while I go out with Brian."

"How about you, Chuck?" Brian called. "Wanna come with us?"

"Go ahead. Maybe I'll make the next trip."

Vivian began picking up the paper plates from lunch, and Chuck offered to help. When they finished, they sat on the porch drinking ice tea. In the yard the children had found the croquet set and were playing their own version of the game. Joslynn, the baby, was wobbling around the lawn dragging a mallet and holding a ball. Jeremy, the oldest, was trying to explain what he thought were the rules to his sister, Jackie, who was laughing and running in circles, hitting first her ball, then his.

Vivian spoke. "You know what I'm thinking, don't you, Chuck?"

"I've got a pretty good idea."

"Don't do it. Don't sell and move away." He didn't answer. After a moment, she went on. "I know it's your house to do with as you please, but we'd all miss it, especially at times like this."

"I can see that." His voice was sad.

"Whatever the trouble is, it'll work out. Is Dawn still in love with Gareth?"

"That's not it. She might still feel guilty about his death, but I think she's getting over that. No, I just think I'm better suited to being single."

"Okay. I won't talk about it anymore."

In the middle of the afternoon, Dawn, Josh and Cliff returned home just as Brian was sailing into Quiet Cove. Carl shuttled in on the dinghy and came up to the house.

"Who's going out on the next trip?"

"I'm going," Vivian said. "It's your turn with the kids. Dawn, do you want to come too?"

"Love to," Dawn replied. "I'm not taking your place, am I, Chuck?"

"No. Go ahead. I can sail any day."

Josh and Cliff headed for the beach to take a dip and Vivian and Dawn went out to the sailboat in the dinghy.

"Welcome aboard," Brian announced, happy to have the chance to skipper more passengers.

Five minutes later they were rounding the island and feeling the roll of the swells beneath the boat. The two women sat on the foredeck.

"I'm concerned about Chuck," Vivian said. "He seems so depressed."

"I know. It worries me, too."

"A couple of weeks ago he told me he was thinking about selling the house and I asked what was wrong. I thought maybe something had gone wrong between the two of you. But he said no, that wasn't it. It was his problem and he didn't want to burden you with it."

"That's about what he said to me, too."

"I hope it's all right, but I also said I thought you'd be willing to share the burden. He said you'd already offered."

"That's true. I . . . I have an idea what part of the problem is, but I don't want to go into it. It's really his business. But what I don't know is how deep the problem goes."

"If only he'd see how much all of us care about him."

"I think he knows that, but it's funny. The more he sees our concern for him, the more he pulls back, as if he feels unworthy."

"It must be hard on you, Dawn."

"It is, and there's only so much I can give. First I lose Gareth and then Charlie. Now I'm losing Chuck. It's a different situation, but it hurts nonetheless. I've got the book coming out and the exhibit, which is less than two months away. To top it off, I'm leaving for Moscow Monday night. It's not that I'm interested in anybody else—hell, that's the last thing I need right now—but I tell you, I haven't got the energy to keep worrying about Chuck."

"I understand," Vivian said, "you've got to take care of yourself." She paused for a minute, then said, "Damn! Why do people get so screwed up? I mean reasonable people, ordinary people, people like us. We all want somebody to love . . . somebody who'll love us, but we make such a mess of it."

"We do, don't we."

By the time they returned, Chuck had started the fire in the grill, and Carl was rolling potatoes in aluminum foil for baking on the grill. Josh asked if anyone wanted a beer from his cooler, and Dawn said she could bring over some wine. Carl asked Chuck if he had the makings for martinis. Pretty soon they were all standing on the porch with the drinks of their choice, watching the shadows lengthen across the yard. Vivian cooked hot dogs for the kids and Carl brought out a tossed salad Vivian had made and seven filets mignons. When the potatoes were done, he cooked the meat and people settled into the chairs around the tables. After dinner the adults tried a round of croquet, but soon it was too dark.

"It's almost time for the fireworks," Josh said. "If we go now we can get a spot on the wharf next to Marblehead Yacht Club."

"Where do they shoot them off?" Chuck asked.

"From the causeway that goes out to the Neck," Brian said. "And there's a surprise, too. Wait 'til you see it."

Leaving the dogs behind in Chuck's house, they went in two cars. This time Josh and Cliff rode with Chuck, and Dawn with Vivian. Again, because of the crowds, they parked a distance away and walked to the harbor. Most of the people on the wharf knew each other, Marblehead being a small town, and old friends were catching up on the latest news.

Dawn found a place near the rock wall beside Carl and Vivian while Chuck, as if to make a point, was on the opposite side of their group talking to Josh and Cliff.

"So what's the surprise?" Chuck asked Josh.

"Look out there at the causeway. It's starting now."

Chuck saw the sputtering red glow of a road flare, and then another about a hundred feet away, followed by still another. Soon the entire causeway was lit with flares at hundred-foot intervals. When the lights reached both ends of the causeway, they continued on around the harbor as property owners and yacht clubs ignited flares. Within five minutes the entire Marblehead Harbor was a necklace of hundreds of hissing, sparkling red lights.

"Quite a sight, isn't it?" Josh said. "It's called the Illumination of the Harbor."

There were two flares on the wharf, one not ten feet from Chuck. He looked at the members of his group, the family that claimed him as one of theirs, and each glowing red face was smiling in awe at the spectacle.

Suddenly a rocket shot into the sky and exploded in a cascade of red, white and blue sparkles, then another and another. Jeremy stood in front of his dad while Carl put his arm around Vivian. Josh clandestinely took Cliff's hand. Brian, engrossed in the display, didn't resist when his mother, standing behind him, put her hands on his shoulders.

Chuck watched them sadly, then reached down and scooped up Jackie and Joslynn in his arms. "There now," he said, cuddling them to his chest, "you can see better."

"Thanks, Uncle Chuck," Jackie whispered in his ear. He smiled, knowing beyond a doubt that he would never hurt a child.

After the fireworks, Carl and Vivian were anxious to get home and put the children to bed. Everything had been packed up before the fireworks, so it took them only minutes to put their children's playthings into the back of the van along with the empty containers that had held the day's meals.

Vivian rolled down her window and said plaintively, "Let's do it again next year, Chuck."

"We'll see. Have a safe trip home."

As they pulled away, Dawn and Brian thanked Chuck for a wonderful day and crossed the lawn to their house. Only Josh and Cliff seemed to be in no hurry to leave. After the goodbyes, they returned to the porch.

"You guys want a nightcap before you take off?" Chuck said.

"Why not," Josh said. "I think there's still a few beers in the cooler." He fished in the mostly melted ice for a beer. "Chuck?"

"No. I'm having scotch."

"Make mine a Coke," Cliff told Josh. "I'll drive."

Chuck returned to the porch with his drink and sat down next to Josh. Somewhere in the distance, maybe from Salem or Beverly, they could hear the fireworks of yet another community. The sky was clear and a warm breeze was blowing. No one spoke for several minutes.

"Josh, I want to ask you something and I don't want you to take it the wrong way."

His half-brother looked at him, wary of what might follow. "I can't promise, but go ahead."

"I know you loved Dad a lot and I'm not asking you to say anything against him," he paused for a moment, "but when you were young, did he ever show you any affection in ways you didn't want?"

"Is this one of those damned 'What turned you into a queer' questions?"

"Oh!" Chuck said, surprised. "No. I wasn't even thinking about that."

"It's okay if you want to ask," Josh said, annoyed, "but just ask it straight out."

"That's not it."

"Then what's it about?"

Chuck took a deep breath and said, "I think Dad abused me when I was young."

"Christ, Chuck," he said, his face screwed up like he was smelling something bad. "What do you mean?"

"When I was ten, just before Mom and I left, I remember Dad coming into my bedroom and touching me, playing with me."

"My dad? Huh, no way."

"It's hard for me to believe, too, but that's why we had to leave here, why Mom took me to Rochester."

"You've got it wrong, somehow. He just wasn't that kind of guy. Have you said anything to Vivian about this?"

"No."

"Well, don't. This is crazy. You ought to drop it right now. You've crossed some wires somewhere back in your memory. Dad would never do anything like that."

Chuck didn't answer, and the three of them sat in silence. Finally Chuck spoke. "Maybe I did get it mixed up, but I had to ask."

"Well," Josh said, still angry, "it's a hell of a thing to say about somebody."

Chuck didn't know what to say, but Cliff turned to him and broke the silence.

"Chuck, what a heavy thing to carry around."

Chuck nodded his head. "You don't know how heavy."

THIRTY-SEVEN

It wasn't until Monday evening, when Dawn was seated in the coach section of her British Airways flight to Moscow via London, that she realized how frightened she was. Ever since Gareth's death, uncertainty had surrounded the reason he was in the wrong place at the wrong time. Maybe he was just taking a walk or going to a store. Nobody could blame Dawn for that, not even Dawn herself. But he could also have been on his way to Krubinski's to arrange for the use of the poster. Then, as far as Dawn was concerned, his death would be her fault and she'd have to bear the guilt for the rest of her life. Not knowing the truth was hard, but her limbo of uncertainty was better than the hell she would have to endure if indeed she was guilty. On this trip to Moscow, if she was successful, she would learn the truth, and the possibilities terrified her.

She attached her seat belt and looked out the window. Soon she heard the cargo doors slam and lock and the whir of the mighty jet engines spinning to life. There was a slight jolt as the tug attached to the nose wheel began to push the 747 away from the gate.

Dawn tried to tell herself that knowing about Gareth once and for all was better than not knowing, but she was so sure of what she would discover—that his death was her fault—that she wanted to unhook her seat belt and rush to the door while they were still on the ground.

A thought crossed her mind. Could it be that Chuck was withdrawing from her because some primal instinct deep within his animal nature warned him that she was dangerous? "Stay away from her, man, she's a black widow." If that's the case, she said to herself, it's for the better. I don't want another man dead on my account. I've already got two.

Gareth was the second one. Her father was the first. In the dark days following Gareth's death, when she thought the weight of her depression could be relieved only by taking her own life, a psychiatrist attempted to have her see the parallel between the two deaths. At the end of the first session he had said, "By blaming yourself for Gareth's death, you're reliving your childhood belief that you caused your father's death."

Frustrated and distraught, she had screamed at him, "Christ! I'm not stupid. You don't have to be a goddamned doctor to see that." He ended the session by giving her a prescription for Prozac and another appointment. She left, filled the prescription and never went back.

What she didn't tell the doctor was what happened that night before her father was killed. If she had, he would have known Dawn was not reliving anything. She *was* responsible for both deaths.

Dawn closed her eyes and let the roar of the engines, the vibration of the cabin and the thumping of the wheels as they sped over the runway carry her back to the night before her father died, when she was fourteen.

Dawn lay on her bed and let her eyes roam about her bedroom, not looking at anything in particular. On the wallpaper border around the ceiling, Winnie the Pooh characters danced around the room as they had done since her parents had bought the house ten years before. The house was a three-bedroom ranch in Warrington, Florida, only a few miles from her father's base at Pensacola Naval Air Station. Surrounded by pine trees with lawns composed more of pine needles than grass, the house was within walking distance of the bay. Most of Dawn's friends were Navy brats, and all attended Warrington High.

Her mom was okay, but was always yakking at her to stand up straight and hold her shoulders back. Her dad was cool, but only if she did exactly what he wanted. He'd been a lot more fun when she was little, before he'd left for Vietnam. Now, since he'd come back, if she wore her skirt a little too short or a tube top that showed off her bust, he'd throw a fit. One day her friend Jerry came to the house wearing an antiwar T-shirt. Her dad exploded, called him a long-haired hippie, and ordered her never to see him again.

The phone beside her bed rang and Dawn picked it up. "Hello."

"It's me."

"Not now, Jerry. Dad'll be home in a minute."

"Will I see ya tonight?"

"I told you already. Why are you calling again?"

"I like to talk to you."

"I've got to go, Jerry," Dawn said, clutching the phone to her ear and craning her neck to look out her bedroom window. "Dad's pulling into the driveway."

"Don't go. Shut your door. He won't know who you're talking to."

"He might pick up in the kitchen. Bye. See you tonight."

A door slammed. "Anybody home?" her dad shouted from the kitchen.

"Hi, Daddy. Mom's gone shopping. Said she'd be back by five-thirty." She could hear him coming down the hall. He knocked at her already open door. "Come on in."

"Hi, darling. How was your day?" He was wearing his khaki uniform but had removed the tie and rolled up his sleeves. He was handsome, with prematurely gray hair.

"Okay." Dawn sat on the edge of the bed. "How was yours?"

"Same old thing. Trying to find enough holes in the clouds to do spins and stalls without bumping into another plane." She could see his eyes move disapprovingly over the clothes she was wearing: hip-hugger jeans and a tight-fitting scoop-necked blouse with short sleeves. Each morning he left for the base at five, so he wasn't there to voice his objections to her choice of clothes.

"Better get some decent clothes on soon. Tonight's family night at the club."

Dawn scowled. "Didn't Mom tell you? I'm not going."

"Come on, now," he said, frowning. "What d'ya mean, not going? It's family night. We always go."

"I've made other plans. Mom should have told you."

"Well," his voice rose, "you can just unmake them."

"No, I can't," she said defiantly, "and I don't want to anyway."

He walked into her room and put his hands on his hips. "You're not going out on a school night, that's for damn sure."

Dawn gave him a cocky expression. "I wouldn't exactly call studying for a final exam going out."

"Studying? Who with?"

"Friends."

"Is Jerry one of them?"

"Probably."

"Okay. That's it." Now he was mad. "Forget about it. He's too old for you. What is he, seventeen?"

"No," she said angrily. "He's only sixteen."

"That's still too old for you. You're not going out now or ever with Jerry what's-his-name."

"Just because his dad's enlisted." She could see by the way he pursed his lips that she'd struck a blow. "You don't seem to mind me talking to the older boys at the Officers' Club."

"I don't trust them any more than I trust Jerry, but at least they dress decently. And look at the way you're dressed. They let you come to school that way?"

"What's wrong with this outfit? Mom helped me pick it out."

"Then I guess I'd better have a talk with you *and* your mom."

"Yeah. Just give us an order, Commander Olson. Tell us what to do."

"If that's what it takes, I will. For starters, get dressed in something that's respectable. You're going with us to the club."

"No!" she shouted back at him. "I'm not, and you're not going to make me."

"Then, goddamnit, little lady," he leaned forward, his head almost in her face, "I'll lock you in your room."

"You'd better nail the windows shut, too."

Her mother was at the door. They hadn't heard her come in. "Hey! Hey! Hey! Take it easy." They stopped yelling and looked at her. "What's wrong?"

"Tell him," Dawn demanded. "Didn't you say I could study tonight with Jerry?" Dad, red-faced, stared at his wife.

"I said you could study with your friends for the exam tomorrow. Will Jerry be there, too?"

Dad jumped in. "Now why the hell would Jerry be studying with her friends? He's two grades ahead of her."

"Mom, I specifically told you I would be studying with Jerry tonight."

"You mean just the two of you, studying?"

"Well, we might go for a Coke."

"Look! That's all beside the point," he said with a restrained voice that sounded even angrier. "This is family night at the club, the night we do things as a family." He was speaking more to his wife than to Dawn. "And that's what we're going to do."

Her mother turned to her. "I'm sorry, I'd forgotten it was family night when I said you could study with friends, and by the way, I didn't understand it was just one friend when you asked me."

"Well, I'm sorry you got it wrong, but I've already told him to come by and pick me up."

"Well then," her dad ordered, "call him and tell him to forget it. You're going with us."

"I'm not going with you." She stamped her foot. "If you won't let me see Jerry, I'll just stay home."

"Stay home, then. To hell with doing things as a family. But let me warn you, if I come home and find Jerry here, I'll wring his ass and beat your butt."

Mom pushed him out of the room and shut the door. Dawn could hear them arguing in their bedroom. After half an hour, they left. Dawn opened her door and wandered into the kitchen. Mom had left a note with instructions for dinner—a hamburger in the meat keeper and salad stuff in the crisper. She threw the note in the wastebasket and returned to her room. Dejectedly, she slumped onto the bed and picked up the phone.

"Jerry?"

"Hi, Dawn. Can I pick you up?"

"They won't let me go out."

"I thought you said you could."

"That was Mom. Dad said no. Damned near bit my head off."

"Can I come over?"

"No. I don't think you should."

"How 'bout if I meet you in your backyard? Then you're not going out and I'm not coming in."

"Well, maybe it'll be okay, but you'd better park around the block. They know your car."

"I'll be there in ten minutes."

Family night, because it was a weeknight, would be over at eight, so Dawn knew she was safe for at least an hour. She slipped out her bedroom window, leaving it open, and met Jerry in the back corner of the yard behind a thick pine grove. Sitting on the ground, they were not visible to neighboring windows or passersby on the street. While his right arm was wrapped around her shoulder, with his left hand he deftly knocked a Marlboro free from its pack and lit it with his Zippo. He offered one to Dawn, but she shook her head. For half an hour she complained about her father while Jerry nuzzled her cheek and neck with kisses. When the hand that was around her shoulder grazed the bare skin above the scoop neck of her blouse, she automatically brushed it away. She sat cross-legged, picking up pine cones and throwing them down hard as emphasis to her anger. Finally, tired of complaining, she turned her lips to Jerry and let him kiss her.

The car was halfway up the driveway before she saw it. Giving Jerry a push that sent him onto his back, she raced to her bedroom window. She scrambled inside, closed the screen and was sitting at her desk, her history book open in front of her, when her father arrived at her closed door. He knocked apologetically.

"Dawn? Could I talk with you?"

"There's nothing to talk about."

"Please open the door."

She got up and opened the door. Standing there, head cocked to the side, she looked at him disgustedly. When she didn't speak, her dad said, "I want to apologize." Still she said nothing. "May I come in?"

Dawn sighed, then turned, walked to her bed and sat down. Her father sat in the desk chair. For a full minute they said nothing. Twisting a strand of hair, she stared at the floor while he looked at her. Then, "Dawn, it may not look like it, but the reason I said what I said about Jerry is because I love you. You're young and I don't want you to get into something with somebody like Jerry until you're old enough to handle it."

"What d'ya mean, someone like Jerry? You don't even know him."

"I may not know him, but I was sixteen once myself. There was only one thing I wanted from a girl as pretty as you."

"Ugh! That's disgusting. He's not like that, even if you were."

"Dawn, please listen. I'm not trying to be mean. You're a very beautiful young woman. You have class. I don't want you to get involved with someone in a way you'll later regret."

"So what you're saying is you don't want me to be a pothead and don't want me to get pregnant. Why don't you just say it?"

Her father's eyes dropped to the bedspread and then to the floor. A line of pine needles led from the bed to the window.

"Would you stand up for a minute?" His eyes narrowed.

She looked at him suspiciously. "What for?"

"Just do as I say." He reached for her wrist, but she jerked it away and stood up herself. He looked at the back of her jeans. Some pine needles clung to her pants. "So, you did go out."

"Sure. I went for a walk."

"Out the window?" He was livid. "So you could get back in without being seen?"

"Whatever you say, sir." She stretched the "sir" sarcastically.

"You can knock off that cocky attitude, little lady." He brought his face close to hers and glared. "You were out in the yard with Jerry, weren't you?"

"It's none of your business."

"Oh yeah? I'm making it my business. You're grounded for two weeks. No going out except for school. No friends over and no telephone calls in or out."

She stared at him, jaw clinched, determined not to cry in front of him. After he stormed out of the room, slamming the door, she burst into tears and buried her head in her pillow.

The next day at eleven twenty-three, Dawn was called out of her history exam to go to the office. The principal, Mrs. Cranshaw, and the assistant principal, Mr. Terrell, were both there. Dawn entered, cautiously, her eyes darting fretfully about the room.

"Dawn, I'm so very sorry to have to tell you this." Mrs. Cranshaw took both of Dawn's hands and guided her into a chair. "There's been an accident at the base. It was your father. He's been killed."

Dawn looked up, frozen. All she could think of saying was, "Where's my mother?"

"She's at home. The chaplain's there, too. Mr. Terrell will drive you home."

Dawn started to get up, then faltered and sank back into the chair, limp and shivering. Mrs. Cranshaw caught her and, kneeling on the floor, put her arms around her.

Almost incoherent, Dawn mumbled over and over again, "I didn't say good-bye. I didn't say good-bye."

A military funeral was held three days later. Dawn stood beside her mother, both dressed in black. Her mother leaned on the shoulder of a friend and wept constantly. Dawn, standing tall, remained stoic.

Two weeks later, Dawn went to her English teacher's classroom when school was over. That day in class her teacher had handed back the poems each student had submitted as part of a homework assignment. At the bottom of Dawn's poem Miss Alvarez, her teacher, had written, "Dawn, please see me after school."

"Do you still have the poem?" Miss Alvarez asked. Dawn placed it on the desk. "Would you like to tell me about it?"

Dawn liked her. She had a kind face.

"It's about this Greek myth. About Icarus. I wondered what it would be like to be his daughter, so I made that part up."

"Would you read it aloud to me?"

Dawn shrugged her shoulders. "Sure. It's called 'Icarus's Daughter.' " She cleared her throat.

> "Icarus had a daughter who sent him on his way.
> She made his life unbearable by what she wouldn't say.
> She wouldn't say she's sorry, she wouldn't say good bye.
> So off he flew to find the sun, to find a way to die."

"I like it," Miss Alvarez said. "It's well written. How did you happen to write it?"

Dawn looked down at the desk. "I don't know, I guess I just imagined it. Maybe Icarus did have a daughter."

"Maybe. In the poem it sounds like his daughter blames herself for his flight to the sun, for his death."

"I know. It could have happened that way, if she'd said things that hurt him. Maybe he didn't care whether he lived or died."

"Dawn, tell me about your father."

"My father? He's . . . he's dead." For the first time since the accident, tears came to Dawn's eyes. The frozen expression melted and she began to cry. Miss Alvarez held her for several minutes until the sobbing stopped, then drove her home.

As the giant 747 soared eastward into the night, Dawn looked out the window at the clouds below, lit by a quarter moon. To herself she said, "So off he flew to find the sun, to find a way to die." Again tears came to her eyes, as they had almost twenty years before.

THIRTY-EIGHT

Chuck was glad he hadn't gone to Rochester over the Fourth, because it had been fun showing off his house. But he wanted to see his mother's face when he told her about the suppressed memories that had come back, flooding into his mind. "I know what happened, Mom." A hundred times a day he rehearsed it. "It's all come back to me. Dad came into my room at night, didn't he? You mean you don't know? How could you help but know? It happened several times. And only once, the last time, did you protect me."

No, he thought, that's too much. He couldn't say it that way. "Mom, you knew what he did. You saw him that night you came into my room. He was doing it and you saw him. So you hit him with the lamp. I remember it all now. But why didn't you tell me? Why did you keep it from me, and pretend it never happened?"

He wanted to see her expression when he confronted her, see how she fit into the equation. And it couldn't be done over the phone. He needed an excuse that could get him to Rochester before they got into his real reason for going. Mom's birthday was July ninth. That would be his excuse.

He called her late Monday afternoon and asked if he could come up the next day to help her celebrate her birthday. She said she wasn't celebrating it, but he could come up if he wanted. By the tone of her voice Chuck could tell she suspected it wasn't her

264

birthday that was bringing him to Rochester, that there were other reasons.

Just before hanging up, he said, "And Mom, I won't be alone."

"You're bringing a young woman? Ah! That's the reason you're coming. You want me to meet her."

"Not exactly. I'm bringing Bear."

"Oh." There was disappointment in her voice. "Are you planning to bring him into my house?"

"I don't know what else I can do."

"Is he clean?"

"Very."

"Well, I'm not buying dog food."

"Don't worry, I'll bring it."

"You're not going to tell me the real reason you're coming, are you."

Chuck said, "It's your birthday."

"You want to talk some more, don't you?"

"Yes, I do need to ask you some things."

"Okay. See you tomorrow."

The next morning he and Bear drove to Rochester, Chuck driving and Bear riding shotgun. After an hour of watching the passing scenery, Bear lay down and put his head in Chuck's lap. A morning coffee break allowed the dog a chance to circle the parking lot and thoughtfully examine each bush for the scent of previous visitors. At just the right spot, he stopped to pee. When they reached the New York state line, they turned into a Burger King and had lunch on the tailgate of the truck. Bear could have eaten his hamburger in one bite, but Chuck tossed him one small piece at a time, making the dog's lunch last as long as his. Back on Interstate 90, the road carved its way through steep hills on each side of the road. Suddenly Bear woofed at something out his window. There on the hillside was a herd of deer grazing on the grassy slope. Bear danced on the seat and whined at Chuck to stop and let him out. "Sorry, big guy. Can't do it." After a while he lay down again and slept with his head on Chuck's leg.

Chuck drove with his left hand on the wheel and his right embedded in Bear's fur. As the miles rolled by, Chuck went around and around about what to say to his mother. When he thought about the nightmares, his divorce from Michelle and his problems with Dawn, his anger boiled. He wanted to throw it all in his mother's face. Then, a quarter-mile down the road, he knew that was wrong. It wasn't his mother who'd abused him. And how could he tell her that it was partly his fault, that he may have done something to lure his father into his room? But why hadn't she told him about that night and the smashed lamp? By the time he made his midafternoon coffee stop, he was so confused he almost decided to turn around and go back to Marblehead. No. He'd come this far. He'd go the whole way.

It was after six when they pulled into Rochester, wending their way through residential streets to the home in which Chuck had spent his teenage years. The house was a sturdy Victorian with clapboard sides and wide porch. The driveway ran along the left side of the house to a garage so small it would accommodate only a compact car. The yard had been recently mowed, and Chuck pictured his mom pushing the nonmotorized lawn mower back and forth across the grass. He pulled into the driveway and tooted the horn. As he was hooking the leash onto Bear's collar, he saw his mother come out the front door.

He met her on the front walk. She had changed from her uniform and was wearing a blouse and slacks.

Harriet assumed her somewhat rigid stance, letting a wary smile be her welcome. "How was the trip?"

"Long, but not bad." He stopped far enough from her to avoid the awkwardness of greeting one's mother without a hug. Bear, however, approached with his usual majesty, ready to receive his pat on the head. He was ignored. "I had good company," Chuck said. "If you don't mind, I think I'd better walk him up the street a ways. Then we'll join you."

"Suit yourself. Got the dog food?"

"In the truck. I'll bring it in when we come back."

When he returned to the house, he smelled the rich, spicy aroma of meat sauce with garlic. "You remembered my favorite dinner."

"Thought you'd like it." He caught her smile as she turned to stir the iron kettle. "Got time for drink if you'd like one." She'd always had two drinks before dinner, a custom he'd inherited.

"Sounds good to me. I brought some Johnnie Walker Red. Can I fix you one?"

After dinner he took Bear for a final walk while his mother cleaned up the kitchen. When he returned they remained on the porch, sitting side by side in the wooden swing that hung from chains attached to the ceiling. Bear emitted a long groan and collapsed on the floor beside them.

As they swung leisurely back and forth, Chuck wondered if this was the time to tell her why he'd come. Too soon, he decided.

Instead, he said, "Happy Birthday!"

"Bah!" she said with a wave of her hand. "Don't mention birthdays."

He continued, "So, you're a year away from retiring at sixty-five."

"Naw. I could retire now if I wanted to. I've got over thirty years in. But I'll wait another year. With social security and my pension, I'll do pretty well."

"Will you stay here?"

"No. I'll sell the house. Maybe go to Arizona. Some of my friends have retired there."

For several minutes they swung in silence. People passed on the sidewalk and Harriet waved hello. One couple had a golden retriever, which Bear raised his head to observe. Is now the time? Chuck asked himself.

"I see you drove the truck. Still got that little sports car?"

"I've still got it. Bear rides easier in the truck."

"How's the house working out for you?"

"It's coming along."

"You decided to stay?"

"I don't think so."

Enough of this small talk, Chuck thought. If I'm going to tell her, it might as well be now.

"Mom, I know what happened that night the lamp got broken." He turned slightly toward his mother. "It's all come back to me."

His mother's feet hit the floor, stopping the swing. She sucked in her breath. Her eyes became instantly fearful.

"You came into my room and picked up the lamp and smashed it over his head." Harriet's hands, folded in her lap, began to shake.

"He'd come into my room, and he was touching me, fondling me. You smashed him with the lamp." Chuck turned to face directly at his mother. "Isn't that right?"

"Yes. Yes." She jumped up and ran into the house. Chuck followed. His mother was standing at the kitchen table, her hand pressed against her mouth. Wild-eyed, she looked at him hysterically.

Torn between anger and compassion, Chuck stopped at the other end of table, leaning on it with both hands. "Why did you hide it from me all these years? Why didn't you tell me?"

"I . . . I thought you'd forgotten about it. You never asked. At first I thought you would, but you never did. Then, after a while, I figured you'd forgotten."

"Forgotten?" His jaw clenched, he shook his head. "Never forgotten. Maybe I didn't remember it for thirty years, but it was always there. How could I ever forget what Dad was doing to me, touching me and fondling me, when you came in and hit him with the lamp?"

Suddenly Harriet's eyes opened wide and she stared at him with disbelief.

"Your father? Charlie? Oh God! Oh my God!" She keened the words and gripped the edge of the table for support. "That . . . that wasn't your father. That was someone else."

THIRTY-NINE

It was midafternoon on Tuesday when her plane landed in Moscow and close to five when her taxi rolled up the wide curving drive to the Cosmos Hotel. Twice they had been stopped by the police for a random inspection of the cabbie's papers. Each time the officer, gently patting his open palm with his billy club, found a discrepancy in some document. The driver gave him a few rubles for discovering the flaws in his papers, agreed to have them corrected the next day and was allowed to go on.

After the second time it happened, Dawn, exhausted from the trip and frustrated with the delays, asked the driver why he didn't get his papers in order. "Isn't it expensive," she asked, "bribing the police?"

In broken English he responded. "It is. But if I fix one thing, they find something else. It is not my papers that are wrong. It is the police."

At the hotel Dawn wrestled her luggage past the penetrating eyes of the security guard posing as a doorman and into the hotel. More than a hundred people of many different nationalities milled about the huge showpiece lobby of this former USSR state hotel. Some were tourists who followed their guides like obedient sheep. Others were independent travelers looking as tired and haggard as Dawn. Ten more tedious minutes in line at the registration desk finally got her a room on the sixth floor.

At the sixth-floor concierge desk, she picked up her key and pulled her bag down the carpeted hallway to her door. Inside, she immediately went to the bathroom and started water for a bath. As the tub filled, she dialed Professor Neleginski's office.

"How nice to hear from Mrs. Ireland." It was the voice of an elderly man. "Yes, tomorrow at eleven would be fine."

She hung up and submerged herself in the hot water.

The particular campus of Moscow University where Neleginski had his office was situated high above the Moskva River in one of the seven gigantic Camelot-like towers Stalin had built. The taxi drove her up the wide tree-lined boulevard, depositing her at the entrance at ten-thirty. It was good she got there early, because it took her half an hour to find his office.

She knocked and a white-haired man in his seventies opened the door. "I am Nikolai Neleginski. Welcome to Moscow. Please come in." Stooped and wearing a coat that was threadbare at the elbows, he gave her a warm smile. There were three desks in the office, one of which appeared to be Professor Neleginski's, and a window overlooking the boulevard.

He took Dawn's hands in his. "You are as beautiful as Professor Davies said."

"He spoke of me?"

"When did he not speak of you?" He looked at her and, as if reading her thoughts, his smile faded to sadness. "I'm sorry it came to this. He loved you deeply."

Standing there, her hands still in his, the fear and remorse she had been holding in welled up and she began to cry. Gently, the older man took her into his arms and held her. After a few moments, Dawn eased back and, drying her eyes, said, "Thank you."

The professor brought up another chair and they sat at his desk. They talked some more about Gareth and the seminar he had been teaching, then Neleginski asked, "Is there anything I can do for you?"

Dawn took a deep breath and explained how she had asked Gareth to contact a man named Demitri Krubinski regarding the use of a poster he owned. She also told her newfound friend about the guilt she felt for possibly sending Gareth to his death. The older man nodded as she spoke.

"And you have come to Moscow," he said, "to find out the truth. You are a brave young woman."

She asked him how she might go about finding Krubinski. "I can tell you what I told Gareth. It's not much, but it may be a way to begin." He suggested she go to Dom Knigi, a store on the New Arbat Street, that sold posters as well as books. "If this Krubinski is a dealer in poster art, they will know about him."

As she was leaving, the professor again took Dawn's hands. "After you have found him, come back and see me. Tell me what he said." For a moment Dawn felt she was talking to Charlie.

New Arbat is one of the spoke roads that radiate outward from the Kremlin. She ate lunch at the Praga restaurant on Arbat Street, then walked over to New Arbat. At the Dom Knigi she spoke to a middle-aged woman who seemed to be one of the managers. Yes, she knew Krubinski, but why did she want to see him? Dawn explained that she wanted to discuss the use of one of his posters in a book and an art exhibit. She told her that she had met with Mr. Krubinski a year earlier but had not been able to contact him since. This seemed to satisfy the manager, who left abruptly and went into an inner office. She spoke with a man behind a desk and then returned.

"We will try to call Mr. Krubinski. We cannot guarantee we can find him, but we will try. Here," she said, handing Dawn a slip of paper, "this is our telephone number. Call us later this afternoon and I will tell you what I have found out." Before Dawn left, she gave the woman the telephone number of the Cosmos Hotel and her room number, "In case you need to call me."

With an afternoon to kill, she walked up New Arbat toward the Kremlin and around the wall to Red Square. Across from Lenin's tomb, she went into GUM, the state department store, and bought a variety of foods to take back to the hotel for dinner. Suddenly she was overcome with jet lag, and finding an entrance to the Metro, Moscow's subway, she went down the steps and onto a platform that looked liked an elongated chapel in a cathedral. Soon she was speeding beneath Moscow, bumping elbows and sharing seats with Russians who had the same blank expression as subway riders the world over. She changed trains twice and finally arrived at her stop for the Cosmos Hotel.

Back in her room, she laid out her dinner: bread, cheese, mustard, sliced cucumbers, a meat ravioli and a small bottle of vodka. She unscrewed the vodka cap and poured a small amount into a glass, then walked to the window.

"So far, so good," she said aloud and toasted her progress with a sip of vodka. "But I'd better call the poster store before I fall asleep." She dialed the number and asked for the manager she'd talked with in the shop.

"Yes, we were able to reach Krubinski." Dawn's eyes opened wide. "But he was unwilling to allow us to give you his phone number. Instead, he said he will call you tomorrow morning at ten. I told him you were staying at the Cosmos Hotel and gave him the number."

"So there is no way I can telephone him?"

"He prefers to do it this way."

"Well, thank you for your help. You have been very kind."

Dawn hung up. "More waiting."

FORTY

It was someone else?" Chuck's voice rose above his mother's anguished screams. Staggering, he sank back into the kitchen chair behind him, the scenery of his reconstructed memory shifting and crumbling around him. His mother slumped into another chair and buried her face in her hands. Chuck, his eyes blinking, his breath coming in quick gasps, stared blankly at the woman he thought he knew. In an instant the past had changed, catapulting the present into confusion. For what seemed like an eternity, they said nothing.

Gradually Harriet's sobs diminished, but she sat there mute. Chuck, not knowing what to say, went over to her, bent down and hugged his mother. On his knees he took a deep breath and spoke softly.

"So it wasn't Dad after all."

His mother shook her head slowly. "I was always ashamed to tell you. But Chuck, I would have in a second if I'd known what you were going through, that you had it so mixed up."

"Then do you know who it was?"

She didn't answer. Again she began to cry aloud. "I'm sorry, Mom. It must have been an awful experience for you, too. I'm sorry I dragged it up again, but I have to know." Now she was weeping uncontrollably.

"How did he get in?" Chuck implored. "Did he break in? Did you call the police?" She covered her face with her hands. "Mom, it's okay. Look at me." She lifted her eyes to his face. She was as white as marble.

Gently he put his hand on her shoulder. "What happened after you hit him and drove him down the stairs? I remember hearing you fighting with him. Did he hurt you? Did he try to ra . . . ah, assault you or something?" She shook her head no. Chuck had to get it all out. "There's something else you probably don't know. He broke into our house five or six other times and did the same thing to me."

Harriet stared at him, a crazed look in her eyes. "Stop!" she yelled. "I can't stand any more." She hit the table with her open hand.

Bear, already agitated by the tension in the room, leaped to his feet from his place beside Chuck and began barking.

"Bear! Down!" Chuck took the massive head in his hands and pulled him toward him, rubbing him behind the ears. "There, there. It's okay." And to his mother, "You did all you could do, Mom. You drove him out of the house."

"You don't understand," she whispered. "Just let me sit here for a while."

Chuck went back to his chair, crossed his legs and continued petting the dog. After a couple of minutes Harriet got up and moved to the sink, where she splashed cold water on her face. "I'm fixing a drink. Do you want one?" He nodded.

A minute later they were sitting at the table, each with a glass of scotch, while Bear resumed his position spread out on the floor at his master's feet. Harriet stared at her son for several seconds, then closed her eyes for several more. Still with eyes closed, she began.

"I'm going to tell you something I've never told another soul." Chuck, not moving, waited. "That person . . ." she took a deep breath, "that person that came into your room was a man I was seeing."

Chuck raised up in his chair and gazed at her with disbelief. "Seeing? What do you mean, seeing?"

"An affair. We were having an affair."

"Your lover? It was your lover that came into my room?"

"All right, lover, if that's the way you want it."

Chuck twisted in his seat. "Your lover?" He felt nauseous.

"Yes, dammit. And don't get sanctimonious on me. It was a long time ago. I was young then. Thirty-two years old. Hell, I was ten years younger than you are now. Charlie was away more'n half the time. I knew he had this girlfriend in Paris."

The son could feel the bile climbing in his throat. He took several deep breaths, then stared at his mother. "Oh, God, I'm gonna be sick." He got up and went to the sink, bracing himself on splayed arms over the drain. Retching, he vomited once, twice, then let his head hang down as he swallowed hard to gain control. "Mother, please tell me what this is all about. This man, your lover . . ."

She wheeled in her chair, interrupting him. "You've got to understand. With your father away all the time on those flights to Paris, I had no one else but this man, and Chuck, until the last time, I knew nothing about what he was doing to you."

"It's hard to believe," Chuck sighed. "He comes into my bedroom five or six times, this man I always thought was my father. And he does disgusting things to me. And you didn't know?"

Harriet wiped her eyes with the bottom of her apron. "Okay, don't believe me, but I'm telling you that I didn't know about it until the last time. I had to have slept through the others. But this once I did wake up and he wasn't in the bed."

"Oh, shit, Mom. I can't believe this."

"Just listen!" his mother said, her voice back to normal, the voice of a trained nurse. Only this was his mom. But Chuck listened.

"When I realized he wasn't there, I figured he'd gone to the bathroom. When he didn't come back, I got up and looked downstairs. There was no one there. Then I came up to your room. I opened your door and there he was. I was dizzy with rage. I grabbed the lamp and struck him, then drove him down the stairs, fighting with him the whole way. I could have killed him. I kept on yelling at him and striking at him. That's when he said it."

"Said what?"

"That if I ever told anybody about it, he'd see that I got fired from the hospital and never get a job anywhere else."

"And how could he do that? All you had to do was call the police."

"How? Ha! He could do whatever he damn well pleased. He was one of the up-and-coming doctors at the hospital."

"A doctor? Christ, a doctor?"

"Yeah, a doctor. And I was a nurse. It happens more than you think."

"Did he force you? Threaten to get you fired if you didn't go to bed with him?"

"No. Do you really want to know the details?"

"You've started. Let's get it all out."

She took a sip of scotch, sat back in her chair and exhaled a long breath. "I was in love with him. Things were going badly with Charlie. I'd found out about his girlfriend and I had a hunch he was about to dump me. Anyway, this doctor was young—he was about my age—and he was good-looking. There was only one problem. He was married. But so was I."

"And he was nuts. He was a—what do you call 'em?—a pedophile."

"I know that now, for God's sake." She closed her eyes and shook her head hard. "Look, I was young. I was lonely. I was afraid Charlie was going to leave me. And . . ."

"And he knew you had a little boy?"

Her eyes filled with horror. Swallowing hard, she said, "Yes, I think I told him about you."

"Did I ever meet him?"

"No. He'd always come late at night when he finished at the hospital. I was afraid someone would see him. He'd park up the street and walk to the house. You were asleep. The first night he came he asked if he could see you. I guess I'd boasted about what a beautiful child you were. I left the light on in the hall and opened your door. When I was sure you were asleep, he peeked in. And that was it."

Chuck locked his fingers behind his head and closed his eyes. "So how did he manage to sneak out of your bed and come to my room without you knowing it?"

"Are you sure he did?" The tone of her voice suggested that

maybe he was imagining it. "Are you sure there were other times?"

"I haven't the slightest doubt. I've lived with it in my nightmares for thirty years. He came into the room, this man I knew was my father, hushing me to be quiet, and put his hand on my chest to hold me down. The first couple of times he just played with me, then he started to lick . . ."

"All right. That's enough. I don't want to hear it." She was suffering. He could see it.

"You didn't answer my question. How did he sneak . . ."

"I *know*. Why did it go on so long without my knowing?" She waited for several seconds before continuing. "When he'd come over, I drank a lot. I was scared and I felt guilty. I drank too much. He'd always bring a bottle so we wouldn't use any of Charlie's." Then she looked up at her son and her eyes filled with tears. "I'm sorry, I'm so very sorry. I didn't know what he was doing. Please believe me. It was such an awful time." Her eyes pleaded with him through her tears.

The anger he'd felt moments before dissolved in compassion. After all, this was his mother. Finally he said, "I do believe you, but do you know what it's been like for me? Do you know that it has so screwed up my idea of sex and love that I can't make it with someone I love? That's why Michelle left me. I was such a bastard. When she'd get passionate, I . . ."

"No more, please! Don't tell me."

"I want you to listen. When she'd get passionate, I'd feel like she was being a slut and get so angry I couldn't do it. I'd say things and call her names. Now there's another woman, a beautiful, wonderful woman named Dawn, that I'd love to marry, but I'm afraid it will happen all over again."

"I had no idea," Harriet murmured. "I'm so sorry. I thought it was something lost in the past, that you'd forgotten about." She stretched out her hand across the table, reaching for his hand. He extended his and their fingers touched.

"There's still something I don't understand," he said. She pulled back her hand, expecting another blow. "On the days after this guy came into my room, Dad was always home. That's why I thought it was Dad who came into my room. I figured he got back from his flight late and came in to say good night and that's when he started touching me. The next day when I'd see him he didn't act like he'd done anything bad. I couldn't understand it."

"He hadn't."

"But why was he always there the next day? That's what got me confused."

"He always telephoned me from Paris before he left. It was something we worked out, kind of a tacit accommodation. He'd call so he wouldn't find me in a compromising situation, in exchange for me not confronting him about what he did in Paris. I could tell from the sound of his voice over the wires that he was still there. I knew that meant he couldn't get home for at least twelve hours. Those were the nights I told the doctor he could come to the house."

"And the next morning when I got up, he was there."

"Yes, but he was asleep."

"I see." Chuck took a deep breath as he pondered his mother's explanation. "On that last night, or maybe it was early morning, I remember you and Dad arguing. I thought you were still fighting over his being in my room."

"We had a fight, all right. He found something that belonged to the doctor—a sock or undershirt, I don't remember—in the bed, so he accused me of having an affair. He was right, of course, but I realized he was looking for an excuse to tell me he wanted a divorce. I told him I knew about the young woman in Paris. Then when he said I wasn't fit to be a mother and there was no way he'd let me keep you, I blew up. Later that day I packed our bags and we left."

"I see now. There were two people and two fights. I put the two together."

"When he came here to the house to try to get you back, there was no way I was going to let it happen. He was going to marry that other woman. I'd be damned if she was going to be your mother. He was away all the time anyway. He only wanted you to spite me."

Chuck thought about that for a while. He could understand his mother's bitterness, but he also knew there was another side to his father, the side that he had learned about in Marblehead from Vivian, Josh and Dawn.

"It's all over, Chuck. Everyone is dead—my guy, the woman from Paris, Jacqueline, and now your father."

"I know. It's just that all the anger comes back when I think about those times." Again, she reached out both hands across the kitchen table to her son. He took them in his hands. "But we sure can screw things up." He looked at her. "Still, I wish you'd told me."

"So do I."

Holding her hands tightly, he fixed his eyes on hers.

"Who was it, Mom? What was the doctor's name?"

She held his stare, but the pain returned to her face. Almost imperceptibly, she shook her head. "I don't remember."

"How could you not remember? You remember all the other details as if they were yesterday."

"I don't remember. What difference does it make anyway?"

"I'd like to know."

"But why? It's all over. It was years ago. The harm's been done. We can't change that."

"I want to know."

"Why?"

"I want to find the sonofabitch."

The muscles in her jaw clinched. Her hands began to shake as he held them. "The man is dead. Leave well enough alone."

"I'm not sure I believe you. You've deceived me so much."

Harriet inhaled in quick, halting breaths and began to weep.

"I don't remember his name. I *won't* remember."

Chuck looked at her sadly and pulled his hands away.

FORTY-ONE

Dawn picked at her food she'd bought at GUM, but fell asleep before she finished half of it. She awoke again at eleven, got up and undressed from her street clothes. Then she lay in bed reading for two and a half hours, finally dropping off to sleep. When she awoke it was nine-thirty in the morning. Quickly, she showered and dressed.

At ten o'clock the phone rang. She leaped to answer it.

"Is this Mrs. Ireland?"

"Yes. Mr. Krubinski?"

"Yes. We've lost touch with each other over the last several months. I'm afraid the fault is mine. I've found in necessary to move around a lot." He paused, then added, "Are you still going through with the deal we talked about regarding the use of the Alexander Apsit poster *The International?*"

"Yes, and that's why I'm calling now. I need desperately for us to sign the agreement I sent you so you can ship the poster. Would it be possible for me to meet with you?"

"I think we could do that, but not here." There was a pause. "Do you know the Smolenskaya Square?"

"Yes, I was near there yesterday."

"There's a Metro stop at the square, so it shouldn't be hard to get there. I'll meet you in front of the Ministry of Foreign Affairs at two o'clock."

"And what about the contract? Can you bring it?"

"Yes. How do you want to handle payment? I'd appreciate dollars. What was it we discussed? Seven hundred and fifty U.S. dollars?"

"I can do that. I look forward to seeing you."

"And Mrs. Ireland, I have some other posters you might be interested in. I'll tell you about them."

"Good. I'm always interested in posters of good quality."

"Until two, then?"

"Two it is."

She hung up and stared into space. He said nothing about having met with Gareth last December, she thought. Either Gareth never made contact or if he did, he never got there. "Well," she said out loud, "I'll find out at two."

Too restless to stay in the room, she left the hotel and walked to the Metro. An hour later she was at the Smolenskaya Metro Station. It was only eleven-fifteen, so she ambled up Arbat Street looking at the shops selling everything from matrioshka dolls to Soviet medals and army uniforms. Back again in the square, she went to a second-floor restaurant across from the Ministry of Foreign Affairs and ordered lunch. Looking out the window at the ministry, she noticed it was identical to the university building where Neleginski's office was. About one-thirty she crossed the street and walked back and forth in front of the entrance to the ministry.

"Mrs. Ireland?" a voice asked tentatively, behind her.

She turned. "Ah! Mr. Krubinski."

He smiled. "It's good to see you again. Let's see if we can sit down somewhere." He led her across the street to a bench at one side of the square. They sat and faced each other.

"I've had a hard time reaching you," Dawn said. "Can you tell me why you have become so elusive?"

"I have discovered a trove of original posters from the early part of this century. Unfortunately, our mafia also knows I have them and is anxious to make them their own."

"Are you afraid?"

"I'm cautious."

"Are these the posters you said I might be interested in?"

"Yes. We'll talk later about them. I have the permission contract right here." He began opening his briefcase.

Dawn placed her hand on his and said, "Before you get it, there's something I must ask you." He stopped unlatching the case and looked at her. "When I didn't hear from you, I asked my partner, Professor Davies, to see if he could find you when he came to Moscow last December to lead a seminar. Did he get in touch with you."

"Why, yes, he did. And we made an appointment to meet in the lobby of the Ukraina Hotel. I waited long past the hour, but he never came." Dawn began to shake, and her face turned ashen. Krubinski looked at her, concerned. "Is something wrong, Mrs. Ireland? Are you all right?"

"I'm sorry," she said. "Just give me a minute." She took several deep breaths. "Can you tell me the date of that meeting?"

"Well, yes. It's still on the contract. I dated it the day I was to meet your partner." He opened the briefcase and rummaged through it. "Here it is." He looked at her again. "Are you sure you're all right?" She nodded, hesitantly, and he removed the sheet of paper. "It was . . . yes, seventeen December."

The lights went out. The world stopped turning. The next thing Dawn knew, she was bent over with her head lying on her knees. Mr. Krubinski was standing over her, bracing her so she wouldn't fall forward. She stirred, and he helped her sit up and lean against the back of the bench. He had given her his handkerchief and she was wiping her forehead.

"Should I call a doctor, Mrs. Ireland?" he asked, concerned.

"No. I'll be okay in a minute."

"What is it?"

Dawn held up her hand for him to wait. Then, after a moment, in a shaky voice, she said, "Of course you didn't know. Who would have told you?" She tried to gather herself together. "Professor Davies was killed on December seventeenth. According to the police report, it was on Ilyinka near the corner of Varvarka Street. He was murdered, robbed."

"My dear lady. I am so sorry."

"Mr. Krubinski, I must ask you. Is that near the Ukraina Hotel?"

He looked at her with sad eyes. "Yes, it is between the hotel and the Metro station. He must have been coming to see me."

"Yes, he must have been." She sighed and let her hands fall to her lap. It was over. The months of uncertainty. The endless days of hoping it wasn't her fault. Now she knew. And with the knowing came an odd sort of calm. The anxiety was over. She *was* guilty of his death.

"Mr. Krubinski, if you will give me the contract, I'll sign it. I have the money here." He handed it to her and she signed it. "And here is your seven hundred and fifty dollars. How soon will you ship the poster?"

"Within the week. Now, what about the other posters I spoke of?"

"I'm very interested in them, but we must save that for another time. Is there some address where I can reach you?" He wrote it on a piece of notepaper and gave it to her.

"Be careful of that address," he said.

"I will. Good-bye, and thank you."

In the morning Dawn was in Professor Neleginski's office. She sat in a chair next to his desk and told him about her meeting with Krubinski. As she talked, the professor nodded. When she came to the part she dreaded, she raised her eyes to his. "Gareth never got to meet him," she said, her voice wavering. "He was killed as he walked to the hotel from the Metro station."

The older man continued nodding, then stopped. "So you think it is your fault he is dead."

"What else can I think?"

He was nodding again. "I know what you mean. I know that guilt."

He raised his eyebrows as he looked at her. "I was seventeen in 1944 and already a corporal in the Russian army. We were advancing on the Germans near Minsk. My squad came upon a German machine gun nest in one of the stalls of an old stone barn. They had us pinned down. It was night and I was ordered to crawl to the building and drop a hand grenade into the stall. In the darkness I became confused and dropped the grenade into the wrong stall. Immediately after the grenade exploded, our troops charged for-

ward. The machine gun fired and eight of our men were killed."
He stopped and looked at her. "It was my fault."

"Did they blame you for it?" she asked.

"No. I then raced back to the barn and dropped a grenade in
the right stall. The firing stopped."

"So you were able to redeem yourself."

"Yes, in the eyes of my sergeant. He thought there were two
machine guns and that I had gotten first one and then the other.
But as we passed by the barn I looked inside. There had been only
one gun and I had missed the first time. Only I knew the deaths
were my fault."

Dawn sat quietly for some time, then she asked, "How does a
person live with guilt?"

"I would have gone to each boy's parent or wife and begged
their forgiveness, but I didn't know who they were."

"So what did you do?"

"After the war I found a priest who was hiding from the Com-
munists. I asked him the same question you are asking. He said
only God can forgive you, so I made my confession and begged
God's forgiveness."

"Did he forgive you."

"Yes, because that's what he does." He raised his head so he
could look directly at her. "But it is hard to feel forgiven."

FORTY-TWO

The next day, with every issue addressed and every memory reviewed from each of their perspectives, Chuck let the matter rest. But two secrets were left unrevealed. Chuck was unable to tell his mother that, as a child, he'd felt a pleasurable excitement when her doctor friend had touched him. The memory of that was so debasing he could hardly admit it to himself.

And Harriet kept her secret. The name of the doctor.

That evening, to break out of the loop of endless arguing, they went out for dinner. For the occasion, Harriet assumed the dignified composure of the Director of Nursing at Rochester Community Hospital and Chuck relaxed into his usual mode of laid-back, casually dressed financial consultant. Only Bear showed his agitation. Afraid that Chuck was leaving him in this strange house never to return again, he put up such a barking fuss that they took him with them in the pickup truck. He was content to curl up on the seat while they ate in the restaurant, knowing that the truck was a part of home.

While they were eating, a strange thing occurred. They talked and joked not as mother and son, but as two adults. Chuck began to see Harriet as an attractive, successful woman with many friends and a commitment to a job she liked. And she began to see him as a personable yet lonely middle-aged man who was very competent in his field.

Over dinner, Harriet said, "Tell me about the woman you say you love."

Chuck, caught off guard, didn't know how to begin. "Well, she lives next door in McIntyre's old house. She's divorced and has a fifteen-year-old son." As he spoke, his voice softened and he smiled slightly. "She's got her own company. And she's beautiful. Oh, and her name's Dawn Ireland."

Harriet watched her son. "I can see you think a lot of her."

"I do, but I'm afraid if I get serious and fall in love, I'll screw it up like I did with Michelle."

"You've never really said what went wrong between you and Michelle."

"I started to and you wouldn't let me,"

"I think I can handle it now," she said.

"Okay." He paused for a moment, then said, "I couldn't perform."

"Hmm. And you think it was connected with what that guy did to you?"

"I didn't know it at the time," he said, "but yes, I do. Whenever sex got hot, I'd get turned off."

"Can I put on my Director of Nursing hat for a minute?"

Chuck laughed, "Sure. Go ahead."

Harriet looked at him seriously. "I think you're probably right. I've seen a few child abuse cases over the years and I know they can be devastating. But they're not insurmountable. Have you thought about getting some professional help?"

"You mean, like a psychologist?"

"Yes, or some kind of group counseling. We offer it at the hospital," she laughed, "but that'd be a heck of a commute."

Chuck smiled at her joke. "Michelle wanted me to get help, but I never did. Maybe I will now."

"I wish I'd said this to you years ago, Chuck. I'm so sorry. Sorry I was so absorbed in my own problems, I didn't see yours."

Chuck gave her a tender look, an offering of his forgiveness. Then he asked, "What about you, Mom? How come you never got married again? You were in your early thirties when we came here."

"I don't know. At first there was the legal fight with Charlie to retain full custody of you, then getting started in a new hospital. We were lucky your Aunt Ruth took us in. Of course it was the old family house, but Mom and Dad had left it to her. I went out some and yeah, there were a couple of guys I almost married. After you left for college I even moved in with one of them. It didn't last long. He drank orange juice from the bottle and put it back in the refrigerator."

"What's wrong with that? So did I."

"But you were a teenager. He was forty-five."

"Oh." Again they both laughed.

"Then Ruth died ten years ago and I had the house to myself. I kind of liked it that way."

Later, as Chuck was paying for dinner, he said, "Happy Birthday, Mom. This has been great."

"Oh. It is my birthday, isn't it?"

"See, I've given you a party in spite of you're not wanting one."

"Are you still mad at me?"

"Maybe, a little." There was still the resentment that she had kept him from knowing his father. But he was willing even to reconsider that. "I guess I'm still mad you aren't the perfect mother I thought you were."

"Well, I'm not. I've made a lot of mistakes and I'll probably make a lot more."

"Same here," he said, laughing.

It was nine o'clock Thursday morning when Chuck awoke. So much for his early start on the long drive home. As soon as he began putting his scattered clothes into his overnight bag, Bear commenced his nervous barking, afraid he was going to be left behind. He continued until Chuck put him in the truck, where he sat contentedly while his master ate breakfast. Harriet walked her son to the pickup truck. Chuck climbed in and opened the window.

"It's been a hard two days," he said to his mom, "but I'm glad we did it."

"I don't bend easily—I guess you've seen that—but I *am* truly sorry that bastard messed up your life and I didn't help you find your way through it."

"Well, maybe I'm through it now."

"If not now, you will be soon," and she leaned through the window and actually kissed her son.

By the time Chuck and Bear crossed into Massachusetts about five-thirty, a sudden outburst of rain slowed him to forty miles an hour. Minutes later it stopped as quickly as it started, and he speeded up again. Bear had curled up on the seat and was taking a nap. Chuck fumbled with the radio dial, up and down the AM and the FM bands, until he turned it off in disgust.

Alone and feeling bored, he found himself thinking about Dawn, how much he longed to see her. She'll be home this weekend, he thought. Maybe I should tell her that I know the cause of the nightmares and why my marriage to Michelle was ruined. He wondered what she would say. He wondered if he'd have the courage.

FORTY-THREE

Dawn returned to Marblehead and immersed herself in the final preparations for the exhibit at the Boston Museum of Art. In her spare time, covered with sweat from July's hotter than normal days, she filled orders for the Air France posters. As her Moscow trip faded into the past, she distanced herself from the pain of knowing she was responsible for Gareth's death. It was always there, however, just below the surface of every smile, waiting to gnaw at her for undeserved happiness. It was easier to reprimand Brian for staying out too late than to share his joy of having completed an entire Stephen King novel.

She saw Chuck occasionally and waved hello. Sometimes he'd start across the yard as if he wanted to talk, but she'd dash quickly into her house as if she heard the phone ringing or left something on the stove. Clara looked at Dawn in confusion when Brian, rather than she, hooked up her collar for a walk. "I can't go, honey," she would say to the dog. "Too much work to do." Then she would almost cry at the disappointment in Clara's eyes. But it was better than meeting up with Chuck and Bear at the end of the driveway and heading out to the swamp. As days passed into weeks, she anesthetized her pain by embracing despondency.

At the end of July, the phone rang. It was Vivian.

After the initial hellos, Vivian said, "I guess I can't break an old habit. Friday's August first, so I'll be out there today to do Chuck's monthly bills. I missed one month and I don't want to do that again. He tries to talk me out of coming, but the truth is, I like sitting up there in Dad's old study paying the bills just like I did when he was alive—his pictures still on the wall, the old green shade over the desk lamp—it's a way of keeping in touch." She waited for a moment, then added, "Does that sound weird, Dawn?"

"No. I miss him, too."

"I was thinking. I should be able to finish the bills by noon. What say we have lunch together? I want to hear what happened in Moscow."

"There's not much to tell, but lunch sounds good, if you don't mind leftovers."

"This is my treat. I'll come by when I finish and we'll go down to the Rio Grande. I haven't eaten there in months."

At quarter to twelve, Dawn heard Vivian calling to her through the screen door. "Anybody home?"

"Come on in, Viv. I'm just about done here."

Vivian walked into the workroom. A floor fan was catching a breeze from the cove and sending it across the room. "I'm starved, so I came early."

Dawn looked at Vivian's pastel green cotton dress, "Don't you look nice. I'd better change." She wore a halter, shorts and sandals.

"No. That's perfect for this weather." And laughing, she added, "I like to sit at the bar. If it's the usual lunchtime crew at the Rio Grande, they'll love it."

They parked across from the YMCA and walked one block to the restaurant. Conversation stopped among the six or eight men at the bar as they watched the two women enter and find a seat, then they went back to talking about their work or their cars or their boats.

"See?" Vivian whispered. Dawn looked at her and shook her head.

"What'll it be, folks?" the attractive bartender asked as she placed a basket of tortilla chips and a bowl of salsa in front of them. She was wearing tight denim shorts, a blue workshirt with *Jose Cuervo* embroidered over the pocket and a Native American choker inset with a turquoise stone.

"Hi, Fran," Vivian said to her longtime friend and one-time classmate at Marblehead High School.

"It's been a while, Viv. How are things in the burbs?"

"Okay, but I like coming home to Marblehead." Vivian turned to Dawn. "Chardonnay? We'll celebrate having lunch together." Dawn nodded. "Two chardonnays and the lunch menu."

As Fran turned away, Vivian asked, "So tell me. How did things go in Moscow?"

"I really don't want to talk about it, Viv. How're the kids?"

Vivian looked worried. "Oh, it was that bad, huh?"

"Yes," she said quietly.

Fran set the two glasses of wine on cocktail napkins in front of them. "We've got a special today—blackened tuna fajita."

Dawn looked at Vivian. "Sounds good to me."

"Me, too," Vivian said. Fran went to the computerized register and punched in their order. "Tell me what happened," Vivian asked. "You got back two days earlier than you planned."

"I got what I wanted, so I came home. Found the guy, Krubinski, who owns the poster, and we signed a contract to use it in our book and at the exhibition. Also met the professor who was working with Gareth on the seminars." She took a drink of wine, then set the glass down. End of subject.

Vivian waited for a moment. "Okay, now tell me what you're not telling me."

Dawn gave her a quick glance, then looked down at her glass. After a moment, she said, "I found out what Gareth was doing when he got killed." She spoke so softly, Vivian had to lean closer. "He was on his way to Krubinski's."

"Oh!" Vivian said sadly. "I'm sorry. And that means . . . ?"

"That means he was running my errand. Doing the job I should have done." She took a sip of wine. "Well, at least I know now. I'll just have to live with it."

Vivian looked at her and then down at the menu that was still on the counter, then back at Dawn. She blinked her eyes hard. "God!" she said, drawing out the word. "I just had the strangest feeling . . . like we'd done this before." She stared down at the open menu, then squinting, as if searching her memory, looked back at Dawn. "We were sitting on your bed. That's it. And we had a scrapbook open and we were looking at pictures of you and your dad. Remember?"

Dawn slanted her eyes toward her. "No. When?"

"Years ago. The second summer after you and your mom moved in."

Slowly Dawn nodded her head. "Oh, that. Now I remember. I showed you the poem I'd written about Icarus's daughter."

"Right," Vivian said.

"I see what you're saying. I was blaming myself for my dad's death, like I'm doing now for Gareth's. I suppose I am, but so what?" Her voice rose enough to cause the men across the U-shaped bar to lift their heads. Dawn looked at them, then lowered her head toward Vivian. "I know all this stuff," she said in a forced whisper. "That doctor I went to last January tried to tell me the same thing. But you're all missing the point. I'm not dreaming that I'm responsible for their deaths because of the way they died. It's the other way around. Their deaths are alike because I *was* responsible for both."

Fran arrived, placing two sets of plates before them, one containing a dollop of sour cream, shredded lettuce, chopped green onions and salsa and condiments for the fajita, and the other a covered dish of warm, soft tacos. Then she brought two sizzling platters of blackened tuna with slices of grilled onions and red and green peppers.

"*Bon appétit*, as they say in Spanish."

"Thanks, Fran," Vivian said. "It looks great."

Dawn began picking at her food, cutting small pieces of tuna and cooling them in the sour cream. Vivian put a little of everything on a taco and rolled it up. The cream and salsa ran down her fingers as she took a bite.

Vivian wiped her hands and cooled her mouth with a gulp of water. "When you showed me the poem," she said, concentrating on the preparation of her next fajita, "you told me never to tell your mom about it. Did you ever show it to her?"

"No. You know what those four years were like before I graduated. We couldn't talk about anything without having a fight. That's why I married Paul right after high school—to get out of the house."

"What's it like now between you and your mom?"

"She was here last fall with Martin for a couple of days. That's her husband. He was on business in Boston. They stopped by the house for lunch, then went up to Brighton to see Brian."

"Not much of a visit."

"Long enough." She nibbled some more at her fish. "I know I sound bitter, but Dad's dying knocked a hole in our relationship. I'm not sure why. Maybe I wanted more attention than she was able to give, or," she laughed sarcastically, "maybe she was trying to give me more than I thought I deserved. It all came to the same thing. We couldn't talk then and we can't talk now."

Vivian gazed around the bar. Some men had left and others, plus some women, had come in. "It's hard to talk here."

"Just as well."

Vivian picked up the bill, which was tucked into a collection of hot sauce bottles, looked at it and laid a few bills on the counter. "Thanks, Fran," she called, and, taking Dawn's elbow, "Come on, we're leaving." Dawn didn't object.

Outside, as they walked to the car, Vivian said, "I've never seen you so down. No, that's not true. You were about gone last winter after Gareth died." They came to the car and got in. Vivian turned the car in the opposite direction from Quiet Cove.

"Where're you going?"

"Out to Lighthouse Point, where we can talk without a lot of people around." They drove in silence across the causeway to Marblehead Neck and then to the far end, where the light tower rose a hundred and twenty feet above the rocky promontory. They got out and crossed a grassy slope to a marble bench placed there as a memorial to a past Marbleheader. They sat.

"It makes me sick to see you this way," Vivian said, an urgency in her voice. "You're tearing yourself apart. It's not fair to you and it's not fair to Brian." At the accusation about her son, Dawn shot her a glance, but said nothing. Vivian took her hand. "Please look at me. We've known each other for more than twenty years. Maybe we've grown apart some in the last few years, but I love you. I can't stand to see you doing this to yourself. You are too lovely a person."

Dawn looked toward the water. Three sailboats in full sail swept smartly out of the harbor, picking up speed from the freshening breeze on the ocean side of the point. She wanted to go home— she wanted Vivian to stop talking—she wished she could be out there on one of those sailboats. She didn't know what she wanted.

"Dawn, listen to me." She looked back at Vivian. "Whether you're to blame or not to blame for your dad's and Gareth's deaths, it's time to make peace with yourself."

"Yeah," she said sarcastically. "And what if I don't want to?"

"Okay, then." Vivian's voice was suddenly angry. "Go on letting us down, the people who love you: me, Brian, Josh. And, I might add, your editor and the people at the museum."

Dawn was quiet for a few moments, then turned to Vivian. "It's that bad, huh?"

"Yes, and we're all worried about you."

Emphasizing each word, Dawn said, "Believe me when I say, if I knew how to make peace with myself, I would."

"It's not that hard." Before Dawn could respond, Vivian hurried on. "You start by making peace with other people."

"Viv, I appreciate what you're trying to do, but I'm up to my neck in work and frankly, I'm exhausted. Anyway, I'm not mad at anybody. I've got no one to make peace with."

Vivian again took her other hand. Her voice was earnest. "Start, Dawn, by making peace with your mother."

Dawn sighed and slipped her hands free. "You're a good friend, but that goes too far. What's between me and Mom is none of your business. I know you're concerned and I'll see what I can do about being a better person, but leave my mother out of this. Now, I've got to get back. I'm expecting a call."

That night she took leftover broccoli, slices from a turkey breast she'd grilled two days earlier, portobello mushrooms and garlic and made a pasta that she kept warming on the stove for Brian's return home. He and Mike were working at a neighbor's house cleaning brush from a back lot. When she heard him say good-bye to Mike in the driveway, she began setting the table.

"Hi, Mom!" he called, slamming the screen door.

"Don't slam the door," she yelled.

"Sorry."

She looked at him as he came into the kitchen. His shirt was torn and his face smeared with dirt. A twig still clung to his hair. He pulled out a chair to sit down and knocked over the one next to it. Collapsing into the first chair, he reached back with his left hand and righted the other one. Dawn suppressed an urge to throw her arms around him and kiss him.

"What a day!" he said, letting his head fall backward over the back of the chair. "Hot as you know what. But he paid us fifty dollars each."

"Good for you." She was carrying plates to the table. "Dinner's ready, but it can wait if you want to shower."

"Oh, umm, Mike and I are going to a show . . . if it's okay. We'll get a hamburger on the way."

She set the plates down hard on the table. "No, it's not okay. You've worked all day and you need to eat." He pursed his lips. "I don't want you going out tonight anyway. You've got to get up early to help out at the children's camp."

"It's the early show, Mom. I'll still be in by ten or maybe eleven."

"I suppose Mike's planning to drive."

"How the hell do you think we'd get there otherwise?"

"Don't get smart with me."

Brian jumped up, knocking the chair over again, and stomped out of the kitchen. Livid with anger, she watched him go, then went to the stove and turned off the burner under the pasta. Pretty soon she heard the water come on in the shower upstairs. She remained by the stove, clutching its corners to steady herself. As another wave of anger hit, she grabbed up the pot and dumped the pasta into the sink. Then she sat down at the table, holding her head in her hands.

Five minutes later, maybe ten, Brian came to the kitchen wrapped in a towel.

"I'm sorry, Mom. I'll eat dinner here."

Without raising her head, "No you won't. I threw it out."

He stood in the doorway for several moments. "I didn't know you had dinner all ready. Mike and I'd had such a good day working and earning all that money that we wanted to celebrate."

He waited for a minute for her to say something and, when she didn't, crossed to her side. "I'm sorry I lost my temper," he said.

Tentatively he placed his hand on her shoulder. "Please don't be mad at me."

She clasped her hand over the hand he'd put on her shoulder. Slowly she raised her head. Her eyes were red from crying, her cheeks stained with tears. She turned in the chair and hugged him around his waist. "I'm sorry, too. I'm not mad anymore."

"I'll stay home."

"No. It's okay now. I'm all right. You go to the show with Mike. I'm sorry I blew up." She wiped her eyes with one of the napkins from the table.

"Are you sure?"

"I'm sure. Go ahead now."

"Thanks." And he was racing up the stairs to get dressed.

When he left, Dawn went to her room and dug out the scrapbook from the top shelf of her closet. She hadn't looked at it in more than twenty years. There were the pictures of her with her dad and mom when she was growing up, the newspaper article about his crash and the obituary. Stuck in the back page was the poem. She read it and then read it again. Taking the scrapbook and poem with her, she went to her workroom and turned on the computer.

Dear Mom:

How long has it been since I've written you? Now that I think of it, I've never written you. Imagine that. Only called when I was coming to the West Coast and felt I had to make an obligatory visit. I didn't think you wanted to hear from me. I knew I didn't want to see or hear from you.

Tonight I was looking though a scrapbook I made before Dad died, pictures of the three of us having a good time together. What ever happened to that? How did we lose it? I know it was when Dad died, but why?

I'm faxing this to you so you'll get it before I have time to change my mind. I'm also faxing a poem I wrote after he died. I hid it from you so you wouldn't know how I felt.

If you're there and get this fax, please read it.

Mom, I'm sorry that we haven't talked, really talked to each other all these years. I love you. Dawn.

She went to her address file and faxed off the letter and poem before she could change her mind.

Half an hour later her phone rang.

"Hello, Dawn?"

"Mom?"

"I got your fax." Pause. "It's beautiful." Dawn could hear her mother weeping as she talked. "I was afraid to write you. The few times we've been together were like standing on the edge of a volcano. I was as anxious to get away as I think you were."

"I was," Dawn said, tears in her eyes. "I was always afraid you'd start talking about Dad and break down and cry. I couldn't have stood that."

"I felt that way, too. I know how much you loved him. I tried never to talk about him."

"And he was there, between us," Dawn said, "every time we were together."

"I missed him so much. After the funeral I wanted to hug you and cry with you, but you didn't shed a tear. So I cried by myself in my bedroom with the door shut."

"I was afraid to be with you, Mom, because of what I'd done. That's why I never showed you the poem, the one I faxed to you."

"I read it. You wrote it soon after the accident. I guess you meant it to be about you and your dad, but it doesn't make sense. In your poem, Icarus's daughter caused her father to fly too close to the sun. She caused his death."

"What do you mean, it doesn't make sense?" Dawn said. "We had that awful fight the night before he was killed and I wouldn't make up."

There was a moment's silence on the line. "I'd forgotten about that," Dawn's mother said, "and it must have been awful not having had a chance to make up, but that's got nothing to do with the accident."

"It doesn't?"

"No. They recovered the plane. They found a leak in the hydraulic system."

FORTY-FOUR

Chuck was coming down the stairs from the study where he'd put in a couple of hours' work after Vivian left for lunch. He'd missed thanking her for doing the bills because he'd been in the side yard pruning sucker branches from the apple trees. As he passed the front door, he was surprised to see her pulling into Dawn's driveway. He stopped to watch. Bear caught up to him and helped watch. Dawn got out of the passenger door, slamming it harder than necessary, and stormed into her house. Vivian waited for a minute, backed out to the street and left.

"I wonder what that's all about," Chuck said to Bear. "Looks like they had an argument."

He went into his kitchen to prepare a sandwich for a late lunch. The sound of the refrigerator door opening drew Bear. Both sets of eyes were searching the glass trays for leftovers when Chuck heard someone coming up the steps from the garage. He looked up to see Vivian at the door.

"I just saw you drive away."

"I know." She crossed to the kitchen table and sat down. "I went around the corner and parked by the boat shed. Didn't want Dawn to see me coming in here." Her voice was curt.

"I'm glad you came back. I wanted to thank you for doing the bills."

"You're welcome. I like doing them." He could see she was

upset, so he closed the refrigerator door and took the chair beside her. Bear lay down pressed against the refrigerator door.

"What happened out there in the driveway? Dawn looked mad."

"She was. That's why I'm here. I'm worried about her."

"Is something wrong?" Chuck asked. "I've hardly seen her since she got back from Moscow."

"I hadn't seen her in a while either, so I asked her to go to lunch. You weren't here right after Gareth died, but she's almost as depressed as she was then. I told her so and she got mad."

"What's it about?"

"She found out that Gareth was killed on his way to see the man who owns the poster, the one she's using in the book. So she blames herself for his death."

"She's told me there might be a possibility of that."

"Well, now she knows for certain. So she's blaming herself for both her dad's and Gareth's deaths. It's an obsession." Vivian, as much at home in what was once her father's kitchen as in her own, got up and went to a cupboard. "Would you like a cup of tea?"

"No. But I'll make myself a sandwich while you're making your tea."

Five minutes later they were back at the kitchen table, Chuck with a bottle of beer, munching on a cheese and lettuce sandwich. Vivian sipped her tea, Bear sitting between them.

"After lunch," Vivian said, "I drove her out to Lighthouse Point so we could talk. I felt so sorry for her. She looked terrible. I told her there wasn't much she could do about Gareth's or her father's death, but she could start getting her life back together by making peace with people around her. When I mentioned making peace with her mother, she exploded and told me to mind my own business. I don't know what to do now."

"There's not much I can do. I've tried some friendly overtures, but she turns and runs away."

"I love her so much. She's practically my sister and such a lovely person. I hate to see her this way."

"I know how you feel," he said sadly, "believe me."

Vivian looked down at Bear and rubbed his forehead. Bear, however, was concentrating on Chuck's cheese sandwich and didn't seem to notice. His master tossed him a small piece of cheese and the dog caught it in midair.

Vivian sighed audibly and shrugged her shoulders. Then, changing the subject, "When I came this morning, I expected to see a FOR SALE sign in the yard. You haven't sold it already, have you?"

"It's not on the market."

"That's good news," she said, smiling for the first time since she arrived. "Does that mean you're staying?"

"I might. For the time being, anyway."

"Hmm. What changed your mind?"

He lifted the bottle to his lips and drank. When he set it down he was smiling. "It's a different house. It seems friendlier."

"Come on, now," she said disgustedly. "Tell me what's happened."

"I found out Dad wasn't such a bad guy after all."

"I told you that."

"I know, but when I went up to Rochester for Mom's birthday, I discovered that most of the stuff I believed from childhood about him wasn't true." He left it at that. Telling her that it wasn't his dad who'd abused him would have been too much. "He even paid to send me to college."

"I'm so glad you found all that out. Why did you think Josh and I and Dawn loved him so much?"

"I know that now, but it took me some time. When Bear and I got back from Rochester and drove into the driveway, the house looked different. Like I said, it looked friendly. So I decided to stay for a while."

She placed her hand on top of his. "I'm relieved. None of us wanted you to move away."

"Thanks," he said and kissed her on the cheek.

Her face brightened. "That means we can have Dad's birthday party."

He frowned. "Birthday party?"

"His birthday's August ninth. I wanted to have a party just like we always did, here, with the whole family, but with you selling the house it didn't seem right. Now we can do it."

"Isn't that just a touch morbid?"

She ignored his question. "We'll decorate just like we used to. Dad'd want it that way."

At eleven-thirty on August ninth, Vivian's van pulled into the driveway. Chuck and Bear crossed the yard to meet them. Carl came around from the driver's side, opened the sliding door and undid the seat belts for the three kids. Before he could back out, they were tumbling out the door and hugging Bear. Vivian called to Chuck to help her and went to the back of the van. Out came a dozen hydrogen-filled balloons, on which HAPPY BIRTHDAY, CHARLIE was written. She handed the strings to Chuck. "I'll get the rest of the decorations. Take those up to the porch."

Brian and Clara came out the back door of their house, the dog rushing down to play with Bear and the children, and Brian coming to the porch. "Can I help?"

"Sure," Chuck said. "Hold these while I tie them to the railing."

Vivian came up the steps carrying more decorations, and said to Chuck, "I see you've got the grill going. Good timing. The food's in the van." When Chuck finished tying up the balloons, he went with Vivian to the van to get the food. As she opened the back door, she said, "I hope you don't mind, but I invited Dawn. We couldn't have a birthday party for Charlie without inviting her."

"That's fine with me. Do you think she'll come?"

"I hope so."

She handed Chuck trays of hamburger patties and a bowl of potato salad, and sent him on his way. She brought a covered cake tin containing the birthday cake.

Carl was attaching a Mylar banner across the front of the house. The words "Happy Birthday" were repeated again and again in brilliant colors. Beneath the banner he stretched a piece of brown wrapping paper bearing Charlie's name in bold letters. When everything was ready, they went to the front lawn to admire their handiwork.

"Pretty good," Vivian said, her hands on her hips. "I think Dad's impressed, wherever he is." There was general agreement.

At the sound of the screen door closing on Dawn's porch, conversation stopped. They all turned to see Dawn walking briskly

toward them. Her full ankle-length dress of thin rust-colored material flowed out behind her. A breeze lifted her blond hair. She was
smiling.

Chuck, feeling the excitement she used to arouse in him,
watched her crossing the lawn. He found himself smiling in response to her smile and wanted to rush to her and take her in his
arms. But he didn't, and his need to control himself left him feeling empty.

But Vivian ran to Dawn and gave her a hug. They stood there
together, talking and laughing softly, until Carl called to his wife.

"Come on, Viv, don't keep her all to yourself."

Vivian turned, smiled and, taking Dawn's hand, led her to the
group.

"Hi, Dawn," Carl said. "How do you like the decorations?"

For an instant, as she turned toward the banners and the balloons, her eyes connected with Chuck's. The flicker of a smile
seemed to ask for something that he was afraid to let himself believe. Then she was speaking.

"They're beautiful, Carl. Only one thing's missing." Carl
looked as though he was about to ask, What? when Vivian moved
past him, putting her arm around Dawn. Silently they looked at
the banner, their heads tipped until they were touching. Then,
blinking her eyes, Dawn said to Vivian, "I'm glad you wanted to
do this. Thanks."

At that moment an unfamiliar red Miata convertible with the
top down drove into the yard. Josh was driving and Cliff was waving. They parked, but instead of getting out, Josh sat up on the
back of his seat and called to the group.

"How do you like my new car?"

"Ooo! I like it," Dawn responded.

"I decided to spend some of the money Dad left me. Just the
thing a Boston real estate agent should drive, don't you think?"

Carl laughed, "If he's got only one client at a time."

Brian ran to the car and exclaimed his latest word for total ap-
preciation. "Ragged! Can I sit in it?"

"Sure. Hop in." Josh got out to make room for Brian.

"You've got to take me for a ride later," Brian shouted to him, but Josh had joined his sister and was looking at his father's birthday banners.

"It's almost like it used to be," Josh said.

When his nephew and nieces saw him they left Bear and Clara and ran to him. "Hi, Uncle Josh. Give us a piggyback ride." Jeremy tried to tackle his leg and Jackie pulled on his arm. Little Joslynn stood by coyly, waiting for Josh to pick her up, which he did.

Cliff shook hands with everybody and gave Vivian a hug.

They walked onto the porch and Chuck asked for drink orders, beer or wine. When he started for the kitchen, he asked Josh to help him. His half-brother seemed cool to the request, but complied reluctantly.

When they were out of earshot, Chuck said, "I want to apologize." Josh lowered one eyelid and looked at him warily. "I'm sorry for what I said about Dad. I was wrong." They stood across the kitchen table facing each other."

"*I* told you that."

"And you were right. I know for certain I was abused by some man, but he wasn't Dad."

"How the hell could you even think it was Dad?"

"He used to come into my room when he'd get back from a flight and kiss me good night. Then one night this guy started coming in and playing with me, and I confused the two of them. The point is," Chuck said weakly, "I found out from my mom it wasn't Dad."

"Who was it?"

Chuck looked down at the table. After a moment's pause, he said, "This is hard because it makes my mom look bad, but the truth is," he raised his eyes to Josh, "he was a friend of Mom's."

Josh wrinkled his nose in disgust. "Ugh," he uttered and turned away.

"It's not as bad as it sounds. She knew nothing about this, and when she found out, she kicked him out of the house."

"Still, to be seeing a man who'd do that to a child . . ."

"Okay, she was dead wrong about that, but I can tell you, as a mother she was the best."

"So this happened at the time they got divorced. It wasn't just because Dad had met Mom in Paris. He must have known about your mom's boyfriends."

"Look, I don't want to argue about what did and didn't happen between them. The point is, I'm sorry for what I said."

"Okay. Let's get the drinks." Josh pulled open the refrigerator door roughly and started getting bottles. "How many beers was that?"

"Three. I'll get my own."

Josh opened three bottles and took them to the porch. Chuck was pouring two glasses of wine when Dawn came into the kitchen.

"Do you have a Coke for Brian and some juice for the kids?"

"There's Coke and orange juice in the fridge. I'll get it."

"No, let me."

They faced each other as they turned toward the refrigerator.

"Hi," Chuck said.

"Hi." She looked at him and smiled the same way she had on the lawn.

"Aaah," Chuck uttered, unable to find words.

She put her hand on his arm. "When Vivian called to invite me, she said she'd told you about what happened in Moscow. Things are better now. I'm okay."

"I'm glad. I'm doing better, too." Her hand was still on his arm.

"You've got a good sister," she said.

He nodded, "I know."

Removing her hand from his arm, she said, "I'd better get the juice for the kids."

"I'll get Brian's Coke."

They smiled and went about their tasks.

After hamburgers and potato salad, a cake inscribed "Happy Birthday Charlie" was set on the porch table. There were no candles on the cake and no one started the birthday song. Instead, they just stood in a silent circle around the cake: Cliff beside Josh, who was holding Vivian's hand, then Chuck, Dawn and Brian, and finally Carl, holding in each arm a squirming Jackie and Joslynn. Jeremy had his arm locked around his dad's leg.

Chuck looked to see if anyone else was going to say something, and when no one appeared to be, he spoke. "Seeing I'm the new-comer here, I want to say a few words about my dad. I regret that I grew up never knowing him. For me he's always been the forty-year-old man whose lap I sat on looking up at the picture of him in front of his P-47 Thunderbolt. God! Forty. About my age now." He paused to reflect on that, then went on. "Now, thanks to all of you, I've come to know him in his later years. I can see he was a kind and loving father and friend. Happy birthday, Charlie."

"Happy Birthday, Charlie," everyone said quietly.

Jeremy squeezed himself to the front of the circle. "Can we have some cake now?"

"Yes, darling," Vivian said. "We'll have some cake." She began slicing the cake while Dawn scooped out ice cream, serving the children first, then the adults. Bear and Clara, who had done very well picking up pieces of hamburger dropped by the kids, now followed them to the lawn, ready to assist them with dessert.

"That was beautiful, Chuck, what you said about Dad." Vivian took a chair beside him, and set her coffee cup on the railing.

"Thanks." He looked down as he collected his thoughts, then turned toward his half-sister. "I've found out some things about Mom, mine, that is, and Dad. I can see now I was really out of line when I made their divorce all Dad's fault. It wasn't. I apologize for what I said."

She smiled at him. "That's okay."

"There's more if you want to hear it."

"No, I don't think so." Neither spoke for a while. "Like we said, it was a long time ago."

"Well, I want you to know that I don't blame Dad."

"I know that, and I don't blame your mom." She laughed. "I have enough trouble as it is trying not to blame Carl and the kids. I don't need to take on other people's problems, especially when those problems occurred before I was born."

Like the Fourth of July party, the group split up to play croquet and badminton—Chuck had found a set in the basement—or to go for a sail. There were always two or three on the porch taking time out to rest or have a beer. Chuck was sitting beneath the umbrella drinking a beer when Cliff and Josh approached. Cliff had his hand in the center of Josh's back and was actually pushing him in Chuck's direction. He stood up to meet them.

"Josh tells me you apologized for what you said about Charlie." While Cliff was speaking, Josh ignored both of them, his eyes studying the roof of the house.

"That's right."

"And he also said that the damage had been done when you said it and no apology was going to make things right." Chuck acknowledged this with a nod. "Now I have something to say. Josh? Are you listening?" Josh sighed, then gave his partner a condescending look. "All right," Cliff continued. "Do you have any idea how hard it must have been for Chuck to tell you the truth about what happened, that he had been sexually abused, and by a friend of his mother?" Again Josh looked away. "And on top of that, to tell you that he was sorry for having suggested that your dad—his dad too—might have done it."

Josh glared at Cliff. "Are you through?"

"For the time being, yes."

"Good. Now I have something to say." His face shook with anger as he looked at Chuck. "*Your* dad, huh? You don't even know him as your dad. All those years when he saved that room of yours, hoping you'd come back. But no. You didn't come back. How hard would it have been to come and see him? No, you stayed away nursing your hatred. Hell, he had to die and give you the house before you'd come back. And you have the fucking gall to stand with us, Viv and me, around that cake and say what a wonderful man he was. You're nothing but a goddamned fake." With that, he started down the steps, speaking to Cliff over his shoulder. "I'll be in the car when you're ready to go."

The words hit Chuck like a body blow, shattering the fragile confidence the day had brought to him. He sat down on the railing and watched him walk away.

"I'm sorry," Cliff said. Chuck nodded but said nothing.

The party ended a short time later when everybody gathered to cut free the balloons—everybody but Josh, who was sitting in his bright red car his father's money had bought him. Those on the porch watched with a mixture of joy and sadness as the HAPPY BIRTHDAY, CHARLIE balloons rose higher and higher, until, as tiny black dots against the afternoon clouds, they disappeared into the sky.

When the cars had driven away, Chuck was in the kitchen cleaning up.

"Can we help?" He turned toward the kitchen door. It was Dawn and Brian.

"That's okay. There's not much." They'd used paper plates and plastic spoons and cups.

"If you've got a garbage bag, we'll collect the stuff on the porch." Chuck handed them one and they left. Her presence helped revive his spirits. In a couple of minutes they returned.

"Brian wants to ask you something," Dawn said.

Chuck let the spatula he was scrubbing drop into the soapy water and dried his hands. "What's that?"

"I wondered if Mike and I could take *Thunderbolt* for a sail tomorrow, maybe go up to Manchester?"

"It's fine with me if it's okay with your mom."

Brian turned toward his mother and she nodded yes. "You're a better sailor than I am," Chuck laughed, "so she's safer in your hands than mine."

"And we were also wondering if you would mind if we spent the night on the boat so we could get an early start?"

"I don't see why not." The words caused Brian to beam.

Dawn spoke to him. "Do I have to call Mike's mom to let her know it's okay?"

"Oh, yeah. I forgot. Could you do that now?"

Dawn smiled and picked up the kitchen phone. While she was talking, Chuck asked, "How long a sail is it to Manchester?"

"Depending on the wind, about two to four hours."

"Have you got everything you need: compass, chart, things like that?"

"Uh-huh, and Mike's got a cellular phone he's bringing."

Dawn hung up. "She says okay, but be sure to check the weather in the morning."

"We will," Brian called as he ran for the door.

Suddenly the kitchen grew quiet. Chuck and Dawn looked at each other awkwardly. Then he stuck his hands back in the soapy water, searching for the spatula, and Dawn tied up the top of the garbage bag.

"Viv says you might be staying for a while."

"That's right," he said, rinsing the spatula and starting on the coffee pot. "I took the house off the market."

"What changed your mind, if I might ask?"

"I like it here. Now that I've put so much into the house, I'd hate to have somebody else move in. It feels like a home, and I've never really had that feeling about other places I've lived."

"I'm glad you're staying. Brian is, too. Well, I'd better be getting home."

"I'll walk you to the door." Drying his hands on a towel, he followed her through the house to the front door. He held open the screen for her. "It's good to see you, Dawn. I'm glad you came to the party."

"So am I."

She was less than three feet from him. It would be so easy to reach out and take her hands in his. The sun setting behind the house was sending long shadows across the lawn and turning the trees to gold on the island beyond the cove. The air was soft, the breeze quiet and her smile warm. She stood there beyond what the rhythm of their parting allowed and still she remained, he looking at her and she at him. Then she turned and walked away.

At the step, she stopped. "Good night, and thanks."

FORTY-FIVE

Like most homes in Marblehead, Dawn's had no central air conditioning. Open windows and the sea breeze were enough to cool the house most nights. But Saturday night was one of the two or three nights a summer when she could have used an air conditioner. By morning it was hotter than it had been the evening before. She awoke early, with perspiration sticking the sheet to her bare back and strands of hair to her forehead. Rolling onto her stomach brought a brief respite as the sweat on her back evaporated, yet it didn't last long. The morning sun streaming into her room added to the heat, but also to the beauty of the day.

She got up and walked to the window. Still half-asleep, she took a deep breath, circled her arms over her head and slowly let them down as she exhaled. Five times she repeated this maneuver, then leaned on the sill and gazed at the harbor. Not a leaf was stirring, and the water in the cove was as smooth as glass. "Not much of a day for sailing," she said to Clara, who was still curled up in her chair. At the sound of Dawn's voice, Clara perked up her ears. Then Dawn noticed that *Thunderbolt* was gone. She shook her head and smiled. "Talk about eager. They must have motored out of the cove. Probably sitting out there in Salem Sound waiting for a breeze."

Dawn went to her closet and put on her white terrycloth robe. A flick of her hands brought her hair out of the collar and allowed it to fall outside the robe. When she started down the stairs, Clara leaped from the chair and was hard on her heels. Together they trooped to the kitchen, where Dawn made coffee, then out the front door to get the paper. Soon they were seated on the steps, Clara stretched out in the sun and Dawn reading the paper. When she reached page three of the first section, she spoke to Clara.

"Get the coffee, will ya, honey? I'll take mine black."

Clara cocked her head, not understanding the request.

"Oh, all right. I'll get it myself." Dawn got up, went to the kitchen and returned to the top step with a mug of coffee.

Sunday. What did she have to do? There were several orders for Air France posters that had come in during the week. She could pack those for shipping. As for the exhibit, since it was the weekend, there wasn't much she could do except worry about it. Her mind told her the first order of business was getting breakfast and walking Clara, but her body remained sitting on the steps. She leaned back on her elbows and stretched out her legs, carefully tucking the robe around them. Closing her eyes, she listened to the birds and allowed the languid August morning to calm her get-busy mind.

Her thoughts drifted to last evening's parting at Chuck's door. I thought he was going to take me in his arms or at least say something, she said to herself. He looked like he wanted to. But what would I have done if he had? She knew the answer. She would have gone into his arms. Hmm, she wondered. Then what? I might have stayed. Brian was no worry. He was spending the night on the boat. It would have been so easy.

It wasn't falling in love that worried her. She already loved him. It was he who had pulled away from her. *Maybe he's still not ready.* If he wasn't, she wasn't sure she had the energy to start up the relationship again, only to have it break off.

But she did feel stronger. Vivian had been right. All those years of nursing anger toward her mother had been more of a drain than she'd realized. And all because she thought that she, Dawn, had caused her dad's death. How different life would have been if she'd shown the poem to her mother as her teacher had urged her to do.

But what if Chuck were to have an accident? And it was her fault? Did she have the strength to face that? Or was she always going to be the cause for every effect in the life of those she loved? Suddenly she was seized by another thought.

What if it was Brian who had the accident?

The ringing of her phone suddenly filled her with terror. She ran into the house and grabbed up the receiver.

"Yes?"

"Hi, Mom."

"Brian. Are you all right?"

"Sure. Why?"

"Where are you?"

"Sitting in the boat. Thought I'd try out the cellular phone. Guess it works okay."

Dawn closed her eyes and took a deep breath. "Yes. It seems to."

"Well, see ya."

"Wait!" she shouted into the phone. "Tell me where you are. What's happening?"

"Not much. We're out a ways. Got the sails up, but there's no wind."

"Are you coming back in, then?"

"Oh no. The wind's supposed to come up."

"Did you eat breakfast?"

"Yeah. I gotta go. I can see some ripples on the water behind us. Maybe it's a breeze. Bye!" He hung up.

Dawn sighed and looked down at Clara. "I don't know if I can manage this." The dog tilted up her head and wagged her tail. "Okay. Let's get some breakfast."

After they ate they walked out Cove Road to the point. A southwest breeze had come up, and *Thunderbolt* was nowhere to be seen. Let them go, she said to herself, and headed back to the house to fill the orders for the posters.

Concentrating on counting, rolling and stuffing the posters into shipping tubes, she lost track of time. The printed address labels were laid out in order on the worktable and she was carefully affixing the right label to the right tube. The curtains at the window lifted gently as a cooling breeze refreshed the room. She stretched and wiped her brow with a Kleenex. It felt good. Then back to work. Nine labels remained on the table when suddenly the curtains billowed and a wind scattered the labels onto the floor.

"Oh, hell," she said. "Now they're all out of order."

She started to pick them up when she noticed how dark the room had become. Going to the window, she closed it against a substantial breeze. Outside, the tree branches were beginning to thrash and fallen leaves were blowing across the lawn.

"My God!" she said aloud. "It's a storm."

She raced to the phone and dialed Mike's cellular phone. It seemed to take forever, but finally it began to ring. After eight rings she could hear the circuit flip to a different ring and then an electronic voice said, "Your party is unable to answer or has left the receiving area." Then the line went dead. Frantically she tried it again. Maybe she'd dialed the wrong number. Again the same electronic voice. She hung up and ran to Chuck's house. Heavy drops of rain were beginning to fall.

Opening the screen door, she rushed in. "Chuck! Are you home?" No answer. Running up the stairs, she called again. "Chuck!"

"Dawn? I'm in the study. Come on up."

She hurried down the hall to the study.

"They're out there and it's starting to storm," she said leaning against the doorjamb. He got up from the desk and went to the window.

"That blew up in a hurry."

"It's starting to rain," she said, out of breath. "I called them and they didn't answer."

"What's the number?" She gave it to him and he tried it on the study phone. They waited while it rang. Then Chuck hung up. "Not able to answer or out of the receiving area," he said.

"That's what I got, too." She looked at him. "I'm scared, Chuck. Something's happened to them. I know it." She began pacing back and forth across the study. "What was I thinking when I let him go out there? He's only fifteen."

"Dawn," he said gently. "Stop for minute." He placed his hands on her shoulders. Her blouse was wet from having run through the rain. "Tell me. When did they say they'd be back?"

"Not until this evening. The weather was fine this morning. I had no idea it would get like this."

"Look, it's only one o'clock. They were going to Manchester. They're probably there now, tied up in the harbor. Maybe they've gone ashore and left the phone on the boat."

She twisted out of his grip and began pacing again, chewing on the knuckles of her right hand. "You don't know that. How do you know that?"

"I'll find out." Chuck dialed information and asked for the harbor master at Manchester, got the number and called it. After a few moments he was talking to someone, giving them a description of the boat and the two boys, then he hung up. "They'll check and call me back in a few minutes."

"It came up so quickly. I was packaging posters in my workroom. I wasn't paying attention to the weather."

"Let's go downstairs and wait there." He turned off his computer and, taking her elbow, led her to the stairs. When they got to the kitchen, the phone was ringing. Chuck picked it up.

After listening for a minute, he said, "Okay. Well, please be on the lookout and call me if you see them." Pause. "Good idea. Do you have the number?" Pause. "I'll call them right away."

"The boat's not there. They gave me the number of the Coast Guard."

Dawn came to his side. Her eyes were red. She was rigid with fear. He held her by her shoulders. "Look. We'll find them. Brian's a sensible guy. They probably headed in somewhere as soon as they saw the storm coming."

She said nothing, just stared at him.

"Does Brian know the number of your cellular phone?"

She nodded several times, then said, "Yes, I think so."

"Then run up to your house and get the phone. Bring it back here."

Dawn hesitated for a moment, then hurried to the door. She stopped briefly on the porch to survey the harbor, but *Thunderbolt* wasn't in sight. Then she sprinted to her workroom, got the portable phone and came back to Chuck's kitchen.

He held his hand over the phone as she came in. "I've got Coast Guard Search and Rescue in Gloucester." Then back to the phone. "That's right, it's a sailboat, O'Day 22 . . . Out of Marble-head . . . No, not a marina. Out of Quiet Cove where we moor the boat . . . Two boys, age fifteen and sixteen. Brian Ireland and Mike—I don't know his last name. Brian's a good sailor . . . They left this morning, early . . . Telephoned by cellular phone about nine. They were in Salem Sound . . . Yes, they have life preservers. No radio, just the phone . . . Yes, we've tried calling several times. No answer."

Chuck listened for a few moments, then asked, "Can you send out one of your boats?" Pause. "How long will that be?" She could see him getting mad. "An hour?" He listened again, then said thanks and hung up.

"He said he'd send their boats as soon as they returned from another mission north of Cape Ann."

"An hour?" Dawn cried. "Christ! That might be too late."

"He also said he'd notify other vessels in the area on the VHR 16 emergency channel as well as the police and fire department rescue teams along the coast."

She came to him and gripped his arms tightly. "We've got to find him." She was shaking with fear.

Suddenly, Chuck moved her back and picked up the phone again. "I've got an idea." He turned the phone on speaker and dialed a number.

"Hello, Francis?"

"Hey there, Chuck. If this is about an electrical problem, it's Sunday. I'll get back to you in the morning. If it's about fishing, let's talk."

"I need your help. Brian, Dawn's son, and a friend are out in my sailboat."

"In this weather?"

"Yeah, and they're not answering their cellular phone."

"Do you know where they went?"

"They were going to Manchester, so they're somewhere be-tween here and there."

"Well, quit talkin'. Let's go get 'em. Meet me at the boat ramp behind Devereux Beach in ten minutes. Bring your portable phone."

Chuck hung up. "You got the phone?" She held it up. "Let's

go." Not stopping for rain gear, they ran down to the garage and got in the truck.

They arrived at the boat ramp in time to see Francis backing his boat trailer down the ramp. The sky was heavy and a strong south-west wind was blowing over the road and into the sheltered harbor, whipping up whitecaps.

With Francis giving the orders, they slid the boat off the trailer and into the water. Chuck held the bow line while Francis parked his pickup. Then they were off. Chuck asked Dawn for the phone and called the Coast Guard. The duty officer had no new informa-tion for them, but Chuck gave him the number of the cellular phone. Then he handed the phone to Dawn. Sitting with her back to the wind and rain, she held a piece of canvas over her head and began dialing Mike's number. Chuck stood beside Francis at the central console. She could hear them talking as she tried again and again to reach Mike's phone.

"It's a southwest wind about twenty-five knots," Francis shouted over the engine's roar. "Twenty-five knots is not all that bad, but we're getting some pretty heavy gusts. The rain doesn't help, either."

"I hope to hell they've put in somewhere."

"Don't worry. We'll find 'em. If they're still out here and com-ing from Manchester, the wind's right in their face. They're having to tack all the way."

When they reached the mouth of the harbor, Francis gave the two hundred-horsepower Evinrude full throttle and the Aquasport lifted out of the water. Waves began slamming against the hull as they chased the rolling swells across Salem Sound. Dawn glanced out from under the canvas to see that they were passing Children's Island to starboard and Eagle Island to port.

Fifteen or twenty minutes later she felt Chuck's hand on her shoulder. He said something that was lost in the wind.

Pulling the piece of canvas aside, she twisted up to look at him. "What?"

"Anything?"

"No. It rings seven or eight times and then a voice says your party must be out of the receiving area. Christ, maybe they've been swept out into the ocean."

"Not likely," Francis yelled. "They've probably dropped the phone overboard."

Dawn gave him a frightened look and went back to her phoning.

Fifteen minutes later, with the lighthouse on Bakers Island off their starboard beam, they were able to see Manchester Bay behind Great Misery Island.

"There's a sail!" Francis yelled, pointing to the left of the bow. Chuck leaned next to him, so his eyes could follow Francis's pointing finger. He reached behind him and squeezed Dawn's shoulder. "There's a sail."

Immediately she jumped up. "Where?"

Chuck pointed. "That looks like *Thunderbolt*, don't you think?"

Rubbing the rain from her eyes, "The sail looks right."

Francis pointed the Aquasport toward the sail and the three of them clung together by the wheel, their eyes fixed on the same distant spot. With each minute the sail grew larger and the possibility that it was the boys stronger. The boat was sailing without a jib, but they would have taken that down because of the storm. Four minutes later they were certain. It was *Thunderbolt*, sailing briskly on a port tack. They were within a hundred feet of the sailboat before the boys noticed them. As Francis throttled back to the speed of the sailboat and began paralleling its course, two surprised faces turned toward them.

"Ahoy!" Francis called.

Brian, half-rising from his seat by the tiller, yelled back, "Mom? Chuck? What are you doing out here?"

Dawn was so mad she couldn't answer. Chuck shouted, "Looking for you."

"For us? We're right here."

Dawn found her voice. "We've been calling and calling you. Why didn't you answer the phone?"

"It's in the cabin somewhere. We didn't want to get it wet." As Mike ducked into the cabin, Dawn quickly dialed his number again. A moment later, Mike emerged from the cabin holding the phone. "Hang on a minute," he shouted. "It's ringing. Hello."

"Hello, Mike. This is Dawn." Mike's eyes shot across the water toward her. "Mike," she said in measured tones, "the whole point of taking the damn phone was to be able to keep in touch. How can we keep in touch when your phone is shut up in the cabin?"

She heard him say, "Here, Brian, I think it's for you."

"Hi, Mom."

"Brian, you have put us through hell." She emphasized each word.

"I'm sorry. We *were* on our way home."

Dawn, furious, punched the OFF button.

"Wrap up those sails, boys," Francis bellowed, "We're towing you back."

Brian, dejected, dropped his shoulders and brought the bow into the wind until the sail luffed. Mike uncleated the main halyard and let the main down, then furled it. Francis came alongside and passed a line to Mike, who secured it to the bow cleat.

The engine roared, and they began the sluggish job of towing the sailboat back to Marblehead against the howling headwind. The rain beat against their faces, requiring them to constantly wipe their eyes. They were thoroughly drenched. The boys had the roughest ride, as the bow of *Thunderbolt* slammed down hard against the waves.

Dawn sat on the seat, her lips pressed tightly together and her arms folded. Chuck stood beside her, his arm on her shoulder. "At least we found them," he said, attempting to assuage her anger.

"Absolutely no remorse," she snapped. "And did you see that expression when we told them to lower the sails? We were interfering with their fun. They have no sense of the trouble they've caused."

"Speaking of trouble," Francis said to Dawn, "you'd better call the Coast Guard and tell 'em we found 'em."

A minute later she said, "I got them. They're sending out the word on the emergency channel and notifying the local rescue teams." She got up and stood by Chuck at the console. "I don't know. Sometimes I think he's too much for me. I say no, and he sulks. I say yes, and he takes advantage of it. And today, if we hadn't found them, they might never have gotten home."

Dawn glanced back at the sailboat. The two boys, looking like outraged victims, were hunched at the stern, bracing themselves on the gunwales against the bouncing of the boat. She tapped

Chuck's arm and gestured toward the sailboat. "I hope they suffer."

Francis turned to have a look, then laughed. "Typical fifteen-year-olds." Dawn shot him an angry look. "When I was that age," he went on, "I took a bunch of guys in my dad's boat out to Children's Island and we built this big fire to roast hot dogs. Next thing we knew the harbor police were pulling up in their launch and arresting the bunch of us for trespassing. Was my old man mad."

"He should have been," Dawn said. "Teenagers have no consideration for the feelings of others, especially their parents."

"Yeah, like I said, they're fifteen-year-olds."

The telephone in the pocket of Dawn's shorts began ringing. Surprised, she took it out and flipped it open.

"Yes?"

"Ah, Mom?

"Yes," her voice clipped.

"This is Brian."

"I know. What do you want?"

"Mike and I were wondering, after we tie up, if we could spend another night on the sailboat? If Chuck doesn't mind."

Handing the phone to Chuck, she said, "Do I kill them now, or wait 'til later?"

"Brian? This is Chuck."

"We were wondering if you'd mind if we spent another night on the boat. With the rain and all, it'd be neat."

"Hang on a minute." He looked at Dawn.

Shaking her head, dismayed, she said, "I don't care. I'd probably kill him if he were in the house."

"Have you had anything to eat?" he asked Brian.

"Oh yeah. There's food left from last night. Anyway, we had a big lunch in Manchester before we left for home." Chuck decided not to relate this to Dawn.

They left the boys tying up to the mooring in Quiet Cove, and motored to the boat ramp at the end of the harbor. There was still enough high water to reach the ramp, and Chuck jumped over the side to hold the boat while Francis backed down the trailer. Soon the boat was winched aboard the trailer and Francis drove the truck up the ramp. Chuck and Dawn came to the driver's window.

"Thanks, Francis. They'd still be out there without your help."

"Glad to do it. And Dawn, don't be too hard on the kid."

"I'll just kill him slowly."

The truck and trailer left and Dawn and Chuck got into his pickup. She sat on the far side of her seat, saying nothing. They reached Chuck's garage and he bleeped open the door. When he turned off the engine, he got out and went to Dawn's side to open her door. She just sat there, staring straight ahead. Her wet hair was plastered to her back and traces of makeup darkened the edges of her eyes. She began to shiver. He touched her arm, and guided her out of the truck. Standing in front of him, her shoulders bent, her arms hanging loosely at her sides, she burst into tears.

"Come upstairs," he said softly, but she continued to stand there, shivering and sobbing, oblivious to his presence. A pool of water formed around their feet. Finally he took her elbow and led her to the stairs and up to the kitchen. Easing her into a chair and taking a towel, he knelt in front of her and began to dry her face and hair. She opened her eyes and looked at him. Her terror was palpable.

"I'm so afraid," she sobbed. "I almost lost him."

FORTY-SIX

Dawn continued weeping, her shoulders shuddering with each sob, her fingers clenched in her lap. Tenderly, he wiped the tears from her cheeks. Then it started again, the shivering, her arms and hands jerking involuntarily. Chuck got up and went to the entrance hall, returning with a blanket.

"You're freezing. Better go into the bathroom and get out of those wet clothes." He handed her the blanket. "Here. It's yours. The one you gave me when I fell off the boat."

She remained seated, staring up at him vacantly. Carefully, he took her arm and helped her stand, then guided her to the bathroom and handed her the blanket. "Get out of those things and wrap yourself in the blanket." She took it. "Do you need help?" She shook her head and walked into the bathroom. Chuck returned to the kitchen. A few minutes later, barefoot, with the blanket wrapped around her shoulders, she came into the room. She had stopped crying.

"Have you got anything I can tie this with?" She was holding the blanket closed across her chest. He nodded, removed his belt and encircled her waist with it, slipping the end through the buckle. It was far too big, so he tied the end in a half-knot around the buckle. As he worked, she ran her fingers through his wet hair.

"You'd better change, too."

"You're right. Will you be okay for a minute?" She nodded and let him lead her to the sofa in the living room, where she sat down.

Bear, who had been watching them with grave concern from the time they'd come into the house, followed them and sat by her side. Moments later Chuck returned wearing his bathrobe. His hair and beard were tightly curled from a brisk towel rub. Dawn was petting Bear's head.

"We missed lunch. Can I get you something to eat or would you like a drink first?

"I'll take the drink."

"Be right back." He started for the kitchen.

"Chuck, would you mind going over to my house and getting Clara? She's been alone there for a long time."

"Sure." Bear's eyes tracked him until he was sure he was going outside, then he bounded up and followed him. Chuck threw a rain slicker over his shoulders and together he and Bear crossed to Dawn's house. Clara was waiting just inside the door. Chuck opened it and she bolted onto the porch. She chewed Bear's collar for a second, then ran into the yard to relieve herself, Bear following. A few minutes later the three of them entered Chuck's house. When Clara saw her mistress, she raced into the room uttering her combination whine and howl that sounded like a human saying hello. Chuck left them to their lovefest and went to the kitchen. He returned with the drinks and two large rawhide bones for the dogs. Delighted, the dogs curled up behind the sofa, chewing and occasionally growling as one tried to steal the other's bone. Chuck sat beside Dawn on the sofa. Her eyes remained closed and he wondered if she'd fallen asleep. Then she spoke.

"For a couple of hours there, I thought my world had come to an end. I thought I'd lost him. All that wind, those huge waves and the rain. I was terrified the storm had swallowed him up and I'd never see him again. If something happened to Brian I would simply take my own life. I'd do it in a minute. Without a second thought." She hunched up so she could reach her drink, which sat on the coffee table. She sipped it, then returned it to the table.

"I was mad at him when we found him, and the little twit didn't even seem to realize he'd done anything wrong. That I can live with. I know Francis is right. He's just being fifteen. That's not what hit me." She turned to look at Chuck. "It's that I thought I'd lost him." Again tears came to her eyes. She placed her hand on Chuck's arm, then turned away and leaned back against the sofa.

"So, what has it been," she said opening her eyes and staring at the cold fireplace, "eight months since Gareth was killed? Then Charlie in April." She paused. "You see, if anything had happened to Brian it would've been too much. And it would've been my fault for letting him go out in the boat."

She reached for the glass and touched it to her lips. Without looking at him, she continued, "Here we are side by side, almost afraid to touch each other, and two months ago I was telling you how much I loved you. You said you loved me, too, but this awful thing, whatever it is, was getting in the way. I tried to tell you we could handle it, but you pulled away. So," she said, forcing a laugh, "chalk up another loss for me."

She set her glass down and, tucking her legs beneath her, faced Chuck. "Right now I want to rest my head on your shoulder. I want you to hold me and tell me you love me. That you want to care for me the rest of my life. That you want to be like a father to Brian, at least a good friend." She stopped and stared intently into his eyes, her face contorted with pain. "But I'm not going to do that. I can't risk having you love me again, and then leave me. I can't survive another loss."

Chuck's face reflected Dawn's pain. Each time he started to speak, the words he contemplated seemed empty, so he said nothing. He, too, wanted to reach out and pull her to him, but he didn't dare. So there he sat, his drink in one hand, the other on the arm of the sofa. Dawn looked at him for a long time, then stretched out her legs and leaned back.

Sitting two feet apart, each with their own thoughts, they were silent for several moments. Then Chuck spoke. "Last month when you were in Moscow, I was at my mother's in Rochester." She nodded. "Mom had her birthday while I was there, but that wasn't the reason I went." Dawn glanced at him briefly, then relaxed, glad to have the subject shifted away from her. "I wanted her to confirm something I was sure she knew."

He thought for a moment how to begin. "The night when we said we loved each other and I ran home, I had the same old nightmare, but with a difference. From the time I was ten I dreamed it was a dragon that came into my room and terrified me. That night I dreamed it was a man and he held me down, and . . . he started playing with me." He paused. "I want to tell you this, but it's difficult. And it's not pleasant." He looked at her.

"Go on."

He took a drink, then set his glass down. "In the dream, this man started licking my stomach, going further and further down each time." Embarrassed, he shot a glance in her direction, then went on. "Finally, he took me in his mouth." A long pause. "The dream was so real it started me wondering if maybe it really had happened.

"Two weeks later, the night of the nor'easter, when I came home dressed in your blanket there, I was up in my room and happened to pick up one of my old books, the *Gingerbread Man*. It's about this gingerbread boy that everyone wants to eat, but he runs away."

"I know the story. I read it to Brian when he was little."

"Then you know at the end the fox tricks him into riding across the river on his back and catches him in his mouth. As I was reading this, the memory came back to me of what had happened the night before we left Marblehead. A man *had* come into my room and did just what I'd dreamed about."

"So it was more than a dream."

"I'll say. Well, as he was doing it, Mom came into my room and hit him with the Bugs Bunny lamp, smashing it. You know, the one that's glued back together?" Dawn's eyes opened wide, but she said nothing. "Mom pushed him out of the room and down the stairs. I could hear them fighting for a long time. To hide from their screaming, I distracted myself by drawing a penis on the gingerbread boy. The drawing's still there. That's when I knew for certain he'd come into my room."

Dawn winced.

"There's more. You see, I assumed it was Dad who'd done it. Sometimes when he'd come home at night from a flight, he'd come in and kiss me good night. Oh!" He stopped as he remembered something else. "And another thing, this playing with me happened five or six times. I realized that when the memory came back. So you see why I was so surprised that you and the others loved Charlie so much. I'd lost the memory of what had happened, but not the anger for him."

"No!" she said emphatically. "It couldn't have been Charlie, whatever you say."

"Wait. I'm coming to that. When I told Mom what Dad had done, she went nuts. She said it wasn't Dad. It was someone else."

"I'm sure she did. Did she say who?"

He took another deep breath. "No, she didn't. But what's important is, I know it happened and I know it wasn't Dad."

Dawn placed her hand over his. "So that what's been tearing you apart." She stopped abruptly. "Oh, gosh, Chuck, is that why, when we were making love, you got upset?"

Chuck squeezed his eyes closed and pressed his folded hands against his chin. For several moments he remained rigidly quiet. Then he spoke. "It wasn't what *you* did. It was that I wanted you to do it. I wanted you to do it just like I wanted that man to do it when I was a boy."

Dawn thought for a moment, then said, "And you were bad for wanting him to do it?"

"Yes! I was bad, not just because I wanted him to, but for making him do it. I thought that he could tell I wanted him to, and . . . and that's why he did it. *That it was my fault.*"

After a moment's silence, Dawn, in a voice barely audible, said, "Do you still feel that way?"

He started to say something, then stopped. After a moment he started again. "I'm not sure. I only know that it still feels like I caused him to do it."

Dawn stared into space for a long time. Gradually she began to smile. "Aren't we a pair."

"How so?"

"The way we blame ourselves. You for causing that man, whoever he was, to lust after you." Chuck started to interrupt. "No, wait. And me for causing Gareth to get killed."

"I don't see what you mean."

She sat up and looked at him. "I never thought about this before, but the way we're blaming ourselves is one hell of an ego trip—that we're so powerful we can control what other people do."

Now Chuck smiled slightly. "I guess it is a little presumptuous to think I had that much power over a grown man, unless he was really sick."

"Whether he was sick or not, you thought you were controlling him."

"Yes, I guess I did."

She grew serious. "While we're making confessions, I've got one, and I didn't realize it until just now. When Mom told me that Dad's accident was caused by a leaky hydraulic system, for an instant I couldn't accept it. All those years I believed that I had so much power over him, I could cause him to crash his plane simply because I didn't say I was sorry."

Chuck smiled. "You *are* as bad as I am."

"Yes, just as bad, but in a little different way."

"Do you still feel bereft of your power?"

"No," she laughed. "Relieved."

"Huh!" he grunted from a sudden realization. "So do I."

For a while they each sank into their own thoughts, then, simultaneously, reached for their drinks and took a sip.

Leaning back on the sofa, Dawn said, "I like this, sitting here beside you, except that it's like sitting on the edge of a cliff."

"Is it?"

"Uh-huh. I'm afraid I'll fall back in love with you and you won't be able to take it. I'm afraid you'll run away again or say something mean."

"Right now I'm dying to hold you, but I don't know what would happen. I might make a mess of it and I might not. At least now I know what was screwing me up." He turned toward her. "On the way home from Mom's I could feel the difference. I felt lighter, like a load had been lifted off me. I realized that most of my life I've felt like a victim. Then I began to get this new feeling, that I wanted to find the guy that did this and kill him. Well, maybe not actually kill him, but beat the shit out of him."

"I've never heard you say things like that before."

"I never realized I could be so mad at somebody."

"Do you think you'll find him?"

"I'd like to. I'm sure Mom knows his name, but she's not telling. She said he was dead. I don't believe her."

"Hmm. Maybe she's afraid of what you'll do."

"I doubt that's it. I think there's more to it than that." Chuck got up and picked up the two empty glasses from the table. "How about another drink?"

"Didn't you say something about food a while back?"

"I did. I've some hamburger patties in the refrigerator. Come on out to the kitchen and we'll have our second drink while I cook them."

"Sounds good to me."

The smell of cooking hamburgers brought the two dogs to the kitchen. Dawn sliced tomatoes and onions while Chuck watched over the meat. Soon they were munching thick burgers, with mustard and ketchup running down their fingers. Chuck had cooked an extra one that they split in two for the dogs.

After dinner they stood at the front door while the dogs circled the yard.

"Thanks for tonight, Chuck."

"Do you have to go?"

"I'm okay now. I think I'd better."

The wind had let up, but the air was heavy with moisture and the treetops were shrouded in fog. A distant foghorn sent its deep bass sounds rolling across the water. Standing next to each other, their shoulders touched, sending a deep tremor through each of their bodies.

"The foghorn," Dawn said in a dreamy voice. "It reminds me of that old movie *Titanic*. Remember the scene when the huge ship was sitting still in the water with the lifeboats drifting away while the boat's deep whistle blasted again and again? God, but that was a lonely scene."

"I remember it, too." He leaned so his shoulder and arm were pressed harder against her. "When I hear a foghorn way out at sea I can imagine it sitting on top of its buoy that's bobbing about in the waves, its anchor line running deep into the black water and nothing around but darkness. That's loneliness to me." He could feel her body shudder.

The dogs came up onto the porch. "Think I can make it to my house in this blanket?" she laughed.

"No. I think you'll step on it halfway across the yard and have to run the rest of the way nude."

"My, what would the neighbors say?"

"Probably, 'Hurrah!' Look, I've got five beds in this house. Surely we can find one for you. The boys are taken care of out there in the boat, so you don't have to worry about Brian. And if you stay here, you can be the first to try out the new Jacuzzi. What do you say?"

"That's a very compelling offer. How can I refuse?"

"Good. Bear," he called. "Clara. Come on in. We're all spending the night here."

Chuck got sheets for the king-sized bed in the master bedroom—he purposely avoided calling it Charlie's room—and together they made the bed. Then he showed Dawn how the Jacuzzi worked and started the water for her.

"I'll be in my bedroom if you need anything. Just holler."

Smiling, she waved. "Night, Chuck."

He and Bear climbed the steps, leaving Clara somewhat confused, standing by the door. Finally she turned and followed her mistress into the bathroom.

Chuck took off his bathrobe and lay down, pulling the sheet over him. He stretched out on the bed with his hands locked under his head and listened to the water filling the tub on the floor below. After several minutes it was turned off with a clunk that rattled through the house's water pipes, and he heard the powerful roar of the Jacuzzi pumps. Closing his eyes, he could imagine the jets of hot water erupting from all sides of the tub and surging against Dawn's recumbent figure. Her hair would be caught by the jets behind her head and driven around her shoulders and over her breasts. The side jets would bubble over her stomach and the jets by her feet would send a million fingers of hot water racing up her legs. He threw the sheet off his body and sighed. He was sweating.

Eventually the Jacuzzi was turned off and silence again filled the house. The only sound was the distant foghorn belching out its lonely warning. He tried to recall if he had left her a towel, but he knew he had. No, he told himself, no excuses for going down there.

He was almost asleep when he heard Clara tripping up the stairs and coming into his room. I guess she wants to sleep with Bear, he thought. Then he heard Dawn's voice at the top of the stairs.

"Chuck? Are you awake?"

"I'm awake. Come on in." He pulled the sheet over him.

The hall light came on and Dawn, dressed in one of Chuck's extra-large T-shirts that she'd found in the bedroom, tiptoed into the room.

"How did you like the Jacuzzi?" he asked.

"It was great. You haven't tried it yet?"

"No." Pause. "Are you okay?"

"Yeah. It's that damn foghorn."

"It's mournful, isn't it?"

She sat on the side of his bed and gazed at him. The light was behind her head, so he couldn't see her expression.

When she began to speak, her voice was pensive. "I know you love me and I love you." He nodded. "And I know there's a good chance you're still as confused about this sex thing as you were before you learned you were abused. But I'm willing to take a chance that both of us can get the best of it. Am I crazy?"

"No. Well, a little crazy, but so am I."

"I want to crawl in there with you."

"And I want you to."

"But listen. There are two things. First, I'm off the Pill and I don't know where my diaphragm is."

"And I haven't got a condom."

"So you know what that means. Okay."

"I know what it means. It means a hell of a lot of pressure's off me."

"If you say so. The other thing is, I don't want you to say something that'll hurt me. If you start getting funny feelings about bad memories, just tell me. Don't freak out. What you went through is horrible and powerful. It's not going away in one night. So if something goes wrong, just tell me and we'll talk about it. If you yell at me, it's all over between us, because I'm not strong enough right now to be yelled at. Is that fair?"

"Fair."

Dawn went back to the hall and turned off the light. He heard more than saw her pulling the T-shirt over her head and coming to the bed. He could sense the weight of her body on the mattress beside him and feel the heat of her stomach and legs as they

pressed against him. As his eyes became accustomed to the dark, he saw that she was propped up on an elbow looking at him. Her other hand began to stroke his head, her fingers combing his hair and beard. She leaned toward him and kissed him gently. When he put his arms around her body she eased herself on top of him, continuing to kiss his lips and nose and eyes. They rolled onto their sides facing each other. Chuck let his free hand wander over her breast and down her side. He could hear her breathing growing heavy, or was that his own?

"I love you," he said between their kisses.

"I know. I love you, too." A moment later, she whispered, "move your hand down. Yes, that's right. There, yes, there. Now touch me." As she spoke, she slid her hand down his stomach and gently caressed him. "I want to touch you, too."

"Oh, yes."

"Kiss me." And he did, open-mouthed, their tongues working against and around each other. "Don't stop touching me."

"Don't you stop either. Ohh, yes, that's just right," he moaned.

"Oh, it is, it is."

The bed began to roll with their movements. Their two hands became intertwined, so it was hard to tell whose fingers were doing what. Their words, "Yes, yes, yes," spoken in chorus, began to catch in their throats, eventually turning to groans of pleasure as they fell onto their backs, each with a long deep sigh.

Chuck started laughing first. Then Dawn.

At the end of the bed were the silhouettes of the two dogs, gazing at them with fixed admiration.

FORTY-SEVEN

Dawn awakened with a start until she realized the warm body spooned up against her backside was Chuck's. Then she relaxed into the folds of arms and legs and joined him in the game of footsie that had been the cause of her waking up. His foot traced the outside edge of her foot, back and forth, while she rubbed her toes against the top of his other foot. Soon his leg began to slide up and down over her leg as he pressed against her bottom. Like a cat stalking its prey, his hand crept around her side to cup and massage her breast and nipple. Lazily, she rolled over to face him and was immediately pulled into his arms. They kissed and kissed again.

Releasing her lips from his, she whispered, "Save it for tonight."

"Aww," he pleaded.

"I'll find my diaphragm. It'll be worth it."

"Promise?"

"Promise," she said, getting up, finding the T-shirt and heading for the stairs. "I'll use the other bathroom."

"Wait. What are you doing today?"

"I've got a ten o'clock appointment at the BMA, so I'm not just running out on you."

"You'd better hurry. I'll put our wet clothes in the dryer so you'll have something to wear home, then get your breakfast. Come down when you're ready."

"Hey. You're a pretty neat guy."

An hour later she was running across the yard to her house to dress for work. They'd agreed to have dinner together at his place at seven, Brian included.

When she left, Chuck picked up his morning paper from the front walk, got a second cup of coffee from the kitchen, wiped the water off one of the porch chairs and settled into it to enjoy the cool of the morning. Down in the cove, Brian and Mike were crawling out of the cabin, stretching and scratching. He waved, but they didn't see him. Bear and Clara, standing beside him, also saw the boys, and Clara's quiet whine indicated a hope that they would come up to the house and play with her. Chuck had finished the first section of the paper when Dawn came out of her house and got in her car.

"Have a good one!" he called.

"You, too." And she was gone.

Chuck picked up the second section, then laid it down. How his life had changed in one weekend. Here he was waving good-bye to Dawn and excitedly looking forward to her return. Not at all like the time a few days before when he thought she was walking out of his life as she crossed the lawn. And the way they made love last night, how she came up to his room because she wanted him, because she loved him. It really was making love, each giving love freely and naturally to the other.

His thoughts turned to the night ahead. They'd use the master bedroom. He laughed, thinking it was time for him to leave his childhood bed on the third floor and move to a grown man's master bedroom. And tonight she'd have her diaphragm. Suddenly his eager anticipation slipped, like the earth at a faultline, sending a quake through his stomach and jarring the serenity of his morning. His eyes winced. His body grew tense. It's too soon, he thought. Rapidly, the ordered pattern of his thinking began to cross and criss-cross, shooting this way and that in a thousand directions at once, until all thought gave way to mindless, undirected fear. He sat there, unable to move.

How long? He didn't know. Gradually he came to himself, Chuck Carver, sitting on the porch with the paper in his lap and the dogs asleep beside him. His mind was working again, but his residual fear started searching for something to worry about. His eyes moved about him: the expanse of lawn, the porch deck beneath him, the house behind him. How was he going to pay for all of this? It had been simple enough when he was going to sell it and move back to Alexandria. But now, obviously, he was going to stay. He'd run up thousands of dollars repairing and sprucing up the old place and now he had a sizable mortgage, plus the one for the condo in Alexandria. His three consulting clients were enough for the simple, ordered life he'd had before, but never enough to maintain a home and lawn like this, to say nothing about repaying the mortgage he'd incurred.

And that was another thing. He was losing a client because the bank was being gobbled up by one of New England's larger banks. That would leave him with only two other accounts. He should have been out scouting new business this summer instead of tearing up and rebuilding this stupid porch.

Bear had risen from his nap and was staring at Chuck. The dog whined softly. When Chuck didn't respond, Bear put his paw on his arm and looked at him with pleading eyes. Clara noticed Bear's entreaties and got up also.

"Not now," Chuck said, removing the paw. "Later."

Bear raised his other paw and put it on Chuck's lap.

His master looked at him. "No!" He tossed the paw off him.

"Woof!" Bear demanded, and Clara joined him with her combination yawn and howl. Soon they were both barking insistently.

"All right. All right. I'll put my sweats on and we'll go for a walk."

They went up the road to the swamp, now deep in its summer foliage. When the dogs were released, they raced ahead and Chuck had to hurry to keep up. Fifteen minutes later they reached the high point on the other side of the swamp and Chuck sat on the rock outcropping. The dogs joined him, one on either side. He found two dog treats in his pocket, left over from a previous walk, and passed them out. Appreciatively, the dogs chewed and drooled and picked up the pieces they'd dropped.

"You're good guys," Chuck said, putting his arms around their necks and hugging them.

As he looked out across the treetops, he recalled the last time he was there with Dawn. So much had happened since then. Fantasies of loving her, holding her in his arms, lying together in bed, all had become reality. The house had been transformed. He'd gotten to know the family he didn't know he had, Vivian and Josh.

He even had a fishing buddy. But most important, he'd discovered he'd been sexually abused when he was ten and that it had been the chunk of iron sitting next to his compass that had steered him off course his entire adult life.

Knowing what had happened was a help, but the fear and lack of confidence associated with it were still there. He wasn't going to overcome that in one night. He'd promised to tell Dawn when he was afraid. Tonight, then, would be the first test.

Walking the dogs home, he began to plan his day's work. No sense in spending time with the client he was losing, he told himself. Then it hit him. If the two banks were being merged, then all the programs he'd designed would have to be merged with those of the large banks. Who understood those programs better than he? By the time he got home, he had decided to call the two banks and set up appointments to present a proposal for merging programs. Then he'd have to get busy and write the proposal. When he reached the porch steps, he took them two at a time and within minutes was sitting at his computer.

At seven Dawn and Brian called into the house from the front door. "Anybody home?"

"In the kitchen."

As they entered Brian said, "That smells good."

"Hope so. It's roasted chicken with vegetables. It's got another half-hour to go. Bring that cheese and cracker tray and we'll sit on the porch. Dawn, how about a gin and tonic?"

"Perfect."

"Brian, Coke?"

"Sure."

While the two adults sat on the porch, Brian played ball with Clara and Bear.

Sitting next to each other, Dawn took Chuck's hand while they discussed the events of the day. Her time had been spent with the audio-guide people preparing the script for the tour through the exhibit. It had gone pretty well until she discovered she needed to do some additional research on one of the posters. Chuck told her about his idea to merge the programs of one of his client banks with the bank that was absorbing it. When the news of the day had

been shared, they relaxed in their chairs and watched Brian playing ball with the dogs.

"I like this, sitting here together," her voice mellow.

"Me too. Home after a busy day. Your son playing in the yard.
The dogs fed. A delicious dinner roasting in the oven."

"It's almost like . . ."

"Yes, it is," he broke in quickly.

"By the way," she said, squeezing his hand, "I found it."

Chuck had only a momentary shudder, then said, "What about
Brian?"

"I gave him money for the second show at the Warwick, here in
Marblehead. He's delighted. When I told him I might be late, he
said, and I quote, 'Don't worry, Mom, I understand. I'll see you in
the morning.' "

"Hmm."

"He likes you."

After dinner, Brian took off for the movies and they cleaned up
the kitchen. Hand in hand they climbed the stairs to the master
bedroom, the dogs following.

At the door, Chuck said, "Okay, guys, I'm shutting you out."
They looked at him with disbelief, but lay down when the door
was closed.

Chuck, still holding her hand, pulled her toward him and they
kissed. "I feel like my parents are away and I've invited my girlfriend over."

"I think you just closed the door on our parents." They laughed,
but not too loud. "So you haven't tried your Jacuzzi yet."

"No."

"It's big enough for two. Want to give it a try?"

While the tub was filling, Chuck undressed Dawn one garment
at a time, caressing the portion of her body that was revealed when
the item was dropped to the floor. He almost forgot the Jacuzzi
when he removed her bra. Then she undressed him, pushing him
back onto the bed to pull off his pants and underpants. Chuck
turned on the pump and joined Dawn in the swirling waters, he at
one end and she at the other. They slid down until their heads
were just above water, a movement that necessitated sticking their
knees ungracefully up in the air. It was only a matter of seconds
before their toes crept up each other's legs to begin a gentle mas-

sage. Dawn closed her eyes blissfully. But the more Chuck became aroused, the more his tension grew. When Dawn opened her eyes and saw the muscles in his jaw working, she suggested it was time for bed. They dried each other and went to the king-size bed.

He lay down, tense as a band of steel, and put his arms behind his head. She sat cross-legged beside him, running her fingers through his hair. They said nothing for several minutes.

"It's not as easy as I thought," Chuck said.

"Tell me," she said lovingly.

"It started this morning. When I thought about our making love tonight, I got so scared that everything else seemed to go bad. Every trouble I could imagine popped up: the house, the mortgage, the lack of business. I wanted to run away."

"What'd you do?"

"Took the dogs for a walk," he laughed slightly.

She smiled. "And?"

"We sat on that high rock in the swamp, you know, where we stopped that time. I fed them dog treats and we looked at the world."

"Was it nice to look at?" she said as she lifted his head to place it in her lap. He assisted by raising up so she could slide her legs under his shoulders.

"It seemed to bring things back into perspective." She was rubbing his temple and pressing his head against her bare stomach. Slowly he began to move his head back and forth against her, sometimes turning it far enough so he could kiss her smooth skin. "You smell good."

"So do you," she said. When she bent over to kiss his stomach, her breast came close to his mouth and he leaned up to kiss her nipple. She raised up for a moment, smiled tenderly, then bent down again so he could continue. "We don't have to do any more than this," she said calmly.

But he was ready for more. "Come down here with me." She moved out from under him and stretched out beside him.

"I love you," she whispered.

"I know." He looked into her eyes. "I love you, too."

"Do you know how nice this is for me, to be here with you?"

"Yes." His voice was tense.

"Good. I'm glad you're taking this seriously." He looked at her askance. "Because it's time for my diving lesson."

"Your what?"

"Lie on your back." With a dubious scowl, he rolled onto his back. "Now you've got to take this very seriously," she instructed. "This is no laughing matter. If you make the slightest wrong move, I could fall and break my leg or my head. Ready?"

"I don't know what for, but yes, I'm ready."

She knelt on her knees. With the first and second fingers of her right hand she began walking down his chest. Once she pretended to trip herself in his chest hair. Chuck smiled. Getting up, she resumed her journey to his penis, which was pointed cannon-like toward his chin. Tracing her finger around the head and down the sides, she tested it to make sure it was good and solid.

"Seems to be in good shape," she announced. "Don't you think?"

His smile broadened as he shook his head in amazement.

"Uh-uh! I told you this is serious business. No smiling and absolutely no laughing. I might break a leg. Ready?"

"Ready." He fixed a grim expression on his face.

Dawn's fingers walked to the base, climbed on top and with wobbling steps inched their way to the tip. Then, with small jumps that became higher and higher, her finger-person bounced on the diving board, eventually making a graceful dive all the way to Chuck's mouth.

Chuck laughed out loud and the finger-person disappeared into his mouth.

"Oh-oh! You've swallowed her." Frantically, Dawn rolled on top of him and drove her tongue into his mouth. "I've got to save her," she exclaimed between laughs and kisses. Locked together, they began rolling first one way across the bed and then the other. Soon he was between her open legs and they were making love. Their orgasms exploded with such loud groans that the dogs began barking outside the door.

When they fell back onto the bed, they were giggling with joy. Suddenly, Chuck grabbed her and pointed down below his stomach.

"Look. Look what you did. You broke my diving board."

FORTY-EIGHT

The September 2nd opening of Dawn's exhibit at the Boston Museum of Art of was only a week away, so her days were spent with last-minute preparations. The first night would be a preview that she and the museum director would host for press and invited guests. Chuck was busy too now that the merged banks had accepted his proposal. His days were spent designing the programs that would link their two systems.

But Chuck's and Dawn's nights were their own. The first week after Dawn's diving board game, they tried to maintain a semblance of decency by sleeping in their own beds at least every other night, until Brian told his mother he didn't mind spending the night alone. From then on, they'd stayed together every night. Their lovemaking was an act of playful intimacy, sometimes wild and sometimes quietly tender. Sometimes they just kissed each other good night, she falling asleep on his shoulder or he pressed up against her back. A few nights had started with Chuck feeling anxious, his mind a mile away. When that happened, she sat beside him in the bed, stroking his head and asking him to tell her what was wrong. Once it was the delay in the acceptance of his proposal to the two banks that were merging—he was sure they'd gotten a bad report from one of his references. Another night it was closer to home. He was afraid that when she really got to know him, she'd see he wasn't the man he pretended to be, and leave him. She would listen without speaking and when he was finished, take him in her arms either to sleep or to make love.

Every morning Dawn returned to her house to dress for work, so she could tell herself she hadn't actually moved in with Chuck.

Chuck was alone when his mother called. Dawn was working late and Brian was at his house.

"Hi, Mom. What is it?" A call from his mother was rare. It usually meant trouble, like the time two years before when she'd fallen on the ice and broken her leg, or a tragedy, like the death of her sister a few years back. It had been only a month and a half since his visit and not much could have gone wrong since then. As usual, she got right to the point.

"There's something I want to tell you, something I *need* to tell you." The strain in her voice was obvious, so unlike the cool, commanding tone she usually used. "Do you have a few minutes?"

"Sure. What is it?" He reached a kitchen chair with his left foot, hooking its leg and pulling it to the counter where the phone was. He sat down.

"I've got to go back a few years for this to make sense. That night when I found him in your bedroom—you know what I'm talking about, don't you?"

"I know."

"I was horrified. I wanted to kill him. Instead, I just drove him out of the house." Pause. He could hear her labored breathing. "Before he left, he threatened me. If I ever breathed a word of what he'd done, he'd see to it I never worked as a nurse again. The next morning, Charlie and I had our big fight, and you and I left for Rochester. It was awful. I was confused and desperate. I was running away from everything, my house, my job, my friends, and I had no idea if I'd be able to make a go of it on my own. Before I could think about what that doctor had done to you, I had to be sure that Charlie and his wife-to-be didn't take you away from me. And there was also the fear that the doctor would do something, even in Rochester, to keep me from getting a job.

"But I did get a job and Charlie didn't get custody of you. Then time slipped by and I never got around to reporting the doctor. You seemed to have forgotten about it—I know now I was wrong about that—but at the time it seemed like a dead issue. So I let it go. I'm sorry. I wish I'd been stronger, but I wasn't and I'm sorry."

Chuck broke in, "I wish you'd been stronger, too. I wish it'd never happened, but it did."

After a moment of silence, she went on. "I didn't think about that night and what the doctor had done to you until you came up here a few weeks ago. Then it all came back."

"But why wouldn't you tell me his name? Hell, Mom, it was years ago. Why are you still protecting him?"

"Protecting him? That's the last thing I'd do."

"Then what is it?"

A long pause. Chuck remained silent. He could hear her voice break when she spoke. "Because I was still afraid. When you reminded me about that night, it wasn't only the horror of it that came back. It was the fear that that man would ruin my life. It made no sense. I thought I'd put the whole thing out of my mind, but I hadn't. It was my fear that kept me from thinking about it."

"Are you afraid now?"

"Yes! It's just as real as it's ever been, but now I know it's foolish. He can't hurt me now." Then, blurting out her words, "Chucky, the reason I'm calling is to tell you his name."

He waited.

"His name is James Haslett. He's a pediatrician."

"Christ! Not a pediatrician."

"Yes. A children's doctor."

After he'd hung up, Chuck continued to sit by the phone. He wished Dawn would get home so he could tell her about his mother's phone call. He wanted her sitting beside him, listening to him and telling him about her day. She'd said seven o'clock. It wouldn't be long now. A casserole was keeping warm in the oven and a salad was in the refrigerator. He made himself a drink and was walking into the living room when he remembered the list of physicians included in the information packet he'd received for a new HMO. He was transferring to one in Massachusetts, his new home.

The two dogs watched him head up the stairs and decided to follow him, thinking maybe it was time for bed. Instead of the bedroom, he went to the study and sat at his desk. Bear and Clara slumped down on the floor beside him. The papers were still on the desk, the application form on top waiting for him to fill it out. Beneath it was a booklet listing all the doctors associated with the plan. He ran his finger down the list of names.

There it was. J. HASLETT, PEDIATRICIAN. He had an office in Salem. Chuck made a note of the telephone number and put it in his wallet. He would call for an appointment the next morning. He was surprised at how calm he felt. No hysteria. No rage. Just cool determination to see the man, make sure he was the right person, then confront him.

As he sat there, he thought again about his mother's phone call and the courage she'd had in making it. Picking up the phone on the desk, he dialed her number in Rochester.

"Hello, Mom? Chuck."

"Hi." Her voice cautious.

"I didn't thank you for calling me."

"I'm glad you called me back." She sounded relieved.

"I understand now why you couldn't tell me. I'm sorry I got upset."

"It's been a hard time for both of us. What are you going to do now that you know?"

"I'm not sure. He's still here. Has an office in Salem. I'm going to go see him and, if he's the right guy, tell him I know what he did. Don't worry. I'm not going to kill him, although sometimes I think I'd like to."

"If you decide to press charges, if that's still possible, I'll be your star witness. He can't hurt me now." She laughed. "Hell, I'm retiring in eleven months."

"We'll see what happens. I'll let you know."

"If it's too late to press charges, just kick him in the balls and tell him it's from me."

He laughed loudly. "I'm glad I'm getting to know you."

The first appointment Chuck could get was three days later at twelve noon. The receptionist had asked why he wanted the appointment, but Chuck said it was a matter he could discuss only with the doctor. He arrived at the office on time and found a seat in the waiting room. Two mothers were there, one with a baby girl of about eighteen months and the other with a boy who looked to be about six. As Chuck worried over what he would say to the doctor, the little girl worked herself off her mother's lap and toddled over to him. She stopped about five feet away and, with her thumb in her mouth, stared at him. Chuck stared back. Then he smiled. She smiled. Then he made a face. Giggling, she turned and ran back to her mother.

He picked up a copy of *People* magazine, but didn't read it. His mind was still rehearsing what he would say. A nurse came around the corner. "Mrs. Templeton? This way, please." The mother picked up the little girl and followed the nurse.

Chuck's eyes wandered over to the young boy, sitting beside his mother and looking at a copy of *National Geographic.* Every so often he'd tug on his mother's arm and point to a picture in the magazine. If she knew what I know, Chuck said to himself, she wouldn't be taking her son into that office. How many, many children has he violated?

Again the nurse approached. "Hi there, Jimmy. You and your mom want to follow me?" Jimmy and his mother rounded the corner behind the nurse. Pretty soon Mrs. Templeton came out with her daughter and left.

Meanwhile, Chuck rehearsed. "Dr. Haslett, I have reason to believe you . . . you"—what? That's no good. "Dr. Haslett, thirty years ago you had an affair with my mother, and . . ." That won't work, either. This is ridiculous. He's simply going to deny everything I say and probably threaten me with a lawsuit. I shouldn't even be here. I should be hiring a detective to build a case.

Chuck thought about Jimmy, the young boy who'd just gone in. He's about four years younger than I was when it happened. Chuck could see himself lying in his bed, listening to the sound of the man's footsteps on the stairs, knowing what he was going to do. He could remember the revulsion that seized him in the morning when he was sure his mother could tell how bad he'd been. He could still feel the pressure of the man's hand on his chest, holding him when he licked and touched him. And the man was Dr. Haslett.

He decided that when the nurse called him he would go into the office and sit down across from the doctor. He would start by telling him exactly what had happened without pointing the finger at him. He would say his mother had an affair with a doctor, a pediatrician, who used his mother to gain access to himself. He'd explain how this doctor would come into his room, and how, over a six-week period, he'd sexually assaulted him. And how his mother had found the doctor in the very act, and hit him with a lamp, driving him from the room. Finally, he would tell him that the man had threatened his mother never to breathe a word of it to anyone. Then he would wait and see how the doctor responded.

"Mr. Carver? Doctor Haslett will see you now."

He took a deep breath, got up and followed her to the office at the end of the hall.

She held the door open for him. "Step right in and have a seat."

Chuck walked into the office. A woman in a white lab coat looked up at him and smiled. "Hello."

"Oh," he said, momentarily disoriented. "I'm sorry, there's been some mistake. I'm looking for Dr. J. Haslett."

"I'm Dr. Jane Haslett."

Chuck laughed uncomfortably, "I was thinking of James Haslett."

"I'm afraid you've got the wrong person."

Seized with a momentary dizziness, he steadied himself on the back of the chair. "Do you mind if I sit down?"

"Please." She gestured to the chair against which he was leaning. He sat. Her expression was warm and congenial. About his age, she had brown hair and wore glasses and a light blue blouse under her coat. "I can see you're confused."

"I am. I was expecting a man, much older." Chuck started to rise. "I'm sorry to have taken up your time."

"Please." Again she gestured for him to be seated. "Can you tell me why you wanted to see Dr. Haslett?"

"I'd rather tell him personally. It goes back a long way."

"Is this something that happened in your childhood?"

"Yes, when I was ten."

"Well, Mr. Carver," she laughed warmly, "I *am* a pediatrician. I deal with children's problems all the time."

Chuck relaxed and leaned back in his chair. He studied her for several moments. Would she understand? He desperately wanted to tell someone the story, the *whole* story.

"I've plenty of time to listen. You're the last patient this morning. Why don't you tell me what's on your mind?"

So he did, from beginning to end: the horror, the terror, the revulsion, the anger, even how good it had felt when the man took him into his mouth. Then he told her about his marriage to Michelle that ended in divorce. How he couldn't accept her coming on strong to him. How he was unable to maintain an erection when they made love. And how he covered his humiliation by calling her a whore.

"When did you remember what happened to you when you were ten?"

He was surprised that she knew he had blocked it out. "That's exactly what happened. I'd totally forgotten about the sexual abuse. It was as if it'd never happened. Except for the nightmares."

"Uh-huh, and it was messing up your life."

"Yes, it was."

"And what caused you to remember it?"

So he told her about his father's death, his coming back to Marblehead and the continuing nightmares. Then about the discovery of the broken lamp and the *Gingerbread Man* book in which he'd drawn a penis. The more he talked, the more the words tumbled freely from his lips.

"So it all came back?"

"It did, like a freight train."

"What's it like now that the memory's returned?"

"Well, the nightmares are gone, but I still feel that it's only a matter of time before people'll see through me, that I'm rotten inside. Then they'll leave me or fire me." He laughed. "Apart from that, I feel pretty good. I've found a wonderful woman I love who is willing to stay with me through my occasional craziness. I can even make love again."

"It sounds like things are getting better. But why did you want to see Dr. James Haslett?"

"I'd rather not say."

She removed her glasses and set them on her desk, then looked at him. "You're not the first person, Mr. Carver, to come to this office looking for Dr. James Haslett. There have been others. You see, I know why you're here."

"You know? How do you know?"

"He was my father. He sexually abused me from the time I was ten until I was thirteen."

Chuck lowered his eyes and shook his head despairingly. "Yes. I guess you do know."

"By the time I was twelve I tried to escape from the horror of what he was doing by getting into drugs. It helped by letting my mind go blank, but after a while I couldn't stop the drugs. When I was thirteen, I finally got the courage to tell my mother what was happening. She was furious, not at my father, but at me. How could I say such things about him? He would never do anything like that. Well, at least it got me into counseling and I was lucky enough to get a doctor who believed me. She helped me get off drugs, too.

"I moved out of my parents' house because they couldn't handle me. For me it was an escape from my father. I lived with my grandmother, my mother's mother. It was easier there, because she was as convinced as I that her daughter's doctor husband was a creep. One day at school when I was a senior, two kids I didn't know very well, a boy and a girl, came up to me and asked if Dr. Haslett was my father. When I said yes, they told me what he'd done to them. The same thing he'd done to me. The three of us went to the doctor who'd been my counselor and together we decided to press charges against my dad. All hell broke loose. My parents disowned me. Even my grandmother said I was wrong to go to the police. The other parents, however, got behind the case and we had a trial. He was convicted and sent to prison."

Chuck looked into her eyes and saw the same pain he had known for years.

"You talked about the feeling of rottenness," she went on. "I know that too. During those years when he'd come into my room, he'd tell me I was his little princess, that I was so beautiful he couldn't stay away from me, that I was special. I knew it was wrong, but it was exciting, too. For a year or so. Then it got sick. He wanted me to do things I didn't want to do and he threatened to tell Mom if I didn't do them. I hated him, but I feared him even more. That's when I started doing drugs."

It was almost more than Chuck could bear. Tears came to his eyes as he listened to her.

"I'm telling you this for a reason," she said calmly, fixing her eyes on his. "I used to think it was my fault, what he did. That I seduced him to show I was better than my mom. He even called me his little seductress. And what he did felt good. So it must have been my fault."

"Yes." Chuck was nodding his head slightly. "I was sure it was my fault, too."

"I thought so." She paused. "I want you to hear this. Are you listening?" He nodded. "It is never, never, never the child's fault. Do you hear that?"

"Yes."

"The job of an adult, especially a parent, is to care for children and protect them, to do the right thing for them. And when a grownup violates that trust and takes advantage of a child's innocence, it is never, never the child's fault."

Chuck put his hands to his mouth, leaned back in his chair and exhaled a long breath. The tears began to flow down his cheeks and into his beard. His body shook with sobbing.

"Thank you. Thank you," he cried.

After three or four minutes, he dried his tears. Dr. Haslett handed him a sheet of paper. "Here're the names of two counseling centers in Boston that work with people who've been sexually abused. You're fortunate that you've recovered your memory of the abuse and that you have someone, the woman friend you mentioned, who will see you through the hard times. But the effects of abuse go deep, and it takes a long time and the support of other people who've been through it to give you a full recovery. I strongly recommend that you check out these centers and get into one of their programs. I did."

"I should have done it years ago. I think that's what Michelle, my ex-wife, wanted me to do."

They looked at each other, kindred spirits, and both began to smile.

"Thank you."

"You're welcome."

At the door, Chuck turned back to her. "Where is your father now?"

"Dead. He committed suicide in prison."

FORTY-NINE

The east foyer of the Boston Museum of Art was aglow from hundreds of miniature bulbs in the cut-glass chandelier that hung from the ceiling two stories above. White marble walls, bare except for an enormous triptych of Renoir dancers, added to the ethereal quality of the room. Men in black tie and tux and women in cocktail dresses or evening gowns gathered in the entrance hall, drinking champagne and greeting friends. Some were museum trustees, some donors, and a few were collectors. There were press representatives and TV people with cameras. Others were city and state officials who knew the value of being seen at such an event. It was the cocktail reception for the opening of *European Poster Politics: 1910–1940.*

Brian had been there since the middle of the afternoon, when he'd arrived with his mom. Dawn had last-minute details to attend to and told Brian to entertain himself until the evening. He went for a walk and found a trading card shop where he exchanged several green pictures of George Washington for those of a variety of hockey stars. At five-thirty he returned to the museum, going directly to the office of Joe Lee, the designer who had worked with Dawn. Here he changed into his rented tux. Now he waited in a corner of the foyer, the tux coat covering a T-shirt bearing the likeness of Albert Einstein, and the pants hanging in folds over black and white Nike basketball shoes. When he saw Josh and

Cliff showing their invitations at the door, he waved and rushed over.

"Whew! Finally somebody I know," he said by way of greeting.

"Hi, Brian," Josh said. "Nice outfit."

"Thanks. Mom hasn't seen it yet. I left the pleated shirt and black tie downstairs."

"She'll be surprised," Cliff said. "Bet she likes it, though." His medium brown complexion was set off by the cream color of his form-fitted jacket that buttoned to a narrow circular collar. Josh wore a dark blue suit with fine white stripes. The slender coat, cut long with a narrow collar, had four buttons, the top three of which were buttoned. His shirt was purple and his wide tie a solid amber.

Brian eyed his friends' clothes with admiration, but said nothing. Just then, Vivian and Carl came up to them.

"Hello, everybody," Vivian said, feeling slightly self-conscious in her very short black cocktail dress embedded with black sequins. Her arm rested on Carl's. His tux was traditional.

"The big event at last," Carl said. "Where're Dawn and Chuck?"

Brian said, "Mom's getting dressed and I don't know where Chuck is."

"Hi, sis. You look great," Josh said. "Lemme see if I can hijack a cocktail waitperson for you. Be right back." Josh disappeared into the crowd. A minute later he was back with a young man bearing a tray filled with glasses of champagne. Everyone but Brian took a glass.

"Go ahead," Vivian said, winking at Dawn's son, "tonight's special." Brian hid his smile and took one. "How's your mom doing?" she asked. "Excited?"

"Uh, I guess so. We left the house and had to go back for her dress, then she went through a red light on the way in."

"Brian?" a voice said behind him.

He turned. "Grandmother!" He ran to give her a hug. "I didn't know you were coming."

"It's a surprise. I wouldn't have missed it for anything."

"Then Mom doesn't know?" His grandmother nodded. "She'll be surprised, all right."

"Hi, Mrs. Olson," Vivian said. "Remember me?"

"I thought that was you, Vivian, but I couldn't be sure. It's been such a long time. I'm Ellen Fraiser now."

"It has been a long time. I was eighteen when you left Marble-head."

"You and Dawn were such good friends. Are you still close?"

"Very."

"Did she tell you we had a long talk on the phone the other night? After all these years we're friends again, not just mother and daughter."

"I'm glad. She'll be so pleased you're here."

A group of people began descending from the balcony on the escalator, four men and a woman. A ripple of applause greeted them from the crowd below and the man in front acknowledged it with a regal nod. The man was James Campbell, the director of the museum, but all eyes were fixed on the solitary woman—Dawn.

Her silver sheath dress, sleeveless and with a plunging V neck, followed the lines of her figure, from her broad shoulders to the tops of her ankles. Reflecting the lights of the chandelier, it glittered with thousands of tiny silver platelets. At her neck she wore a triple-strand choker of black pearls. Her blond hair fell freely over her shoulders.

At the foot of the escalator, the five people drifted into the crowd, Dawn moving quickly toward her son and friends near the door. Then she saw her mother and stopped.

"Mom!" She went to her and they embraced. "I'm overwhelmed. You came."

"Of course. I guess I should have told you, but I wanted it to be a surprise. You look absolutely wonderful."

"Thanks. Your being here makes everything complete." Then, turning to the group, "Hey, everybody, this is my mom."

Vivian put her hand on Dawn's arm. "Your gown is stunning."

"And yours is verrry chic," Dawn replied.

Brian examined his mom's gown. "It's like a coat of mail, only the chunks of metal are smaller."

"I hope that's a compliment," she laughed.

"Yeah, it's pretty."

Then Dawn looked at him. "Where's the rest of your outfit, the shirt and tie?"

"Don't you like this? It's my own creation. It's me, Mom."

She shook her head. "It surely is."

"So," Carl jumped in, "it's the big night, huh, Dawn?"

"That's right, Carl. Did you meet my mom, Ellen Fraiser?"

"Glad to meet you. I'm Vivian's husband." Then, to Dawn, "What do we do now, stand around for a while?"

"It'll be starting soon." Dawn let her eyes rove over the crowd. "Where's Chuck?"

"Not here yet," Brian said. "At least I haven't seen . . ." He paused as his eyes fell on a tall man being admitted by the door guard. The others followed his line of sight and stared at the person in the tux coming toward them.

"Chuck?" Dawn questioned.

His beard was gone. He was clean-shaven.

She watched him, wide-eyed, as he came toward her, his skin slightly red from the unaccustomed scraping of a razor. He seemed taller, his gray curly hair quite dashing, his shoulders broader, his frame more erect. Mesmerized, she began walking toward him, then hurried into his arms. He caught and hugged her, then held her at arm's length.

"Dawn, you're absolutely breathtaking."

She looked up at him, leaned her head to the side and looked again. "I like it. The beard was nice, but I like this better. I can really see you."

"It's a little scary. I've got nothing to hide behind." She smiled again and kissed his cheek, then led him back to the group. Vivian touched his cheek and nodded her approval. Brian said he liked him better with the beard.

Josh was standing at the back of the group, staring at him. Chuck saw him and uttered a tentative, "Hi."

"Hi." The tone was flat and Chuck couldn't tell if Josh was still angry at him. His half-brother continued to stare.

"You . . . you look exactly like Dad in his wedding pictures. He was about your age then."

Vivian caught her breath. "It's true."

Chuck laughed, nervously, "Well, I *am* his son."

"I see that," Josh said. "I guess I always thought of you as some-one who just barged into our family."

"I did, in a way."

Josh was shaking his head, still amazed. "You look so much like him. I can't get over it."

"I know this guy," Cliff said, "and that sounds like a compli-ment."

Josh nodded and Chuck smiled. "Thanks, Josh."

There was a general sigh of relief as the group acknowledged the reconciliation.

Dawn took Chuck's hand and led him to her mother. "Chuck, I want you to meet my mom, Ellen Fraiser."

Each let their eyes rest on the other for a moment, then Chuck said, "I'm glad to meet you. I knew I would, but I didn't think it would be this soon."

Ellen looked first at him, then at her daughter, then back to Chuck. Nodding her head, she said, "I think it's time we got to know each other." They smiled.

There was a tap-tap-tapping sound on a microphone, and a voice rose above the rumble of conversation in the foyer. "Ladies and gentlemen. If I may have your attention." It was James Campbell. "We're here tonight for the opening of an exciting new exhibit, 'European Poster Politics, 1910 to 1940.' But first I'd like to ac-knowledge some of the distinguished guests who are here this eve-ning."

He began mentioning the names of trustees and donors, then top government officials of Boston and Massachusetts. As he droned on, Chuck leaned his head next to Dawn's and whispered, "I'm proud of you." She looked up at him and smiled. "I wanted to get here before it started, but the shave took longer than I'd planned."

"It's worth having you a little late just to see you without a beard."

"I wanted to get here in time to ask you to have dinner with me at the Boston Harbor Hotel when the reception's over. Just the two of us."

"I'd love to."

The voice of the director cut into their conversation. "And now it is my pleasure to introduce Dawn Ireland, who co-produced this exhibit with her partner, Dr. Gareth Davies. As many of you know, Dr. Davies died tragically last December, and the task of completing the show fell to Ms. Ireland. By the way, she has signed several copies of the book that accompanies the show and it may be purchased in the gift shop at the end of her private tour. Ms. Ireland."

As applause echoed through the foyer, Dawn came to the podium. Smiling confidently, she took a minute to look across the expectant crowd. Then she spoke. "There should be two of us here this evening . . ." Her voice caught in her throat. She dropped her eyes, swallowed and went on, her voice trembling slightly. "But, as Director Campbell said, Dr. Davies, who gave so much of his time and talent to the book and the exhibit, died last December. Dr. Davies was an outstanding scholar and a dear friend. I am proud to have had the opportunity of working with him over the last few years until his untimely death. He is deeply missed by all who knew him."

Dawn paused, then, letting her eyes move over the assembled people, she regained her composure. "Posters are raw art," she began, "often splashed out oh paper in the evening, printed during the night, and plastered on the walls of buildings the next morning. Not for the discriminating perusal of the critical art lover, posters are for the populace, to prod them, set them afire and drive them forth in the cause of one political party or another. Tonight, we will travel through time, from 1910 to 1940, looking at European politics through the eyes of the men and women who designed the posters. We will begin with the pre–World War One era, examining the events of that period in various parts of Europe. Then on to the years of the first World War, followed by the twenties, the great depression and finally the beginning of World War Two. As you go through this exhibit, set your imagination free, let yourself be a citizen of Moscow or Berlin or Paris, walking the streets, hearing the crowds. Let the posters capture your mind and arouse your spirit to take up arms against your own special brand of oppression in the name of what freedom means to you." She paused, then said, "Please follow me to the escalator."

Carl leaned his head toward his wife. "I'd follow her anywhere."

Vivian laughed, "So would I."

Cliff sighed, "Now I know how people felt who listened to Joan of Arc. I could stand here all day listening to Dawn and looking at her in that silver gown."

Eagerly the crowd moved to the escalator and into the galleries on the floor above. In each room, Dawn found special anecdotes to tell about the artists or the circumstances that had inspired the posters. The people listened with rapt attention, asking only a few questions, and soon they reached the last room.

"It's been my pleasure to be your guide tonight," Dawn said at the end. Then, raising her voice, "Are you ready to take up the cause, whatever it might be?"

The crowd laughed and applauded.

Museum Director Campbell, reminded the guests about the signed copies of the book in the gift shop, and turned to Dawn. "That was a fine job. I think it's going to be a hit." Then, seeing the chairman of the board of trustees, he whirled away. "Franklin! What did you think?" Dawn listened, but Franklin's answer was lost in the crowd.

The curator, Dr. Christopher Jackson, who had been more hindrance than help, gave her an insouciant nod as he headed toward the exit. "Rather good, Dawn," he said.

Joe Lee, with whom she had worked so closely in designing the show, slipped up to her. "Hey there, Dawn! We've got a winner, huh?"

"Couldn't have done it without you, Joe." He smiled proudly.

Then Chuck was standing beside her.

"It's wonderful. The exhibit's magnificent and the way you presented it was perfect."

"Thanks, Chuck. Give me a minute to say good-bye to these people and I'll meet you downstairs."

A short time later, the circle of friends was standing by the east foyer door and Chuck was explaining that he and Dawn were having dinner together. "I hope you don't mind, Ellen, but it's a special night."

She looked at him and smiled. "I understand."

"You two should go out together," Vivian said, "but not until we've had our chance to congratulate her."

Eventually Dawn arrived, carrying a bag filled with the clothes she'd come in with. Brian took the bag. "Good job, Mom. You had 'em eating out of your hand."

Vivian kissed her, Carl shook her hand and both Josh and Cliff hugged her.

Her mother put her arms around her and whispered in her ear, "I was so proud of you, darling. I . . . I wish Daddy could have been here, too."

Tears came to Dawn's eyes. "Thanks, Mom." Josh gave her his handkerchief, and she wiped her eyes.

Then she took charge.

"Brian, you and Mom will go home in my car. Mom, is that all right? You can drive and Brian can show you the way. Don't wait up for me."

"I'd be happy to drive my grandson home and don't worry, you're not sixteen."

"You're right about that," she said and turned to her friends, "Thanks to all of you for coming. It was fun, wasn't it?" They all agreed.

She put her hand on Chuck's arm and he led her out the door. At the curb was a white limousine with the chauffeur holding open the back door.

Dawn looked past the long Cadillac toward the parking lot. "Where'd you park, Chuck?" she asked.

"Here. This is for you. After all, you're a celebrity."

Her eyes opened wide. "You are too much," she said, "and I love it."

As they drove to the Boston Harbor Hotel, they drank champagne from glasses the chauffeur had poured for them. When they were pulling into the hotel, the chauffeur said over the intercom, "I'll be parked over there to drive you home when you come out." He came to a stop and ran around to open their door.

Dinner was exquisite in the upstairs dining room, and the view of the harbor captivating. Dawn talked for several minutes about the show until her pent-up excitement gradually expended itself.

Chuck asked, "When do you move the exhibit to the next city?"

"In January it'll go to San Francisco, then Chicago and finally to Washington, D.C."

"Will you have to be gone all that time?"

"No, just to set it up and host the opening."

"Have you thought any more about the posters Krubinski wants to sell you?"

"I'd like to get them. But first I'd need to find a secure place to keep them. They're very valuable."

"Maybe we could build a fireproof vault in my basement."

"Hmm. Would you mind sharing your house with my posters?"

He looked at her with an expression that said, Need you ask? Then, "Will you add these posters to your show when you take it to the other cities?"

"No, this one is set, and it matches the book. The new posters will be the core of another exhibit. Want to help me put it together?"

"Sure. Can you use a good business manager?"

On the ride to Marblehead, Dawn rested her head on Chuck's shoulder. They didn't speak, but every so often would turn their lips to each other and kiss. When they pulled up to the house on Quiet Cove it loomed large and dark against the pine trees on the hillside behind. The chauffeur opened their door and they got out.

"Do you want me to keep the lights on the house until you get inside?" the driver asked.

"No," Chuck said, "we know the way." He paid him and the limo departed.

Chuck put his arm around Dawn and walked toward his porch. When they placed their feet on the steps, they could hear whining and barking from the front hall. Chuck opened the door and turned on the lights. Clara and Bear came shooting out onto the porch, wagging their tails, wiggling their behinds and generally letting them know with howls and whines that they had been gone entirely too long.

"Let's walk them down to the beach," Chuck said.

"We'd better or we'll never hear the end of it."

No one was around, so they didn't bother about leashes. When the dogs realized they were heading toward the beach, they raced on ahead. Arm in arm, Dawn and Chuck followed slowly. It was a moonless night, giving the sky an even darker backdrop for the myriad stars. The nearby island hunched like an enormous black beast guarding the entrance to Quiet Cove, and *Thunderbolt* rocked gently on small waves.

Dawn said, "I always wondered why Charlie named the boat *Thunderbolt*. It's such a ponderous name for something as sleek as a sailboat."

"It's the airplane he flew in the war, a P-47 Thunderbolt. There's a picture of him in the study standing in front of it."

"I'm glad you've gotten to know him. He'd be happy with what you've done to the house."

Clara was charging at Bear and nipping his rump, trying to get him to chase her. He'd twist toward her, his jaws snapping threateningly, but she'd ignore them and sweep in for another attack. Finally Bear walked into the deep water, and Clara yapped at him from the shore.

"The real estate person's coming again tomorrow," Chuck said. "I can't get her to give up. I've told her I'm not selling."

"Are you sure about that?"

"Positive."

Dawn moved around in front of him and pressed her body against him.

"You're going to stay in the house?"

"Absolutely."

"Then send her over to see me."

"You're selling?" he said, looking at her askance.

She raised an eyebrow and nodded.

"I'll send her on one condition. That you come live with me."

"Really, Mr. Carver. What would the neighbors say?"

"Congratulations, if we're married." He put his arms around her. "Dawn, will you marry me?"

Her eyes opened wide. "Ohhh, yes!"

Their kiss was so long the dogs came up and sat down to stare at them.

"Let's go home," Chuck said. They started up the drive. The warm glow of the lights on the porch and in the entrance hall welcomed them.

"To our home," Dawn said.

As they approached the house, Clara, by habit, left Bear and headed for her house. Then, seeing everyone going onto Chuck's front porch, she raced across the yard. At the doorway she squeezed next to her big, strong friend, Bear, making sure that she too had a place in this house.